MW00325963

EDDIE'S

A NOVEL **BOY**

ROBERT SCHWAB

This book is a work of fiction. Names, characters, places, and incidents either are products of the author's imagination or are used fictitiously. Any resemblance to actual events or locales or persons, living or dead, is entirely coincidental.

Copyright © 2021 by Robert Schwab

All rights reserved. This book may not be reproduced or stored in whole or in part by any means without the written permission of the author except for brief quotations for the purpose of review.

ISBN: 978-1-7358600-1-5

Schwab. Robert.
Eddie's Boy

Edited by: Karli Jackson

Warren publishing

Published by Warren Publishing
Charlotte, NC
www.warrenpublishing.net
Printed in the United States

For Tyler and Emily,
whose births bestowed the title, "father," on me,
and whose lives have taught me how to live up to the role.
I have tried to make you proud.

Acknowledgments

Writing is my avocation, a calling that does not provide me with a living, but rather consumes non-vocational time that might otherwise be spent with my family. Recognizing that writing is my passion, my family indulges me, supports me, and celebrates my modest successes. For this, I owe them a debt I can never repay, and my first thanks go, as always, to Cathy, Tyler, and Emily, as well as to my early-morning feline writing companions, Sox and Jester. Gratitude is also due my sisters and other family, friends, and colleagues who encourage me and remind me that telling good stories is a worthwhile endeavor. Special thanks go to David Moller, whose experience and optimism have been a guiding light on my writing journey, and to Jayna Ross, who saw the need for this novel before I did, and convinced me I needed to write it.

Hugh Cook has been an invaluable editor who provided encouragement and an editor's eye that helped me shape the story. Mindy Kuhn and Amy Ashby at Warren Publishing have guided me through this process every step of the way with patience and grace and incredible skill. They also had the insight to pair me with Karli Jackson, whose editorial expertise and gentle but persuasive suggestions saved my story and turned this into the book I had imagined from the beginning.

Finally, to my muse, the relentless, inscrutable goddess of my art who is with me always in my mind and my heart, and who will never let me accept anything that is not good enough. Thank you for believing in me.

PROLOGUE

When the clock struck midnight on Monday, April 30, 2007, Dr. Landon Ratliff's fortieth birthday had been lost, thwarting everyone's expectations, including his own. The milestone had been a source of private dread for Landon and a focus of preparatory excitement for the office staff, but both apprehension and anticipation had been for naught. Eventually, Landon would see his elaborately decorated office, but only in photos taken to memorialize the staff's mischief. He would never taste the customized cola cake from Jestine's. It had not even been sliced—in the aftershock, no one had an appetite, and freezing it had seemed way too hopeful. Also lost was the perfect Charleston afternoon that drifted toward a glorious spring evening full of vivid bloom, an evening that should have held promise but did not, since the private happy hour and dinner at The Lot had been canceled. The crowd at The Pour House next door was forty people short for the live show that night. All the hope and joy of the planning and all of Landon's foreboding had been wasted because precisely forty years after the uncomplicated birth of the third child of Eddie and Iris Ratliff, he had been lying unconscious on a gurney in the emergency department at the Medical University of South Carolina with a breathing tube inserted into his windpipe to prevent him from choking on his own vomit.

The day's festivities had commenced early and, as it turned out, spectacularly. Just after midnight, Landon was awakened from an unusually fitful sleep by the doorbell. Anticipating coworkers determined to enjoy a full twenty-four hours of making him squirm, he ignored the first ring, hoping but not expecting to send them away disappointed. In the brief silence that ensued, he considered the more appealing possibility that perhaps the bell signaled delivery of a gag gift, that a wheelchair or a cane would be waiting on his porch in the morning. The second ring dashed that hope and induced him to assess what he was up against (there had been no laughter, no catcalls, perhaps in deference to the neighbors). From his bedroom window he spied no crowd, so he crept downstairs and peered through the peephole at the first truly breathtaking birthday present he had ever received during his all-too-rapid journey to middle age.

On the porch, bathed in a halo of yellow light, stood Luna Quinn, his latest love interest, clad in an oversized T-shirt short enough to declare that it was paired with nothing more than panties. The cool, night air provided strong evidence that the T-shirt was all she was wearing above the waist. Her reddish-blonde hair was tied back with a huge birthday bow, and she was clutching a balloon bouquet, a satin pillow, and a bottle of wine.

Unfortunately, he would remember none of this, nor any of the subsequent hours when he happily traded rest for the opportunity to at last take Luna to bed. He would retain no recollection of the gift of waking to find Luna gone, a note on the pillow thanking him and wishing him a beautiful day, with a promise to meet him on James Island for the party later that evening. Gone, too, would be the rushed shower, skipped breakfast, and race to make the 7:30 a.m. admissions committee meeting.

Had he recalled how distracted he was when he got behind the wheel, he would surely have scolded himself, but of course that memory was gone too. After briefly pondering how a woman who did not own a car had gotten from Queen Street to Ford's Court dressed only in a T-shirt and panties, Landon had rubbed his eyes and recognized how exhausted he was. It would be a long day. He had slept less than two hours, by his reckoning. Lowering the window might have helped keep him awake, but his fatigue amplified the morning chill, so he chose warmth while devising a plan to steal some sleep before the evening's revelry began. He pulled out onto Meeting Street determined to find an unoccupied call room after lunch.

From here forward, amnesia was his friend, erasing the blare of the truck horn and the lancinating pain of the airbag shattering his left thumb just before his head struck the doorframe, cracking his skull and rattling his brain around inside its protective covering. After that, there was nothing for him to remember; he lost consciousness immediately but remained upright, held in place by the seatbelt that surely saved him from further injury. His ruined car settled on the southeast of the Four Corners of Law, its passenger-side tires resting on the slate sidewalk in front of St. Michael's Church.

Several witnesses came to his aid and offered comfort to the truck driver, a kind man who was visibly distraught and blamed himself, despite the general agreement that Landon had run a red light and left no opportunity to avert the crash. Both vehicles appeared to have been obeying the speed limit. Police and rescue workers arrived quickly, unencumbered by traffic snarls at this early hour. Some worked efficiently to extricate Landon from the wreck, protect him from further injury, and get him on his way to definitive care at the hospital. Others interviewed bystanders, directed traffic around the mess, and began restoring order. All the while, the sun rose higher in the sky, illuminating the scene with the clear light of a spring morning that would elevate the spirits of nearly every citizen of Charleston but ultimately fade into a collective memory of what a fine spring it had been. For one citizen, however, April 30, 2007, would prove to be a singular day, remarkable and yet somewhat indistinct for all time.

CHAPTER ONE

L andon was drowning, strapped to a board. Something had scalded his throat, searing him as if he were on a spit. There was hissing, ringing, squawking. Voices, maybe. Something burned in his arm.

"Dr. Ratliff?"

He was being lifted, strangled by something hot that had him by the throat. A woman's face emerged from the gloom. His arms were bound. He needed to cough. Tears filled his eyes.

"Try not to fight the ventilator. You're in the hospital."

The hissing and squawking and dinging. Ventilator. Suctioning. Restraints—he struggled against them, arms and legs. He needed to pee. Something hard was in his mouth. He couldn't swallow.

"Try to relax, Dr. Ratliff. We're going to try to get you off the ventilator today."

His mind wandered to catching a large bluegill when he was five or six. The fish had swallowed the hook, and his brother held it while he yanked the hook out. He remembered how the fish's eyes bulged as the hook emerged along with the stomach and a length of intestines streaked with blood.

❖❖❖

The noises were familiar when he awoke the next time. The hiss of a ventilator, its alarm when he coughed, and voices murmuring. The stiff, raw, caustic burn in his throat—he was intubated. And restrained. The burn in his groin was a catheter. It made him feel like he had to pee.

"Dr. Ratliff?"

It was a nurse. Landon wanted the breathing tube out. There were tears in his eyes. He thought of the fish again.

"Nod your head if you understand me."

He nodded. It hurt to nod.

Another face. It was Dr. Fanning. "Landon, try to relax." His voice sounded strong and good. "You're in the ICU. You had a car crash. They're going to extubate you now."

They, who? He wanted Fanning to take care of him. More voices, but he wasn't listening. Something tickled, then burned, then he was coughing. Alarm bells, he was lifted, the hook was coming out, then suctioning, like a snake, hissing and sucking, gagging him.

He could swallow but didn't want to. His throat was stripped and raw. His thumb ached—the whole arm did. His groin was on fire.

"Don't touch that, Dr. Ratliff," the nurse said, pulling his hand away. "We'll take the catheter out when you're more awake."

Landon tried to force his eyes open, but the effort exhausted him. A lemon swab tasted like nectar, and he gaped (*like a fish*, he thought) while the nurse moistened his cracked, crusted lips. His head felt thick and battered. Hands were at his neck, sliding a mask onto his face. Misty oxygen filled his nose and mouth. A hard, thin tube creased his tongue—he knew it was in his stomach, sucking out the acid, but couldn't remember what the tube was called.

"Take a big, deep breath for me," the nurse said, her kind face materializing in the dusky room. Was it night?

He took a breath, felt a twinge of pain in his chest.

"Good."

He heard other voices, snatches of conversation, but his head felt stuffed with cotton. At least the pillow was soft. Something touched his chest—a stethoscope. Now they were lifting his gown. Pressing on his legs.

"Can you wiggle your toes, Dr. Ratliff?" A male voice.

Landon obeyed. His toes worked. It did not hurt to move them.

Fanning hovered over him, his brow furrowed. "Get some rest, Landon. I'll check in on you later this morning." A hand engulfed Landon's elbow. "You're in good hands, Son."

Oxygen mask susurration had replaced the clang and hiss of the ventilator. The mist was soothing, like the pillow. He tried to nestle his head in better, but that hurt, so he lay still, sore and stiff but not so much in pain. Just spent, as if he'd run fifteen miles on a sticky day. Parched—his torn throat rebuking him with every attempted swallow. He wasn't comfortable, but maybe he could sleep. What else was he going to do?

Landon woke for the third time; the room was brighter. Sunlight glared behind closed blinds, the lights were off, and it was noticeably quiet. Sensing that it would be best to remain still, he allowed his eyes to roam. Ceiling, bedside right (monitors, IV, ventilator), bedside left (door, brighter hallway), foot of bed—two chairs, one occupied by Luna

Quinn, who rose and approached the bed smiling. He lifted his head but only briefly.

"Hey, sleepyhead." Luna's forced smile comforted him. Her perfume smelled like orange blossoms. His eyes were welling up.

"Hey," he croaked, embarrassed by the weakness of his voice. He realized then that the oxygen mask was gone, replaced by a thin, rubber tube with two prongs stuck in his nose. Not uncomfortable, he noted, or maybe less uncomfortable.

"Should I get the nurse?"

He shook his head, regretted it immediately. A vise had him, just behind the ears. Luna's eyes signaled fear. Her fingers brushed his shoulder. "Are you hurting?"

"A little." His arm was heavy and wrapped below the elbow—a splint encased his forearm and hand. The catheter still stung. He reached across his body, and Luna took the bait, tangling her fingers in his. He wanted to hold on, but his back ached from the effort. The hiss of a distant ventilator reached his ears.

"Let me pull the chair up," Luna said, scurrying to sit closer. She settled his uninjured arm on the smoothed bedclothes. He tilted his head so he could keep her in full view. His head objected to movement, but the pain faded quickly.

Luna leaned in very close. He counted her freckles while her green eyes welcomed him. He wanted to run his finger down her nose and trace her lips, but he couldn't muster the effort and feared the pain. It hurt to smile.

"Landon, do you know who I am?"

He nodded and then winced. "Luna."

He would have given a month's pay for the smile that she laid on him then, for the tilt of her head that splayed a few tendrils of hair from her loose ponytail, though he might have demanded a refund after her reflexive hug that sent tongues of fire through his chest and behind his eyes. He couldn't stifle the moan.

"Oh, I'm so sorry," Luna said. "Let me get the nurse." She was up and out by the time he recovered enough to open his eyes. A ventilator alarm started clanging, probably next door. Someone was getting extubated or suctioned or something worse.

"She'll be right in," Luna announced, a smile plastered on her face. Her voice cracked a little.

"I'm okay," he whispered. "It's okay." He wanted to kiss her, but his head refused to leave the pillow. It hurt to raise his eyebrows, but he did it anyway and puckered as best he could, guessing he looked anything but inviting and hoping Luna wouldn't think he was having a stroke.

She got the hint, and he got a careful kiss, warm and sweet as the April air. His throat was killing him. "Water?" he asked.

Luna scanned the room. "I don't know—are you allowed?" Her hand skimmed her forehead and landed at the back of her neck. She raised one finger, turned, and left the room. Landon heard her speaking in the hallway, and then she appeared in the doorway. "Someone's getting it. I'll be right back."

He ran his furred tongue over his lips, tasting the remnants of Luna's lip gloss, sweet and fruity, remembering all the patients he'd examined in this ICU, how their breath was always musty and stale. Now, *he* was one of those patients, so what happened to *Dr.* Ratliff? His teeth felt coated, thick. He realized then that the tube was no longer in his stomach, no longer creasing his tongue. They must have removed it. That was a good sign. The head of the bed was elevated to protect his injured brain. That wasn't such a good sign.

A man in scrubs entered carrying a plastic cup filled with water. Luna trailed behind. "Good afternoon, Dr. Ratliff." He plunged a straw into the cup, then held it to Landon's searching lips. "Slowly, now. Don't rush it." The water was liquid gold, seeping into his tongue, saturating every cracked inch of his mouth. There was nothing to swallow after the first sip, but he sighed and swallowed anyway, then tried to ignore the pain of the second sip working its way through the seared tissue of his corrugated throat and down to his shrunken stomach.

"Tanya will be here in just a minute," the man said. He was a technician, but Landon couldn't place his name. He knew Tanya; she was a good nurse. Smart, good looking, funny. He was in good hands.

"Today is May 1," the technician said. "You're in the ICU at MUSC." He pronounced the hospital name as *musk*, the acronym that everyone used for Medical University of South Carolina. It was May 1—Landon had forgotten about his birthday. He was forty now. "My name is Isaac." That was it—Isaac. "I'll be here until seven if you need anything." He handed the cup to Luna.

Tanya appeared in the doorway, rubbing cleansing gel on her hands. "I'll tell you," she said, approaching the bed, "some people will do just about anything to avoid a birthday party." Her skin was the color of a perfectly-creamed cup of coffee. She still wore an Afro, but she could pull it off. "I'm Tanya," she said, offering her hand to Luna, who introduced herself and returned Tanya's bright smile.

"Sorry it took me so long to get here," Tanya said, tilting her head in the direction of the adjoining room. "We had a little accident over there." She turned back to Luna. "You look familiar. How do I know you?"

"I'm a volunteer reader here," Luna replied. "I don't think we've met."

"That's right." Tanya wagged a finger in the air. "You were here with Mrs. Newman a few weeks ago."

"Zelda? She was so sweet."

"You're the sweet one. Sitting and reading with these patients. I know you brighten their days."

"I get as much out of it as they do," Luna said. "And—I met Landon here."

Tanya laughed. "Mixed blessing." She patted the corner of his bed then turned her attention to the monitor, inspected his IV line, and adjusted the oxygen cannula that Luna's kiss had dislodged. "It's May first," she recited. "You're at MUSC. Can you tell me your name?"

"Denzel Washington," Landon said, hazarding a grin.

"Well, then." Tanya pressed a hand to her hip. "You'll have to excuse us, Luna. I'm about to close that door so Denzel and I can get busy. I'll lose my license, but sacrifices must be made."

Everyone was laughing. Landon's chest and head were protesting. "Landon Ratliff," he said, trying and failing to suppress a cough that made his head throb.

"Darn." Tanya shook her head. "Might as well keep working then." She motioned for Luna to sit. "What do you remember, Dr. Ratliff?"

"Nothing."

"You were in a car crash yesterday morning. Do you remember any of that?"

"No."

"Anything from last night or this morning?"

He yawned. That hurt too. "I remember the oxygen mask, and I think I remember being extubated." He smiled through the pain. "I remember how to pee—can I get this catheter out?"

Tanya nodded. "Should be able to. I'll ask Dr. Schneider for an order." She gave him a sidelong glance. "Can I trust you? I don't want to be changing any sheets before I leave at seven." She folded back the sheet. "Move your fingers for me."

"What happened here?" he asked, wiggling the fingers on his left hand.

"Broken thumb. Needs surgery." She exposed his feet. "How about your toes?"

He obeyed then nodded when she touched his ankles and asked if he could feel her fingers. Same with his hands and arms, chest and face. "Any double vision?" she asked.

"Nope."

She smoothed and tucked his bedclothes then wetted a washcloth and mopped his face. "You can do this for him as often as he likes," she told Luna. "You won't hurt anything. If the cannula comes out of his nose, just put it back in like this."

"Thanks," Landon said. His tingling face wanted more already.

"So what's the last thing you remember?" Tanya asked, then after waiting a beat, she added, "What's my name? And don't say Aretha Franklin."

"Tanya Matthews."

"Good. What do you remember?"

His head was aching. "Sunday." He turned to Luna. "We went to brunch, didn't we? Or was that last week?"

"We went Sunday, remember?" Luna said. "That new place on Linguard?"

"Yeah, you found it in the paper, right?" He touched his forehead, afraid to rub or squeeze.

"What was the name of it?" Tanya asked, raising a hand to stop Luna from answering.

"Cak's Table?"

"Yes!" Luna said, clapping.

"Very good," Tanya said. "Remember what you ate?"

"Grits with bacon and arugula and some kind of peppers. Poached egg on top."

Tanya tilted her head, eyes wide, brows up. Luna smiled and nodded. "That's right. Hatch peppers from New Mexico."

"Peppers? In April?" Tanya widened her stance, hands on hips. "Ain't no peppers growing in New Mexico in April."

"The chef said they freeze them," Luna said. "But they're even better fresh in August."

"Unbelievably good," Landon added. "You gotta try them."

"What about after that?" Tanya asked. "What did you do?"

He rolled his eyes, stared at the ceiling. Nothing was coming to him.

"Remember Sunday night?" Luna asked. Her hopeful expression made him feel as if she were trying to coax an answer to a quiz.

Nothing came to him. He shrugged. "I don't know."

A crowd of white-coated men and women had gathered in the hall, signaling time for afternoon rounds. Tanya excused herself to join the group. The drone of the ICU drowned out their voices. Luna touched his arm; her smile seemed forced.

The neurosurgical team filed in, led by Dr. Alan Schneider, a big man who had played college football somewhere in the Midwest. Landon had learned that fact from Dr. Fanning, and Schneider had confirmed it reluctantly, making Landon like and respect him even more. He was forceful but only as arrogant as a guy who operated on brains needed to be. His team was small today—one junior resident and two students—which meant Landon was doing well. The chief resident was probably rounding on the sicker patients and would report to Schneider later.

"Ratliff, good to see you awake," Schneider said, squeezing Landon's hand. He nodded to Luna, who had pressed herself against the wall in the suddenly crowded room. Schneider turned to one of the students, a bleary-eyed young man wearing ill-fitting scrubs beneath a wrinkled, white coat. "What do you notice about this room, Mr. Neal?"

Neal looked around. His fellow student, a tidy-looking woman, wore the satisfied expression of the teacher's pet. Landon hoped Schneider wouldn't call on her; he favored students with quiet confidence. "The room is dark and quiet," Neal said after a minute.

Schneider gave him a thumbs-up. "Correct. Why is that?"

"Reducing stimulation post-concussion."

"Exactly." Schneider turned to Landon. "Can you tell me the date?"

"It's May first. That means it's Tuesday."

"Know where you are?" Schneider was shining a light in Landon's eyes now. The glare made him wince.

"Charleston. MUSC. The ICU," Landon recited.

"How about your name?"

"Landon Ratliff."

Schneider smiled. "I think that head bonk did you some good, Ratliff. You seem smarter than you were before." He patted Landon's arm. "Ms. Duval, what does the conventional assessment of a patient's orientation usually entail?"

"Person, place, date," she replied.

"Why did I reverse the order in this case?"

She paused. Neal looked tired. "You had already greeted the patient when you came in, so this provided a test of short-term memory?"

Schneider nodded. "Exactly." He pulled up a chair close to Landon. "Let me fill you in, since Tanya tells me you don't remember much. Not too surprising—you took a good whack. You came in yesterday morning unconscious, pretty low on the coma scale, and got intubated in the emergency room. CT showed a parietal skull fracture"—he turned to Luna and patted his head on the rear left side to indicate the area—"but no bleeding in your brain or inside the skull. We repeated the CT this morning, and it looks the same. The skull fracture probably saved you. Why do I say that, Mr. Neal?"

"The force of the impact was dissipated into the bone, which did not damage the brain as much."

Landon smiled. He loved the give-and-take of Socratic teaching; it was sometimes intimidating when he was a student, but he had enjoyed the challenge, and as the teacher, he was known for challenging the students, pushing them to become better physicians. *Was that all gone now?* Duval looked impressed. Schneider gave another thumbs-up.

"We'll see how you do tonight," Schneider told Landon, "and if all goes well, we'll get you out of the ICU tomorrow and then home Friday."

"Can I go back to work?"

"Not for a couple weeks at least. Trust me, Ratliff, you won't feel like it, and it isn't safe."

"But I feel fine." That wasn't quite true, but he'd worked through sickness before.

"Sure you do. Lying still, in bed, with the lights off, no TV. Believe me, this is going to take a while. We'll repeat the CT in two weeks. If it's okay and you can function, we'll think about it."

"How about running?"

Schneider shook his head. "Not a chance. Nothing strenuous for two weeks. No driving, nothing. For the next couple of days, no TV, no cell phone, no computer. We have to let your brain recover."

"Can I at least get the catheter out? I'm pretty sure I can use a bedpan."

Schneider's laugh was brief but booming, like a cannon shot. "I can help you out there. Already ordered it. Any other questions?" He raised his face to Luna then back to Landon.

"What about my thumb?"

"Oh yeah. You shattered it at the base. Ortho wants to pin it. Probably tomorrow or Thursday. The trauma guys will probably be by later, too, but I think they'll sign off. We'll get physical therapy to come and see you tomorrow. You hungry?"

"Not really."

"Well, I ordered clear liquids, but we can advance your diet as you tolerate it. Don't be a hero about the pain meds either." He rose and stretched. "I'll see you in the morning." He nodded to Luna, and the parade vanished through the doorway.

"We'll get that catheter out in a few minutes," Tanya said, then followed the team to her other patient.

"Are you okay?" Luna asked. He nodded but knew his face betrayed him. No work, no running. Can't even drive. What was left if he couldn't work? Was he still a doctor? "Seems like things are going well?" Luna offered. "Home Friday is pretty good?"

"Yeah." The glare around the window shade was intensifying as the sun sank toward the horizon. "What time is it?"

Luna looked at her watch. "A little after six."

"If you need to go, it's okay."

"I'll stay if you want. Maybe you need to rest. It won't be dark for another couple hours."

"I need to call my mother."

Luna eased herself back into the chair. "Dr. Fanning called her last night. He thought she needed to know. Besides, you can't use the phone—Dr. Schneider said."

"What did my mom say?"

"I don't know for sure. She was upset, asked a lot of questions. Dr. Fanning was great. He was here all evening."

Landon nodded. Good old Mike Fanning. Always around when you needed him. "She's not coming out here … is she?"

"No. Not right away anyway." She searched the room. "Would you like some more water?"

He nodded, bypassed her offer of the straw, and then grasped the cup himself. After filling his mouth, he pressed his lips together to moisten them. His head didn't like being turned. "Do you see any lemon swabs, Luna?" She looked around, a puzzled expression on her face. "They look like big Q-tips, but they're wrapped up." He ventured a slight turn toward the bedside table. "There they are," he said. "Can you get me one?"

The lemony swab on his lips and Luna's smile added to his growing and welcome sense of comfort. "Dr. Fanning sent a message from your mother. She wanted me to give you a kiss for her." She tossed the spent swab in the wastebasket. "Lemon is one of my favorite flavors." Her hands cupped his face as if it were a baby bird while she touched her delicious soft lips to his.

"Things seem to be returning to normal."

Landon smiled, immediately recognizing Fanning's voice. Luna turned and Landon saw him standing in the doorway, still wearing his white coat.

"Good to see you again, Ms. Quinn," Fanning said, offering his hand.

"Luna, please, Dr. Fanning."

"It's a deal, but only if you call me Mike," he replied, still grasping her hand. "How are you holding up?"

Luna blushed and hooked a wayward strand of hair behind her ear. "I'm fine now. Landon's awake."

"So he is." Fanning approached the bed. A huge smile creased his face, accentuating his jowliness. Landon felt once again like a fish, this time one about to be devoured by a pelican. "How are you, Landon?" Fanning's voice cracked before he cleared his throat.

Landon felt his eyes welling up. "I'm good. Sore, but okay."

"Landon?" Luna interrupted, "I think I'll get going." She hoisted her backpack. "You two need to talk, and I have a cat to tend to." She leaned in and kissed him again. "I've got some papers to grade too." She shook hands with Fanning. "I'll let you two chat. It was nice seeing you again."

Fanning nodded. "Lovely to see you."

"Thanks for being here," Landon said. "See you tomorrow?"

"Right after class," Luna said, tapping the air above his nose. "Get some rest."

Fanning watched her walk out the door. He waited a moment then turned back, his eyebrows arched above his glasses, a nearsighted pelican once again.

"Thanks for being here," he mocked. "This sounds serious."

Landon smiled. He was getting used to the pain. "Don't overdo it. I'm sick."

"She seems special." Fanning eased himself into the chair. "She was here almost all day yesterday."

Landon nodded. "She told me you talked to my mom."

"Yes, and Luna was the one who suggested that. How long have you been seeing her now? This seems lengthy for you; you've mentioned her several times these last few months."

"What did my mother say?"

"Don't change the subject." Fanning pushed his glasses up. "How long have you been dating?"

"We've been out a few times." He tried not to smile, but Fanning's grinning face reflected such relief and joy—he was a true friend. "Okay, I met her in January, but seriously, we haven't been out much. She teaches creative writing at the college, and she's working on a novel. Her schedule is as bad as mine."

Fanning pursed his lips and nodded in mock seriousness. "Hmm. February, March, April," he counted on his fingers. "Three months, heading into four …"

"Okay, okay." Landon was chuckling, but his head was reminding him to remain still. "Can we talk about something else? How was my mom?"

"Upset but managing. She's quite a lady too. Did Luna fill you in?"

"On what?"

Fanning raised his chin. "Probably not." He cleared his throat. "Your father's ill, Landon. In the hospital, too, so your mother can't come here."

"What's wrong with him?" His father had been hospitalized back in February. The diagnosis of pancreatitis had not been surprising, given his long love affair with cheap bourbon, but for the most part, he had avoided the health problems that typically accompanied a lifetime of smoking and drinking.

"Not sure. Some stomach problem, according to your mother. I told her I'd keep her updated about you." Fanning smiled. "I confess I painted a rosier picture than your condition warranted last night. I didn't want to worry her too much. And now I look like a genius."

"Schneider said I couldn't use the phone," Landon said. "What's that all about?"

"Post-concussion, you know that. Limited sensory stimulation. Schneider's fanatical about it. And I think he's right, by the way."

"Two weeks off work? I've got that grant proposal to finish up. The deadline is June fifteenth."

Fanning feigned shock. "How *will* we get along?" He pushed his glasses up again. "Listen. You've had a serious blow to the head. You need to rest and recover. Take it a day at a time but resign yourself to being out of commission for at least a couple of weeks."

Isaac breezed into the room carrying supplies on a small tray. "Hi, Dr. Fanning. Sorry to interrupt, but we've got shift report in fifteen minutes. I'd like to get that catheter out."

Fanning rose. "Don't let me stand in the way, or Landon would have *me* catheterized." He patted Landon's arm. "I'll check back with you later. Get some rest."

Fanning sat at the nurse's station flipping through Landon's chart. The updated CT reports were there now. The brain scan report noted the skull fracture and the absence of bleeding in or around the brain. It was mysterious; jostling the brain could affect so much but show so little.

Fanning had reviewed all the scans last night with the radiology resident on duty. All of them. Even the neck, chest, pelvis, and abdomen scans that the trauma surgeons always ordered, blithely irradiating the entire body just to make sure they didn't miss anything. And then they had missed it anyway—and so had Fanning. The radiology attending had found it this morning and had called Fanning first.

He closed the chart as the trauma team approached. Dr. Zohar, the new trauma chief, led the parade. A meticulous dresser, he was never seen outside the trauma suite in his scrubs, and he insisted that his team do likewise. Absent the white coats, they would have resembled a collection of prep schoolers wandering the halls.

"Dr. Fanning," Zohar murmured, flashing remarkably white teeth that contrasted with his mocha skin. "How is Ratliff?"

Fanning replaced the chart in the rack and shook hands with Zohar. "He's awake and talking. Seems much better."

"Excellent. Have you spoken with him?"

Fanning shook his head. "I haven't. I just informed him that his father is hospitalized back home in Virginia, and I didn't think he needed more to worry about."

"I understand." Zohar nodded. "But we're planning to do the MRI in the morning, prior to his orthopedic procedure." He plunged his hands into his pockets. "Would you like me to tell him?"

"I'd rather you didn't. Let me tell him in the morning after he's had a good night's sleep. I'll be here early."

Zohar pursed his lips. "Fair enough, but I'd like to be here as well. I don't want Ratliff thinking I withheld information from him. Shall we say six?"

"You don't have to be here," Fanning replied, knowing if the roles were reversed, he'd feel the same way. Zohar's smile made further discussion unnecessary. He extended his hand, and Zohar gripped it. "See you at six." He remained standing until the group disappeared into Landon's room, then he slumped into the chair. It was time to call Mrs. Ratliff and tell her the good news about her son. The bad news could wait until tomorrow.

CHAPTER TWO

L una loved Wednesdays; one afternoon class, no office hours, so the morning was free for grading papers, preparing a lesson plan, or lately, working on her novel. After two days of sitting vigil at Landon's bedside, though, none of these options sounded as good as the opportunity to talk with a friend. So today, the writing would have to wait because she was meeting Diana for coffee.

She finished watering the jungle of plants on her piazza, lugged her bike down to street level, then rode north to Beaufain, where a steady stream of inbound traffic persuaded her to dismount and walk the last few blocks. The bike rack at Cup of Joe was half full. Inside, students with early classes or uninteresting night lives sat pecking away at laptops or cell phones, ignoring one another by mutual agreement. One or two tables held students engaged in human conversation.

There were two unoccupied chairs in a corner. Luna tossed her backpack into one and her helmet into the other. Diana joined her just as she was shaking her hair out.

"I still can't believe you ride a bike in a skirt," Diana said, offering a quick hug. "Looks great with the jean jacket, though." Diana was dressed for tennis in the white

Wimbledon bomber jacket that looked as if it were made for her. Luna considered taking up tennis every time she saw her in it.

"You just tuck it under you," Luna replied. "Beats walking and no carbon emissions." She nudged Diana toward the back of a short line.

"Okay, Mother Earth." Diana rolled her eyes. "At least I drive a hybrid."

Diana Vacker was Luna's assigned faculty mentor at College of Charleston. Despite mutual efforts to maintain professional distance, she and Diana had become close and met regularly for personal as well as professional conversation. Diana had proven to be a nonjudgmental listener as well as a source of wisdom and guidance. Luna respected her accomplishments and intellect and loved her sense of style.

Although Luna had always been the envy of her friends for her "casual prettiness," to her, Diana epitomized effortless, simple beauty. She was a true blonde (a bonding point since Luna prided herself on her own natural red hair) with a face that seemed designed for smiling. Her eyes always seemed to conceal a funny surprise. Bronzed from years of tennis, she wore the uneven, natural look of someone who enjoys being outdoors rather than someone who works at having a tan.

Armed with cappuccinos, they maneuvered through the tables a few minutes later and landed in the nook Luna had laid claim to earlier. Luna moved her backpack to the floor and settled into the spongy chair. Diana was scanning the crowd, a puzzled look on her face.

"I'll never understand how staring at your phone is better than conversation. Guess I'm showing my age." She turned her attention to her coffee. "This foam is so pretty, I almost hate to drink it."

"Not me," Luna said, displaying an exaggerated foam mustache that she slurped from her upper lip. "They'll make you another one, you know." She dabbed the remnants with a napkin while Diana chuckled. "So, how was Savannah?"

"Pretty, like always," Diana replied. "Especially this time of year. Mark was on the phone every day. Some deal in Amsterdam. It was nice to get away, I guess." She scooted forward in her seat, balancing her cup on her knees. "How was Landon's birthday?"

"I wish I could say memorable, but that would be a cruel joke."

"Sorry." Diana offered an overdone grimace then leaned even closer. "What happened?"

"Well … a lot. First of all, Landon was in a car wreck on Monday morning. He's in the hospital, and he missed his birthday completely."

"You're kidding." Diana's eyes narrowed. "You aren't kidding."

Luna shook her head. "I wish I was."

"Is he okay?"

"Getting better. He fractured his skull and was on a ventilator, but he's off now. Awake and talking but pretty banged up. He broke his thumb." She had never seen Diana look so pained. "Sorry to lay all this on you. I've been pretty much living at the hospital the past couple of days."

"I'm so sorry," Diana said. "Poor Landon. This is awful."

"I know. To tell you the truth, I feel partly to blame."

Diana tilted her head. Her eyes narrowed, but she said nothing. Luna recognized the look. She was waiting for more.

"I kept him up most of the night—before the wreck. I think he fell asleep driving." She wasn't certain about divulging her birthday surprise to her mentor at first, but as she began to describe the plan, each detail widened Diana's smile. The change in mood was welcome and overcame Luna's concerns about propriety.

"You didn't ride your bike in your underwear, did you?" Diana's wicked grin made the question seem hopeful.

"Uh, no. Still a little chilly, and getting arrested for indecent exposure wasn't part of the plan. I wore sweatpants and stashed them with my backpack and bike."

"So?"

Luna sipped her cappuccino, savoring the flavor along with the anticipation and delight on Diana's face. She knew it couldn't last. "It was so special, Diana. Our first time. Only Landon can't remember anything about it. He has amnesia from his head injury."

Diana's expression fell. She moved her cup from her lap to the side table then steepled her hands under her chin. Luna felt her eyes filling up; she reached for her napkin.

"I'm so sorry," Diana said. "That's sad. Poor Landon. But Luna, none of this is your fault. It just happened."

"I know." She rubbed her forehead. "Can I be honest with you, Diana?"

Diana gave her a flat-eyed look. "You have to ask?"

"I don't really *know* how I feel right now. Sad, confused, angry—I'm not sure. I mean, things were going so well … Now what? I want to help, but I don't even know him that well." She shifted her gaze and stared into her coffee cup. "I wish I could take back all the jokes I made about Landon turning forty."

"Careful. Forty is young to some of us, you know."

Luna waved her off. "I'm sorry. He seemed so worried about it. That's why I planned the birthday surprise. I thought it would take his mind off his age. I guess the car wreck did that. It took his mind off everything, including us." She dabbed her eyes again. "Maybe I'm making too much of this. He's getting better, and I've got things to do anyway. My novel won't write itself. At least classes are almost over … But, what if he needs something?" She smiled. "I'm sorry, Diana. You must think I'm losing it."

"No, of course not. Confusion is understandable, but it's only been a couple days, and you just slept with the guy, even if he can't remember it. This never seemed like a casual fling, the way you've talked about him. Seems to me, your novel can wait. He needs you, and I've always thought you were very interested."

"I *am* interested, but still. I don't know—the truth is, I don't even know him that well. I thought about what you said last week. A single man at his age is usually divorced, gay, or weird."

"Well, now *I* feel guilty about joking about his age. Anyway, gay seems unlikely, based on recent events."

Luna laughed. "I can say for certain that he is most definitely not gay."

"Divorced?"

"He says not."

"You asked?" Diana's smile was close-lipped and secretive.

"It came up. But now he's hurt, so what happens to us? What if things don't work out? I can't just walk away, but I can't spend all my time helping him either. I don't want to still be an assistant professor when *I* turn forty."

"I know, and you know I think you're doing great, and you know I think you worry about this too much. But let's not worry about it now, okay? What about Landon? How badly hurt is he? What's the prognosis?"

"Seems like he's getting better already." Luna shrugged. "He can't work for a while. I don't really know."

Diana said nothing for a moment then scooped some foam from her drink with her finger. "I can only imagine how strange this must be, Luna. But still, you seem to be getting way ahead of yourself. This isn't like you. Could it be you're moping about the birthday surprise?"

That stung, but Luna had learned to pause, to process what Diana had said, because she was wise and caring and honest—as honest as Luna fancied herself to be. She waited until Diana had finished her sip.

"Maybe a little. I put a lot into that surprise, and now it's gone. He can't even remember the first time we slept together."

"Hmm. As I said, this guy sure sounds like someone you care about, and you know this isn't his fault," Diana said. "Does anyone really know whether his memory will come back?"

Luna shook her head. She wasn't holding out much hope and didn't know if that was realistic or evidence of more sulking. She hated whining, especially to Diana.

"The future is anybody's guess, Luna, but it seems to me this relationship *does* matter to you. Right now he's hurt, you're hurt, and there's an awful lot going on. Things happen for a reason. Maybe it's time to catch your breath, reflect a little. It's normal to want some time for yourself. You aren't married to the guy. He's got family and friends, right?"

"No family here, but he has friends, I guess."

"Well, let them take their turn." Diana tilted her head, her eyes searching for Luna's. "Be kind to yourself, but don't punish Landon—or your relationship—for something that neither of you could control."

Luna nodded. If the gift was lost, maybe it was replaceable. Another reason to hope for a quick recovery.

It was a short ride to her office, but Luna took her time. Although she loved her talks with Diana, after today's conversation she needed to clear her head. Landon's upcoming birthday had provided a long, welcome diversion from her own impending milestone. But now his birthday was behind them, and its aftermath served as a constant reminder of time's fickle nature. Soon enough, she would turn thirty, and her life wouldn't be as she'd imagined it when she finished school—or even last week, for that matter.

She pedaled through the arch into The Cistern Yard, circling beneath the canopy of live oaks under the stern, watchful façade of Randolph Hall. Graduation was ten days away. Her third faculty procession already.

The grounds crew was busy planting fresh annuals. She knew they would overplant, partly to cover the dying daffodils but mostly to exceed the expectations of parents who cared nothing about the normal rhythms of nature, and whose substantial investment in their child's education carried an unspoken expectation of a fairy tale landscape as a backdrop to the commencement proceedings. Although she would have loved to stop and help plant, she resisted the urge and pedaled on, coasting among the eclectic mix of brightly colored buildings that served as classrooms and administrative offices. The campus always lifted her spirits. So did her own cramped office on the upper floor of a coral-colored stucco and brick house at the corner of George and Glebe Streets. The office opened onto the upper piazza, her sanctuary, where she graded papers, read, or held office hours. Her desk inside served as a repository for unopened mail and the desktop computer she generally ignored in favor of her laptop.

Her assistant was not at her desk in the foyer. Luna checked her mail cubby and climbed the stairs that led to her office. The small chalkboard mounted on the door held a message in flowing script: "Call Mike Fanning as soon as you get in."

"As soon as you get in" sounded ominous. Luna fumbled with her key in the balky lock then rummaged through her backpack. Her sister Fox regularly berated her for leaving her cell phone on silent mode, for being inattentive to what ought to be a constant, reliable source of communication. But Luna liked being incommunicado. She craved time for herself. The phone had recorded two missed calls from Fanning: one at 9:15 a.m., another at 9:30 a.m.

Fanning answered on the second ring, his booming voice immediately reassuring. As always, he thanked her for calling and inquired about her morning as if this were a social call. Luna noticed her heart racing as he cleared his throat. "I need to speak with you about Landon," he said. "I'm afraid it's not good news."

She swallowed. "I'm listening." The breath she had been holding escaped as she spoke, making her voice sound inappropriately sultry.

"I spoke with Landon this morning, and he asked me to tell you," Fanning said. "When he came into the emergency department after the crash, a number of X-rays and tests were done to make sure he didn't have other injuries, and one of the tests—a CT scan—showed something that needs further investigation."

"I'm still here," she said after a pause. "I don't really know what to ask even."

"I know. I'm sorry to drag this out, but I'm trying to give you some context."

"What is this 'something' that needs investigating?"

"We're not sure. It's in his left kidney, and it could be a hemorrhage—bleeding—or it could be something else."

"Like what?"

Fanning exhaled. "The radiologist thinks it has the appearance of a tumor."

"*Cancer?* Isn't Landon a little—" She knew better. Forty wasn't too young. Neither was thirty.

"We don't know anything for certain yet. The MRI— another imaging study—was done this morning. Landon is in surgery having his thumb repaired. We should know more this afternoon. Could you come over? I think it would help if you were here when I speak with him."

"Did he ask me to come?" She immediately wished she could take that back, unsure if she sounded eager or exasperated.

"Not specifically for this purpose. But I know you're a great comfort to him."

"You don't think I'd be intruding?"

"Certainly not. Ms. Quinn—uh, Luna—I won't lie to you. I suspect this news will be unwelcome, and your presence would be very helpful to Landon … and to me."

"My class ends at three. I can come any time after that."

"I can adjust my schedule to whatever time works for you."

She felt tears welling up, a mix of fear and tenderness. She was scared for Landon, but it felt good to be needed. "I'll come straight after my class," she said, wondering how she could teach anything worthwhile today. Exams started next week; maybe she could give her students a free day to catch up on their papers.

CHAPTER THREE

Landon's new room was larger and less cluttered than the ICU room, but it was full now—Fanning, Zohar, Luna, and half a dozen residents and students—and yet Landon felt more alone than he had ever felt in his life. The news this morning had been unsettling but uncertain enough to allow for some hope. When the sedative from surgery had worn off, he'd learned that the MRI had dashed that hope. Luna had been with him when Fanning and Zohar arrived to deliver the news. Their feigned optimism hadn't fooled him, even though he understood, because he had done the same thing with patients many times. Doctors aren't supposed to be pessimistic, especially when no one really knows how things will turn out. Why take away hope?

At least they had told him privately rather than in front of a cluster of students and residents he might have to see and teach in the future—if he had a future.

"Dr. Ratliff is forty-eight hours post closed head injury from a car crash," one of the students recited now. "He suffered a fractured thumb that was repaired today. Vital signs and mental status are normal. Physical therapy reports some minor balance issues but no motor deficits."

Landon held his tongue. Therapy had been torture. His tolerance for bright light had been poor, and his head pounded and swam while the therapist remained unfailingly upbeat, apparently blind to his suffering.

"He underwent MRI evaluation of a renal mass today. It appears to be an incidental renal cell carcinoma that will require further evaluation and treatment after discharge."

Landon was stuck on "incidental." Oh, by the way, Dr. Ratliff—you have cancer.

Dr. Zohar stepped forward. "Any laboratory workup of the tumor that is pertinent, Mr. Jackson?"

The student glanced at his clipboard. "Calcium, blood count, liver functions are all normal."

"Why does that matter, Ms. Petty?" Zohar asked another student.

"The results suggest there has been no spread of the tumor outside the kidney," she replied. "The prognosis is better if the tumor is contained."

"Precisely." Zohar turned to Landon. "I will leave it to Schneider whether you go home tomorrow or Friday. From our standpoint, you're ready. He will arrange follow-up for your head injury, and you can schedule follow-up with the urologist for your tumor. I assume you have instructions for your thumb?"

Landon shrugged. He was still contemplating "your tumor." Zohar made it sound so chummy, like a teddy bear or a favorite pillow, tucked in among his other injuries. There was nothing very chummy about his thumb right now. The anesthesia was wearing off.

"Perhaps they haven't rounded yet," Zohar said. "We'll catch up with them later or first thing in the morning. Any questions?"

Landon shook his head. "I'm fine. Thanks for everything." He tried to sound grateful, even though he felt about as lucky as someone struck by lightning. He had only one question, but he wasn't sharing it: *Why me?* There was no answer to that one, and he didn't want to sound whiny, especially with Luna in the room.

Zohar's team filed out, each member regarding Landon warily; one of the female students offered a quick smile. *Must be a girl thing*, Landon thought. Luna had been doing that repeatedly and looking at him as if he were wearing a sign around his neck proclaiming that he, Landon Ratliff, age forty, was now a cancer patient.

Fanning pulled up chairs and waited for Luna to settle before taking his seat. Landon shifted in the bed, hoping that Luna wouldn't feel compelled to pat or rub his aching arm. She apparently didn't and instead crossed her arms and folded them in on herself. Her eyes roamed elsewhere; she chewed on her pouty lower lip. Fanning looked exhausted and old.

"I spoke with your mother just before I came over," Fanning said now. "I told her only that you were improving and that more tests were being run. Do you want me to tell her?"

Luna turned toward him. Landon struggled to find his voice. "No, not yet. I'll wait until I know more. She's probably worried enough anyway."

Fanning's jowls quivered and spilled over his splayed collar. "Sure. Things will be clearer in a day or two."

"Anything more about my dad?"

"She said he's improving. Should go home soon." Fanning cleared his throat. "Said it was pancreatitis."

He wasn't surprised. Alcoholic pancreatitis often recurred, especially when the patient continued drinking. He guessed his father, a Vietnam veteran, was at the VA hospital in Richmond, where Landon had done rotations in medical school. Things there never changed much; students and residents still provided too much unsupervised care, joking thoughtlessly and unkindly to ease the stress. Those jokes were always about the old guys, skinny men with sallow complexions, barrel chests, and nicotine-stained fingers, with shiny, hairless skin that betrayed their poor circulation, and bellies sagging with fluid their failing livers could not keep from spilling into their abdominal cavities. They were difficult patients, isolated by war experiences, illness, and lifestyle choices and by the sense that they deserved better than what they were getting. Now his father had become one of those men.

"I'll call her as soon as Schneider lets me use a phone," Landon said. "For sure when I get home, unless he's had my phone removed."

"You should probably be cleared in a day or two," Fanning said. "Better to be careful."

Dr. Schneider appeared in the doorway alone. His expression conveyed a degree of distress and respect that touched Landon, even as it reminded him that, for now at least, they were no longer colleagues. Fanning rose to greet him.

"Please sit," Schneider told him. He remained at the foot of the bed. "Well, I don't know what to say about the latest news. I'm sorry, but at least the tumor appears small and well contained. I spoke with Bill Taylor, and he seemed very optimistic."

Taylor was the head of urology, an elder statesman who ought to have retired a while back, or so it seemed to Landon. But he admired Taylor for being well read, an excellent teacher, and always courteous to students, residents, faculty, and staff.

"I assume he recommended nephrectomy?" Fanning asked, then quickly swiveled his head toward Luna. "Removal of the kidney."

"That's one option," Schneider replied. "Problem is, we'd like to avoid general anesthesia after a closed head injury. The data are mixed, but there are numerous reports of decline in cognitive function."

"How long would I have to wait?" Landon asked.

"Ideally? A couple months." Schneider waved off Fanning's offer of his seat. "Taylor didn't recommend waiting that long, so he suggests you consider RFA."

"RFA stands for radiofrequency ablation," Fanning explained to Luna. "A procedure where a catheter is threaded into the kidney and the tumor is essentially burned away."

"Sounds awful," Luna said.

"How effective is it?" Landon asked.

"Very effective if the tumor is small, which this one is," Schneider said. "For tumors less than three centimeters, the cure rate with one treatment looks to be about eighty-five percent. Less than one percent fail after a second treatment."

"What then?"

"I guess you could have the nephrectomy."

"The RFA procedure is done under light sedation by an interventional radiologist," Fanning said to Luna. "It's not painful, takes less time, and recovery is much quicker."

"It's your decision," Schneider said, shoving his hands into his lab coat pockets. "In fact, you can go home and think it over. You did well at therapy. You can go tomorrow." He glanced at Luna then back at Landon. "It might be helpful to have someone at home with you, just in case."

"In case of what?" Landon felt his face reddening. He didn't want Luna or anyone else to have to babysit him. But *especially* not Luna.

Schneider shrugged. "You never know, Ratliff. You could lose your balance or maybe just need a little help. You probably won't feel like fixing meals. Just little stuff. Just for a few days."

"I can help him," Luna said. "I don't live far away, and if I need to stay with him, I will."

Schneider nodded. "Just a day or two, I think."

"I'll run by the store tonight and get some things," Luna said to Landon. "Stock up your fridge. We can make a list."

Schneider smiled. "Seems like you're in good hands, Ratliff. I'll see you in the office on Friday, and we'll do some cognitive testing then. Repeat CT in two weeks and repeat cognitive testing two weeks after that."

"What about work?"

"Not until after the CT and only if you're asymptomatic. I'd plan on two to four weeks off. Spring is a beautiful time to relax, Ratliff."

"Can I travel?" Maybe he could go home.

"Short car trips only when necessary. No air travel for at least a couple weeks. Recovery time is variable. Take it easy through the weekend and see how you feel. See you in the morning before you go." He shook hands with Fanning and with Luna and was gone.

Fanning cleared his throat. "Landon, I need to share something with you—I hope you won't be angry with me."

Landon said nothing. Right now, he was angry with the world, but he had never been angry with Mike Fanning in his life.

"I took the liberty of calling Ramon Flaco. He's the best urologist I know, and your best friend's father. I thought he might be able to help." He bowed his head. "I should have asked your permission first, before sharing your condition with anyone else."

A pang of regret crept into Landon's muddled mind. He hadn't kept in touch with Dr. Flaco, who had mentored and helped him long ago, before he had decided to switch from surgery to critical care. He hadn't spoken to his "best friend" Enrique in far too long either. Enrique had befriended him in medical school, the first day of anatomy lab, when Landon was staring down at a cadaver, still wondering what a dock builder's son was doing trying to become a doctor.

"It's okay, Mike. I appreciate you calling. What did he say?"

Fanning forced a smile. "Well, he was shocked of course and sends his best wishes for a full recovery. He recommends Quentin Lake for the tumor. Lake's at Tulane."

"Are they back in New Orleans?"

"Oh yes." Fanning turned to Luna. "The medical school, along with the hospital, was devastated by Katrina. You probably knew that."

"I knew about the hurricane," Luna said. "Landon told me he did his residency in New Orleans. You were his teacher."

"Mike went back there to help after the hurricane," Landon said to her. "They had to move the medical school to Texas."

"I didn't do much," Fanning said. "Anyway, they're back home, and Flaco thinks you should go there as soon as you're able."

He swallowed. His throat still burned. "I could just do it here, couldn't I?"

"Sure. It's your decision."

"Nothing much left to hide now." He waved a hand over his bed. "My ass has been hanging out for everyone to see all week anyway."

Fanning chuckled. "True. Your dignity has been battered a bit. Think it over. You've got a couple weeks at least until you can travel, and Schneider doesn't recommend you embark on treatment immediately."

"He's crazy. I can't take four weeks off."

"He said two to four, Landon," Luna said.

"Take it one day at a time," Fanning said.

"But my grant. The admissions committee—I'm taking over as chairman."

"Perfect timing." Fanning smiled. "The admission letters went out a month ago, and new applications won't come in until fall. Most chairs cancel at least one summer meeting— sometimes two."

"I wasn't going to do that. We've got work to do."

Fanning rose from his chair and peered at him over his smeared glasses. "Work that can wait." His enormous, jowly, closed-mouth smile seemed patronizing right now, though

Landon knew better. "Relax and heal, my friend. I know relaxing doesn't come easily for you, but you need it to help you heal. The medical school will be there when you return." He turned toward the door. Luna forced a smile when he touched her lightly on the shoulder. "As Schneider said, you appear to be in excellent hands." He paused in the doorway. "Dr. Flaco asked if you wanted him to inform Enrique."

"What did you tell him?"

"I told him I'd ask you. I'd already presumed enough, I think."

"It's okay. He can tell him."

"Are you sure?"

"Yes. Enrique will spaz out, but not to his father." He felt Luna's eyes on him but didn't want to meet her gaze. "He would want to know, I guess. Tell him that I can't talk on the phone yet."

Fanning stared at him for what seemed like a long time, then smiled and nodded to Luna. He left without saying more.

Landon closed his eyes; he wanted a hole to crawl into. Who would finish the grant? Maybe he could postpone the committee until the end of May. He had to be better by then—he was on the schedule to attend in the ICU. He had never called in sick; during medical school, he had spent one memorable night delivering babies between episodes of vomiting. He felt fine.

No, he didn't. His head felt like a dirigible with a jackhammer pounding away inside. Everything hurt. Curling into a ball and sucking his thumb would be too obvious, but it sounded pretty good right now. His thumb hurt like hell. It felt like they rebuilt his whole arm. He couldn't cry or scream—Luna was here. He didn't want her staying with him either. Well, he did, but not to watch over him. He wasn't that old yet, was he? Cancer patients were supposed to be old. He didn't feel old. He wanted his mom.

CHAPTER FOUR

L andon awoke early Saturday morning, even though
the conditions were ideal for sleeping in. A light rain
peppered the roof, pattering through the leaves of the
magnolia outside his bedroom window. Cloud cover muted
the daylight, sparing his eyes and wounded brain. His bed,
his sheets, his pillow all felt fresh and familiar after the
institutional sleeping arrangements he thankfully had not
grown accustomed to. His thick blanket provided just enough
protection against the morning chill.

The bed felt almost perfect. He wished Luna were there
beside him instead of sleeping in the guest room. That might
have been torture, though, since sex was still forbidden.
Things had been going so well with Luna, and now she was
his nursemaid. He wasn't sure she'd ever want him after this,
and he definitely didn't want pity to be the emotion luring
her to his bed. At least he was thinking about sex again;
perhaps this was some additional evidence of his recovery.

There were clear signs of improvement. He had passed
the cognitive and physical testing yesterday, so Schneider
removed the ban on telephone usage. Television and
computer remained off-limits until the headaches subsided,

but with the telephone embargo lifted, he had been able to call home and speak to his mother last evening. It had been a difficult conversation; he was glad Luna had gone home to tend to her cat.

The news about his father was sketchy. He would likely be discharged on Sunday if he was able to eat. His mother had sounded tired and older all of a sudden. Landon tried to reassure her—he was doing better, and Luna was helping a lot. He smiled when his mother expressed her admiration for "this new woman" amidst poorly disguised probing questions about her that he was happy to deflect.

He had not told his mother about the cancer. Despite having rehearsed what he might say, her broken, tired voice and obvious relief at hearing from him made delivering more bad news seem cruel. So he had decided to wait until today, but now he wondered if it might not be better to wait until his father got home. That way, at least one burden would be removed from his mother before Landon replaced it with another. Or would it? He recalled his father's prolonged convalescence after his own car crash, back when Landon was just a teenager. He'd rebroken the leg that had been shattered in Vietnam, and it healed slowly. His father had retreated into pain pills washed down with his customary daily dose of beer or whiskey, reciting some mysterious mantra from his military days about "seventy-five, dead or alive" whenever the pain became unbearable. He had been grouchy and unpleasant to everyone in the family. Landon remembered finding his mother crying late at night when his father's relentless meanness finally wore down the stoic façade she wore for the sake of her children. Now, when his father came home from the hospital, he would be her problem exclusively. Maybe it would better to tell her today and let her assume one additional burden at a time.

Even before breakfast, he had again changed his mind about telling his mother. The recollection of his father's mysterious mantra had occupied his thoughts for a while, offering hope that his memory was at least partially intact. He remembered hearing the mantra again on his first visit to New Orleans. The man who uttered it died before Landon could discover its meaning. And although he had long ago given up on learning the source and meaning of that strange phrase, its reappearance at least diverted his thoughts from injury and illness for a time. At least until unsettling news yanked him back into reality, forcing him to process the information and settle on a course of action (which included not telling his mother yet) that seemed sensible and logical.

The news had come by telephone while he was making coffee. The call was from Dr. Taylor; Landon had expected to hear from him yesterday.

"Sorry it's taken so long," Taylor said. "I've been reviewing your studies in detail. Last night, I called Dr. French and had him take a look."

Landon smiled. Ben French was Taylor's closest friend, the recently retired chair of radiology, and yet Taylor addressed him by his last name.

"He confirmed my diagnosis," Taylor continued. He cleared his throat. "Excuse me. Dr. Ratliff, it appears the tumor extends a bit further than we thought."

Landon's heart skipped and raced. "Metastatic disease?"

"No, no, no. I'm sorry. No evidence of spread to other organs." Verbal backpedaling seemed to weaken Taylor's voice. "Nothing in the renal vein either." He forced a cough.

"Sorry. But on the MRI, there appears to be extension into the perinephric fat."

That meant the tumor had grown out of the kidney, at least a little bit. That made the prognosis worse, but how much? He couldn't manage more than an anemic, "So?"

Taylor seemed to understand. "Based on the tumor size and its extension, I would recommend partial removal of the kidney instead of an ablation procedure. Dr. French is reviewing the literature today."

"Dr. Schneider thinks I should avoid general anesthesia because of the head injury."

"For how long?"

"I'm not sure. A couple months maybe."

Taylor grunted. "That's too long to wait. I suggest you seek a second opinion. My own experience with trauma victims suggests that when surgery is required, it is done, and I don't recall serious problems with the anesthesia."

He didn't hear much of the conversation after that. He appreciated Taylor giving up part of his weekend to try and be helpful. He also knew medicine was not an exact science. He himself had provided countless patients with apparently conflicting options and had done so because he felt obligated to offer as much information as possible. Now as the recipient, he was unprepared for the rapid heartbeat and jitteriness that ensued, for the anger he struggled to conceal as he begged off further conversation, concocting a headache that required rest.

In fact, his head felt better today, and the barely perceptible dizziness that made him walk as if his feet hurt was perhaps improved as well. The soreness in his thumb persisted, but his ribs and left leg ached less. He was healing up, at least in some areas, while a tumor that could eventually kill him was growing, extending outside the kidney, minute by minute.

Raindrops spattered the window that looked out across the small yard toward Meeting Street. Cars were visible through the recently trimmed privet hedge, approaching or leaving the same intersection where his life changed—forever—in the time it took for his heavy eyelids to drift downward. Now he wanted answers, definitive answers. He wanted someone to tell him what to do. Schneider had done that, but he hadn't known the full extent of the disease. Taylor had said it was a more invasive tumor. That sounded riskier than general anesthesia after a head injury.

Overhead, he heard footsteps, then the creak of the bathroom door that he'd never taken time to oil. No time now to check the internet for answers. Luna would remind him about Schneider's instructions, and anyway, reading made his head hurt. He contented himself watching gravity working on the raindrops, pulling them free of their landing spots on the window, releasing them to travel a seemingly random path to the sill.

"You okay?" Luna asked, once she had poured herself coffee and joined him at the kitchen table. "I thought I heard the phone."

"Yeah." He knew she wouldn't pry, and although technically his answer could suffice, she deserved better. "It was the urologist." He kept his eyes on the window. "He thinks I should have surgery instead of the other procedure." He turned and could not suppress the smile he had planned to force. Beneath a hastily constructed, perfectly casual sloppy bun, her remarkably large eyes now looked enormous, asking the question that she seemed to hope he would not keep private. She was pretty, even in the morning.

"It's okay," he said. "Doctors don't always agree."

"Why does he think that?"

"He's an old guy, thinks the traditional approaches are better."

She tilted her head. Her eyes narrowed. A tiny furrow split the space between her eyebrows. "Are they?"

He shrugged. "For some types of tumors."

"Yours?"

He drained his cup with a prolonged gulp. "It's not clear, Luna, and you heard Schneider—he thinks general anesthesia is risky."

"Are you worried?"

"No, why?" He rose and busied himself in the cabinet. "You want more coffee?"

"You look worried."

"I'm fine." He turned and forced his mouth into what he knew was an unconvincing smile. "Just got to figure out the best course of treatment."

"Why don't you call Enrique or his father? They're urologists. You haven't spoken with them yet."

He nodded. She had to remind him. "Yeah, I should. I'll call them later today."

She tilted her head again, her eyes searching for his. He looked away, scratching absently at his neck. When he looked back, she was sipping her coffee and staring past him at the rain.

Luna declined his offer of breakfast. She seemed eager to head home, even more so than the day before. The rain had picked up a little, prompting Landon to offer his car—

forgetting, once again, that he no longer owned a serviceable vehicle. Instead, she borrowed a rain jacket, mounted her bike, and pedaled north into the shower. For the first time, he was glad to see her go. He took that as another sign of improvement in his health rather than a reflection upon their relationship; she seemed to want some private time too.

Newspapers still in their plastic wrappers went into the recycling bin. Luna had done the remaining dishes last night. The coffee pot had already been rinsed. He considered a shower, then realized he was dithering, so he forced himself to sit down and call Enrique. He must have gotten the news by now. Probably procrastinating, trying to figure out what to say. It had been far too long since Landon had called him. Neither had made enough effort to keep in touch, but Enrique was married and had three children, so at least he had an excuse.

Enrique had it made, having followed the career plan laid out by his father, Dr. Ramon Flaco, now a semiretired urologist in Miami. After completing residency training, Enrique had opened the satellite office in Naples, and under his father's astute direction, the practice had thrived and grown into the largest in southwest Florida. Enrique and Amy had children, attended mass dutifully, and built their waterfront mansion on land purchased by Ramon twenty-five years earlier.

That could have been Landon, too, had he not changed his mind about becoming a urologist. That trip to New Orleans during his internship had changed everything. He met Dr. Fanning and discovered his love for critical care— and for a Tarot reader who played rubboard in a Zydeco band. The love for critical care had lasted, fortunately, though sometimes he wondered how his life might have been different. It would sure be strange now—a urologist with kidney cancer. It was even stranger trying to picture himself living in a waterfront mansion with a wife and children.

Amy answered on the second ring. The years had worn down the high notes a little, but her voice still brought a smile to his face.

"How *are* you? Enrique and I have been frantic since we heard the news. We wanted to call, but Ramon said you couldn't use the phone."

"Yeah, I know. Don't worry about it, Amy. I'm okay, I guess."

"Enrique is going to be sorry he missed you. He's operating today."

"On Saturday?" Enrique was never known for his love of hard work.

"Don't ask. He grumbles all week when it's his turn, but the practice is so busy, here in 'the land of the leg bag.'" Her laugh took Landon back to their school days.

"Well, you're probably busy. I can call back."

"Not at all. Ramon's at baseball practice, and Libby and Hector are at the club. Thank God for tennis lessons." Then she added, in an awful impersonation of Marlene Dietrich, "And so, I have the place to myself. Some wine, a bubble bath, a few bonbons. You aren't disturbing anything, darling."

Actually, it was easier for him to talk with Amy. He had always felt comfortable around her, always marveled at the way she listened and cared, no matter what he had to say. She listened now, offering only an occasional exclamation of surprise or anguish as he related the events of the past week.

"Landon, I am so sorry," she said finally, when he had told all he could stand to share. Her voice cracked and was interrupted by sniffles. "God, I can't believe it."

"It's okay. I can't either. I'm sorry to ruin your Saturday."

There was a pause. "You aren't ruining anything. We get so caught up in what we're doing. I feel terrible for you, and I'm sorry we haven't kept in touch better."

He felt a headache coming on. "I haven't exactly been beating a path to your door either."

"Enrique will want to talk to you."

"Tell him I'll call him. Or I guess he can call me."

By the time he extricated himself from Amy's well-intended but increasingly annoying apologies, instructions, and encouragement, he was too tired to call Enrique's father. His head felt full and tight, the dull light seemed more intense, and squinting made his headache worse. The glacier glasses were on the bedside stand upstairs. A nap sounded good. He wanted to shade his eyes, but not with a casted arm, and he needed his good arm to hold the stair rail. So he kept his head down and stared at his nonslip hospital socks making their uncertain way up the stairs to his bed.

CHAPTER FIVE

Landon's rain jacket still dangled from the coat hook beside Luna's front door a week later. She arrived home carrying a bulging sack of groceries, provisions for the meal she'd been looking forward to with increasing anticipation over the past few days. The jacket confirmed her distraction—she'd had several opportunities to return it—and reminded her of the promise she'd made with Diana about today.

Hazel was hiding. Luna called to her, made little kissing sounds, but knew the cat was punishing her for her absences, and so she soon abandoned the effort. Instead, she set about restoring the sanctuary they both had missed. She tossed the rain jacket into the closet and put on her favorite Tony Bennett music.

The calendar needed some attention too. May 6 was last Sunday, so she tore off pages until she reached Saturday, May 12. Graduation Day—one of her favorites and extra special this year because Diana had agreed to come for brunch.

After putting away the groceries, sifting the litter box, and replenishing Hazel's food and water bowls, she opened the windows to admit the thick, heavy air. Then she turned her attention to the piazza garden. The tea olive tree was blooming, filling the balcony with the scent of apricots. Cascades of colorful blooms spilled from the hanging baskets of bougainvillea that adorned each corner. But she had neglected the washtub filled with bulbs. Ordinarily, the tired-looking tulips would already have been replaced with vibrant annuals to contrast with her beloved gardenia, which would soon explode with the snow-white, fragrant blooms that always reminded her of fresh sweet cream. Her bulbs would just have to forgive her this year, and they'd have to be patient. Final papers, a novel, and a boyfriend who needed her were higher on her list, and the novel hadn't gotten much attention lately either.

Things were definitely looking up, though. Landon was improving; most of her visits this week had been social calls, but he'd seemed glad to see her. He still had some headaches but otherwise had little pain, and his balance was better. Unfortunately, his memory was not. She wondered now if she should have left the balloon bouquet in his house when Landon came home from the hospital. At the time, she thought it might confuse him, but now she wished she'd used it as a conversation starter.

She pruned here and there and swept the piazza before sinking into the wicker rocker and closing her eyes. The apricot smell carried her back to California. Tony was singing "Lazy Afternoon." Sounded like a great idea, but not today. Graduation was at four, and Diana was coming at noon. A short nap sounded awfully good. She hadn't slept so well this week, worrying about Landon.

Enough of that. Hopefully, the weather would cooperate—May in Charleston could be glorious or stifling;

graduation called for glorious. As did brunch, which Luna hoped to serve on the piazza. She stood on the threshold, eyes swiveling, chewing her lip. The outdoor space would add a picnic quality to the meal; indoors would be cooler, though.

Luna had lucked into her apartment on her first day in Charleston. The owner's prerental renovation had eliminated the claustrophobic enclosed spaces so characteristic of the city's architecture. Larger windows allowed daylight to flood the single open space that contained the kitchen and living room, now divided only by a curved, granite-topped island that served as preparation space and as the everyday dining area. (For special occasions, she had a side table that converted into a dining table that accommodated her mismatched, flea-market folding chairs perfectly.) The living area contained a futon, two straight-back sitting chairs, and Luna's favorite: a brown leather Morgan reading chair and ottoman that had been a graduation gift from her sister, Fox.

No time for lounging right now. Hazel was still sulking, and Luna wouldn't give her the satisfaction of searching for her. Instead, she pulled out the heavy cream and placed a saucer full on the island. Ordinarily, she shooed Hazel off the island, disgusted by the thought of cat ass sitting where she chopped vegetables, but she knew the cat loved sitting up high, perched on the edge, surveying her territory like a majestic lion. The combination of cream and her personal pride rock should prove irresistible.

She busied herself in the kitchen until finally, two pointed ears appeared at the bedroom doorway. Luna tried to hide her smile in her tea cup, then turned her back, staring out the window until finally she felt Hazel's fur against her leg.

The cat glided back and forth like a sentry, never looking up, ignoring the cream until she had firmly established her indifference. Her tabby fur was the color of a faded Dreamsicle and needed brushing this morning.

"Well hello, sweet kitty," Luna said at last. Hazel marched on, turning only when the full length of her tail had tracked across Luna's leg. Finally, she circled the island, sat, and surveyed the living room briefly, then leaped up and closed in on the saucer, only then allowing a faint purr to escape. Luna smiled and stroked Hazel's sleek back while she lapped up the cream. Hazel had made her point; domestic tranquility had been restored. It took very little to set things right again. Luna wished people were more like cats.

Diana arrived right on time bearing a spring mix bouquet and looking so pretty in her sky-blue summer dress, her hair pulled into a casual up-do that seemed easy and perfect.

"Hey, there," she said now, handing Luna the bouquet. "I hope you don't mind—I know you have your own beautiful flowers."

"Not at all. I meant to get some this morning. I'm way behind on my gardening." She pulled a vase from the cabinet and filled it. "Would you mind putting this on the table outside? We're eating on the piazza." She still had to stifle a smile every time she said piazza; in California, it was a porch or a balcony, but she had become thoroughly Charlestonized over the past three years.

"The table looks beautiful," Diana said. "Your olive tree has gotten so big."

"Yeah, it has. It needs some attention, though. Everything does. Can I pour you a glass of lemonade?"

Diana nodded and smiled. She turned and began to weave through the living area. "This place is so you, Luna. You've done a beautiful job."

"Don't look too close. Anything that looks like dust might be."

"Stop. It's not like you haven't been busy. She paused by the desk where Luna's journal rested on her laptop. "How's your novel coming?"

"Don't ask." She handed Diana a glass. They touched glasses and sipped. Diana's satisfied smile made Luna want to laugh.

"It's not wine, but it'll do," Diana said. "Should we sit here?"

"No, let's sit outside. It's such a beautiful day." Luna grabbed the charcuterie board she'd thrown together and led the way.

They chitchatted through the appetizer course, commenting on the weather, Luna's flowers, the merits of gouda versus cheddar, and whether capicola had really ever been part of a live animal. Diana was so funny; Luna loved her delivery, the way something would come to her mid-sip, and how she'd struggle to avoid gulping, eager to make another hilarious pronouncement.

The main course was ready, warming in the oven and cooling in the refrigerator, and when it came time to plate the food, Diana insisted that they do it together. She gushed over the menu: crispy crab cakes, blueberry coleslaw, and coconut rice.

"Wow, this is really beautiful, Luna," she said, once they had returned to the table. "Everything looks perfect. Did your mother teach you to cook?"

Luna laughed. "No. That's funny. My mother was not and is not a cook." She stabbed a blueberry. "My oldest sister did the cooking. She taught me a little, but mostly, I just used cookbooks and experimented. Lots of disasters. How about you?"

Diana shook her head. "Nooo. I do not cook. Well, spaghetti or something once in a while, but if I cook too often, Mark gets suspicious." She smiled broadly, her entire face seeming to light up. "I order a mean pizza, though."

Luna gazed out at the street below. "Seems awfully quiet for graduation day."

"Oh, it'll pick up. It's early. I love graduation."

"Me too. I'm going to every after-party tonight."

Diana's eyes caught hers, then shifted away. "Be careful, Luna. You wouldn't be the first faculty member whose career was derailed in a fraternity house."

"Who?" She straightened and leaned into the table. "Tell me."

"No one I know," Diana said, waving the question off. "I was warned when I started here, and I've taken the advice. It's best to keep your distance from the students, at least socially. Don't forget—you're still young enough to be hot to these guys."

That comment felt better than she had expected. She hoped it didn't show. "Don't shortchange yourself, Diana. I see the boys looking at you too."

Diana shook her head. "No. Maybe in a Mrs. Robinson way, which isn't a compliment in my opinion. You're much closer to their age, and … well, please be careful."

She recognized what Diana wasn't saying, knew she was struggling to keep the agreement they'd made on the phone yesterday—to take a break from sickness and illness, to focus on graduation and her students, just for a little while. It was too late now. She tried to shield her face. "It's good advice, Diana. Thanks. I know how vulnerable I am."

Diana said nothing. Luna knew she wasn't the type to change the subject. She would do what she always did—be a friend, listen without judging, and let the conversation go where Luna wanted it to go. Her eyes were kind, but reflected Luna's pain.

"It's okay," Luna said. She looked away. "You've been great all day, but I can't just ignore everything that's been going on. It would be so easy to do something stupid." She dabbed at a tear in the corner of her eye.

"Luna, after today, school's out." Diana's eyes were locked onto her now, but Luna saw nothing but kindness.

"I know that. So?"

"So, have you thought about getting away? Maybe you should take a trip."

Luna smiled. "Great minds think alike. I *am* taking a trip."

Diana sat forward. Her eyes narrowed. "When … where? With whom?"

"Tomorrow. Beaufort. With Landon." She saw Diana flinch. "I know—it seemed like a good idea last weekend. He was so pitiful. As soon as I suggested it, I had second thoughts. Am I being too pushy? I don't want to smother him, and it might be weird with him hurt and all. I thought he might forget about the idea, but he didn't. His memory seems better."

Diana's brows came up, but Luna cut her off. "Not that much better, Diana. He still doesn't remember his birthday."

Diana looked away. "Beaufort's beautiful. Where are you staying?"

"Cuthbert House. I stayed there last summer. It was nice."

"I've heard that. Never stayed there, but I love the town." Diana fiddled with her napkin. Luna felt relieved when she finally looked up. "You haven't mentioned this trip, Luna. Has this been bothering you all week?"

"I've been complaining enough. I didn't want to trouble you with this. Besides, I talked to my sister about it."

"What did she say?"

"Oh, she thinks it's a great idea. She says I'm overanalyzing, says I should loosen up and just go for it. I'm not like her, though. She doesn't think about people's feelings enough."

"Seems a little harsh. I've never met her, or Landon, for that matter, but I've heard you talk about her, and you seem close."

"Do you think this trip is a good idea? Don't you think it might be too much?"

The look Diana gave made Luna wish she could take that last comment back. "You know me better than that, Luna. It doesn't matter what I think. This is *your* decision. What do *you* think?"

"I don't know. Part of me feels bad for Landon, and part of me feels bad for me, for us. Things were going so well. Now, I don't know whether I'm pushing too hard or being too casual about all of this. I'm not entirely certain about any of it. I'm not writing, either. At least the semester is over, so I don't have to worry about preparing lectures." She felt tears welling up. "I know I'm getting older, but not *this* old. New relationships are supposed to be fun."

"Haven't you and Landon had fun?"

"We used to. I can't remember. I know he can't—" Luna paused and stared into her plate. She heard Diana take a big breath. When Luna looked up, she was waiting, elbows perched on the table, chin resting on her interlaced fingers.

"It isn't Landon's fault that he can't remember your birthday surprise, Luna. It seems like you're punishing him—and yourself—over this. You do what you want about the trip, but if you decide to go, try to be positive. Otherwise, you aren't being fair to Landon, and that's not like you."

Luna nodded. "You're right. I owe him better than this. It isn't his fault."

"Sounds like he wants to go?"

"Yeah. He's excited about it. It's a beautiful place."

"Well then. Seems like an opportunity for some new memories."

Luna smiled. "Maybe. He's getting better. Who knows?" She sat up straight. "I'm sorry for being so whiny, Diana. I think Landon needs me, and that feels good, but I'm sick of tiptoeing around, wondering if he's okay, wondering if I'm doing the right thing."

"It's okay. You're not Mother Teresa. Anyone would feel this way. I get tired of taking care of Mark when he's sick, and he's my husband." Diana rested her hands in her lap. "Luna, I don't give advice—you know that—but here's what I think: you aren't saying no, so it sounds like you want to go. So go, and do your best to make it fun and romantic and everything you want. If it doesn't work out, well, maybe that's a message you need to pay attention to."

Luna settled into the chair. Diana was right. This trip was important and not just for Landon.

CHAPTER SIX

The cable stays on the Ravenel Bridge convinced Landon that putting the top down had been a bad idea. Glaring at him like a giant spider web in the brilliant sunshine, the stays, along with the drone of the wind and the staccato appearance of oncoming traffic, mounted a relentless assault on his still-tender brain, reminding him that he was not as well as he'd hoped. Sure, he had traded the glacier glasses for his Ray Bans, a welcome if timid emergence from the land of the disabled, but halfway across the Cooper River, he affirmed Dr. Schneider's recommendations as prudent rather than overcautious.

Luna's flapper-style beach hat was providing both sun protection and hair containment. Nevertheless, the unfettered hair danced in the wind like gasoline-fed flames, licking occasionally at his shoulder. Her Wayfarers were the originals and black instead of tortoiseshell, so at least he and Luna weren't sunglass date mates. Usually chatty, she seemed preoccupied this morning, but in a happy way, as if she were harboring a surprise. Probably enjoying the opportunity to drive, particularly since she had rented a convertible for their adventure.

He closed his eyes until they had crossed the bridge, but their eastward route kept the sun in his face. He didn't want to complain; he had already killed the radio, clearly a setback for Luna's road trip plans. "How'd you find this place?" he asked, hoping to divert his mind from the sensory assault.

"*Southern Living.* Best new beach restaurant. The brunch menu looks fantastic. A little out of the way, but I love the name."

It wasn't long before they reached Sullivan's Island. For once, he appreciated its narrow, inadequate roads that prohibited anything resembling speed. They crawled along the main drag lined with restaurants and beach boutiques selling upscale knickknacks for people with money to spend. Out of the wind and no longer facing the sun, he felt his headache subsiding. Their destination, The Wayward Daughter, was in a two-story frame house, freshly painted blue, with gleaming white porches facing the harbor. Luna became visibly giddy when they scored a table on the upstairs porch.

Landon gladly yielded the view to her, choosing the seat that kept the sun at his back. "So are you the wayward daughter in your family?" he asked, mulling over the menu while the aroma of fresh coffee enveloped him.

She smiled. "I think so. I'm the one who traveled farthest from home."

He tested his memory. "You're the baby, right?"

"Just like you, only I'm the fourth of four." She had removed her sunglasses, and the climbing sun drew a squint that crinkled her freckled nose.

"Everyone back in California?"

"My parents are there and two of my sisters. My oldest sister, Tule, lives in Lake Tahoe, on the Nevada side."

"Julie?"

Luna laughed. "Tule—with a *T*."

"Unusual name. Must be a story there."

"Yep. Tule is a fog that blankets the central valley of California from fall to spring."

"Your sister's named after fog?"

Luna laughed. "That's nothing. My sister Sutter is named after the smallest mountain range in the world, the Sutter Buttes, and Fox is named after a theatre in Visalia."

Landon leaned in closer. "So what about you? Named for the moon?"

His question hung in the diminishing space between them while Luna slowly leaned in until their noses were almost touching. Her green eyes promised mischief. "Yes. I was born on Halloween, and the harvest moon that year was enormous."

She sat back. "The real story is our crazy parents, central valley vagabonds. Anyway, let's order—I'm starved."

He was hungry, too, and although he loved breakfast, the shrimp roll and Frogmore Chowder caught his eye, and he didn't regret the choice. Luna chose a sticky cinnamon bun speckled with pecans and drizzled with caramel and then coaxed some fresh whipped cream from the waitress.

"If you're really sweet, I might share the middle with you," she teased, after she had smeared the cream evenly and sliced into the sticky mess.

He smiled. "I think road trips agree with you." He'd almost forgotten how playful and fun Luna could be. The crash seemed to have changed things a lot, but who could blame her? Who wants to care for an invalid? "I'm glad you thought of this trip."

She finished chewing her first bite then gave him a slow head tilt. "Me too."

The food helped; he hadn't felt up to preparing a full dinner alone last night. Fortified now by good coffee and an excellent meal, basking in the glorious sea breeze that tempered the impatient sun, he was content to hear about happy students, fawning parents, and raucous after-parties. They nibbled and lingered as if they had nowhere to be, and since check-in wasn't until late afternoon, they really didn't. A newspaper and a hammock would have complemented the meal perfectly, but he knew he wasn't really up for reading the paper yet.

"Tell me about Beaufort," he said, when Luna turned to the remains of her breakfast. "When were you there?"

"I went last fall. A guy I was dating suggested it, and it was really nice. I went by myself actually," she added, a touch that Landon appreciated. "I started working on my novel there. It's beautiful and quiet. Nice restaurants along the bay. The Cuthbert House is this old mansion. The new owners are restoring it. It's old but nice."

"Sounds *nice*." He tilted his head as he mocked her. She laughed.

"Okay, okay. How about lovely?"

"I liked quiet. I need to catch up on my emails and work on my grant."

"I thought you were going to do that yesterday," she said, abandoning the fork and scooping whipped cream with her finger. He accepted her offer, enjoying the taste and feel of her skin on his lips. "You need a break, Landon. *We* need a break." She dipped her head and peered at him, her enormous green eyes shaded beneath the beach hat's oversized brim. "All work and no play isn't good for us." A buttery smile lit up her face. "I suggest hand-holding, long walks, romantic dinners, and lots of bed rest."

Landon liked the sound of "bed rest," though he wondered what she meant by it. Luna had put up with a lot for him since the crash. Maybe this trip would give him opportunities to show his gratitude, and maybe they could get back on track. If that all went well, this place sounded like a perfect setting for their first time sleeping together. He raised her hand to his lips and then smiled. "I concur. I'll have to pace myself, though; I'm still a patient, you know. You working on your novel?"

"We'll see. I need to work on a Fourth of July trip I'm planning with my sisters."

"Why?"

"I volunteered."

"No, I mean why are you taking the trip?"

"You sound like my sisters," she said, furrowing her brow. "We never see each other, and we're sisters. Don't you get together with your siblings?"

"Nope." Luna seemed to be waiting for more. "Doesn't seem to bother them."

"Does it bother you? Maybe you should suggest it."

"Nah. My sister would never go for it. I haven't talked to her since her daughter was born, and she's nine or ten now."

"You're kidding!"

He shook his head. "I'm not. She doesn't have anything to do with any of us. She hates my dad and blames the rest of us, including my mother."

"Blames you for what?"

"Who knows?" He picked up his fork. "Can we change the subject? I believe it was you who offered the middle of the cinnamon bun."

She pointed her fork like a sabre. "I believe I said *share*, mister. She divided the spongy, sticky dough, speared the larger piece, and presented it to him. He gobbled it directly from her fork.

"Did you talk with your mom?" she asked.

He liked the way she cradled the coffee cup in both hands. After a sip, she'd press her lips together, savoring the taste. "Yes, but I didn't tell her about the tumor." He raised a finger to stifle her response. "I'm waiting until after I talk with Dr. Lake tonight; at least then I'll have a better idea of what I'm up against."

She tilted her head; her large eyes registered everything but revealed nothing. A corner of her lower lip disappeared behind her upper teeth. "Is your father home?"

"Yes. He's on the mend. But it won't last. He'll drink himself into trouble again."

"Is he always in and out of the hospital?"

"No, but I think Father Time is catching up to him." He motioned for the check. "He's been abusing himself—and everyone around him—for a long time."

He didn't mention closing the convertible top. Luna had been chattering again about riding in the open air, and since the brunch had made him a little sleepy, he figured he might be able to nap, or fake it anyway, and keep his eyes closed. Besides, he had begun to think his headache had more to do with hunger than injury, and he had solved the hunger problem. Luna always encouraged his naps, following

Schneider's instructions, so he wasn't worried—at least, not about the car ride.

The conversation with Lake was a different matter. Today he would get yet another opinion about how the tumor should be treated. So far, no two physicians seemed to agree, except no one was recommending chemotherapy or radiation, which was at least something to celebrate. Nevertheless, the difference between having a kidney removed and having a procedure while sedated was significant.

The sun and wind were still assaulting his apparently vulnerable brain, and Luna seemed content with silent driving, so he closed his eyes, unsure whether sleep would come, and if it did, whether it would bring respite or nightmares.

He awoke later with a start, stiff and sore. Above the roar of the wind, he heard Luna's laugh and felt her hand on his arm. "Hey, sleepyhead. How was your nap?" This must be how nursing home patients feel when family members visit. At least his head didn't hurt.

"Where are we?" He returned to an upright position, testing for pain along the way. The road was making a sweeping curve to the left. Seemed like an exit.

"Almost there."

There was no hint of the sea. The road was like most in South Carolina—a narrow two-lane with gravel shoulder abutting overgrown scrubby grass fading into fields or yards or woods. Houses were more frequent now. The airbase loomed, and traffic lights and strip malls served notice that they were in Beaufort. A sign pointed to Parris Island. He held his tongue but wondered what Luna had seen in this place.

At last, they turned off the main road and dove into a warren of lanes too narrow to be called streets. The houses were shabby with neglected yards. Then there was an old brick wall, a colonial-looking churchyard, and they turned into a gravel lot behind a towering L-shaped building. "This is it!" she announced. She parked beside a man loading luggage into an SUV. "I called ahead for early check-in, and we got lucky."

The house smelled of fresh paint, but there was little evidence of construction. The owners were friendly people who greeted Luna like an old friend, even though they were obviously busy turning over the rooms and cleaning up after breakfast. "Don't forget happy hour," they called as Landon and Luna negotiated the narrow stairway to the second floor, Luna weighed down like a Sherpa, Landon hoisting a single small bag with his one good arm. Their room was off the balcony and overlooked a small, brick courtyard that contained a bubbling fountain and three wrought iron tables with chairs. An ancient live oak dripping with Spanish moss provided shelter.

"No bay view, but it's quiet and the bathroom is huge," Luna said, shedding the bags and flopping onto the bed. "And the bed is great."

The bed sounded tempting, but he needed to use the bathroom. It was large, as advertised, and had been updated with a glassed-in shower for two. Somehow it was difficult to imagine a passionate rendezvous that included a trash bag taped over his cast.

"Up for a walk?" she called from the balcony when he emerged.

"Shouldn't we unpack?" He had hoisted his bag onto the bed. He felt her searching hand on his back, then around his waist. Straightening and turning, he met her lips and folded himself into her hug, his face caressed by her wondrous hair that smelled of lime and coconut.

"Later," she whispered. Another kiss. His suitcase went to the floor as his foot found the door and nudged it shut. Her fingers played at his buttons. She paused once, but he pressed a finger to her lips and her quizzical expression melted away, replaced by a conspiratorial smile that he knew mirrored his own. It was time. What Schneider didn't know wouldn't hurt him.

It *was* a good bed, although it didn't need to be. She was gentle and careful, which seemed considerate rather than tentative, overcoming his self-consciousness and allowing his instincts to take over. Afterward, she snuggled and purred, burrowing into the hollow of his neck while he stroked her back with his good hand. His head hurt, but only a little—a small price to pay. His arm felt fine. He was more tired than the energy expenditure would have suggested, but then, he was out of practice.

"You okay?" she asked after a minute. Her fingers plucked at his chest hairs.

"Better than that."

Her head came up and those big eyes found his. "Really? No headache?"

Seemed like a good time to lie. "Nope. I feel great. A little tired, but that's your fault." He raised up and kissed her forehead.

"May thirteenth," she murmured, then whispered it into his ear.

He smiled. "I know."

"Just want you to remember this."

"Don't worry about that. If my brain is that damaged, I'm done for. This was unforgettable." He was expecting something more than the forced smile he got, but wasn't up for a serious conversation right now anyway. Plenty of time for that later.

When he awoke, his headache was gone and so was Luna. The bags were still on the floor. It was almost four; he had slept for more than an hour. He rose in stages, testing each movement, anticipating pain that never came. The room was bright, yet he felt fine without his sunglasses. So there was progress.

Luna was not on the balcony. The bathroom was empty. She must have gone for a walk. He splashed a little water on his face, then opened his laptop. Maybe he could flop on the sofa and get some emails finished.

Reading was easier now, but routine mail or the obvious junk that he used to delete without hesitation still gave him pause, making him wonder if he was missing something.

He'd barely made a dent when the door eased open just a crack. "I'm up," he announced as Luna breezed in. Her face was flushed, and she was smiling.

"How was the nap?" She braced herself on the sofa arm and leaned over to kiss his forehead. "Guess I wore you out, huh?"

He turned back to the screen and smiled. "Is that a challenge?"

"Later. It's time for happy hour." She ducked into the bathroom. Water splashed in the sink. "They have decent wine, and it's a good way to meet the other guests."

"Why would I want to do that?"

"Stop, Mr. Anti-social." She leaned into the room while she toweled her face. "You'll like the owner. He's a very interesting guy. Knows a lot of history. Right up your alley." She sat beside him and planted a soft kiss on his cheek. It felt good. "What are you doing anyway?"

"Work. Trying to clean up my inbox."

"Just do what I do—delete, delete, delete. Cleans it up in no time." Her arms circled his chest. Red hair tumbled across his line of sight. He was done for, and he really didn't mind.

"You're distracting me," he teased, closing the laptop.

"No offense, but it's not too tough." She pushed him onto his back and wormed her way onto his chest. Her hair shrouded him, creating a private tunnel for their faces. Her eyes always made him smile.

"Why don't we skip happy hour?" he asked, sliding his good hand along her hip.

She smiled. "Tempting, but you need to be careful, and I need some wine." She pulled him to his feet. "Come on. We've got all night."

"It has to be a real happy *hour*. I'm supposed to call Dr. Lake."

They locked the door and headed for the lobby. She skipped backward ahead of him, flashing a naughty grin. "Perfect. Gives you an excuse to duck out early, and since you'll need some privacy, gives me an excuse to stay behind for a second glass."

Landon took her hand, feeling better and far luckier than he would have guessed.

CHAPTER SEVEN

The wine was mediocre, a Merlot from an up-country winery near Greenville, but Luna accepted her second happy-hour glass with pleasure and settled on the comfortable sofa that placed her between Jack and Mona, the hosts, and as far as possible from the Conways, the nightmare couple squeezed together on the love seat nearest the front door. It was Sunday night, so most of the guests had departed that afternoon.

"He seems to be getting along pretty well," Jack said to Luna. He and his wife had purchased Cuthbert House eighteen months before and had already shared its fascinating history as well as details about the extensive renovation that was beginning to wind down. Landon had seemed to enjoy their company and had whispered some very funny comments about the Conways before excusing himself to go make his phone call. His cast had advertised injury, and although Landon had rationed as little information as possible, Luna was relieved for him when he was finally able to escape.

"I think he is," Luna said. "Seems better every day."

"Those head injuries can fool you," Frank Conway said in the booming voice that fit his blocky appearance.

"When I played, we had two guys leave the team because of concussions. Can you imagine? Had to give up football altogether."

Luna smiled, resisting the urge to ask whether Frank had ever fully recovered from his own head injury.

"One less thing to worry about with our Lexie," Lisa Conway chirped. She had a singsong, grating voice and seemed incapable of speaking without invoking the name of their only child, the astonishing Lexie Conway, whose life history was now burned into the memory of everyone in attendance. They'd all been fascinated to learn that at this very moment Lexie was completing her packing and eagerly anticipating her parents' arrival after a triumphant first year at the University of Florida. There, she had just missed walking on as a cheerleader but nevertheless successfully pledged a sorority, thereby bolstering Frank and Lisa's contention that she was a remarkably resilient woman with a bright future. Hopefully that future would take place back home in Rockford but probably not until after graduate school—perhaps law school.

Whew. It was exhausting for everyone. Now Jack smiled and left it to Mona to redirect the conversation while he went to fetch more wine from the kitchen. Luna sank deeper into her chair, marveling at the Conway's parental pride, certain that her parents had never regaled a gathering with stories about Luna or any of her sisters. The wine was seeping into her brain as she killed time, letting Landon make his call. It had been a gamble, jumping his bones like that. Fox would've been proud of her. She was proud of herself, and cast or no cast, the sex had been good—maybe not quite as good as his birthday, but pretty good for a guy who just got out of the hospital. Afterward, it occurred to her that he might not have been cleared for sex, but he hadn't complained. Doctors don't know everything, anyway. She wouldn't worry about that now. Now, they had a memory, and she wasn't going to let anything ruin it—even the lost birthday memory. She'd never forget it, didn't want to, but for Landon, it didn't exist. And now, she didn't need to bring it up, really couldn't bring it up, not without making him feel bad. Maybe she should have told him before. She still wondered about leaving the balloons in his bedroom. Maybe she shouldn't have thrown them out.

"I bid you all a good evening," Jack declared upon his return. He handed Mona a half bottle of the Merlot. "We'll see you all at breakfast in the morning." Luna waved off Mona's offer of a refill, eager to extricate herself from the tiresome recitations of overly involved parents. She knew Mona's breezy personality, a perfect complement to Jack's professorial demeanor, would be more than a match for the Conways.

It was too soon to return to their room, so she strolled east along Bay Street, determined to clear her mind. Maybe Fox was right about overanalyzing. It was time to relax and enjoy being a young couple together on a romantic getaway. Diana's advice had been right on target too; Luna was glad she'd listened to her and decided to make the best of this trip. It was just what she and Landon needed.

The last of the sunlight glared off the sound, where a few boats were straggling into port. She'd had just enough wine; everything catching her attention seemed fascinating. It really was a beautiful evening—a little cooler, with a seductive breeze carrying the sweet scent of gardenias. She crossed the street and headed for the waterfront, a manicured, grassy area that skirted the patios of the restaurants, where the early dinner business seemed brisk.

She wondered how Landon was faring. Diana had been right about something else too. She—Luna—*had* been sulking, *had* been selfish, whining about how things had changed with Landon. He had to be going out of his mind, stuck at home, unsure about ever feeling well again, and worrying about the tumor growing inside him. Hopefully, this getaway would help him as much as it was helping her. The call with Dr. Lake should help too—he always seemed to feel better when he knew the plan.

Speaking of plans, she needed to get on the July trip before her sisters changed their minds. Fox was supportive, but the other girls were a greater risk. Tule would have to travel, and Sutter would have to care—significant barriers for each of them. Nevertheless, they had agreed, so now it was on Luna.

She had originally imagined a travelogue of their childhood, visiting Fresno, Sacramento, Visalia, Lodi— all the places their vagabond parents had lighted briefly in their futile pursuit of theatrical fame, never staying anywhere long enough to provide their daughters a sense of home. Mercifully, Luna had come to her senses before revealing this plan, which might have scuttled the idea of a reunion for all time.

So now she had settled on Sonoma Valley, a wine-tasting trip, something they might all agree on, at least for a little while. Merlot was everyone's favorite, and what better way to overcome the starchy discomfort of familial unfamiliarity than intoxication?

The smell of food reminded her that brunch had been some time ago. Landon's call was probably over. A moonlight dinner with a view of the sound awaited, followed by a reprise of the afternoon's interlude.

It was a short walk back to Cuthbert House. She tiptoed across the upper porch in the gloaming and flattened herself against the wall like a spy, listening for Landon's voice. There was no need to interrupt his conversation; it would be easy to kill time in a rocking chair. The door was ajar, though, and at first she heard nothing from the darkened room. Then came the sound of water splashing in the sink. She slithered inside and tiptoed to the bathroom. Landon's head was under the faucet, water pounding his face and head. She stood silently while he turned the water off, fumbled for the towel, and then raised his head. He looked away when he saw her, covering his face with the towel, but she had already seen his red, swollen eyes. Landon had been crying.

CHAPTER EIGHT

On Wednesday evening, Luna sat waiting in a restaurant bar. She had a view down King Street, and things didn't look promising for Charleston's night life tonight. Rain hammered the slate sidewalks and asphalt, stippling the street as if millions of tiny flashbulbs were going off all at once. The evening rush hour was over, so traffic was fairly light, but shoppers were undeterred, many braving the elements in hastily manufactured rain suits fashioned from dry cleaning bags or trash bags purchased at the first clap of thunder.

The storm had struck without warning, a steady curtain of rain that washed the color from the street scene, which now resembled a sepia photograph. Luna wondered if Diana had been caught off guard; she said she was going to do some shopping, and if the storm had soaked her, her customary punctuality would be pitted against her desire to be "put together" for any social occasion.

A moment later, Luna discovered that she needn't have worried when she spotted Diana's blonde hair bouncing beneath the maroon canopy of what appeared to be a College of Charleston umbrella. She waved uselessly as Diana rushed past the window.

"Hope I haven't kept you waiting," Diana gasped, smiling at the hostess who relieved her of the dripping outerwear that clashed noticeably with her dress. "Jeez, what a storm."

Luna couldn't resist. "Was that a C of C umbrella?"

Diana groaned. "Don't rub it in. I needed protection, and fast. So, it was either a drowned dress or that hideous jacket and umbrella. Maybe I'll keep it in my office and invite the dean over."

"Good idea." Luna giggled. "You'll be promoted in no time."

Diana grabbed the drink menu. "Very funny. Enough about fashion—or my lack of it. What are you having?" She poked the menu in the direction of Luna's wine glass.

"Malbec."

"I'll have the Malbec," Diana said to the waiter, then leaned in across the high table. "Any particular reason?"

"Nothing dramatic. Hoping for some inspiration." She raised her glass without sipping.

"You must be writing," Diana said.

"You might call it that. I'm typing words, then deleting them mostly."

Diana accepted her glass and touched it to Luna's. She sipped, nodded, and pressed her lips together. "Yum. Excellent choice. So how are things with you and Landon?"

"Okay, I guess. I'm not really sure. Why?" She felt her face reddening.

"Sorry. Maybe that was a little blunt," Diana said. "I just wondered since you cut your trip short."

"Landon's request. He was too distracted to relax." She ran her finger around the rim of the glass. She didn't want her voice to crack. "I can't blame him actually."

"What happened?"

"He talked to the doctor in New Orleans. The tumor is small, but it's grown outside of his kidney, which makes it a T-something or other—"

"Tumor?" Diana looked stricken.

"Oh God, I'm sorry, Diana. I haven't told you." She had violated Landon's privacy but figured it was too late now. "Landon has a tumor in his kidney. They found it on one of the scans they did after his crash."

"That's terrible." Diana clutched at her neck. "The poor man."

"I know. That's bad enough, but it gets worse." She had promised herself not to cry, but felt the tears coming. "The tumor has grown outside of his kidney. That means he only has a sixty percent chance of living five years." She grabbed her cocktail napkin and dabbed at her eyes.

"What?"

Luna swallowed, struggling to find her voice. "I know." She managed a weak shrug.

"What's next? Chemo? Radiation? Do they cut it out?"

She had never seen the deep furrow that appeared between Diana's eyes. A sip of wine strengthened her voice. "Depends who you ask, apparently. He's gotten two or three opinions. He's settled on going to New Orleans next month to have some procedure that's supposedly safer for people with head injuries."

"What's he up to now?" Diana's sip seemed to catch her off guard. She sputtered and stabbed at her mouth with a cocktail napkin. "I swear. I am worse than a child sometimes."

Luna smiled and offered her a second napkin. "I'm not sure. Home probably."

"You're not sure?" Diana looked away for a moment. "I guess I don't understand. He gets horrible news, and you come back, but now you don't know where he is …?" She scrunched her shoulders, her free hand cupped, palm up, asking to be filled.

Luna's face felt hot. She swirled her wine, tried to force a smile, but it didn't take. "I don't … I don't know. I think we're both needing some time."

"*Now?* After *this* news? Are you sure, Luna?"

"Am I sure? I'm not sure about anything. I offered to be with him. I did. He said he didn't want to drag me down. What do I say to that? I can't force myself on him. I've never done this before. There's no road map."

Diana's silence seemed to demand an explanation that Luna hadn't prepared. "I don't know. Sometimes this all makes me feel so old."

"I'll bet Landon feels the same way."

Luna nodded. "I know. I'm trying, Diana. Maybe we're just too far apart in age."

Diana reached for her glass. "What? Why do you say that?"

"He's ten years older than me."

"He is?" Her eyes flashed toward the window, then back. She took a quick sip. "You probably told me that before."

"Fortieth birthday, remember? Ten years is a big age difference, and it seems even bigger now." She felt herself tearing up again. "That's probably not fair."

Diana handed her another cocktail napkin. "Sorry, I don't carry tissues. Look, I get it, but I'm probably the wrong person to talk to about this. Mark is twelve years older than me."

"You're kidding."

Diana's flat-eyed, thin-lipped look made Luna smile. "Love, love, love kidding about age, Luna. Why would I kid about that? He was thirty-eight and a successful businessman. I was like you—a few years out of college, not really looking for a husband but tired of playing games with men who were still children."

She couldn't resist. "So, which was he?"

"Huh?"

"Thirty-eight and not married." She counted off on her fingers. "Weird, gay, or divorced?"

Diana rolled her eyes. Her smile made Luna feel better. "Divorced actually. Have you figured out which one applies to Landon?"

"Unlucky?" She wondered if that was in poor taste, but Diana let it pass.

"Look, Luna, I don't know what to tell you about the age thing. It hasn't been a big deal for us. Maybe you guys aren't right for each other, but I don't think age is the issue. Cancer might be, but this doesn't seem like the right time to make a final decision." She swirled and sipped. "I can't believe it—poor Landon."

"I know. It's awful, and things were going so well. We had a really fun brunch out on Sullivan's Island. The room was so romantic, and then ..." She felt her face reddening again but couldn't wait to spill it. "The bed was pretty fabulous too."

Diana's eyebrows twitched, and the faintest spark flared deep within her eyes, then gathered strength. "Now we're getting somewhere." She motioned for the waiter. "Drink up, honey. This calls for another round."

By the time Diana gave her an air kiss and folded herself into a taxi, Luna was pleasantly intoxicated and unpleasantly troubled. The rain had slowed to a drizzle that barely merited an umbrella, and the streets were filled with after-dinner strollers, so a ten-block walk home didn't seem risky. Maybe she could clear her head.

It had been forty-eight hours. Should she call Landon? Diana had suggested it. This was really her last free night. Summer session started Friday, so tomorrow night was out; she needed to be rested and fresh. Or did she? They wouldn't do anything of importance in Friday's class, and besides, she'd taught the same class last summer. *Stop acting like an old woman*, she thought. *Call him. You know you want to.*

No. She would wait. Landon said he needed time. She didn't want to seem too eager or clingy. A night snuggling with Hazel and then maybe some writing in the morning. The novel was her ticket to promotion. Associate professor by thirty—that was always the plan. Pretty unlikely now, but at least she could have a manuscript by thirty. Maybe if she didn't hear from Landon by lunch, she could call him and invite him out for oysters. Maybe that would take his mind off his—no, it wouldn't. Nothing would.

She thought again of Diana. Dinner had been a mixed bag—lots of serious talk but some fun too. The way Diana had listened had helped clarify things. She envied Diana's life, though truthfully, she knew little about it. She rarely mentioned her husband, who would be almost sixty now. They had no children. Or health problems. It was so nice to just talk and laugh. The Beaufort trip had started that way.

Queen Street was glistening, dark and deserted, silent except for the gurgling of rain in the downspouts and gutter drains. The air smelled washed and clean, punctured now and again by the rancid perfume of a steaming dumpster. The Mills House glowed pink in the night. She did not pause at Meeting Street, forced herself to not look south toward the intersection where everything had changed. Hazel would be waiting. Hazel needed her too.

CHAPTER NINE

On Thursday, Landon left Schneider's office in the new car he'd bought the day before, just before the rainstorm spoiled the dealer's free detail job. No one at the dealership had questioned his ability to drive with a cast, and except for the usual inquiry about a trade-in, no one had asked what happened to his old car. The crash was becoming old news, and he was very glad to put it behind him.

He'd bought a white BMW 325 convertible, which of course he'd not been able to fully enjoy driving in the rain. His plan to cruise the city, swing by Luna's, and drive out to Sullivan's Island for the sunset had been washed out; instead, he made his way home in the storm, more tentative about driving than he'd hoped. He decided to wait to show Luna the car until after his appointment, when he could share the results of his testing.

Now he was free to drive as much as he wanted. Schneider had said so, and he said he could fly home if he wanted to. Landon had asked because he did want to. It was time to tell his mother—and father—that he had cancer, and he did not want to do that by telephone.

Thursday had dawned sparkling clean and breezy, all sunshine and fluffy clouds. He put the top down and cruised King Street, happy for the traffic lights. During intermittent pauses, he reveled in the leathery seat smell, the invigorating spring air, even the buzz and hum of late morning shoppers. Convertibles were at their best at low speeds and much better in spring and fall than in stifling, summer heat.

As he had hoped, both the CT and neurologic examination had been normal. Overall, Schneider had seemed pleased. He advised gradual increase in activity. Landon planned to ignore that advice, though it was well-intended and probably wise. There had been no ill effects from ignoring the ban on sex, though he and Luna had only had time for one trial. Now, he had a few weeks until he would once again be a patient, and he planned to enjoy pretending to be well for as long as he could.

He turned onto Queen Street, surprised to find that his heart was racing. He felt jumpy in anticipation of seeing Luna. Would she celebrate with him? His injuries were healing. He had a plan to deal with the tumor. Things could be a lot worse. The new car was sporty; she'd like that. Maybe they could just cruise for a while.

There were no parking spaces, and a humorless-looking officer in a highlighter-yellow vest was already marking tires and writing tickets. He circled the block and was about to give up when he spotted a space on Church Street.

On the walk to Luna's apartment, he caught himself rehearsing what to say, checking his clothes. He was grateful for the cast, which left only one hand to tremble, so he shoved that one in his pocket as he climbed the stairs to her piazza.

Her flowers looked fresh and pretty, as he figured she would also. Finally, he rang the doorbell.

After two rings and no response, he knocked. He started to peek in at the window, then caught himself and headed down the stairs. Why hadn't he called Luna this morning? The door to the lower-level apartment opened, and a tall, thin man with disheveled hair and sore-looking eyes shuffled out. He was wearing a rumpled shirt and khakis that showed too much ankle above ragged slippers. "You looking for Luna?" he asked in a friendly way.

"Yes. I'm Landon Ratliff—a friend of hers." He extended his hand, but the man withdrew into the doorway.

"I'm John Davis. You don't want to shake my hand today. I've got the flu or something." He plucked a handkerchief from his pocket and wiped his nose. "Anyway, Luna's not home. Said she got called in to meet with a new recruit or something. She'll be back late this evening. She said to tell you if you came by."

Landon smiled. "Thanks." He turned and headed toward the street, then stopped and raised his good hand. "Nice meeting you. Hope you feel better."

"Thanks. You too." He gestured toward the cast. "I'll tell Luna you came by."

"Tell her I got a new car, will you?"

John stared at him for a moment, then shrugged. "Sure. Congratulations." Landon fought the urge to flee as he turned away. His disappointment at missing Luna had been wiped out by her message left for him. *For him.* He sure wasn't going to share his excitement with John Davis.

Mike Fanning had invited him (and Luna) over for dinner, probably thinking they could either celebrate or commiserate after the appointment with Schneider. Landon had first tried to beg off, then concocted an excuse for Luna, not knowing that she actually would be busy. Now back home and feeling much better, he had the afternoon to himself. He considered a drive to the shore but decided to save that for when he saw Luna again and opted instead to try a run. It had been nearly three weeks; he could not recall such a hiatus in over twenty years, and he wondered, as he laced his shoes, how much fitness he had lost.

The answer came little by little over the next thirty minutes. Even before he reached the Battery, he felt heavy-legged and sluggish, but by the time he arrived at Rainbow Row, his form was gone, a side stitch tormented him, and he was practically gasping. No chance he would run through the pain. Bent over, hands on knees, sweat beading the sidewalk, he picked up a rhythmic patter of rubber on asphalt. A man and a woman ran toward him, veered into the middle of the street, and were gone, upright glistening bodies slicing the air, arms relaxed, stride even. They were chatting as they ran. Landon turned and watched them glide through the tourists until they rounded a curve in the road and vanished. His mouth was sticky, too sticky even to spit. He felt a headache coming on.

He walked to Fanning's house for dinner. The afternoon had been about as productive as most were these days. Chastened and exhausted by his pathetic jog, he'd once again taken refuge in a nap and some aspirin. He awoke groggy and famished. A light snack and a shower refreshed him, and after muddling through a few emails, he had managed to book a flight home for the weekend and call his mother, who was overjoyed to learn of his arrival in less than twenty-four hours.

Afterward, he had wanted to talk to Luna. He didn't want to disturb her meeting, but surely she had some free time? He'd be out of town all weekend. Still he was hesitant, analytical, tossing the phone back on the nightstand and pacing the floor like a middle schooler trying to screw up the courage to ask a girl if she liked him. His indecision may have cost him his opportunity because when he finally called, her phone went immediately to voicemail:

"Hi, this is Luna. I'm unavailable. Leave a message, and I'll call you back."

She was on the phone and soon would discover that he'd called her. He found that disturbing, for indecipherable reasons, and decided not to leave a message. He did not try to reach her again.

Now he was strolling far from her apartment, heading for Fanning's house, pondering the meaning of Luna's failure to return his call. He had checked his phone repeatedly, ensuring that he had not inadvertently switched it over to silent, but he hadn't, and there weren't any messages.

It was a beautiful evening. The breeze carried the sweet scent of hibiscus, one of those long-familiar smells that reminded him of his time in New Orleans. He'd gone there for a medical conference and wound up switching specialties and moving from Florida to learn critical care medicine under Mike Fanning's tutelage. There had been a girl too—a Tarot reader and musician named Gillian. That hadn't worked out, but New Orleans became his adopted home. After his training, he joined the faculty at LSU and then came to Charleston at Fanning's request when he took a promotion opportunity. He loved Charleston, but he'd spent ten years in New Orleans and missed it, more often than he'd ever expected.

The temperature had fallen enough to quicken his pace and help him rationalize his earlier, failed attempt at exercise. It had been less than three weeks since his crash. Maybe it was too soon to push himself. Walking was decent exercise, and it felt good—great actually.

Fanning lived just north of Broad, on a dead-end lane. Like most houses in Charleston, Fanning's was built end-on to the street, a narrow façade revealing little about the design or extent of the building. An alley at the back of the house was canopied by an arbor thick with flowering vines that created a cool and mysterious passageway, while a towering wall of bamboo concealed what he knew from experience was the front courtyard. Except for the narrow spaces separating the house from its neighbors, it might have been mistaken for a townhouse.

"Landon!" Fanning filled the doorway that opened onto the lower piazza running the length of the house. His bristly hair looked as if he cut it himself in poor light, and his clothes pegged him as a man for whom comfort trumped fashion. But his smile, buttressed by his massive jaw and underbite, exuded warmth and genuine welcome. "Right on time, as always," he said, waddling aside to allow Landon to lead the way. He gestured toward the flagstone courtyard, where a glass-topped table held a bottle of wine, two glasses, and a covered dish. A small fountain nestled among the bamboo bubbled softly. Three fan palms standing shoulder to shoulder at the far end of the patio shuddered in a high, unfelt breeze. "I thought we'd have cocktail hour out here. Such a lovely evening."

"Wine okay?" he asked, once Landon had settled into his chair. "I have beer or something stronger, if you prefer."

"Wine's good," Landon said, and Fanning decanted a swallow into his glass, then hovered until Landon had swirled, sniffed, and sipped. "Cabernet, right? This is great."

Fanning nodded, a quick, jerky movement that once again brought to mind a pelican with a bill full of fish. Landon stifled a smile as Fanning sank heavily into his chair, then filled both glasses more than two-thirds full.

"Generous pour," Landon said.

"I'm hoping for a generous celebratory toast." Fanning hoisted his glass. "I hope I'm not setting myself up for embarrassment. How'd it go today?"

He touched glasses with Fanning. "You mean you haven't called Schneider?"

"Touché, Landon." The pelican was bobbing its head again. "I was tempted, I admit. But I resisted. The privacy police would be proud of me."

"Well, then. I'm not accustomed to having something on you, Dr. Fanning. He took a long swallow, savoring the thick berry flavor. "I may hang onto this for a while."

"Fortunately, the famous Ratliff poker face has already given you away. It's good news, isn't it?" Fanning was leaning so close, it looked like he might try to swallow him whole.

Landon smiled. He'd teased Mike enough. "CT and exam normal. I'm free—no restrictions."

"Ha! I knew it!" Fanning exhaled, then coughed. "That is, I hoped I knew it." His eyes were moist. He touched Landon's glass with his. "I'm really happy for you."

Landon sipped, hiding his face in his glass. "It's been tough."

"Excuse me a minute. I've got to tell Sheila. She's been holding her breath all day." He bounded onto the piazza and disappeared inside, leaving the front door creaking on its oil-starved hinges.

Night was descending, turning neighboring houses into phantoms floating between the majestic trees that occupied every green space and coalesced overhead into a jungle-like canopy. Tree frogs and crickets were tuning up. The wine was soothing Landon's recovering brain. He lifted the lid on the dish just as Fanning burst through the door.

"Help yourself, Landon. I told Sheila about your love of clams, and she simmered them in a broth of her own creation—basil, garlic, oregano, early green tomatoes, I don't know what all."

The sauce was thin and red and bursting with tomato flavor that kissed the briny sweetness of the clams. Fanning tore at a warm, fresh baguette and dunked a piece into the liquor, staining his fingers before they could usher the soaked bread into his eager mouth. Landon savored the flavor and added a sip of wine to the mix, silently toasting the culinary genius of Sheila Fanning.

"Wow. That is the best clam broth I've ever tasted," he said as Fanning fished a pair of clams from the dish.

"There is no recipe. I've asked her, and she swears she just adds what feels right at the time." Fanning patted his stomach. "Her cooking has served me and my tailor very well."

A bright light like a massive flashbulb split the air, followed immediately by a crack of thunder that made both men flinch. The stars were gone, and in the glow from the porch light, long streaks of rain scored the air, splattering on the patio like bare feet slapping a tile floor. Fanning scooped up the serving dish, Landon grabbed the glasses, and they ducked onto the piazza just as the rain gathered strength and rattled the upper piazza floor. Gusts of wind threatened to soak them, so Fanning yanked the door open and hustled him inside.

The Fannings scampered about like unleashed puppies, scrambling up and down the stairs with a card table, folding chairs, and a tablecloth. Thunder rattled the windows, temporarily drowning out the steady tattoo of rain on the roof. Landon confined himself to the living room, in obedience to Sheila's mock threats of bodily harm if he so much as thought of assisting them. A new painting, a panorama of Charleston, hung above the fireplace. The city had been captured awash in a golden sunset that illuminated the Ravenel Bridge towering above the broken skyline of the jumbled, low city. Here and there a church spire glowed like a lofty spear point, while an armada of yachts and pleasure boats floated on the bleached aluminum river that disgorged itself into the broad harbor.

"That's Sheila's masterpiece."

Fanning had slipped up behind him. "We were heading home from Folly Beach last summer, just before sunset, when she spotted it. She went back nearly every evening for a month, taking photos, sketching, and doing studies from a little hill off 30."

"It's a beautiful painting, Mike. She's very talented."

"Indeed. Let's go up." Fanning gestured toward the stairway that led from the adjoining dining room. Landon knew the way to the study and sitting room, an open comfortable room at the top of the stairs where a backup venue had been assembled. The room was lined with bookshelves, many of which contained framed photographs of the Fanning children.

"What's Emily up to this summer?" Landon asked.

"Studying abroad—in Spain." Fanning gestured toward the chair opposite the stairway. "Sit, please. She graduates next May. Hard to believe."

"How about your son?"

"Still in Atlanta. Tyler and his wife are opening a bistro in Buckhead." He uncovered the clams, sending a fragrant cloud of steam curling toward the ceiling. "He inherited his mother's love of cuisine. She's thrilled."

Landon marveled at the photos of the family on vacation, images as foreign to his own experience as the Hubble telescope photos of Venus he'd recently seen in a magazine. He caught himself wondering if he would ever have children of his own, and if so, if he'd live long enough for them to remember him.

The room had grown quiet. Fanning's eyes were concealed by the reflected lamplight, but Landon knew his relaxed, attentive gaze was fixed on him. When Landon's head came up, Fanning's eyebrows rose and his mouth twitched slightly. He was waiting—to listen.

"I'm heading home tomorrow." His mouth felt sticky. "I still—well, I haven't told my parents about the tumor." Fanning nodded but said nothing. "I just wasn't sure how my mom would take it. My dad's been sick, but you know all that."

"Yes, well, I think it's best for you to tell them in person, and I'm sure it will be good to be home."

"I wouldn't always agree with you about that, but I think it will be."

"How's your father?"

"I guess okay. He seems to be recovering, as best I can tell. I probably won't be able to catch his doctor this weekend, but maybe I'll get lucky."

Fanning swirled his wine. "Are you staying just the weekend?"

Landon smiled and raised his glass. "You bet. I'm planning to be at work on Monday."

"Schneider okayed that?"

The rain peppering the roof had slowed to a steady patter. "Yeah. Said to start slow, so we'll see. I won't overdo it."

"Yes, you will," Fanning said. "But I'll keep an eye on you, and I suspect you'll know when it's time to quit."

He thought about his run today but kept that to himself. The wine was fabulous; it would be easy to overdo that tonight.

"So," Fanning said, shifting in his chair. "I don't want to pry, so stop me whenever you like, but I'm curious about what treatment plan you've settled on, now that you've spoken with Dr. Lake."

"Well, he recommends the RFA because the tumor is small."

"You sound uncertain. Do you agree with him?"

"How would I know? He's the expert, but the literature seems unclear. Many people recommend surgery because of its high cure rate."

"The European literature is showing impressive results with RFA."

He smiled. "Been doing a little pleasure reading?"

"A little. Lake is top-notch, Landon."

"I know, but this is a T3a tumor, Mike. That gives me a sixty percent five-year survival."

"Hold on." Fanning leaned closer. "The tumor is small—very small—and you're young and otherwise healthy."

"Not anymore." He pointed to his head. "I'm head injured now. That's why Lake doesn't recommend nephrectomy. He thinks the anesthesia risk is too great."

"Sensible. The Scandinavians are reporting greater than ninety percent cure rates using RFA on small tumors and greater success if the procedure needs to be repeated. Fanning sipped his wine. "The odds are strongly in your favor. I think you're taking a skewed view of this."

"What do you mean?" His face felt hot, his eyes watery. "Of course, I have a skewed view. It's my life we're talking about." He looked away.

Fanning was on his feet, circling the table. "I'm sorry, Landon. I had no right—of course, this is awful for you. I guess I'm used to talking to Dr. Ratliff, not patient Ratliff. Please forgive me, my friend."

He nodded, forced a smile, and hooked his hand over Fanning's forearm, hoping to reassure him and terminate this awkward half hug.

Once he had returned to his seat, Fanning cleared his throat. "Why not get a second opinion? Surely Lake wouldn't be offended."

"No, he suggested it—even recommended a guy named Morgan in Richmond, in case I wanted to be near home. I looked him up. Trained here at MUSC back in the eighties, then did a fellowship at Mayo."

"Sounds qualified. It would be nice to have your mother with you through this—wouldn't it?"

"Yes. I was thinking it might be nice to take her back to New Orleans, though." He tore at the bread and dipped it in the clam broth. "I don't really want another opinion. What I want is someone to tell me the one best thing to do, and I guess there isn't one best thing." He chewed, savoring the brine and the spices, hoping Fanning would fill the silence, but of course, he just sat, impassive as an owl.

"I trust Lake," Landon said. "It'll be good to see New Orleans too."

"When do you go?"

"Scheduled for June nineteenth. I'll probably leave on the seventeenth and return the twenty-second if everything goes well."

Fanning had looked away, his jaw set. "Well, I was hoping to be around, but we leave for Europe on the sixteenth." He forced a smile. "Oh well, not much I could do from here anyway, and you don't need a second mother hand-wringing, do you?"

He had forgotten about Fanning's vacation. Two weeks in Europe, insisted upon and planned by his wife. The first extended vacation Fanning had taken since the move to Charleston. So much for the backup plan to ask him to come to New Orleans.

"No, Mike. You'll be sipping wine in Paris, where you should be. It's an outpatient procedure. Lake said I'll be a little groggy for a few hours, and then as good as ever. It's no big deal."

CHAPTER TEN

Fortified by three large glasses of wine, Landon wandered the rain-slickened streets of Harleston Village, heading in the general direction of the college. He had begged off Sheila's offer of a ride home, fabricating the need to walk off her sumptuous dinner before bed, and declined Mike's offer of a ride to the airport in the morning. There were no missed calls or voicemails on his phone. He was on his own, free to reflect upon the evening. Its prolonged snapshot of domestic tranquility had left him feeling cheated—past, present, and future.

The streets were quiet except for the bark of a distant dog. Some of the fraternities and sororities were completely dark, but in many, an illuminated window or two betrayed the presence of summer term students. The faculty would be preparing tonight; maybe Luna was working in her office. The idea took hold in his wine-addled mind, though he had never visited her at work. He recalled her telling him the office was at the corner of George and something.

His hand probed his pocket, checked the switch on the phone again. All along the south side of George, the corner houses had lamplight piercing the darkness from upstairs and downstairs windows but what was he going to do? Peek in the windows? Knock on the door? Unless he saw Luna from the sidewalk, he was going to pass by. So he kept looking, but he didn't see her. When he reached King Street, he turned north, crossed King at Marion Square, and skirted the park, where shadowy figures lurked around the fountain and the firefly glow of cigarettes traced the wanderings of transients unable to camp on the wet ground tonight.

He turned south when he reached Bay Street, where he picked up the earthy smell of the river at low tide. A block later, a faint, familiar siren song pulled him magnetically toward a curve in the road, where a lighted pergola rose above a high wall. His ears had not betrayed him. Someone was playing the accordion.

He stood beneath a dripping live oak, unable to see anything from the street. An Irish ballad competed with the wheezy, cacophonous instrument. The singer's strong, pleasant tenor was camouflaged by a strained Irish accent that made him sound as if he were singing an Irish cop joke. Still, it was good to hear the accordion.

Landon had been an accordion player ever since high school, when his music teacher had introduced him to the strange instrument that gave him an identity and the confidence that eventually allowed him to excel academically. At first, the polkas seemed weird and outdated, but when he became proficient enough to play for parties and weddings, he was hooked. It felt so good to hear the applause and see the joy that his playing brought to his audience.

But it had been three years since Landon had touched his accordion. Back in New Orleans, he used to sit in fairly regularly with Gillian's band, even after he and Gillian had broken up and stopped living together. Eventually, though, work got busier and not playing became a habit, just as practicing had once been. Now his instrument languished in its case in the guest closet, and he was no longer even tempted to play.

He had enough of a buzz to make another drink sound like a good idea. The bar was just inside the entrance, but he wanted to watch as well as listen, so he ventured out onto the patio and found a table with a good view of the stage. There, a bearded, overweight man wearing suspenders and a plaid shirt sang and bounced, ignoring the stool that was useless to an accordion player. His arms pumped like butterfly wings while his legs performed an ugly American version of an Irish jig. A tenor banjo rested on a stand a safe distance from flailing elbows and feet.

Landon ordered a Guinness. As he sipped the frothy, bitter brew, the jangly monotonous music and accumulated alcohol intake lulled him into an uncharacteristically sentimental reverie. The man was a decent player, and the music encouraged the crowd to join in, which had always seemed to be the point of Irish music anyway. Zydeco wasn't like that; it was dance music, "kick back the furniture and roll up the rugs, let's have a party" music that had grabbed him back in high school and not let go, at least until he left New Orleans.

For the first time in years, he found himself wondering about Gillian. Their fourteen-month relationship, his longest by far, had died a slow death of neglect as their disparate personalities conquered what both had thought was love. Neither found time for the other's life, and with little to share, their arrangement unwound to a tearful but not acrimonious ending. Attempts at friendship proved awkward, except when he went, as he did often, to see their band play. Gillian would almost always get him up on stage for a number or two, and it was then that he would be reminded of how they came to be a couple. He never asked Gillian if she felt the same way, but her smiling eyes and writhing body suggested that she did, and he liked to think so, anyway.

A couple's request to share his table prompted Landon to drain his beer and invent a tale about being ready to leave. The cigarette smoke *was* bothering him, so he headed inside and found a corner seat at the bar. The lone adjacent seat was empty, too, and since the crowd was thinning out, chances were good that he'd be left alone to have a second Guinness. He wasn't driving, he was already packed, and he had long ago adapted to inadequate sleep.

Halfway through his second beer, a whiff of strong, floral perfume made him look up from his glass. He had little time to ponder the familiar aroma before a gravelly voice reminded him of its source.

"Look what the cat dragged in." She slid onto the stool next to him, her throaty chuckle spewing a cloud of whiskey and cigarettes that tested his forced smile. "Dr. Ratliff—my, my, my, you are a sight for sore eyes."

"Terri Blair," he said, unable to resist sizing her up. She was still too thin and still dressed like a tramp who had plenty of money. Her tank top gaped at the neck and arm holes, revealing a lacy black bra. Skimpy cutoffs covered only what was required by law, and expensive sandals proudly displayed the pair of tattoos that adorned her claw-like feet: a skull and crossbones and the cross of Calvary. There was a time when he had found her sexy and alluring.

"Buy me a drink, sailor?"

He smiled and motioned for the bartender. "Sure, darlin'—the usual?"

"You remember? How sweet." She leaned into his arm. "What are you doing here all alone, and what happened to your arm?"

He raised his cast. "Car wreck. Broke my thumb. He glanced around. "Where's your date?"

"I'm looking at him—I hope." Her thin, cruel lips unfolded into a slow-motion smile while her blue eyes, a startling complement to her deep black hair, held his gaze like a magnet. The bartender shoved a martini glass between them.

"Rye Manhattan with a twist," he said. "On your tab?"

Landon nodded, then touched glasses with Terri, whose eyes never left him as she sipped and then moaned her approval. Her exaggerated lip licking was predictable and a little pathetic.

"Perfect," she sighed.

"The first drink of the night always is," he said, smirking.

Terri's laugh was interrupted by a wet cough. She held a fist to her mouth briefly, then cleared her throat and gave him a crooked smile. "Sorry. How ladylike. I had bronchitis last week and still have a souvenir."

"Are you sure it's not the cigarettes?"

She wagged a finger in his face. "I have one daddy already, thank you. Besides, I hardly smoke at all anymore. Only when I'm drinking."

He smiled again. "So, a pack a day, huh?"

She nudged him with a bony elbow. "I'm serious. This is my first night out this week."

He offered a good-for-you nod. "What are you up to these days?"

"I just graduated. Finished my MBA at Carolina."

"Really? You quitting nursing?"

She shot him a sour glance. "Past tense, Landon. I quit nursing three years ago. Remember that patient that nearly died? The medication error? That wasn't my fault, you know, but I got blamed for it."

He nodded. He did remember now, and Terri was correct. An IV pump had malfunctioned, but the hospital needed a scapegoat, and the doctor had demanded one.

"Anyway, Daddy was thrilled. He always wanted me to go into business, and Mommy Dearest got to say I told you so."

"Don't tell me you're living at home."

"How much you been drinking tonight? Or did you whack your head in that wreck too?"

He let that pass; she had no way of knowing. He smiled and raised his glass.

"I'm living in a river-view apartment on James Island." She sipped and gave him a closed-mouth grin. "If you play your cards right, you might get to see it. You still down on Ford's Court?"

"Yep. Same house. What are your plans?"

"Tonight or for the future?"

He couldn't suppress a chuckle. Of all the women he'd spent time with, Terri was probably the smartest and clearly the most tortured. He found her wicked and seductive banter clever, where others might have considered it slutty. Right now, anyone would think he was chatting up a good-looking tramp, never guessing that she'd once been one of the belles of South of Broad, a debutante from the St. Cecilia Society, graduate of Ashley Hall. He had learned all of this on their second date, lying half-naked on the banks of the Cooper River under the prettiest full moon he had ever seen. She had been respected at MUSC for her skill and professionalism. Their relationship never went anywhere—she was clearly too reckless for him, and he was far too serious for her—but they'd stayed friendly long after they'd moved on to more suitable conquests.

"I'm playing this summer," Terri said. "And looking for some real estate. I'm opening a business that matches students with internships overseas. Lots of travel, all in the service of the spoiled, you know." She took a long drink. "Guess it takes one to know one, huh?" She fished her phone out of her pocket. "Hey, before I get drunker, let me get your number."

He felt bound to act as if he wanted her number too. As he dug his phone out, the message caught his eye immediately: *Luna Quinn. Missed call and voicemail.*

The ringer switch was in silent position. He must have hit it accidentally—again. He traded numbers with Terri, intending to delete hers as soon as possible, then excused himself to go and do his forty-year-old duty. That drew a laugh and a wet coughing fit that followed him down the short hallway to the men's room.

"Landon, this is Luna. I hope I didn't wake you. My neighbor just remembered to tell me you came by. I saw you called earlier. Congratulations on the new car. I can't wait to see it. Anyway, I'm getting ready to go to bed, but if you get this in the next few minutes, feel free to call."

The time stamp indicated she'd called during his first beer. She had class in the morning, so he wouldn't call and wake her now. She hadn't asked about his doctor's visit, which was a relief. He would get his fill of health talk this weekend. She did say she wanted to see his car, so that was hopeful. Maybe he'd call her on the way to the airport. It was 11:15 p.m.; at best, he was going to get about six hours of sleep, and there was a growing possibility he'd get far less than that, if he couldn't extricate himself from Terri soon. Boy, things had sure changed; there was a time … but that time was gone.

CHAPTER ELEVEN

Two miraculous inventions of the modern world were top of mind for Landon as he jogged from the parking garage into Charleston International Airport the next morning—aspirin, which was damping the worst headache he'd had in a week, and wheeled luggage, without which he would surely miss his plane. Neither occupied his feverish brain for very long, though, because his window for calling Luna was closing fast. Although he dreaded having to ask for help getting his bag into the overhead compartment, he decided to bypass baggage check in order to save time. He was through security in minutes, thankful he wasn't living in a larger city with a jammed airport.

She answered on the second ring. "Hey, Landon, how are you?"

He'd never gotten used to people knowing who was calling. He still said hello, even when he'd seen the caller's name on his phone. "I'm good, Luna. Sorry I missed you last night—I accidentally put my ringer on silent, I guess."

"Oh, that's okay. I took one of the new faculty members to lunch, then showed her around the city. She was great. We ended up meeting some of my friends for happy hour. I could've strangled John, though. He knocks on my door at ten to tell me you came by at noon."

"Well, he said he was sick, so maybe he forgot." *Pretty long happy hour*, he thought.

"You never know with John."

He wasn't sure what she meant by that. He knew Luna had deliberately divulged her plans to her neighbor in case Landon stopped by, but now he found himself wondering if they were more than just neighbors. He checked his watch; the boarding area was full, with no lines or other signs of boarding yet. "Hey, Luna—I'm at the airport and wanted to let you know I'm heading home for the weekend. I need to talk to my parents."

The pause was brief. "Oh. That's a good idea, Landon. I bet your mother's glad."

"Yeah, I guess. I just need to tell them about this face-to-face. I can't seem to figure out how to tell them over the phone."

"Hang on a second," Luna said. He heard a door close, then some muffled sounds. "Sorry, I'm heading out for class."

"If you need to go, I understand."

"No, I'm fine. Just needed to lock the door. So I guess the visit with Dr. Schneider went well?"

He wished he had a free hand so he could slap his forehead. "I'm sorry. I haven't told you." First-class passengers were beginning to board. "Yeah, everything's good. I can go back to work, free to travel, no restrictions."

"That's fantastic. Congratulations. I know this has been hard."

He was in the first boarding group. "Listen, Luna—I'm sorry, but my plane is boarding. Can I call you later? I have a layover in Charlotte."

"Sure, but I'm in class until noon. How about later this afternoon? I should be available. Have a safe trip."

Right away, he wondered why he hadn't continued the conversation. The jetway was packed and smelled like sneakers that had been worn sockless all summer. He easily had ten minutes before he would be seated and subjected to the flight attendant's scolding about turning off his phone. Luna hadn't seemed sorry to go, though. Maybe it was just as well. She *had* asked him to call later.

The line crept hopelessly forward, like a restroom queue at a concert, mocking his fatigue. His head felt swollen, and his mouth tasted like he'd used Satan's toothbrush this morning. What had he been thinking? *Three* glasses of wine and then beer? That was too much any time, never mind after a head injury. Why hadn't he settled for a nice dinner with the Fannings and just gotten a good night's sleep? Maybe today he would actually nap on a flight. Otherwise, his mother would assume he looked and felt this way every day.

The man in front of him looked fit and tanned, dressed in a blazer, khakis, and topsiders, probably heading home after a golf getaway. Before Landon could screw up the courage to ask, the man offered to help him with his bag. The ease with which he hoisted it into the overhead compartment did nothing to ease Landon's continued sense of frailty. At last, Landon sank into his seat and braced himself for his seatmate, who in his mind, would likely resemble a squawking monkey or a hippopotamus and possibly both.

He closed his eyes, partly to discourage conversation, but mostly because he was tired. He felt like a codger—skin sagging beneath bloodshot eyes, breath evil and musty. A quick glance confirmed that his fly was zipped—he couldn't be sure anymore.

He wasn't certain about last night either. It had been so easy, even after two beers on top of all that wine, to pour Terri into a cab, decline her cross-eyed entreaties, and promise to call her when he returned. He had no intention of keeping that promise; she wouldn't remember it anyway, but now his ability to resist temptation, proper though it may have been, made him feel old. A night with Terri might have been just what he needed to put his troubles aside for a little while and pretend he was Landon Ratliff again. If only Luna had been home, or if he'd paid closer attention to his phone …

Luck was with him. His seatmate said nothing and had an apparent gift for falling asleep in cramped quarters. Soon enough, the attendant came by, admonishing the passengers to silence their phones. A longer conversation with Luna this morning was just one more missed opportunity to ponder.

Two short hops were not conducive to napping, but after a decent breakfast in Charlotte, he drifted off on the leg to Richmond, aided by a smaller plane with roomier seating and by continued good fortune that supplied him with a silent, bookish seatmate. The final approach announcement jolted him from deep slumber. They were on the ground almost before he could mop drool from his cheek. Although the overcast sky was encouraging, he fished his sunglasses from his pocket just in case, ducked through the cabin door into the syrupy Virginia air, and made the short walk to the terminal.

Like Charleston, Richmond had a relatively small, convenient airport that allowed travelers to move from plane to car quickly. Most times, for most people, this represented a distinct advantage, but right now, proximity and speed were not necessarily his friend. He knew his mother would be waiting just outside security. She had once again refused his suggestion to pick him up outside of baggage claim, adding that it was shameful to not allow families to pass through security and be waiting at the gate.

It wasn't a hangover giving him a dry mouth now. He drifted out of the stampede from three arriving flights and freshened up at the men's room sink. The nap hadn't done much for his appearance, but at least he could splash a little water on his face and tuck his shirttail. The mirror confirmed his fears. He looked about as old as he felt.

His mother had aged a lot recently, adding a little gray and a wrinkle or two on each of his last three trips home. This time might be worse, given his father's illness. Sick or well, his father always found a way to hang the years on his wife. To be fair, Landon, his brother, and his sister had contributed their share, but through it all, his mother had persevered with an optimism and grace that earned her the nickname Steady among anyone who knew the family. Over the years, Dale had emerged as her successor in the next generation. Good thing, since Landon lived too far away and Molly had put more than miles between her past and current lives.

He saw his mother before she spotted him. She stood off to the side of the corridor, her head swiveling like a periscope. Her huge brown eyes flared with recognition when she found him, and a closed-mouth smile creased her face. He accelerated, reveling in the familiar comfort of her arms as he felt her lips on his cheek.

"My baby," she whispered. He felt her shiver, then lean back. Her eyes took him in, squinting a little. He smiled. She looked well, better than he had expected. He hoped she thought the same of him.

"You look tired," she said as they untangled. "Let me pull that"—she pointed to his suitcase—"so we can hold hands."

She always wanted to hold hands, and he didn't mind a bit. How could he? He'd started it, back as far as he could remember, and except for adolescence, when they'd silently agreed to a moratorium in public, they had continued the tradition whenever they took walks together. He looked forward to it now, when age buffered him from the occasional needling he'd taken as a younger man.

"Hope you weren't waiting long." He knew she had been, even though the plane was on time.

"No. Seemed like years, though," she said and gave him a satisfied smile that made him squeeze her hand more tightly. "I've so wanted to come and see you, Landon, but your grandma was sick, and now—" Her voice faltered a little.

"It's okay, Mom. Dad needed you and Grandma too. I understand. How's Dad?"

They exited the terminal and walked to the parking garage. His mother let go and shaded her eyes against the glare. *Probably left her sunglasses in the car,* he thought, *or forgot them altogether.* Another sign of advancing years.

"I don't know, Landon," she said after a moment. "This last time really got him, but he seems to be getting better. He's not eating much."

"Is he having pain? Pancreatitis becomes chronic, sooner or later, and old Eddie's probably flirting with that by now."

"Don't talk like that, Landon. I know it's hard but give your father the respect he—well, he ought to deserve."

He wished he could take that last comment back. He hated disappointing his mother, no matter how he felt about his dad. She led the way to her pride and joy, the 2002 Honda CRV Landon had bought for her. It was her first new car and the only collaboration with his father that he could recall with any clarity. Fearful that his father would resent and belittle his generosity, he had caught him in a sober moment and enlisted his help as a coconspirator in the surprise. Apparently, recognizing that the relic she was driving at the time was both embarrassing and a threat, he had readily agreed and proved to be a valuable ally, making Christmas 2001 a near-mythological legend among all the Ratliffs except Molly, who hadn't been home for Christmas or anything else in years.

"Don't mention this to your father," she said, once she had maneuvered into traffic, "but I think this last time scared him. He's different—I don't want to say changed, don't want to get my hopes up, but he's not the same man, at least not right now."

He couldn't resist smiling. "What? Is he being nice or something?"

She nodded. "Yes, he is. Even says whiskey doesn't taste good to him."

"Well, amen. Is he helping around the house too?"

"No, I'd really be worried if he was doing that." Her quick smile didn't last. Her lips were compressed into a puckered white line.

"Mom, this seems like good news to me. What's wrong?"

"We're old now, Landon. People don't usually change at this age, unless … I hope I don't lose him, is all."

He reached across with his good arm, turning so he could squeeze her shoulder. She risked a glance, offered another quick smile, then concentrated on the road again. She was a nervous driver.

"Illness can change people, Mom. I've seen it happen to people older than Dad." He settled back into his seat. "Enjoy it as long as it lasts. You've sure earned it."

Conversation ceased as they merged onto the interstate. Landon knew his mother needed to devote her full attention to the heavier Friday traffic. Memorial Day was a week off, but devoted beachgoers were heading east early, so I-64 was packed, and even in light traffic, she had always feared and hated interstates. Once they exited onto Route 33, which snaked through cornfields and then tidal marshes, he knew she would relax, and they could talk more comfortably.

He loved the drive more than he admitted to anyone, and knew that his affection for home was entirely due to the reluctant driver now wrestling with the steering wheel. Without her, home would have been nothing more than a toxic stew that simmered constantly, threatening to boil over at any minute. Somehow, though, Steady had turned it into a place that called him back even as he struggled—without success—to put it all behind him.

The Eddie Ratliff Landon's mother was describing now did not fit with any picture of home that he could conjure. He had not permitted himself to dream of domestic tranquility since he was very young, when his father had repeatedly shattered his baseless hope that each night might prove to be the beginning of sobriety and redemption for the Ratliff family. He would peer out of the living room window, waiting for his father's car to pull into the driveway. Landon might see him sneak a drink from the bottle he kept under the front seat, but more often it was his father's wide-based gait and flushed face that betrayed him. He remembered turning away from the window, heartbroken, night after night, until finally he stopped hoping.

If his father's transformation now was genuine, then Landon knew it was fragile or else his father was sicker than he'd thought. Both might be true, and either way, Landon wondered if the news about his own cancer might be more than his father could handle right now. What if Landon's news drove him back to the bottle? Suddenly, the wisdom of this trip home became suspect, but it was too late. He'd already waited too long to tell his mother. She deserved to know, and he was going to need her.

The car had at last reached equilibrium, which meant they were in the right lane, traveling at sixty miles per hour with three to four car lengths clear in front. The buffer zone behind was far less stable, vanishing as cars approached but restored temporarily as they whizzed by. His mother hated being tailgated but feared slow drivers just as much because they forced her to either slow down or change lanes, and neither option pleased her. Nothing in front now, cars flying by on the left, twelve miles to their exit. Still, it seemed risky to reveal his news. He had only one useful arm to help keep the car on the road. There would be less traffic on 33, but it was pretty much a two-lane roller coaster most of the way.

His mother broke the silence. "Tell me about Luna." She risked a one-second, smiling glance in his direction. "She seems sweet."

"She's good. Summer school starts today, so she'll be busy for a few weeks."

"I don't know what I would have done without her when you got hurt. She and Dr. Fanning kept me from going crazy worrying about you." She flailed in the direction of his cast, missed, then clutched at the wheel again. He smiled, grateful for the effort.

"I'm so sorry I couldn't be there," she said.

"Mom, I understand. I really do. I wished you could have been there sometimes, but I knew you were needed here, and Luna really was fabulous."

"Tell me about her."

"I don't know that much. We hadn't been dating that long before the crash. She was born in California, and her family traveled around a lot. Her parents are actors."

"On TV?"

"No. Stage actors—and not famous or anything. She has three sisters—they all live out there. They all have weird names."

"I think Luna is a pretty name. She teaches at the college?" The car swerved a little and slowed while a tractor-trailer the size of a battleship blew by. His mother flinched but held the wheel steady.

"Right. At the College of Charleston. Teaches creative writing. She's writing a novel too."

"Wow. What's it about?"

"It's a sequel to *Sweet Thursday*. John Steinbeck. She doesn't talk about it much. Says it'll jinx her."

"I always loved Steinbeck."

"Yeah, well, apparently she studied at Santa Clara under some big Steinbeck scholar and wrote her thesis about his social conscience and how that's reflected in his novels."

"I never read *Sweet Thursday*. Guess I will now. Do you have a picture of her?"

"No, Mom. We aren't going steady or anything." This time, her glance came with a conspiratorial smile he'd seen many times, whenever she suspected more than he was revealing. "I read *Sweet Thursday*." He got another glance. "I was curious. It was a good story, I guess." There was the smile again. "I like her a lot, but we're *just dating*." He was glad she wasn't looking at him. His face felt hot.

"Okay, Landon," she said.

"She's a redhead. Big green eyes. She has freckles."

"Hmm." His mother was smiling. "Sounds pretty."

"Yeah, she is." His mind was spinning, trying to exit uncomfortable territory, and at the same time, trying to develop a much more important strategy.

"You never finished telling me about the trip to Beaufort," his mother said. They slowed in anticipation of the exit. The blinker was on, even though they had half a mile to go. "Pat Conroy lives there." The car crept into the off-ramp. He checked the side mirror; luckily, no one else was exiting. "He's a great writer, baby. You'd recognize his stories. It's good to face your demons—helps you understand them better and gives you strength."

He had his own demon to worry about right now. "*The Great Santini* was enough for me. Always felt like I was rubbing my nose in it. If I hadn't been forced to read it, I'd have thrown it in the river."

"Well, next time I come to Charleston, let's go to Beaufort. Did you—"

"Oh hey, Mom." He shifted in his seat. Her glance told him he had her attention. "Are the crabs coming in yet?"

"It's almost Memorial Day, Landon." She looked puzzled. "Seems like a pretty good year so far."

"Can we stop at Swoope's? I missed breakfast." It seemed a harmless lie, but one that he knew would strike at his mother's Achilles' heel—one of her babies needed nourishment.

"I'll fix you something if you can hang on."

"I'm kind of wanting some crabs," he said. Actually, his breakfast still lay heavily in his stomach. The days of late breakfast and early lunch were behind him.

To his relief, his mother smiled. "That's what you get for leaving the Chesapeake. I don't guess your father will mind. I'll call him when we get there."

"I'm going to get you that cell phone we've talked about, Mom," Landon said. After the third "Call Failed" message, he gave up.

"That's why I don't get one of those," she said and gave him that smile again.

He ordered crab-cake sandwiches while his mother phoned home. No fan of eating on the run, his mother had betrayed her desire to get home by agreeing to his hastily devised plan for food to go, unaware that his motivation was to spare her the embarrassment of public grief.

"He's fine," his mother said when she returned. "Want to eat out here?" She gestured toward the picnic tables, empty in the shimmering heat. He chose the one closest to the car.

"Your dad fixed himself a bologna sandwich. He's listening to the Braves' game."

"Still not a Nationals fan, huh? I figured by now y'all might have season tickets." He took an oversized bite. The crispy sweetness of the fresh crab overpowered the tasteless glop of the generic bun and hothouse tomato.

"Your daddy would sooner join the church than drive to Washington, DC, for a baseball game," she said as she bisected her sandwich with the plastic knife he had remembered to request. "He's talking about going to Richmond to a game, though."

"Wow. Maybe we should go this weekend. I haven't been to The Diamond since med school."

"You haven't missed much. That stadium is a shame. We went and saw them play in Norfolk a few years ago with Dale. The Tides' stadium is so much nicer."

"The Nationals are building a new stadium. Over by the Navy Yard. You'll be able to take a boat over from Alexandria."

She rearranged her food and finally took a nibble of her sandwich.

"We'll go," he said. "Maybe I can talk Dad into it."

"Maybe." She shrugged. "Sure sounds nice."

As his courage faltered, he began to rethink his plan. The lunch crowd would probably come and go for another hour. He knew he was going to cry and thought this news might challenge his mother's legendary equanimity as well. Maybe he'd wait and offer to drive, tell her on the way home. But then she'd want to hold him, and they'd end up in a ditch off 33. He felt trapped. This was a bad idea. She wouldn't want to stop again before they got home.

She was watching him eat, a faint smile on her face, happy to be sharing a meal with her son. He took a long swallow of tea. "Mom, I need to tell you something." As soon as the words left his mouth, he felt the aftershocks from three weeks ago, like an earthquake returning to claim whatever was left standing.

CHAPTER TWELVE

I t was like watching a building being demolished by explosives. His mother's face quivered under the weight of the news, held for an instant, then collapsed in a landslide of grief that bowed to public decorum even as it overwhelmed her usually impenetrable defenses. Tears filled his eyes, and he choked back the urge to cry out. He had never seen her like this. For a full minute, she neither spoke nor moved; tears wandered from beneath the trembling hand that shielded her eyes from a world she probably no longer recognized. An occasional lost moan escaped from her constricted throat. Finally, she reached for him, and when their hands met, she was on her feet, pulling, circling, then beside him, her arms clamping him to her. She gave in fully then, sobbing and laying her head against his. He pulled her close, felt her shudder as her world split apart and yielded to an unwelcome invader. His plan to provide comfort behind false bravado had vanished with his announcement, and now he did not even try. Fear and anguish and uncertainty and denial had been trampled by the loss of innocence that was worse than anything he had conjured in his mind. His unshakeable mother had been broken and might never look at him—or the world—in the same way ever again. He couldn't help thinking he'd let her down, even as he knew his part in this had been served to him like the draft notice that had arrived unbidden in his father's mailbox all those years ago.

Car wheels on gravel freed them from their mostly silent, shared misery. He felt a quick kiss on his temple, then a tug at his arm as motherhood sounded reveille. "Come on, baby. Let's go to the car."

He tried to drag his free arm across his face, but a cast was useless for wiping tears, so he bowed his head and mashed his face into his shoulder, pulling free of his mother's tender grasp for just a moment, then reaching for her hand. He couldn't look at her yet, but her grip and her stride were gathering strength, and when he risked a glance, her gaze was forward, and she walked erect with pride and purpose. Her resilience, which might prove fragile but perhaps summoned now out of a sense of duty, nevertheless comforted him. Steady Ratliff would not be broken for long. Tempered by a lifetime of marital pain and disappointment that she refused to give in to for the sake of her children, her powers of recovery now brought a different kind of tear to his grief-scoured eyes.

"I can drive, Mom," he said. His smile did not have to be forced.

She nodded, glanced back, then broke free long enough to deposit the remains of their meal in the rusted barrel that stood next to the entrance. He thought to help, but she didn't need it, so he stood beside the car until she returned. "It's unlocked," she said.

She touched his arm as he was putting the key in the ignition. "Before we go, tell me something hopeful, if there is anything. If there isn't—well, tell me that too. I'm going to need to be strong for your daddy."

"I know, Mom. That's why I wanted to stop on the way. I don't want to be the reason Dad falls off the wagon."

"We'll worry about that later. Tell me something."

"It's a very small tumor." His conversation with Fanning the previous evening came to mind. "The chances of a cure are actually very good, and they don't necessarily have to remove the kidney." He shifted in the seat and reached for his mother's hand. "There's a procedure they can do through a catheter, with radiation, that kills the tumor. It works really well, especially with small tumors." He hoped he sounded more convinced than he felt. "I'm going to New Orleans next month to have the procedure."

"Who's the doctor?"

"Dr. Lake. He's at Tulane. I met him a long time ago, at that conference I went to—remember? Before I moved there? He's the national expert, according to Enrique's dad."

"Have you told Enrique?"

He nodded. Technically, he had, and he sure wasn't going to admit they hadn't yet discussed it. He hoped she wouldn't probe.

"Isn't there anyone in Richmond who can do it?"

"Not as well as Lake. He's done more than anyone."

His mother nodded now; her eyes burned with understanding. "You're right. You go there. Is Luna going with you?"

"I was hoping *you* would go," he said. "If Dad's okay, that is."

Her eyes welled up. She squeezed his hand. Her caress was as soft and welcoming to his cheek as his pillow after a night on call. He smiled and leaned into her hand. "I owe you a trip, Mom, and I'm not sick. We can see the sights, and I'll have the procedure—you don't even stay in the hospital—and then we can be back in three or four days."

"You don't owe me a thing, Landon, and I don't care about New Orleans. I've seen it. I wish we were going for another reason."

"Believe me, I know. You think you can go?"

"You think you can back out now that you've invited me?"

"What about Dad?"

She buckled her seat belt. "He'll be okay. Dale can look in on him. What about Luna?"

He gave her a silent glance and turned to back out, then remembered he didn't have a free arm to sling across the seat. He used the mirrors instead. "We're not married, Mom, and I don't want to always be a patient around her. I want to just be her boyfriend. Anyway, I think this whole thing has been a bit much for her. She's got stuff to do."

"Have you asked her? She seemed concerned on the phone."

"She is, no doubt. No, we haven't talked about New Orleans."

"Don't shut her out, Landon."

"Mom—I can handle this."

He felt her hand on his arm. He touched the brakes. "I know you can, Landon, but you're alone down there in Charleston. What if you need something? Do you know how hard it is for me to think about that?"

"Okay, I promise. I won't shut her out." He found himself wondering now if Luna would ask about going. It would be awkward if she did, now that his mother had agreed to go. Not much romance in a trip with your girlfriend *and* your mom, anyway. She *was* his girlfriend, wasn't she? If not for the car crash, who knows what might have happened? Maybe Luna had felt obligated.

He would ponder all that later. Now he was heading home, and as the curvy ribbon of Route 33 unfurled before them, he took in the scenery as if he were watching a documentary of his childhood. Every barn, every creek looked familiar yet changed—smaller and no longer his, like a jilted lover who has moved on but still looks the same.

It suited him that his mother seemed lost in her thoughts for the moment. He was thinking about home—about what, or more specifically who, was waiting for him there. Anticipation of seeing his father had knotted his stomach, made his mind race for as long as he could remember. It was strange, but he could no longer recall pleasant times with his dad, even though he was certain they'd had some. His mother claimed they had, but after countless embarrassments at youth sporting events, then band concerts, and still later in college and medical school, any memories of parental bonding had vanished in a montage of cigarette smoke, bourbon breath, and slurred obscenities.

"Do you ever hear anything from Darlene?" his mother asked.

He smiled at his mother's attempt to divert his attention, and hers, back to a happier, cancer-free time. Darlene Masterson was his college girlfriend, his first girlfriend, and the only girl to ever get his whole heart, which she'd trampled on eight months later. "No, not since I got into med school. She was working in Nashville and planning to go to business school."

"She was from Luray?"

"Harrisonburg."

"That's right. I should have remembered."

"Mom, it was almost twenty years ago. A lot has happened since then."

"Why'd you two break up?"

He turned toward her with a furrowed brow. She had worried a pile of tissues into a mushroom shape that she continued to knead. Her lips were blanched. "Just went our separate ways, Mom—no big deal." That wasn't true, certainly not at the time. He had never shared the pain Darlene had inflicted upon him, pain that had left him cynical and wary of relationships, but as he turned back to the road, it occurred to him that finally, perhaps for the first time, their breakup really was no big deal.

Cancer was a big deal.

Telling his mother had been a big deal.

And in twenty minutes, facing his father, who now may have been transformed into someone resembling a person who might deserve to be called Dad, and if so, someone whose heart he was about to break—now *that* was a very big deal.

CHAPTER THIRTEEN

Whoever had designed the class schedule for the summer minisessions was a genius, Luna thought as she bicycled back to her apartment. It was Friday afternoon, so after teaching one class to disinterested students who were no doubt focusing on the fast-approaching weekend, she now had two and a half glorious days to herself. Diana never appeared on weekends, and Landon was in Virginia, visiting his parents. Her sympathy for the gravity of his trip was genuine. She hoped he would call, but worrying wouldn't help him or her. No, he was where he needed to be, and she would not permit worry or guilt to ruin what now seemed like a precious gift.

No duties, no obligations, no plans—except what she wanted to do. Besides writing, she would finally get her summer piazza garden planted. First thing in the morning, new annuals would replace the exhausted bulbs, which had taken on an appearance suited only for Halloween.

And after lunch, she needed to finalize the details for the reunion. In six weeks, all four sisters would be together for the first time since Luna's graduation from Santa Clara in

1999. Fox had tried to reunite them in 2001, but Luna was busy with graduate school, Tule had just started a new job, and the idea died of neglect, leaving Fox disillusioned about efforts at familial harmony. Although her enthusiasm had been rekindled by Luna's plan, Fox was now totally absorbed by her engagement and move to Los Gatos to a house that had more square feet than all the homes they'd lived in as children put together. So the trip was Luna's.

Sonoma Valley made a lot of sense for several reasons. Luna liked revisiting California, and Sutter and Tule lived close, increasing the likelihood of full participation. Their parents would be in the area and had agreed to meet for a dinner, but no one, including Luna, was getting her hopes up. Too many previous disappointments.

Her more immediate plan for a leisurely lunch was derailed before it even began, first by unpredictable but welcome intrusions from Hazel, and then by thoughts of Landon that refused to be pushed from her mind. She couldn't deny she was glad he'd called from the airport. He had to be anxious and tense; it would be difficult telling his parents the awful news. Was it easier or harder for a doctor, practiced in delivering bad news but more aware of the terrible possibilities? She recalled the first time she'd overheard him talking with students about a patient, how he'd emphasized the need for empathy, how every patient's illness was unique and personal. Now it was very personal for Landon, and she wondered if she'd let him down. Maybe that's what Diana had been hinting at.

She'd address that when Landon returned. It was time to finalize the reservations. She had considered several hotels, each of which offered something special, but Sonoma had the

Four Sisters Inn, a name Luna couldn't resist, even though she figured Sutter would be merciless about her baby sister's cutesiness. With Hazel beginning to twitch and stalk the keyboard, Luna knew her time was running short, so she chose Four Sisters, canceled the others, and was reviewing the itinerary when her phone rang.

She wasn't certain where she'd left the phone—somewhere in the living room—and in the moment before she located it, she wondered if the caller was Landon.

The name on the phone had brought a flash of disappointment. "Hey, Foxy," Luna said, brushing her hair back as she dropped into the easy chair. "What cha doin'?"

"Not much, Lunatic." Her sister's voice dripped with mock irritation, a ritual that Luna and her sister repeated with every call. Their nicknames, one of many injuries inflicted indirectly by their parents, had helped cement their relationship during their teen years and now provided them with a source of affection and joy that each was certain had never been intended by their parents.

"How's the palace coming?" Luna asked.

"Nearly done. They're starting on trim work in the main house, and the stonework on the pool house is nearly finished."

"Still shooting for an August first move in?"

"I think. The pool should go quickly, but the landscaping is harder to predict. It's been so dry here—good for construction, not so good for planting."

"Tell Elliott to buy some rain or maybe some rain dancers. Probably ought to wait until the pool is finished, though."

"Very funny. How's *your* man? On the mend, I hope?"

"Doing better, although *my man* is a little strong." She ignored Fox's poorly disguised snicker. "He's in Virginia this weekend, visiting his parents. He gets to go back to work next week."

"Bravo. It'll be nice to get things back to normal—sort of."

Luna had been on guard ever since accidentally spilling Landon's secret to Diana. "Yeah, sort of is right. He still has a broken thumb and a cast."

"How come *you* didn't go to Virginia?"

She rose from the chair and headed for the refrigerator. "Well, two reasons." Hazel raised her head, then reconsidered and closed her eyes again. "First, he didn't ask me, and second, I wouldn't have expected him to ask."

"The second isn't a reason. Would you have gone if he had asked?"

"No, I had class today, so I couldn't have gone." She plucked a half bottle of Sauvignon Blanc from the fridge and gave herself a generous pour. "So, there's your second reason, Your Honor."

Fox laughed. "Just looking out for my baby sister. Don't want her to become an old maid."

"We're just dating, Foxy. Must I remind you that I'm not yet thirty?"

"Well, unless my memory fails me, and it never does, that milestone is coming up fast."

"So is your wedding, and I think that's blinded you to the joys of being single."

"Sure, sure, Lunatic. Whatever you say." She offered an exaggerated, sinister chuckle. "The biological clock won't be denied, and besides, I can hear it in your voice."

Luna dropped into the Morgan chair again and threw her legs over the rolled arm. Hazel sprang into her lap. "What are you talking about?" She wasn't sure if she was smiling at her sister, the cat, or both.

"You can't fool me, and you sure can't fool Mother Nature. I've heard you: '*Landon* says blah, blah, blah. *Landon* and I are blah, blah, blah.' You never talked like that about anyone else you were just dating."

"I think you're projecting your own obsession with marriage onto me," she said. "And as for my biological clock, that must be your own ticking in your ears."

"My ears are fine, thank you, and two things they keep hearing about from a certain baby sister are her new boyfriend—and her age."

"What!" She sat upright, sending Hazel scurrying for safety.

Fox was laughing. "We haven't had a single conversation since Christmas where you've failed to mention that you're twenty-nine or not yet thirty. It's on your mind, Luna. Don't deny it. It's okay. I've been there."

She swallowed a sip of wine. "I think you're still there—alone, by the way. Look, I really like Landon, no question, but things have changed a lot, and I don't know what that means for him or me or us. If it doesn't work out, we'll both be fine. Don't make this into something it's not."

"It sure sounds like something, but I'll let you off the hook for now. How's the trip coming?"

"Great. I got the hotel today. Went with the Four Sisters."

"Knew you would."

"Sutter's going to puke." Drinking cold wine in the afternoon made her feel decadent.

"She likes to puke. Gives her a verifiable reason to be unhappy."

Luna snorted, sending Sauvignon Blanc onto her palate and out her nose. She sputtered and scrambled for the tissue box that sat on the island. The phone landed beside the tissues, Fox's searching voice small and distant while Luna recovered.

"Thanks for that," she said, still dabbing at her eyes as she retrieved the phone. "Nothing like white wine to clear out the sinuses."

"Sorry. Give me a signal when you're drinking, and I'll hold my tongue."

"Sure you will. That'll be the day."

"Ha ha." Fox cleared her throat. "What about Monica?"

"Monica who?"

"How many Monicas do you know? Your roommate, Monica—I forget her last name. I thought you were going to try to get together while you're here."

She rolled her eyes, though only Hazel could see her. "No. Monica Brown is now Monica *Yates*. Fourth of July is going to be celebrated in Chicago, where the Yates clan can coo over soon-to-be mother Yates."

Fox chuckled. "It's that time of life, baby sister."

"Don't remind me. Everyone and everything else is."

There was silence on the line for a moment, then, "Okay, Luna. Hey, listen, we're heading to Sonoma for Memorial Day. Anything you want me to do for the trip? Reservations at Bodega Bay?"

"Nope. I'm thinking we just do fireworks in Sonoma on the Fourth."

"Luna my dear," Fox said in her best bad impersonation of their mother. "Don't push your luck. After twenty-four hours together, the Quinn sisters may be generating their own fireworks."

Luna smiled. Fox had always been the insightful sister.

Chapter Fourteen

The journey to Wilton Creek was as familiar to Landon as the sound of his mother's voice, but as he left Route 33 and headed toward the post office at Wake, it occurred to him that little was left unchanged. The trees that lined the creeks and marked the fields were older and larger, and yet it all seemed smaller somehow. Everything he thought he recognized seemed closer, older, dustier, and tired. And then there were the invaders—gated entrances to upscale, waterside developments with names such as The Tides of Wilton and Wilton Marsh. Signs advertising lots costing more than he would earn in the next three years. Dale had driven him through one of these communities during an open house last Christmas, before the guards and gates were installed. They'd reminisced about long summers spent scrounging the scrubby fields and woods where bike paths now wound among luxury homes that would have been mysterious, unimaginable mansions had they existed back then. He had seen it all before, but now he felt as if he were returning to a boyhood home he had not visited in ages.

The high school, which he passed without thought on every trip home and which he had not set foot in since graduation, stirred him this time as if he were paging through his yearbook. He'd begun there as a scrawny freshman with an ill-informed determination to make the football team and be an athlete like his big brother. Four years later, he was playing accordion instead of football, off to Old Dominion University on a scholarship he'd received for winning the county science fair. Some long-dead, rich woman had left a pile of money that turned a dock builder's son into a college student, then a premed, and then, after a lot of time and borrowed money, a doctor.

Just past the big sweeping curve that split 625 off 626, the partially paved road leading to the Ratliff home dove into a tangle of sweet gum and pines strangled by poison ivy with stems as thick as pencils. He made the turn and glanced at his mother, who had gone silent some time back. She was staring straight ahead, a thousand-mile stare that he guessed was about cancer, which for her generation remained a death sentence, the disease of her parents and grandparents that struck without warning and invariably presaged a rapid, painful, and awful death.

The slowing of the car seemed to rouse her. She smiled. "Your daddy is going to be so glad to see you."

There seemed to be some hope that she was correct. The last time he visited, his father had been shrunken and angry; the whiskey had wasted what little muscle his small frame held, while the cigarettes whittled away at his lung capacity. Minimal exertion had left him struggling for air. He had resembled a leather mannequin left out in the elements. Now, after being so sick—what would he look like?

They passed the nearest neighbor's house—the Whitakers, who sold his father some land back in 1966.

The dusty, packed-gravel roadway ran out around the next curve, at the only home Landon had ever known. Over the years, humidity and pine resin had worked on the shingles and clapboard siding, lending a mildewed look to the small house that his father had built with the help of a VA loan. It sat about fifty yards above the creek, on a knoll that was the only suitable spot for a house and what passed for a yard.

He saw his father, shadowed within the screened-in porch, rise from a chair as Landon steered into a rusted carport. He touched his mother's arm. "Let's not tell him right away, Mom. You okay if we wait a little bit?"

She forced a smile. Her eyes were teary, but shining. "Of course, dear. Say hello and enjoy some time with him. I think you'll like this guy."

The screen door swung open, and his father appeared, a smile creasing his sallow, haunted face. Landon allowed his mother to fetch his bag while he swallowed and wiped his sweaty palm on his pant leg. His father's eyes, ringed with the aftereffects of serious illness, were nevertheless clearer than he had expected and shone with what looked like genuine pleasure. The handshake was not as firm as he had hoped, and his father's attempt at a hug seemed disappointingly half-hearted. Landon smelled cigarette smoke in his father's clothes and thought he caught a whiff of whiskey on his breath.

"Hello, Son," his father said. "Come on in the house. How was the traffic?"

"Not bad. It's good to see you, Dad." He paused at the door and waited for his mother to pass inside with the luggage. She kissed his father on the cheek, then scurried inside.

"Y'all sit and visit. I'll get us some tea," she sang out.

They took seats opposite one another on the patio set Landon had given them for Christmas. His parents had been delighted and astounded by the advances in technology that enabled such a combination of comfort and functionality. Between the twin recliners, his father had installed his pride and joy, a high-tech replica of a 1930s Crosley console radio Landon had given him for his birthday a few years back. The volume was low, but the murmur of a ball game could still be heard.

"Is the game over?" he asked, settling in on the sofa.

"Yeah, pretty much," his father said. "The Marlins are terrible. Hell, they won the World Series a few years ago."

"Braves started pretty good this year."

"Yeah, they've stumbled a little lately." His father studied the ceiling for a moment, then cleared his throat. "How you feeling?"

"You took the words right out of my mouth."

"I'm all right, for an old man. Was your car a total loss?"

He nodded. "Yep. I bought a new one yesterday. Well, not new—a 2005. Only ten thousand miles on it."

His father's face looked as if he'd just caught the scent of some bloated road kill. "You get another BMW?"

"They're good cars, Dad. I got a convertible this time."

"Ah, hell, it's your money," his father said and swatted at nothing in particular. His hands shook—just a little. "I had one convertible a long time ago but never again. Leaky and cold."

"They've improved some since then," Landon said.

"I know. So have American cars, but no one seems to believe it. Everybody's driving Japanese or German, seems like."

"Mom told me you've taken to borrowing her car now and then."

A smile mirroring Landon's crept onto his father's face. He glanced toward the door that led to the kitchen. "She doesn't have to tell everything she knows. It's a good car— I gotta admit. Damn thing goes in the snow and ice even better than my old truck, and it doesn't need sandbags in the back to hold it on the road." He smiled again. "Don't tell anyone—especially her—that I said so."

Landon gave him an exaggerated wink. "Your secret is safe with me, Dad."

Right on cue, his mother backed through the door carrying a tray with three glasses of tea and a plate of cookies. "You didn't have dessert, did you, Eddie?" she asked.

"Not much," his father said, plucking a cookie and a glass of tea from the tray. "How was Swoope's?"

"Like always," Landon said. The tea was sweet enough to make his teeth hurt. "Crab is good this year."

"Hell, you got crabs in Charleston," his father replied. "You pick 'em?"

"You know I don't pick crabs, Eddie," his mother said. "You boys can pick all you want. We had crab cakes."

She had made peanut butter cookies, his favorite. A cold glass of milk would have been the perfect accompaniment, but it was too hot and muggy for milk. After a couple bites, his father rose from his seat, both hands pressed into the curve of his arched back. He paced a little, his face starched. Landon knew, and guessed his mother did, too, that his father's corroded pancreas was making its presence felt with searing pain that gnawed at his back and belly, mocking his attempts to find a comfortable position. His father tried straddling the lounge chair, squatting and leaning forward like a catcher, his arms swaddling his abdomen. After a long, silent minute, he rose and headed for the house, easing the screen door closed behind him.

"I hate seeing him like that," his mother said.

"Is he getting some pain medication?"

"He won't take it. Says he doesn't want to get hooked on dope."

"Cigarettes and whiskey must be his limit, huh?"

His mother's eyes narrowed. He leaned close and whispered, "I'm sorry, Mom. I don't like seeing him in pain. But I know he's still smoking, and I thought I smelled whiskey on his breath."

She nodded. "I'm sure you did."

"He's still drinking? I thought you said he quit."

"I said no such thing, Landon. He sneaks a little all day long, even though he denies it. He's probably getting a little snort right now. He's got pints hidden all over the house. Thinks I don't know."

"But, Mom, that'll make his pain worse. He shouldn't—"

"Tell *him*, Landon, not me. He's a grown man; it's his choice. The doctor talked to him, and I talked to him until I was blue in the face." She rose from her chair and shooed a fly away from the cookies. There were no tears in her eyes when she looked at him. "He's got to decide, Landon. I have to take care of me." She settled back into her chair.

He smiled. "You always could handle him, Mom."

"It's different now. I used to fight him, hoping to change him, praying that he'd stop. I thought it was the war that made him do it. Not anymore. Sooner or later, the pain will get too bad or else he'll drink himself to death, I guess." She sipped her tea. "I did what you asked me to."

"What?"

"Al-Anon. I've been going since February."

"That's great, Mom. You sound better about all of this."

"It's not 'all of this,' Landon. It's alcoholism, plain and simple. Lots of people endure it. Some have it worse than we did. It helps hearing other stories, though."

"I used to think it was just us," he said. "I thought no one knew, but they did."

His mother gazed out toward the yard, her face stony and silent. "Everybody knew, and I knew. I saw the pain on your faces—yours, especially. Oh, it hurt Molly awful bad, too, but she got angry. As much at me as your daddy. Dale was the toughest, I think." A tear spilled onto her cheek, and she left it to work its way toward her jaw, which was clenched enough to pucker her mouth. "I could have left him or kicked him out a long time ago. I kept blaming it on the war, making excuses. I guess I was afraid to leave him. I thought it would kill my parents." She chewed her lip. "They knew too."

He sat forward, trying to capture his mother's gaze. "You know you can come live with me anytime you want."

She smiled, and the softness returned to her eyes. "You're my sweet baby, Landon." She shook her head. "I'm not going anywhere. Your daddy's sick, and he needs me. Not like I used to hope—he really does need me now." She fished a tissue from her dress pocket and dabbed her eyes. "I can't just up and move. My new grandbaby is here. My parents are here, and they aren't well. I'm handling this better now, with the counseling. Anyway, your daddy's doing better.

He'll never quit altogether, I don't think, but he is behaving himself. I can live with that."

He glanced at the door; whatever his father was up to, he was taking his time. "How's Sally?" he asked, hoping to settle the ground that seemed to be shifting under him.

"Sweet as a peach." His mother was beaming now. "Six months old last week. Good sleeper. Her hair's pure gold. She has her granddaddy wrapped around her finger."

"Carla sent me one of the Christmas photos. Daddy Dale looks pretty proud."

"You wouldn't believe him, Landon." Her hands were working the air now, flaring and flapping in front of a wide smile. "He's like a mother hen around her. I think he'd breastfeed her if he could." She covered her mouth with her hand, but her squinting eyes broadcast silent laughter.

"I won't tell him you said that." He rose from the sofa. "Where's Dad?"

"He might be lying down or in the bathroom. He's had right much diarrhea since he got home. Is that the pancreatitis?"

He nodded. "Yep. I'll go check on him."

The small kitchen looked so much better ever since Dale had installed new cabinets and the first dishwasher the family had ever owned. The peeling, moldy linoleum was gone, replaced with some type of laminate that resembled a planked, farmhouse floor. He had done a beautiful job, despite his father's dismissive attitude, no doubt triggered by the embarrassment and shame of having allowed the room to decay without ever lifting a finger to intervene. Landon noted a cluster of pots atop low flames on the stove and registered the aroma of home cooking that filled the immaculate space.

The bathroom was empty, and the door to his parents' room was closed, muffling the hum of the air conditioner. He squeezed the knob and leaned into the door gently, pleased when it gave way silently. The window unit must have been on for a while, refrigerating the room. His father was lying on his side, curled up beneath a thin blanket that left his droopy white socks exposed. His slack face was noticeably thinner; he looked like an older version of his high school yearbook photo.

His father was only sixty-four, and yet he was an old man, forced to retire by bad habits that were catching up to him in ways far more serious than simply limiting his ability to work. The wreckage of his life was mirrored in his wasted frame, now as close to peaceful as Landon guessed it ever got. Did his dreams torment him? Did the choices he'd made, the wife and children he'd alienated, the war that scarred him, did all that gather and circle, mocking him, sensing his vulnerability? Was it all closing in as he grew weaker, bearing shame and regret, driving him to seek refuge in alcohol, the very thing that made him weaker and more vulnerable?

He knew his father's retirement was not comfortable. All the years of working for unreported cash were reflected in what must be a pitifully small social security check. His mother's job helped—she liked working part-time in the church office—but with needy parents and now a sick husband, she didn't have time to earn much. Dale handled home repairs that otherwise would have strained their budget.

Landon sent money. His mother objected at first, until the impact of her husband's squandering, heedless ways declared itself and fear displaced pride. After a few months of noticeable comfort, she had sent him a heartbreakingly tender letter of thanks. Dale quickly figured out what he was doing and offered his respect and due for it, which to Landon was worth far more than the modest expense.

He eased the door closed, remembering a philosophy professor telling him once that time was neutral, neither friend nor foe. That only seemed half-right now; time could be either, depending upon how you had invested in it. For someone like Mike Fanning, time delivered the satisfaction of having loved your family, raised good children, and performed useful work. For his father, the accounting was less welcome. For Landon, the accounting was uncertain, and frankly, less concerning than the duration of the investment period right now. He hoped his own horizon was farther off than it felt.

His father's nap proved to be a long one, not an uncommon occurrence, according to his mother. When she excused herself to tend to dinner, he saw an opportunity to talk with Luna. There was no cell signal in the house or anywhere on the property. His mother suggested the home phone, but he worried Luna would not answer a call from an unrecognized number, so he borrowed the car instead and headed for Deltaville, where he figured his chances for a signal were better.

He drove all the way out to Stingray Point, thinking he needed open space in order to transmit the cellular signal, then realized after he got there that what he needed was a cell tower. Nevertheless, the signal was weak but present, and he smiled when she picked up on the second ring.

"Hey, sweetie, I've been hoping you'd call." She sounded a little drunk, but Landon decided to leave that alone. Sweetie sounded pretty good to him.

"Hi, Luna. How are you?"

"I'm good now. How are things in Virginia?"

He exited the car. "Pretty good. Listen, I don't have a great signal, and I'm going to try and walk down by the water here. If I lose you, I'll come back and call you, okay?" He hoped he didn't sound as desperate as he felt.

"No problem. Did you tell your parents?"

"Just my mom so far. My dad's taking a nap. I'll probably tell him at dinner."

"How'd it go with your mom?"

There was no seating at the marina, so he plopped down on the dock, dangling his legs over the gray-green water. "It was pretty awful. She took it hard."

"Oh, I'm sorry. I can't imagine how this must feel for her."

"I asked her to go to New Orleans with me. I think that perked her up a little."

"That's a great idea, Landon," Luna said, maybe a little too enthusiastically. Was she disappointed? Maybe he could still ask her?

"Landon?"

"I'm still here."

"I asked you how your dad was."

"Oh, sorry," he said, still wondering whether he should have invited her to New Orleans. "He's okay—lost a lot of weight and looks weak, but he's nicer than I've ever known him to be. Sounds like things at home are better for my mom. She started going to Al-Anon."

"Wow. That's a big step. Good for her."

"Yeah, I guess." He leaned against a piling and stretched his legs out on the dock. "It's weird. I've been after her to do this for years, but now that she's done it, it feels a little strange, like she's pulling away from him just when he's doing better."

"Maybe he's doing better because she's dealing with it."

He smiled. He sure wished Luna was here right now.

He drove back feeling better, his anxiety about telling his father dampened by the conversation with Luna. She had enthusiastically accepted his offer of a picnic supper on Sullivan's Island Monday evening and insisted on preparing the food. After all, she'd argued, she had all afternoon, while he would be busy on his first day back at work. No invitation to stop by on Sunday evening had been forthcoming, but then, he had not offered, and he *was* getting in pretty late. This plan was better; the picnic would provide an opportunity to show off his car and celebrate another milepost in his recovery as well as give him a reason to obey doctor's orders and curtail the workday. He felt fine and had so much to catch up on, but he didn't want to overdo it. Besides, he knew Fanning would show him the door by early afternoon. By sunset, he would be on the beach with Luna, snuggling and necking and sharing a bottle of wine, he hoped. They both had work the next day, so she probably wouldn't spend the night …

He couldn't suppress a smile that he knew no one but he would ever know about. There was no denying it—he missed her.

His father was up when Landon got home, and supper was ready. If he had harbored any doubt, it was erased now—his parents were officially old people, ready to eat their evening meal by 5:30 p.m. His mother was scurrying about the kitchen, filling serving dishes at the stove and shoehorning them onto the small table that probably served the two of them adequately, but just barely. Steam curled invitingly from the food and coalesced above the table in an aromatic cloud that reminded Landon of his childhood and of the time that had elapsed since lunch.

No one could have blamed Landon for dithering over dinner. Everything tasted like home, especially the fluffy biscuits slathered with butter and bathed in gravy as thick and rich as caramel. But he knew his father's pancreas was fickle; at any moment, it could take exception to any of a multitude of fatty ingredients and destroy the delicate balance of a rare communal meal.

He braced himself with a long swallow of cold sweet tea. "Dad, I got something to tell you," he said, then glanced at his mother, whose face was impassive but slightly constricted around the mouth.

A glance from his father was the only reply; he ate warily, like an injured animal, one arm curled around his plate as if someone were threatening to take it from him. Landon guessed that recent experience had taught him to eat slowly, testing the response between each bite in order to avoid a sudden, overwhelming reaction.

"When I was in the hospital—after the crash—they did a bunch of tests, and when they did an X-ray of my kidneys, they found something."

The silence held everyone in its grip, as if a sudden, unfamiliar sound had interrupted their meal. In the stillness, the wall clock's marking of time sounded like the muffled footfalls of a distant, marching army. Landon wanted something to break the hush. His throat felt constricted. A swallow of tea bought him time.

His parents were frozen—one, an accomplice, the other likely conjuring increasingly terrible speculations about what was beginning to feel like a cruel conspiracy.

"It turned out to be cancer, Dad. I have kidney cancer."

Landon's attempt at a brave smile was doomed from the start. His father looked dumbstruck. His mother sprawled across the table, maximizing her wingspan to gather her brood, even at the risk of dunking her elbow in the gravy bowl. Landon did not want to cry and was determined to regain his composure, which meant first escaping from the comfort of his mother's touch. So he stood and guided her into her chair. Once there, she reached for his father's hand, and he watched him take it with a tenderness that was as astonishing as it was threatening to Landon's attempts to be strong. Now, in what surely had to be one of the worst moments of their difficult lives, they offered each other what comfort they could.

"I told Mom on the way from the airport," he said, trying to buttress his voice as he spoke. His father nodded; his hand, squeezed almost white, trembled slightly. Landon cleared his throat, searching for doctoral authority. "I'm actually lucky, if you can ever call cancer lucky. The tumor is really small. They found it by accident, and it hadn't caused any symptoms even. That makes the chance for a cure much better."

"That's good," his father said. "Can they cure it?"

"It seems so. You remember my roommate, Enrique? His father recommended a guy in New Orleans. He's a national expert, and he thinks the chances of a cure are excellent. He doesn't even need to remove my kidney."

"They just cut the tumor out?"

"No, they radiate it through a catheter, so they don't even have to cut me open. It's quick, and I don't even have to stay in the hospital."

His father nodded, slack-jawed and overwhelmed. The effort seemed to exhaust him. His mother wrapped her arm around his bony shoulders. "There's no one here who can treat you?" his father asked. His voice was hollow and distant, as if he were calling to Landon through a drainpipe.

"There's a guy in Richmond, but the guy in New Orleans is the expert."

"I'm going to go with him, Eddie," his mother said. "Dale and Carla can stay with you."

His father stared into his plate. "When are you going?"

"Middle of June. The procedure is scheduled for June nineteenth. If you aren't feeling well, Mom doesn't have to go."

His father's eyes came up first. His head followed, wobbling a little as he searched for something to fix upon. He settled on something above and behind Landon, gripped the table edge with both hands, straightened his slumped shoulders. "Maybe I should go too."

CHAPTER FIFTEEN

It was about 450 miles from Deltaville to Charleston, but to Landon, lying on a picnic blanket in the sympathetic company of Luna Quinn, it seemed like Sullivan's Island was on a different planet.

"You're kidding," Luna said, leaning on one elbow and sipping wine. "He offered to go with you? That's really sweet."

Landon stifled a laugh. "Not sure I've ever heard anyone call my father sweet, but it was thoughtful of him." He tossed a grape into his mouth. "My mom was conflicted about the idea, though."

The furrow between Luna's brows reappeared, and she tilted her head, asking the prettiest silent question he'd ever seen. He wanted to kiss her—had wanted to ever since their first and only welcome-back kiss at Luna's apartment this afternoon. Instead, he sat up cross-legged and brushed back the hair that had taken advantage of her head tilt, letting his hand linger on her cheek then slide to her neck. Her smile was encouraging.

"She doesn't want to divide her attention but doesn't trust him alone yet," he said.

"Did she tell you that?"

"Pretty much." He pulled another grape free and dangled it in front of Luna's lips. Her face relaxed into another smile as her mouth opened, her lips brushing his fingers while her eyes stayed locked on his. "I didn't tell you. My mom joined Al-Anon."

"You did tell me, Landon. On the phone."

"Oh. Well, what do you think?"

"Good for her. Maybe you should follow her lead."

He grimaced. "You sound like her. She tried to drag me along on Saturday."

"Why wouldn't you go?"

He wrapped both arms around his knees and stared into the surf. The tide was retreating, yielding broad swaths of beach teeming with scuttling creatures searching for a tidal pool or burrowing into the damp sand. "I don't know. A couple reasons. Dad and I went fishing, and I didn't see what one visit would do anyway."

In his peripheral vision, he saw Luna rearranging the blanket. He smiled. She always wanted eye contact and now sat squinting into the setting sun. He knew she wouldn't put sunglasses between her eyes and his. "Wouldn't one visit introduce you to the concept? Maybe you'd like it?"

"I liked fishing with my dad."

"I'm glad." She nodded, then waited just a moment. "They have Al-Anon in Charleston, too, you know."

"Can I tackle one problem at a time, Luna? Cancer and a head injury are higher on my list right now."

Her hand felt cool on his forearm. "Of course. But I think you ought to consider it—for later. You aren't alone. Lots of people go through this with alcoholic parents. Group therapy works."

"Your parents aren't alcoholics, are they?"

She shook her head. "No. Neglect is and was their form of abuse. But I've been to counseling, and it helps. You should try it."

"I don't know—isn't Al-Anon for people living with alcoholics? I mean, I'm not really in that situation anymore."

"Yes, you are, Landon." She leaned in—all eyes and red hair and freckles. "You *are* living with it." He felt her hand slide across the back of his neck, then a quick squeeze. "Okay, enough of that. How was the rest of the weekend?"

"It was good. Dad and I talked a little—a lot, compared with other times, I guess. I went with my mom to visit my grandparents."

"Your mother's parents?"

He nodded. "Yeah. My dad's parents are dead." He knew what Luna was going to ask. "I didn't tell them about the cancer. Grandma hasn't been well lately. Mom said she'd tell them later."

"How about your brother?"

"Didn't see him. He was in Okracoke camping. He and his wife go every year, and this was their first chance since their daughter was born."

"You're an uncle?" The setting sun was becoming fierce; she rummaged in her beach bag and retrieved her sunglasses. "That must be so fun."

"I can tell she's going to be a great kid, but she's only six months old. Her name is Sally."

"I like that name. Did she go camping with them?"

"Yeah. Breastfeeding, you know." He shook his head. "Can't imagine camping with a little baby. Can't imagine *having* a little baby either."

"Totally," Luna said. "But nieces and nephews—seems like renting kids. When you get tired of them, you just take them back." She nudged him onto his back and flopped down beside him, bracing herself on her elbows, letting her hair tickle his face. Her eyes locked onto his. He tangled his fingers in her thick hair and pulled her face to his. "For when you have other things to do," she whispered just before their lips met.

The beach was getting busier, locals as well as Charlestonians who made the drive over to enjoy an after-dinner stroll, their cars lining the highway each evening as if there were a festival or a rock concert taking place. Landon didn't care; his customary discomfort with public displays of affection apparently did not apply to Luna Quinn.

Luna stuffed the beach bag, and he grabbed the wine, and they wandered down the surf line, holding hands, searching for shells. She recounted her continued quest for her personal holy grail—an intact keyhole sand dollar; its description left him smiling and confused, so while he sipped from the bottle like a wino, she knelt in the sand and drew the design with her finger. He recognized it as a common offering in Folly Beach surf shops, an observation he kept to himself.

Their shadows threw long stripes across the retreating surf as afternoon faded into twilight, downshifting toward sunset. Only the gulls resisted, wheeling and fracturing the gathering stillness, crying like exhausted children protesting the surrender to bath and bed. Fatigue was beginning to bear down on Landon as well. His flight home had been delayed, and he'd slept poorly, his mind unable to stop grappling with how different home, his parents, his former life now seemed. His father's illness, like his own, appeared to have changed everything, and although he had to admit some of the changes were healthy, he could not deny how unsettling it had been—the absence of tension, his mother's disengagement—all of it had left him feeling like a battle-scarred veteran discharged stateside without adequate preparation.

And then there was work, or more accurately, a day spent pretending to be an associate professor of medicine at MUSC. His first day back had been mostly discouraging. After a tastefully low-key welcome reception attended by the divisional faculty and staff, he'd been eager to get to work, only to discover that his "work" was a charade. Nothing came easy, including his efforts to look busy. He'd been unable to concentrate and felt liberated and guilt-free when he left early, pretending to be frustrated by the need to follow doctor's orders.

Enough of that. Luna was brushing wet sand from her knees, reaching for his hand, and accepting the bottle of wine with a big smile. Her let her sip, then pulled her to him, his interlocked hands coming to rest in the curve of her lower back. He felt her arms encircle his neck, the weight of the bottle pressing one arm into his shoulder just before he tasted the faint remnants of wine mingled with the sweetness of Luna's luscious lips. A stubborn wave defied the retreating tide and washed over their feet and legs, wetting them to midcalf and leaving behind a little sand as it gathered what it could carry from the beach and hauled it away into the timid surf.

The next morning, lying alone—to his dismay—in his bed, he remembered that kiss, which had proven to be but one of many to follow in their journey from the beach to the car.

Once there, they necked like high schoolers before acting their ages for a few minutes until Luna nearly wrecked his new car by planting her moist and still-eager tongue in his ear just after they traversed the Ben Sawyer Bridge. A dazzling sunset and the nondriver's share of wine had worked their disinhibiting magic. It was dark by the time they reached his house.

Their lovemaking, initially desperate and urgent, soon settled into a tender, languid rhythm that Landon found astonishingly pleasurable, his now-sated physical yearnings replaced by unfamiliar relaxation and gratitude bordering on what he guessed was joy. Luna seemed happy and satisfied. They lay nose-to-nose, her eyes shining in the darkness, an occasional contented wordless murmur marking their otherwise silent communion.

There was work tomorrow, though, and she had chosen practicality over passion, resisting his alternately clever or sweet attempts to persuade her otherwise. So he drove her to her apartment, where they shared one last incredible kiss that left him breathless on the piazza, then dazed and befuddled on the drive home. Once there, he checked his phone twice, fought off the urge to call her, then drifted off into a deep, dreamless sleep.

Now, prodded by the clock's digital face that blinked silently like a judgmental owl, he threw off the covers and forced himself into an upright position, wondering if Luna would be free this afternoon. He shook his head, trying to recall who he was or what his life had been like a month ago.

CHAPTER SIXTEEN

Landon was trapped. He didn't mind all that much.

"Are you nervous?" Luna asked.

"This is a dirty trick, you know," he said. He knew his half-hearted efforts to appear vexed couldn't mask how thrilled he was to have her beside him in his car again.

"It was your decision, Dr. Ratliff." Her eyes and smile reflected the delight they shared in teasing one another. "Made of your own free will."

"Well, I still say Saturdays are for sleeping in." He wanted to add *together* but let that pass. They had a three-day weekend ahead of them, and she hadn't made any excuses so far. Things looked hopeful.

He pulled away from the curb and headed west on Queen. It was a glorious morning. The birds were in full voice, interrupting their songs occasionally to squawk at chattering squirrels who seemed oblivious to the clinging humidity. It promised to be a stifling day but wasn't yet, so a drive in the convertible was enticing.

Traffic was light, so he slowed long enough to give her an exaggerated sidelong glance. "I will say, my free will looks a lot like a pretty redhead with big, green eyes this morning."

Her eyebrows came up, along with a hint of a pout. "Could be worse, you know. You could have a warty old conscience nagging away at you every time you try to have fun."

He nodded and immediately thought of Enrique. He had called Landon yesterday. Their conversation had been awkward and guilt-provoking, reminding Landon how neglectful they'd both been toward a friendship that once had seemed solid and deeply important. Between apologies that sounded forced, Enrique had offered bland encouragement. He urged Landon to fight, to keep a positive attitude, once offering a pathetic homily about how burdens were allocated based upon our ability to bear them. Landon had stifled the urge to deride Enrique's familiar ploy of pretending to be a devout Catholic when the situation called for it or when his parents were around, but the conversation had reminded him how his friend's paternal, judgmental fussiness had nearly derailed their friendship on more than one occasion, most dramatically during their one trip to New Orleans together so many years ago. And now, just before Landon was heading back to New Orleans for treatment that he hoped would save the life so profoundly altered by that first visit, Enrique and Amy were coming to Charleston to see him. He had a week to get ready, and no religious platitudes to help him. He just wished he were looking forward to it.

"You were kidding about the free will thing, weren't you?" Luna asked, filling the silence before they'd even reached the river. "Because you have to want to do this, Landon. I don't want to feel like I'm forcing you."

"I was kidding," he said. "But I'll admit, I'm glad you're coming with me."

"Why?"

He smiled. "Can't take a compliment, huh?" He knew better.

"No, I'm wondering why you wouldn't go alone."

"I'm not saying I wouldn't, just that I'm glad you're along."

"Why?"

She was relentless, but even the discomfort felt good somehow. "I don't know. I guess I'm a little scared. You make me feel safer."

"What are you scared of? You recommended this to your mother, right? Why haven't you gone before now?"

She looked as if she were enjoying herself. He felt trapped but by someone who wished him no harm. "I don't know. Part of me thinks this might just be a bunch of nuts getting together to make each other feel better. I'm not sure it's for me."

"Wise approach, Doctor. Make the diagnosis without any evidence." Her sarcasm carried a hint of amusement, keeping it safe. "Besides, what's wrong with feeling better?"

"Nothing, but I don't feel bad." He reached for her hand. "In fact, I feel pretty darn good right now."

"I'm glad, but I don't think you feel as good as you pretend to about your father—or your mother, for that matter." Her fingers, interlocked now with his, reassured him. "Isn't she a big part of this? I thought you were curious about why she's going."

The last traffic light before the Ashley River Bridge caught them. "I am, for sure," he said. "I just hope it's better than I think it is."

"It might be much better if you think a little differently about it." She offered a head tilt and an exaggerated toothy grin. "Anyway, that's my opinion. Not that you asked, but I figure, why deprive you of it?"

He laughed. The light changed, and he accelerated toward his reluctant adventure, certain only that he was grateful for his companion, opinions and all.

The church was a simple, brick structure tucked into a clearing just large enough for the building and a small parking lot. It seemed to have been built for a congregation that lacked ambition or hope or both. Hand-lettered directions on a cardboard poster led them to a room where a young woman greeted them.

"I'm Carol." Her smile seemed genuine, though Landon thought her eyes were as sad as a basset hound's. She was about his height and looked fit, as he had, long ago.

"Landon Ratliff." He noted her strong handshake. "This is Luna Quinn."

"We use first names only here," Carol said, smiling at Luna as she accepted her hand. "I'm so glad you've come. Help yourself to coffee or a donut, if you like. We'll get started in a minute. The literature on the table is free for the taking, although we always accept donations." She indicated two battered folding chairs on the far side of the wooden table that dominated the room. "It's up to you whether you speak or just listen."

The meeting was small, so they stood out like new freshmen at a frat mixer. Luna looked as if she might begin socializing. "Coffee sounds good," he announced, then shifted his gaze to the urn that dispensed oily, black coffee into foam cups too small for people who surely needed a jolt rather than a nudge before a meeting like this. Someone approached Luna, who drifted into an introduction that he wanted no part of, so he concentrated on the fill indicator, which always reminded him of an old-fashioned thermometer. He passed on the crusty sugar, stained with someone's thoughtless after-stir plunge, and on the brown canister of powdery *whitener*, reminding himself once again that Clorox was a whitener as well.

"All right, everyone!" Carol clapped her hands as she settled in at the head of the table. "Let's get started." She raised her voice over the shuffling of the group organizing itself around the table. "We have two new visitors this morning." Besides Carol, there were four other women and one elderly man, whose presence alleviated Landon's unfounded fear that he was attending a women's support group.

"As you all remember, new visitors are welcome to speak or not, as they choose." She turned and offered Landon and Luna a big smile. "We're very glad you've come and hope you'll come back. Would you like to introduce yourselves—first names only, please?"

Landon deferred to Luna, as he would have to anyone right then. "I'm Luna. Nice to meet you."

"Hi, Luna." The response sounded grim, though the faces were friendly and attentive. He prayed she wouldn't continue, setting a precedent he wanted no part of, and when she gave a little wave to the gathering, he moved to fill the opening she'd left him.

"I'm Landon." He nodded and showed his palm briefly before shifting his gaze to the floor, anticipating the droned, mechanical response that followed immediately.

After that, it all became noise, a background accompaniment to his unfocused, unjustifiably cynical mind. Something about someone's daughter's drinking. Something about a husband or ex-husband. There were nods from the group, occasional supportive declarations, delivered as if the speaker were testifying during a church service.

He wanted to escape but feared that leaving would come with too high a cost. His plans for Memorial Day weekend included Luna, and he had agreed to stick this out. He couldn't imagine why he had ever suggested this to his mother. What was she possibly getting out of this meeting? Something, he guessed, because she certainly seemed different.

The speaker was laughing now, and the group laughed with her. That seemed strange, to be laughing about living with an alcoholic. His father was a lot of things but funny wasn't one of them. He thought about all the times his father had embarrassed him, the times he'd made his sister cry, and couldn't conjure up a reason to smile, let alone laugh.

"Would you like to speak?" Carol's voice broke the reverie. Landon shifted in his seat and looked at Luna, who turned to the group.

"Well, I'm Luna, and I'm here to support my boyfriend. Thanks for having me." She turned to him and the group did likewise. He tried not to blush. This wasn't Luna's fault, and he knew he could pass, but decided against it. He liked the way it sounded when she said boyfriend.

"I'm Landon." His voice seemed weak, so he cleared his throat, swallowed, and started again. "I came to see what this is like. My mom started going to Al-Anon back in Virginia, and I wanted to try it." The coffee was cold, but his mouth was dry. "I just came to listen." No one responded. "My mom seems different—more detached or something."

"What about you, Landon?" the man asked.

"How about Landon?" someone else asked.

Carol smiled again. "We try to focus on ourselves, Landon, rather than talking about others. Would you like to say more? We don't know much about who brought you here."

Landon turned to Luna. "I can let her tell you."

"No, Landon," Carol said, "I mean, who is the alcoholic in your life?"

"Oh, I see. It's my dad." Everyone was quiet now. He nodded. "But that's not really why I came today. I just wanted to see what it's like—for my mom." Luna's watery eyes made him think the weekend was still in play. He nodded again and gave Carol a wave, hoping she would move on.

Carol took the hint, and the meeting finally wound down. When he walked through the door and squinted into the glaring sunshine, he got a sense of how paroled prisoners must feel. His face ached from offering insincere responses to the repetitive urging to "just come back" or "keep coming." The brochures were already curling in his sweaty hand, and the book tucked under his casted arm—which was due to be liberated in a few days—had at least given him an excuse for not shaking or touching or hugging. Luna handled the goodbyes, moving quickly in what Landon interpreted as deference to his obvious discomfort.

He backed the car out slowly, trying not to appear too eager or to shower anyone with the baked parking-lot dust. Luna was twisted in her seat, waving like a new bride departing on her honeymoon, but when the tires found pavement, Landon stepped on the gas, throwing her back in the seat and leaving the strange interruption to their weekend behind.

"That was interesting," Luna said, once she had buckled in and tucked her flying hair back into her flapper cap.

"I guess." He knew his answer would only prompt more questions, but since that was true regardless of what he said, he figured he might as well ration his responses and save his energy. In the brief, ensuing silence, though, it occurred to him that he'd rather finish this conversation now and be done with it. "I don't really get it, though."

"It was one visit, Landon. Your first visit. You heard Carol—the first visit is always awkward. You should give it another try. Besides, it sounds like your mother's glad she went."

"We'll see. At least I got a sense of it. Next time I talk to Mom, I can ask better questions maybe."

"Sure, but what about you?"

"What about me?"

"Don't you think this might help you? That's why they asked you to talk about you, rather than about your mother."

"I don't know." They rounded a bend and emerged from the pine forest into a blinding midmorning sun that had them both fumbling for sunglasses. Hiding, even in plain view, felt better to him, in the same way that talking on the phone was easier than doing so face-to-face.

"Sounds like denial or avoidance to me," Luna said.

He shrugged. "I don't know. It was weird and uncomfortable and didn't seem very helpful, but who knows?" He did, but didn't see any advantage in sharing that opinion. "Maybe it *would* help." Not very likely. "I'll think about it." He gave her a quick smile and a wink that she probably couldn't see, congratulating himself on his self-control.

Her hand slid along the back of his neck. "Good." Her hand was better than good, and he rocked his head back, pressing against her practiced fingers. "I'm proud of you for going today. I don't pretend to know what you've gone through, what it's like, but sharing your experiences seems like a good idea. Maybe you can start by sharing with me."

He nodded, trying to appear relaxed despite a mounting sense of being cornered. Suddenly, the long weekend was beginning to seem like a maze that he'd have to navigate, a challenge to be overcome, with nothing waiting on the other side except another week that would mock his newfound inability to concentrate on anything except the pea-sized mass in his kidney and the bruised brain that had led to its discovery. Right now, he couldn't even imagine being able to care for patients or supervise residents and students. He was tired of thinking about his problems—it was exhausting, disheartening work searching for articles about how best to treat kidney cancer, about the odds that he would live to see his fiftieth birthday, and now these Al-Anon folks wanted him to dredge up his damaged childhood? Fuck that. He wanted to laugh and mean it, to run as he used to, and to feel Luna's lips on his, her body against his. Maybe even play some music. He'd done all that, despite his father's drinking; medical school, a successful career—he'd done okay. Most people would say Landon Ratliff had done better than okay. It was the crash and the cancer that he needed to fight. Let his mother talk to support groups if it helped her. Maybe it would help Molly. He was certain his brother would never do it.

"You okay?" She snaked her fingers into his hair.

"Yep." He tried to sound upbeat, hoping the pause had indicated a mutual willingness to change the subject. "How about brunch? We could try that new oyster place on King."

"Oysters sound good, but let's sit near the water. Sullivan's Island?" Her voice was playful. Maybe they'd left Al-Anon behind, at least for a while.

He smiled and turned to her, shaking his head slowly for effect. "No, I've got it. You ever been to Bowens Island?"

Her smile far outdid his, as usual. "No, but I've heard of it. It's a real island, right?"

"Yep. Near Folly Beach. Maybe we should stop off for our suits?"

Her lips landed just in front of his right ear, leaving a loud, wet mark that felt like victory, redemption, and an Olympic gold medal rolled into one. "Perfect. Drop me first, and I'll feed Hazel and play with her a little."

"Good idea. She might not see much of you this weekend."

Luna straightened in her seat. "A little presumptuous, aren't you, Doctor?"

Landon threw his head back and laughed. "Oysters, beer, sun, and surf. Snuggling on the beach, playing in the water. I'd say my chances are pretty good."

"Hmm." She crossed her arms, leaning forward so he could see her exaggerated pose. "Well, we'll see. She leaned in again, threatening to block his view, which amused more than bothered him. "Maybe we'll need to compromise, for Hazel's sake," she murmured, planting a soft kiss on his cheek. "She might be willing to share her side of the bed."

"She can keep her side. I don't plan to need it."

Her naughty chuckle was the perfect overture; the curtain was ascending on the redeemed weekend. Landon urged the car forward, heading east into the rising sun, back into what he had feared was lost. Memorial Day was one of his favorite holidays, the gateway to summer's long, lazy days, drowsy thick twilight, and warm nights. And this year, summer held even more promise—the wonder and glory of sharing it all with Luna Quinn.

CHAPTER SEVENTEEN

T he campus at MUSC was beautiful and green in places, but the Clinical Sciences building, like so much of the complex, was grim and forbidding, standing amid a jumble of hospital and administrative buildings that fit together like a freestyle Lego block project. The mismatched architecture bore witness to decades of evolution and growth. The Department of Medicine lived high up in the brick tower, whose narrow, featureless windows reminded Landon of Richmond's city jail building.

It would be a busy week, he thought as he rode the elevator to the eighth floor. Tuesday already, and he had weekend guests coming. The impending visit made him uneasy. Too much time had passed—too much had changed or maybe not enough. He was still lousy at relationships, and he hadn't paid enough attention to Enrique, Amy, or anyone for that matter.

He'd much rather just spend next weekend with Luna. The long holiday had been nearly perfect, absent the Al-Anon experiment and the break Sunday afternoon that allowed Luna some writing time. He'd actually welcomed the break, thinking he needed it, and then spent the entire time wondering what she was doing, counting the hours until their prearranged meeting at The Vendue's rooftop bar. There, the spectacular sunset had competed poorly for his attention, which was fixed upon how cute a piece of fabric became when fitted to Luna Quinn's remarkably fetching form.

The pulmonary/critical care offices occupied a suite at the end of the hall, a location that allowed both Fanning and Landon to claim corner offices overlooking the nursing school and a weedy-looking green space planted with spindly trees and tall grasses. From the eighth floor, however, they enjoyed a broader view encompassing the Ashley River, the River Dogs Stadium, and the white-gray turreted buildings of The Citadel farther north. To get to his office, he had to first navigate the maze of half-walled, semi-private cubicles that housed the engine of the division—the administrative assistants and business operations people who ran the clinical, educational, and research enterprise.

"Dr. Fanning wants to see you," Landon's assistant, Ellen, called out as he passed. She plucked his Friday mail from the hot file that hung over the half wall. "He's waiting in his office."

Landon smiled to himself as he unlocked the door. It was a familiar scenario after a holiday weekend. One or both of Mike's kids had been in town, and he couldn't wait to share the news of a new restaurant or a beautiful vista Sheila had found.

He tossed the mail on his desk, grabbed the coffee cup he'd forgotten to rinse again, and headed for the break room, hoping someone more thoughtful than he had stopped for pastries on the way in. Armed with a blueberry cake donut and fresh coffee, he found Fanning staring out toward the river. He tapped on the door to signal his arrival.

"Come in, Landon. Come in," Fanning said, gesturing toward the desk that was piled high with papers and journals. "Close the door, please."

This was unusual. Fanning adhered to an open-door policy and preferred to tell his stories standing, spinning and stabbing the air like a weather vane in a storm. Now he lowered himself into his chair, smiling unconvincingly as he regarded Landon through his thick, smeared glasses. "How was your weekend?"

"Good. Had oysters at Bowens'," Landon said. He found a coaster but held onto his donut, wishing he'd thought to grab a paper towel.

Fanning smiled. "We haven't been there since last summer."

"Yeah, it'd been a while for me too. It was Luna's first visit."

"Ah, Ms. Quinn. You've been seeing a lot of her. Things must be going well."

He felt his face getting warm. "Yeah, I gotta admit, we're getting along."

"That's great—she's a good one, I think." Fanning shifted in his chair, then propped his elbows on the desk, interlacing his fingers just below his jowly chin. "Landon, I have something to discuss with you. I'm afraid it will be unwelcome news, so I think I'd best simply spit it out. I want you to take a leave of absence, effective today."

"What?" He had heard him perfectly well. He tried to buy time by taking a shaky sip of coffee after transferring his donut to his casted hand. "Why?"

"You aren't ready to be back at work, certainly not ready to assume clinical duties and—"

"Why do you say that?"

Fanning recoiled at the tone of his voice, his eyes flaring. "I'm sorry, Mike. I don't mean to bark at you. I'm not fully well, I admit, but I'm okay."

Fanning leaned in again. "You're not, Landon. I've watched you. The staff have noticed. You're fiddling around. You haven't answered my emails, and there's no discernible progress on the grant proposal. You missed the fellows' conference Friday."

"God, I forgot," he said, rubbing his forehead.

"I know. It's not deliberate." Fanning patted the air, offering comfort from across the desk. "You've had a serious head injury. These things take time and just how long is unpredictable. I'm glad you feel better, but your concentration is not there yet. I'd be afraid to put you on the clinical schedule, and if you can't do that, well, I'm afraid the other faculty would begin to resent you being around."

He recognized his mentor's careful phrasing. Someone had complained already. "No one has said anything to me," he said. "Who is it? Crenshaw?" Crenshaw had never liked him and probably resented not being named fellowship director.

Fanning smiled. "You know me better than that. I wouldn't tolerate sniping, and even if it occurred, I wouldn't divulge it to you." He rose, circled the desk, and settled into the companion chair. His heavy arm fell across Landon's shoulders. "I've completed the paperwork for you. Ellen has it. I'm recommending six weeks off." He raised a hand to stifle any response. "That'll give you time to complete your therapy, recover, and enjoy the Fourth of July holiday. You'll need to have a fitness-to-return assessment before you come back. Let's touch base when I return from Europe."

"But who's running the division while you're gone? I'm vice chief."

"I've asked Carl to serve in an interim capacity. Nothing official, no title, just watch over things while we're out."

Landon hung his head. Carl Reynolds would love this. Fanning had promoted Landon to vice chief against the expectations of the department chair and despite Reynolds' seniority. Although he and Reynolds worked together collegially, Landon was certain the snub still stung. And now, when he was most needed, Landon had proven himself inadequate in his duties. Reynolds, the worthy heir apparent, would hold things together while Landon licked his wounds in absentia. He was tried and convicted and suddenly felt like an old, sick impostor. "That's it then, I guess, huh?"

He felt a squeeze between his shoulder and neck. "Rest up, my friend. Let your brain recover—it *will* recover with time. Be patient and know that I have complete confidence in you. Work on your grant at home, if you want, as you feel like it, but don't access the site or respond to email. You aren't allowed. I asked Ellen to print out the grant for you, so you'll have it."

There was nothing else to say. Mike was right, even if Landon's pride wouldn't permit him to admit as much to his boss, to his friend. In a full week, he hadn't gotten half a day's work done. He wasn't well yet. It would be a long three weeks until New Orleans, but preparing for Enrique's visit was no longer a problem. He rose slowly, accustomed now to the transient dizziness that accompanied any change in position. He didn't bother forcing a smile; Fanning knew him too well for that.

"There's no rule against visiting," Fanning said after they'd shaken hands. "Stop by whenever you want. I'll be calling you for lunch. I still need your counsel." Landon wasn't convinced, but Fanning's unexpected wink made him smile. "I hope you and Ms. Quinn will join Sheila and me for dinner before we go."

"Sure, Mike. That'd be nice. Thanks." He turned to leave, dreading the gauntlet of support staff between him and the exit. They had all known, probably since Friday, certainly when they arrived this morning. Would Fanning have prepped them? He hoped there wouldn't be a chorus of encouragement, as if he'd lost his job. Better to just grab his things and go. It was only six weeks. By then, it would have been almost three months since the crash, nearly three months since he'd been able to see patients, to actually be a doctor …

Ellen was waiting, folder in hand, eyes searching and maybe a little watery. Everyone else was busy avoiding eye contact. Good. She had marked the pages that needed his signature.

"Here's the grant application, Dr. Ratliff," she said, exchanging folders with him when he had finished signing. She wouldn't call him Landon, no matter how often he asked her to do so. "Call me if you need anything. I can search the website for you, but I can't access your email. I'll screen the snail mail and bring it by each week, if you want."

"Nah, I'll stop by. I'll have plenty of time on my hands. Water my plant, will you?" He knew she would; she always had, even before the crash because he couldn't remember, and now, well, who would expect a brain-injured man to think to water a plant? He leaned into her well-meaning hug, then broke away without making further eye contact. He didn't need help finding the exit.

CHAPTER EIGHTEEN

W arm rain was spitting through gloomy twilight when Landon picked Luna up for a late supper on Sunday evening. She had begged off accompanying him to the airport after lunch, explaining to Amy and Enrique that she had papers to grade and an apartment to reconstruct in preparation for a new week. Landon had no grounds for complaint since she had abandoned her private life for the entire weekend, including Friday and Saturday nights, when she had stayed at his house without excessive prompting. True, Amy was there, and she and Luna were chatting and laughing into the wee hours, and there was significant alcohol-induced disinhibition. But still, Luna had wanted to stay, had wanted him. Waking beside her each morning—her head on his shoulder, one leg curled over his—had provided unfamiliar contentment. He had never enjoyed waking up next to women, despite the extraordinary delight he derived from taking them to bed. Mornings had felt uneasy, awkward; he found himself wanting to get on with his day—alone. Not so with Luna, who was a champion morning snuggler, and one of the rare women who woke up pretty.

Right now, she still looked pretty but also as tired as Landon himself felt. Her smile and kiss were reassuring. At his urging, she had chosen the restaurant, a place he'd never been and where a scene from some movie he'd never seen had been filmed. They sat in the bar at a relatively secluded corner table. Despite the rain, the restaurant was packed, and the nearly empty bar suited their mood better anyway.

"So what did you think of my friends?" he asked, once they were settled and had ordered.

She gave him a look he'd seen before—a tiny, vertical furrow appeared between her now-flattened brows, and her eyes held his in a piercing but still pleasant way, as if she were about to enter unfamiliar territory without a hint of fear. "I feel really bad for Amy," she said, pressing her lips together.

He wasn't surprised by her response. Enrique had looked well—still athletically thin, with just a hint of salt and pepper in his hair—but his demeanor had not improved with age. If anything, he seemed fussier and grumpier than he had in medical school, and there was a sour vagueness to his gaze that Landon had found unsettling. His cynical comments about Charleston, Luna's background and work, and Landon's relationship with women had been ill-timed and poorly disguised as jokes. Amy couldn't hide her embarrassment, particularly when Enrique became defensive and mean with her.

"Well, I think Amy's used to it by now," Landon said, "but I agree it would be hard to live with. I swear, he used to be a lot better. Didn't you love her, though?"

"Love, love, love her. But I think they're in real trouble, and it's sad."

"What do you mean?"

Luna's eyes widened. She turned her head and leaned in, making him feel like a student without the right answer. "Their marriage, Landon. Didn't Enrique tell you?"

"Tell me what?"

Her blank stare made him uneasy. "What did you guys talk about yesterday?"

"Fort Sumter, the war—Enrique talked nonstop about that." Landon had purchased tickets for a tour of the fort, in deference to Enrique's love of history. Amy and Luna had gone shopping instead, as planned. "Let's see—we talked about work, about his kids, about Amy, and about you. He really likes you, by the way."

"Really? It wasn't that easy to tell. He wasn't shy about poking fun at my sisters' names, and I don't think Santa Clara University meets his lofty academic standards."

"He's a snob. Thinks Washington and Lee is the Harvard of the South."

She rolled her eyes. "It isn't even the Harvard of Virginia. So, what else did he say?"

"Well, he thinks you're smart, and—"

"Not me. What did he say about Amy?"

He shrugged. "I don't know. That she was totally wrapped up in the kids and that marriage was hard, but okay, not like dating, though. Sounded like pretty normal stuff."

Luna's brows were beginning to sag. He'd learned that usually meant trouble. She looked disappointed; he felt as if he'd let her down but wasn't certain how.

"I don't think there's *anything* normal about their marriage, Landon—at least not right now."

What little appetite he'd had was gone. "How so?"

"They're having major trouble. Enrique's drinking is a serious problem. He resents having to work all the time but won't do anything about it for fear of letting his father down. He doesn't even eat dinner with his kids anymore."

"Well, building a practice can be hard. Long hours are a part of it, I think."

She shook her head. "No, that's not it. He doesn't want to eat with them. Wants them fed before he gets home. Then he usually has a couple cocktails while she helps with homework and gets them off to bed. On a good night, he'll help, but the good nights are getting rare. Then he wants dinner with her."

"I'm guessing that's not a romantic affair."

"Not at all. He gets drunker, bitches about work the whole time, then they either fight or he just drinks himself into a stupor." She propped her elbow on the table and cradled her forehead in her hand. "He didn't say anything about this? Did he mention the counseling?"

"No. I guess I wouldn't expect him to confess about his drinking. They're in counseling?"

"Just started. Amy threatened to tell his father about the drinking if he didn't go."

Now Landon was shaking his head, trying to recall what they *had* discussed. "He never said a thing about that, either."

"The counselor recommended this trip. Thought it would do them both some good to focus on something else, maybe get a chance to talk with someone else."

"Sounds like Amy did anyway," he said. Amy and Luna had connected right away, bonding in a way that women do, a way Landon admired but did not expect to ever experience. He and Enrique had become spectators before the first glass of wine had been poured.

"She's not the one who needed to." Luna squinted as if trying to look past his eyes into his brain. "How can you guys not talk? You haven't seen each other in five years."

"Yeah. Our ten-year reunion was the last time." He pushed a little coleslaw around with his fork. "We talked, but just about stuff, you know? How would I have known all this? Enrique didn't bring it up."

"Did he seem the same to you?"

He nodded. "Maybe a little grumpier, but Amy seemed good. I asked her about his drinking."

"When?" Luna's eyes softened a little.

"At Market Pavilion when we were dancing—or trying to." He smiled, recalling how he and Amy had waddled around the floor like grandparents at a wedding, watching Enrique and Luna glide across the floor, graceful as gazelles. "She kind of blew it off, so I let it go. You guys were getting along great, so I never brought it up again."

He was relieved to see her smile. "We did get along great," she said. "She's fantastic, but I know she was hoping you guys would talk. She needs Enrique to talk to someone." Luna paused for a sip of water, then gathered her hair into a bundle that she clutched at the crown of her head. "Did you talk about you—your injuries or your cancer?"

Thoroughly chastened now, he felt like a kid who'd neglected a whole list of chores. He stared into his plate. "Not really." Her silence was more painful than the rebuke that never came. He hazarded a glance, and her eyes looked past him again, carrying Amy's pain and her own bewilderment, mirroring his deep, newly recognized sense of inadequacy. How could he have missed the signs? He was a doctor, or at least used to be. Never mind that—was he really any kind of friend? Was Enrique? He couldn't imagine the life Enrique was living, keeping to himself. He had to be in pain, and his supposed best friend, at least at one time, had missed the signs, failed to provide an ear, some comfort, anything. They had gone through the motions, exchanged pleasantries, and let alcohol blanket any emotions that might have shattered the veneer of old friends catching up.

"I don't get it, though," he said. "Enrique invited me to their place in Key West for the Fourth of July. Said the whole family would be there."

"That was the plan. Amy and the kids aren't going now. They're heading to DC to visit her parents while Enrique has some time with his parents."

"Does he know that?"

Luna checked her watch. "He probably does now."

"Well, so much for that. I was planning on going, since you'll be gone."

"I hope you won't change your plans." She rested her hand on his forearm. "You should go. Amy wants you to, to try and help Enrique."

"*Me?* With his parents there?"

"Amy said they really like you. Besides, they won't stay the whole time, if they go at all. Sounds like Enrique's dad isn't much for long visits with his children or his grandchildren." She touched his face, turned it so he was looking at her. Her eyes were tender now, emerald in the low light. "I think he needs you, Landon."

He nodded, trying to summon the resolution and reassurance he knew Luna wanted, and at the same time stifling the nagging doubt that tugged at him. He wasn't sure he was up to this, especially with what he was facing in

New Orleans in a couple of weeks. Who knew what things would be like then?

He knew the answer to that question—no one knew.

CHAPTER NINETEEN

The plane hit the tarmac in New Orleans at a steeper than usual angle, jarring Landon from a fitful, dream-tormented sleep. His arm jerked into the seat back, whacking his still-sore thumb. *At least he hadn't mauled his neighbor*, he thought while assessing his shirt and face for drool.

In this version of a recurring dream, Landon had been hovering over his bed, the stereotypical near-death experience shot. But he wasn't dead, merely anesthetized as Dr. Lake informed his parents the procedure hadn't been entirely successful, that the tumor appeared larger and more aggressive than had been previously thought. The landing had left the ending unresolved.

He felt wrung out and hoped the next two nights wouldn't be like the last two—full of these disjointed movie trailers spoiling his sleep. After all, despite the serious nature of his diagnosis, this was a relatively minor, routine procedure. There was no reason to worry. He needed to be rested and wanted to be alert so he could fully enjoy his return to the city that had changed his life before and would surely do so again. It had been too long since he'd visited, and for the first time in years, he would be a tour guide, an ambassador for the Big Easy.

It wasn't a difficult role for Landon. From his first visit back in 1993, he'd been captivated by the city, especially the French Quarter, where everything and everybody seemed to be celebrating the joy of being alive. The food, the architecture, the music—especially the music—seemed to speak directly to him, calling him home to a place he'd never been.

His decision to move there, made on that first visit, was impulsive and risky, but it had proven to him that his gut instincts were worth paying attention to. He'd never regretted the decision to switch from surgery to critical care, nor the decision to make Mike Fanning his mentor and role model. That had made the subsequent decision to follow him to Charleston a lot easier. But while Charleston was a fine city, it was not New Orleans, and so, on this first visit back, he wanted to be certain to show his guest the best that this grand city had to offer.

His guest wouldn't be his mother, though; it would be Luna, and so he would be escorting a first-timer with the attendant obligation to ensure nothing was missed. He felt a little guilty about his excitement. His mother's resolve about the trip had begun to falter last Monday morning, when their conversation wandered to his father's declining appetite and general fatigue as well as her own mother's latest setback. Sensing trouble, he had called Carla, who confirmed that his mother was overburdened. Carla was out of commission with strep throat, probably a gift from her daughter. Landon's grandfather, never much help on his best days, wasn't feeling well either. According to Carla, Eddie's father looked as if he shouldn't be left alone. He didn't ask about Dale's availability, and Carla didn't offer.

Landon had previously mentioned Mike's European vacation, so that left Luna as the primary player in the lie he improvised to relieve his mother of the additional burden of accompanying him to New Orleans. His mother's guilty tears were short-lived, displaced by obvious relief that gave way to anticipatory pleasure. Danger signals flashed in Landon's mind—she might call Luna, so he had to work fast.

He immediately recognized the potential of five nights in New Orleans with his girlfriend. She *was* his girlfriend, it seemed now, and that pleased them both—he thought. Summer session was over; she was spending lots of time with him, so why wouldn't she agree to go? This was a chance to make up for the truncated Beaufort trip and would be a welcome distraction from thoughts about treatment and prognosis. So after building the case in his mind, he screwed up the courage to ask her. She was understandably surprised by the invitation, but once he explained the circumstances, she seemed genuinely excited.

Now he waited while each row ahead of him rose in turn, adjusted clothing, extracted belongings from the overhead compartment, and then finally made their way down the aisle like condemned prisoners proceeding toward the execution chamber. He continued to scan for unoccupied seats, certain that it had been airline incompetence or intransigence that had forced Luna to take a later flight.

The airport greeted him as if he were a long-lost family member. He had spent the ten most important years of his life in this city. He had learned his profession here and only recently had come to realize how much he'd missed New

Orleans. Why hadn't he returned sooner? He could have come back with Fanning after Katrina and helped tend to his drowned city, but he'd hidden behind the need to stay back and run the division, afraid, perhaps, of how much change the hurricane had wrought. No matter, he was here now—driven by necessity, to be sure—and in many ways, the Crescent City felt as much like home as Virginia.

He made his way to baggage claim, where he hoped both his and Luna's luggage would arrive after what he knew would be a maddeningly long wait. He had offered to check her large bag to make her trip a little easier. It seemed the least he could do, but he was pleased that Luna found it so chivalrous. Now he hoped for time to pull off his plan: he had canceled the rental car yesterday on a whim, as the thought of waiting for her at the bottom of the escalator with a bouquet of flowers had taken hold in his mind. He wanted to surprise her, give her a proper kiss with a hug. Besides, what was the hurry? The Court of Two Sisters served brunch all day. He shook his head and smiled, certain he'd never put so much effort into meeting a woman before.

They hadn't slept together since midweek, a three-night hiatus that now seemed much longer. She had final papers to grade, so he'd busied himself with futile attempts to make progress on the grant but found the time alone haunted with thoughts of cancer and illness and death. He had brought dinner to her each night, then dragged himself back to his desolate bed for another night of fitful, broken sleep.

It was the feel of her next to him he missed most: the soft curve of her hip against his, her hair teasing his chest while her head nestled into the hollow of his shoulder, the rhythmic rise and fall of her breathing as she slept. Best of all was waking up together, when their eyes would open slowly, and they'd smile at one another in the muted gray predawn or a second time in the sun-splashed morning. It was so peaceful; before Luna, he wasn't sure he'd ever really known what it felt like to relax.

Both bags emerged at the typically lethargic pace, so by the time Landon retrieved them and then had a coffee, he had less than an hour to wait. He passed on roses and bought a mixed bouquet, then planted himself behind a column near where the escalator discharged passengers, worrying over his abandoned plan to construct a WELCOME, LUNA sign.

She was wearing a dress he hadn't seen before, a jade-green cottony dress that highlighted her red hair and draped her slender form just perfectly. The tank top showed off her soft shoulders and tender skin that the early summer sunshine had already turned the faintest beige. A white jean jacket was draped over her arm. She seemed lost in thought. He wished he'd worn something a little nicer.

He stepped from behind the column just as she reached the bottom of the escalator. She froze, blinked twice, then she blushed, and a smile lit up her face. She curled her hair behind her ear and bunched her shoulders as he advanced, and then—her perfume, her shining green eyes, her moist, smiling lips, and her arms around his neck. He bent her backward, holding her as if he were the sailor in Times Square at the end of World War II. He felt her laugh, but she held the kiss until he righted her and presented her with the flowers. She blushed again and dipped her chin into her shoulder, glancing at him sidelong through her thick, curvy eyebrows.

"Welcome to New Orleans," he said.

"It just became my favorite city." She buried her nose in the flowers. "This is so sweet. I thought you were picking me up outside baggage claim?"

He shrugged. "I didn't want to wait to see you. In fact, I canceled the rental car. We don't really need it. We can take a cab."

Her shoulders bunched again, and she chewed on her lower lip. "This is so sweet, Doc." She kissed his cheek, and he got another hug that he was happy to return. He let his head fall on her shoulder, felt her lips in his hair. Funny, he had always hated being called Doc, but when Luna said it, it seemed okay. When they separated, she pressed her head against his forehead, her huge eyes staring straight into his, so close he felt as if she could see into his brain. He thought he saw *I love you*, but he didn't hear it. Somehow he couldn't say it, either, though he wanted to. Cleverness evaded him, and she wasn't talking, so he followed his instincts, enjoying the closeness, trying to let her determine the next move, waiting for a sign that came—he thought—when he felt her shoulders shrug again.

"I've got this," he said, evading Luna's grasp for her bag. "It has wheels, you know."

She rolled her eyes. "You need a free hand."

"Why?"

She stopped then, hands on hips, head cocked to one side, eyes giving him the *duh* look, then made a show of taking the handle from him before slipping her free hand into his. "Shall we?" she asked. He smiled.

The cab had great air-conditioning. They held hands, Luna's shoulder against his. He felt his shirt sticking to him and was glad he'd worn a white print, which might help conceal sweat marks. How did women do it? Luna's dress seemed as if it would advertise every drop of sweat, but it looked perfect, even better when she walked, the way it swished and twirled about her legs.

It was a quiet ride. There was little to see riding into the city, and Luna had gone silent. Whenever he glanced at her, she was glancing at him, a bashful smile peeking out from behind hair that refused to behave. He fought the urge to look too excited, pretended to study something outside the window while searching his brain for the right thing to say. He pointed out the Superdome, then the VA hospital and Tulane, unwelcome reminders of the trip's purpose (as if he'd forgotten), but the sights aroused Luna from her reverie, and she became chatty again, providing a delightful diversion that carried them through to their brunch destination.

The next morning, Luna had coffee in the courtyard outside their cottage; it was comfortable in the shade of the towering palm trees and the lush foliage that clung to the brick wall separating their private sitting area from the common area around the pool. No sign of their neighbors, whose cottage shared this patio. Their lights had been on last night when she and Landon returned, but he had squelched her plan to make new friends over another bottle of wine, and she had to admit now, smiling at the memory, his plan had proven far more pleasurable.

Fox answered on the first ring. "Up early for New Orleans, aren't you?"

Luna smiled. It was two hours earlier in California, but she knew her sister's routine, and it never varied; she had timed the call to catch her between her workout and the shower, when she would be watching the news.

"Hey, Foxy. Landon had to go in for tests this morning, so I had some free time on my hands."

"When's the operation?"

"Tomorrow at ten." The chicory-laced coffee was bitter, but better than nothing.

"Tell him best of luck for me. We're pulling for him. How's New Orleans? You got there yesterday, right?"

"Yeah, it's great—we had brunch at Two Sisters—champagne and King cake, yum. Dinner was at Commander's Palace. I loved Preservation Hall. But the best thing, by far, was the streetcar ride. *So* romantic."

"How long did you say Landon lived there?" Fox sounded a little disappointed. "Sounds pretty touristy for a native."

"Well, it was. He said I should see those places. He's saving his personal favorites for later. We're here until Friday, you know." Through the patio entrance, Luna saw a white-haired woman emerge from one of the other cottages and slip silently into the pool. "Hey, Foxy, where do you usually stay down here? We're at the Audubon Cottages. Ever stay here?"

"Nope. Always stay at the Monteleone. You have to go. The Carousel Bar is fantastic."

"That's on the list. Landon said I'd love the bar, and it's the writer's hotel."

"Duh, I'm surprised you aren't staying there."

"Landon chose this, and it's beautiful and romantic and sweet. They have a saltwater pool and breakfast in the cabana every morning. Elizabeth Taylor used to stay here. We're staying in Audubon's old studio."

The other end of the line was quiet, then she heard Fox's throaty chuckle, the one that always preceded a snide comment. "What?" Luna asked, eager as always to play the foil.

"I'm just recalling a conversation back in May," Fox said. She adopted a deep-voiced, serious tone: "God, Foxy, it's not like we're married. I've got things I want to do. A full-time relationship might be too much."

Luna had to laugh. Fox was so funny. "It still might be too much. Who knows what will happen tomorrow, but last night was great."

"Don't buy trouble, Lunatic. Take it one day at a time."

"You sound like Landon."

"*Landon, Landon, Landon.*" Fox was laughing again. "This must be serious."

"Maybe, baby," Luna sang back. "We're having a good time, but it all gets serious tomorrow. Probably tonight—I can't imagine having a tumor and going to get it removed."

"Best of luck. I'll be thinking of you both. So what's up today?"

"Finish my coffee, shower, then off to Faulkner House Books—it's in his old house, where he wrote his first—"

"I know, I know. It's in Pirate's Alley. I'm not illiterate, you know. I read a little."

"*Fortune* magazine doesn't count. Anyway, then I'm off to City Park, to the gardens. We're having lunch at the Bon Ton Café on Magazine Street. Dinner is at Antoine's.

"Ah, that's better. No cocktail hour?"

She drained her coffee and rose to go inside. The woman was gliding noiselessly back and forth through the pool. "The Columns hotel. We went there last night too."

"Now you're talking. The best Sazerac in town. There may be hope for this guy."

"Thanks. I'll tell him you said so. He'll take all the hope he can get this week."

CHAPTER TWENTY

L andon was glad there were no mirrors in the preoperative holding area and grateful for the privacy the tiny room offered. He no longer felt like a middle-aged professional about to undergo a minimally invasive procedure. Tortured, futile attempts at sleep had left him exhausted, and his stomach was rebuking him for passing on a late-night snack. Nothing by mouth after midnight, and he wouldn't be awake enough to eat until noon or later. The holding area was frigid; hunger, fatigue, and a gauzy hospital gown had transformed him into a famished, freezing, feral wretch. Oliver Twist came to mind. He clutched at the flimsy blanket, careful not to dislodge the intravenous line.

A tall African American woman in a scrub suit too large for her willowy frame filled the doorway. "I'm Dr. Kane. You're Dr. Ratliff?"

"Landon." He gestured toward the bedside chair. "This is Luna Quinn."

"I'm Alicia Kane." She shook hands with Luna, who rose to greet her. "I'm your anesthesiologist today. Can I ask you your date of birth?"

"Sure." He waited a second, thinking he was making a joke, but she didn't bite. "April thirtieth, 1967."

"Ever had anesthesia, Landon?"

He recited his recent history, wondering if Dr. Kane had bothered to review his medical record. She explained the anesthetic plan and performed a brief examination, forcing him to expose his inadequate flesh to the merciless cold of the room and her icy stethoscope. Dr. Lake popped in next, smiling and offering bland reassurances that provided no comfort, although Luna seemed encouraged. Finally, Dr. Sutphin, the interventional radiologist who would perform the procedure, stopped in to review what he planned to do.

Then the nurse came in and provided a second tissue paper blanket just before Kane returned to administer Landon's first dose of something. He felt his heart hammering in his ears, his eyelids growing heavy. Shivering and hungry, he recalled a story about freezing to death, how it was peaceful and quiet. Just go to sleep. He blinked hard, clawing at the covers, trying to will himself awake.

"What's up, Doc?" Luna's face filled the space above his bed, her eyes searching and tender, a ghost of a smile on her lips. He felt her hand in his. He was drifting off, his eyes filling with tears. He couldn't lift his head. She leaned closer.

"I'm scared," he whispered.

He thought he saw tears in her eyes as they nearly touched his. He felt her nose and lips brush his cheek. She whispered in his ear; it sounded like "I love you."

He felt his chest open up, his head spinning. His body seemed to have frozen solid below the waist. He didn't want to mumble his reply, but couldn't be sure he didn't.

❖❖❖

Had he dreamed it? Landon wasn't certain, but he didn't think so. Awake now, he saw the empty chair where Luna should have been. His gurney was surrounded by drawn curtains. This had to be the post-op area. A nurse popped her head in. "Thought you woke up. The monitor is going nuts out there." She drew the curtains tight around her neck and whispered. "Do me a favor, Dr. Ratliff, and pretend you're still asleep. Your girlfriend just ducked out to go to the bathroom and was frantic that you'd wake up while she was gone."

He gave a weak wave and a thumbs-up to her query about how he was feeling, then closed his eyes again. It wasn't a dream—Luna had said it, and so had he. Love—did she mean it, or did she say it just to make him feel better? It had worked either way, but she wouldn't just say it. She didn't have to. He smiled.

He heard her approaching. A murmured question to the nurse, then the curtain flapping open. He fluttered his eyes and turned to see Luna smiling, her head tilted with her hair spilling across her brow and onto her shoulder. "Hi, sweetie." She leaned in to give him a gentle kiss. "How do you feel?"

"Pretty good. Sleepy."

The nurse appeared close behind Luna. He coughed, cleared his throat, squeezed her fingers on command, then wiggled his toes, all the while smiling back at Luna, who had moved her chair closer so she could hold his hand.

"Dr. Lake will be in shortly," the nurse said, then vanished behind the curtain.

He had to test his memory, and now was the safest time, when he was still dopey and could claim that as an excuse later if necessary. "Thanks for being here, Luna." He stroked her hand with his thumb, swallowed, and focused on a freckle about half an inch above the tip of her nose. After two false starts, he said it: "I love you."

Her mouth flattened and uncoiled like a snake, her lips parting to reveal a dazzling, sweet smile. She took a big breath. "Do you remember in *Sweet Thursday*, when Doc tells Suzy that he loves her? Do you remember what she says?"

He couldn't remember; he remembered that Luna was trying to write a sequel to that novel, a novel he had read recently. The characters sounded familiar, but that was it. He shook his head.

"Brother, you've got yourself a girl." She touched her nose to his. Her eyes were shiny, her lips moist and delicious. She broke off the kiss and touched his face as gently as if a butterfly had landed on his cheek. "You've got yourself a girl, Brother, and she loves you too."

Dr. Lake's timing could not have been worse; he was accompanied by Dr. Sutphin, and Landon noted immediately that neither man was smiling.

Sutphin spoke first. "The procedure went very well, Dr. Ratliff. As we expected, the tumor was nowhere near the ureter, and I think we got a complete ablation."

"Great news, Landon," Lake said. He was smiling broadly now, glancing from Landon to Luna, his head bouncing like a bobblehead doll.

"Now what?" Landon asked.

"Rest up today, then activity as you feel like it," Sutphin replied. "The incision site just needs a bandage. I'll prescribe some pain pills, but aspirin or ibuprofen are usually sufficient."

"I guess I'm still numb right now. I don't feel any pain."

"Good, but you're right. When the anesthetic wears off, you might feel some pain. I don't think it'll be much. It was an easy procedure."

Easy for whom? Landon thought. Easy to say, but he let it pass. "What's the prognosis?"

Lake jumped in. "Excellent. Good chance of a cure. Wouldn't you say, Chris?"

Sutphin looked a little irritated. "Well, it's never certain, as you know, but I'd say it's likely we won't have to do anything more. Very slight possibility that we'd need to redo this and almost negligible chance of a recurrence down the road. I'd be surprised."

Well, let's not surprise you. Again, Landon kept his thoughts to himself. Luna looked pleased, and so he smiled. "Great. Thanks." He shook hands with Sutphin and then with Lake, who trapped Landon's hand between both of his own.

"We'll do a follow-up MRI in a month," Sutphin said. "You can have that done at home and have the images sent." He clapped a hand on Lake's shoulder before leaving the cubicle.

Lake hugged Luna, then turned to Landon. "You can go as soon as you can walk. By the way, Mike Fanning called a while ago. Hope you don't mind—I told him you did great."

Landon smiled a real smile this time. His back was beginning to ache, but he'd worry about that later. Right now, he had Luna to keep a smile on his face.

CHAPTER TWENTY-ONE

"The flooding started even before Katrina reached land. Water came up the Industrial Canal and flooded the Lower Ninth early. After that, it was just one failure after another."

The cabbie was a sloppy-looking guy, dressed in a shirt too warm for the season and left open over a grimy T-shirt that strained to contain a sizable gut. Tellingly, though, the front seat was littered with newspapers that showed signs of serious use. It had been just dumb luck that he was sitting at the front of the line on Canal Street when Landon and Luna walked up on Thursday morning.

Landon was fully recovered now. He slept the rest of Tuesday away, awakening only to eat a few bites of lunch and a dinner that Luna carried in. Wednesday had been much better. They swam and lounged by the pool in the morning, toured the Garden District (which came with two more streetcar rides), and later dressed up and went for a romantic candlelight dinner at Irene's. A moonlight swim in the deserted pool back at the cottages had predictable consequences that led to deep and satisfying sleep.

Now they were on their way to see the Lower Ninth Ward, which by all accounts had been neglected, if not ignored, in the city's recovery efforts. This cabbie, Horace, was eager to share his encyclopedic knowledge of the storm and its aftermath. Luna peppered him with questions while Landon digested the answers, many of which seemed incredible.

Skepticism vanished when they reached the Lower Ninth, which resembled a village sacked by a marauding, merciless army. Ruined homes squatted on their foundations, engulfed by weeds, as if the dying structure were nourishing the soil. Bleached, exhausted wallboard—still bearing the body count markings left by searchers in boats—was collapsing in on itself, yielding to indifference. Each block contained one—or at most two—such wreck; the rest was dirt, scrubby grass, or a solitary concrete stoop left behind after the wind and water had taken everything else.

"Where did these people go?" Luna asked.

"Scattered. Some left completely. A few got trailers." Horace gestured at a government-issue mobile home standing beside the windowless shell of a partially collapsed, roofless house. "Everybody figured they'd be rebuilding by now. It's a damn shame. That's New Orleans for you, though."

"What do you mean?" Luna was sitting forward now, her head thrust over the seat back.

"Politics," Landon chimed in. "The city fights over whose pet project gets funded while the poor people take it on the chin."

"Bingo." Horace smiled and took a long draw from his two-liter Orange Crush, then glanced in the rearview mirror. "You paid attention when you lived here, sounds like."

"They don't care if these people suffer?" Luna asked, slumping back in her seat so she was facing Landon.

"They don't even recognize the suffering," Landon said. "These people are invisible to them." He turned away, surveying the moonscape through his window. "This is unbelievable," he muttered. "Same with Charity, huh?" he said louder, expecting a response from Horace.

"You seen it yet?" Horace's eyes were in the mirror once again. Landon shook his head.

"That's the hospital, right?" Luna asked. "The hurricane got it too?"

"You want to tell her, or should I?" Horace asked.

"I got this," Landon said. "The floodwaters got into the basement and shut down the power. It took a long time to evacuate all the patients. But then the city and LSU saw an opportunity to get the government to fund a new hospital, so they claimed it was damaged beyond repair. They've never reopened it."

"Even though the army says it's in pretty good shape and even though it would cost less to fix than to build something new, which would take ten years," Horace added. "And so, the poor have nowhere to go while the city and the federal government arm wrestle to see who will get his way."

For Landon, Charity was far worse than the Lower Ninth Ward. As the cab crept down Tulane Avenue, the towering gray façade assumed a spectral appearance, its row upon row of empty windows like the vacant stares of all the lost souls abandoned when the building was shuttered. He thought of the patients he'd saved and those he'd lost. He thought of Deuce, Gillian's friend, his first patient, the guy who'd repeated the mantra Landon had heard from his father;

though he hadn't actually cared for him, he'd cared about him, and that was at least as important. All the Charity doctors, the residents, the nurses—vanished, and for what? Katrina hadn't blown it down, hadn't washed it away. Charity had always been there, and now it wasn't. If the things you counted on could vanish, then could you really count on anything?

The next blow came when Horace dropped them off on Canal. Luna wanted beignets, so they strolled down Decatur, where a dusty, boarded-up door shut down one of Landon's plans for the evening. Three businesses in this one block were gone, likely victims of the same sad story. His favorite jazz spot, Sweet Kathleen's, a shotgun shack of a joint with a long bar and a bank of doors opening onto the parking lot out back, was one of the casualties. Like the others, it had succumbed to the water that flooded most of the rest of the city and then hung around through the disjointed cleanup efforts long enough to choke off the delicate cash flow that had kept the business going. With no lifeline, Sweet Kathleen's and the others had gone under.

After all of that, he should have known better than to suggest a stroll over to Frenchmen Street. Maybe he thought one survivor might ease the pain—except, there were no survivors. Lafayette Passe Partout was gone without a trace. Even the foundation was no longer visible, buried beneath heavy equipment, sacks of concrete, piles of lumber. The lot where the building had stood was unusually large, and when it became suddenly and violently vacant, someone must have capitalized, creating a staging area for repairs of other buildings in the neighborhood. Did anyone remember the rickety building where zydeco screamed from every window, and the out of plumb floors groaned under the weight of a nightly joyous celebration of life? Here was where he discovered Gillian, found that she was more than a nasty fortune-teller called Regula, that music was in her blood, and compassion was in her soul. The bartenders, the bouncers, everyone—gone, washed away, vanished.

"Anybody home?"

Landon felt a gentle tap on his face. Luna was wide-eyed in mock surprise, as if she'd just arrived.

"My name's Luna. I'm from Charleston. Come here often?"

He smiled. The late-afternoon sunlight slanting through the windows caught her hair and highlighted the streaks of reddish gold amidst the deep red. Her eyes still held the wonder and delight of her first seating at the Carousel Bar, where they now sat, sipping and spinning at a barely perceptible rate.

"I'm sorry. Guess I'm a little preoccupied." He leaned in and got the soft kiss he was fishing for. "Today was tough."

Her hand lingered at his collar, her thumb caressing his jawline. "I know. I'm so sorry. Things must have really changed."

"Yes and no. The spirit is still here—you've gotten a pretty good introduction, and if you'd come without me or anyone who'd lived here before, you might not have noticed the changes. You probably wouldn't visit the Lower Ninth, and Charity might or might not catch your eye. But so many other places are just gone. It's unbelievable. Time marches on, I guess."

"It does." Luna glanced toward the window. "I'll bet the cathedral is getting ready to glow." He felt her gaze returning to him, but stared into his drink, hoping but not expecting to change the subject. He'd been avoiding Jackson Square, fearing they might run into Gillian. It was his own fault, talking about how the setting sun turned the cathedral to gold.

"Can I ask you something, Landon?"

"Sure." He had been preparing for the question; she would no doubt wonder why they hadn't yet visited Jackson Square together.

"Do you trust the doctors' prognosis?"

His head came up. The beer taps were drifting by, as if on a gentle current. When he turned, Luna rested her elbow on the bar and cradled her face in her palm. Her expression gave nothing away. His mouth had gone dry.

"I guess so—why?" He caught himself blinking too much and tried to slow his breathing. Luna hadn't moved.

"Do you? I guess I just wondered whether some of your sadness might be related to that as much as to what's happened here."

"What do you mean?" He was starting to feel cornered.

"Relax, Doc." She stroked his arm. "I'm sorry—I don't want to make you uncomfortable. If you don't want to talk about it, that's fine."

He guessed it wasn't fine, tried to recall conversations with Darlene. Was this a rule when you're in love? He couldn't remember any deep conversations with Gillian.

"No, it's okay," he said. "Maybe some of it." He leaned closer, wanting more privacy than a rotating bar full of people could provide. "It's cancer, Luna. I know it can be cured, but I know lots of people who hoped, thought, desperately wanted to be cured, and who weren't. Why should I think

I'm different? I mean, how do you ever really know?" He sipped his Sazerac, felt the burn in the back of his nose. "I'm forty, so either it comes back, or I have a long time to wonder, right?"

"That must be hard."

He knew she was waiting, but he didn't want time or space, so he leaned closer. Her lips touched his forehead, then her eyes locked onto his. "You know what I think we should do?" she whispered.

Luna's perfume washed the Sazerac burn from his nose and palate. He rested his forehead against hers, oblivious now to whatever other patrons might think. His fingers brushed the smooth skin of her bare leg and found the hollow behind her knee. Several interesting possibilities were entering his mind. "What?" He smiled.

Her smile grew wider. "I think we should go see if we can find a certain Tarot reader you used to know."

CHAPTER TWENTY-TWO

S he wasn't joking, yet Landon could not contain a smile. "Why would you want to do that?" he asked. "Why would *I*?"

Luna's eyebrows shot up, and she tilted her head again. "Well, let's start with me—that's easy." She sipped her wine. "First, we're leaving tomorrow, and we haven't really seen Jackson Square—at least, not in daylight—and I want to. This is our last chance to see the cathedral at sunset. Second, you've seen places but no people from your past, and I think you might benefit from seeing someone you know. I'm guessing you don't want to visit the hospitals or medical schools to find someone. And third, I love you." She exaggerated the head tilt even farther, her eyes gaping, so full of wonder and fun that Landon nearly laughed out loud.

"What about me?" he asked, resuming his massage of the back of Luna's knee.

"Your efforts to distract me are greatly appreciated, though futile," Luna began. She stroked her chin and adopted a mock-serious expression. "You, Doctor, are feeling disconnected from a city that has meant a great deal to you, a city that has been through a catastrophe and is changed.

The changes catch you at a vulnerable time, when your own life has changed dramatically, and when your future is more uncertain than anyone would find comfortable. Are you following me so far?" She leaned in, smiling, and received the kiss that he knew she was seeking. "Thank you. Shall I continue?"

"Please." This was not only enjoyable, but her insight was impressive and even more remarkable because he did not feel the least threatened by it.

"So from what you've told me, it seems that this Tarot reader played an important part in connecting you to this city and to your true calling in medicine. And since you lived with her for—how long?"

"A year or so, but who's counting?"

She gave him a sour look, then continued. "Okay, and since it wasn't an ugly breakup, or so you've said, it seems only reasonable to conclude that reconnecting with her might be good for you." She nodded, took a gulp of wine, and raised her head, thrusting her chin toward him.

He smiled. "Okay. Nicely done, counselor. But must I remind you, she was my girlfriend? We slept together. Why would you want me to find her?"

"Must I remind *you*," Luna said, trying to look serious, "that though I am much younger than her—and you—I am not still in high school. Neither are you, mister. And *we* are sleeping together now, and"—she lowered her voice to a near-whisper—"you seem pretty satisfied with me, as you should be." She sat back. "Besides, I'm not suggesting you go alone, unless you really want to, in which case, I might be worried … just a little."

Landon shook his head. "No, thanks. You're with me, sweetheart." He reached for her hand. "Let's go see the square. If we find her, we find her."

They left the hotel and headed for the river, then turned onto Chartres Street. He pointed out St. Louis Cathedral, its white façade now washed with the golden glow of the setting sun. "This is my favorite view of the cathedral. I used to have a drink at Cafe Pontalba just to watch the changing color. So beautiful."

The square was bustling, the colors coming into greater focus as the sunlight dwindled. Luna gravitated toward the garden, then became distracted by the paintings hung along the rails. Landon kept up a steady banter, playing the role of tour guide while he scanned for any sign of Gillian. No table occupied the spot where hers had been (though he hadn't seen her there for at least a year before he moved), but a palm reader's table stood nearby, manned by a young, heavily tattooed woman dressed in shorts and a tank top. No mystery at all; he recalled Gillian's flowing thick hair and elaborate dresses, and guessed she would not approve of this newcomer. Next to her was a man doing caricatures for five dollars each. They seemed overpriced.

"Didn't you come here Monday?" Landon asked. Luna's hand fit his just right.

"I looked at it from Pirate's Alley." She bumped him off stride with her shoulder. "I was waiting for you, and I took too long in the bookshop."

"Any sign of her?" Luna asked finally, when they had passed the buggies and were turning away from the river again.

"No. She used to be over there." He pointed toward Pirate's Alley. "I can't imagine her moving her spot."

Luna shrugged. "Things change."

He gave her a sidelong glance. "No kidding."

Gillian was nowhere to be found, and after watching a guy in dreadlocks play an instrument that looked like a canoe paddle with strings, they strolled through the gardens surrounding Jackson's statue. Luna delighted in the blooms, but his mind was elsewhere. The city looked very much the same, though with fewer residents and more deserted buildings, and the spirit, the vitality remained. And yet, for him, it was completely different. It was no longer his city. He was a visitor, almost a stranger. He had felt some of that in Virginia the last time he visited. Was it possible that he no longer felt at home anywhere? Charleston was fine, it was where he lived, but it wasn't home. He hadn't expected this.

Luna took his hand again. "Thanks for showing me the square. Sorry we didn't find her."

"It's okay. Not sure what I would have said to her anyway."

"Have you spoken to her? Since you left, I mean?"

"No. I haven't spoken to her in years. We talked just before Y2K. New millennium and all that. I can't remember anything since."

She swung around to face him. "What about when you left? Didn't you say goodbye?"

"No. I tried—I couldn't find her. She wasn't here and wasn't at home."

"Maybe she moved."

He shrugged, tried to avoid her gaze, then gave in when she took both his hands in hers. "We didn't date that long, Luna. Eight, no nine years had passed."

"Hang on," she said, tilting her head so far that her ear rested on her shoulder. "Who said, 'must I remind you—we slept together'?"

He had to laugh. Her impersonation wasn't that good, but it was that funny. He dropped her hands and slid his arms around her waist, pulling her close. "Guilty. It was me."

Luna gave him a quick, firm kiss. He leaned in, wanting another. He got the kiss, and a big smile from Luna. "Can we tour the cathedral?" she asked. "Then I want to see where you lived. Maybe she's there."

Landon found the house without difficulty, although it had been disguised with a garish chartreuse trim over a fresh coat of gray. The occupants of the lower level had either moved out or lost their enthusiasm for container gardening because the yard was now a weed lot.

"It used to be yellow," Landon said. "Gillian lived upstairs. There was a kitchen, a bathroom, and a small sitting area plus the bedroom." He smiled. "It was pretty cramped, although I wasn't there much, except for sleeping. Gillian wasn't either; she was either working or playing music and traveling with the band."

"Sounds lonely. Did you ever see each other?"

"Not much. And when we did, we were usually pretty tired." He shook his head. "I'm not sure why we stuck it out as long as we did. Inertia, I guess. Anyway, let's see if she's here." He rang the bell to the upstairs apartment; a metallic, grating ringer from the 1940s echoed behind the door. There was no answer, and no one with intact hearing could have missed that, so he didn't try again. He shrugged at Luna, who slid an arm around his waist as they turned to head back to their cottage. The sun had dropped below the rooflines and the street was bathed in deepening shadow. The tropical air still draped them.

"Landon?" The voice didn't seem familiar at first, but he and Luna located it coming from the porch across the street. "Landon Ratliff?"

She hadn't changed that much, somehow avoiding the damage the years might have wrought. Her hair was shorter, with some gray, but her face was unlined and still pretty. "Wendy," he said. "It's good to see you."

They met in the street and shared a hug. Landon stepped aside to introduce Luna.

"You're still here," he said while they followed her into her ground-level apartment. "Still waiting tables?"

"Pays the bills," Wendy said. She left them in the front room and returned with cans of Coke that they eagerly accepted. "So you back visiting all the old haunts? You moved to Atlanta, right?"

"Charleston." He offered a capsule version of the last four years, though it had been much longer since he'd seen Wendy. He left out the crash and the cancer, then tacked his question on at the end. "Is Gillian still living here?"

Wendy shook her head. "No, she moved out right after 9/11. Somewhere up by the lake. Then she met a guy and moved to Lafayette after Katrina. Had a baby last year. Came for a visit in March." She smiled. "I think she's pretty happy. Looks like you are too."

He smiled. Luna blushed. "Yeah, I am. We are," he said, and Luna nodded. They finished their drinks and rose to leave. "Wendy, it's great to see you. Take care of yourself and tell Gillian I said hello."

Wendy gave them each a quick hug. "You can tell her yourself, Landon." She scribbled something on a piece of paper. "Here's her email address."

The walk to their cottage was silent, a surprise to Landon because he'd expected an interrogation about his feelings or whether he planned to contact Gillian. Luna looked tired. He felt wrung out by the day and had a hint of a headache. He didn't want to think about all the things that had been lost. He was tired of Katrina, tired of thinking about the past, and didn't want to contemplate the uncertainty of the future. So he decided to concentrate on tonight.

First, though, he had something to do. Just before they reached the cottage, he fished Wendy's scrap of paper from his pocket and tossed it into a sidewalk trash can.

Luna smiled. "You didn't have to do that for me."

"I had to do it for me," he said, pulling her close. "I wanted to do it for you."

They showered and changed, then caught a streetcar that carried them far out into the Garden District to the big bend in the river, to his favorite restaurant in the city, Brigtsen's, where they dined at a small table tucked into the corner of the unassuming dining room. They shared a great bottle of wine, then shared increasingly warm kisses on the ride back with the wind caressing them through the open streetcar windows. Canal Street was alive with cars and clusters of people who were either late beginning or early ending another night of revelry. He didn't ask if Luna wanted to stop anywhere, and she never mentioned doing so. He'd seen what he needed to see and now had all he wanted or needed right beside him.

The passageway that led from the mysterious entrance off Dauphine was invitingly quiet and dark. Luna pressed him against the door and molded herself to him from lips to knees. He locked his arms in the small of her back, enjoying the taste of her warm mouth, feeling the swell of her breasts through their wilted clothing. He briefly wondered if they could get away with a skinny-dip, but before he could suggest it, they heard the muffled laughter of a couple having an evening swim. Her took her hand and led them silently toward their cottage.

The refrigerated air refreshed them. Luna escaped his grasp just long enough to light two candles. Then she turned off the lights and led him to the shower. They undressed each other during and between kisses, then soaped away the stickiness of the evening under cool, cascading water.

Their bathrobes lay in a heap beside the bed within minutes. Beneath the silky sheets, he gave himself over to Luna, enveloped in the sensual experience that left no room for past disappointments or future uncertainty. Afterward, as they cuddled and cooed and grew sleepy, he reveled in the now-familiar peaceful, relaxed feeling of having someone he loved snuggled beside him.

CHAPTER TWENTY-THREE

A phone call from his mother awoke them from a contented sleep the next morning—his father was back in the hospital.

"Are you going back to Virginia?" Luna asked, after he had hung up and tossed the phone onto the bedside stand.

She really does wake up pretty, he thought, his troubled mind soothed by the sight of her swaddled in a bathrobe and seated cross-legged atop the comforter. "No. Mom said not to. If they can get his pain controlled, he won't be there long."

"So it's his pancreas again?"

He nodded, his jaw clenched. "Of course. Old Eddie keeps pouring salt—or in this case, bourbon—on his wounds. I can't believe he won't quit drinking."

"Maybe he can't quit, Landon. He's addicted."

"No. He doesn't want to quit. We begged him, over and over. He wouldn't even think about it. Said he'd always drank, and he liked it." Luna's hand was on his shoulder, searching for his neck. "Mom knew, I guess, before she married him, but kids don't get to choose. She used to tell us it was the war, that the war had ruined him. But that's not what Grampa told me. He said Dad was a drunk even before they got married." He felt her hand coaxing his chin up. Her eyes wanted his. "How could you do that? Watch your kids hurting and ignore it?"

"He's hurting too," she said. "I'm guessing he can't help himself."

"Well, if alcohol was doing that to me, I'd get some help."

She hooked her other hand around his neck. Her smile was supportive and unsettling at the same time. "Denial's a big part of alcoholism, Landon. For everyone involved."

Four days later, on Tuesday afternoon, Landon was in Gloucester, Virginia, sitting in the stuffy, windowless waiting room of Dr. Walter Denbigh, thumbing through a worn copy of *Virginia Wildlife* while Denbigh wrapped up the day's appointments. He knew Walter still had to make rounds on his hospitalized patients, including Landon's father, so he was grateful that Walter had made time to visit with him on rather short notice.

Landon had flown in that morning, after his father had failed to improve as expected over the weekend. By the time he arrived from the airport, his father was feeling better, grumbling about being hungry, and finally complying with the nurses' efforts to get him out of bed.

Now Landon sat in the dull lamplight, aware of a faint antiseptic odor wafting through the window opening onto the reception desk. Denbigh was the son of Preston Denbigh, who had delivered most of the babies in Gloucester County— including Molly, Dale, and Landon—during his career and for whom the new obstetrical wing in the hospital had been named. Preston had been Landon's parents' physician, too, and when he retired in 1990, his son inherited the most lucrative family practice in the region. The efforts to carry on his father's legacy had been largely successful, though no one seemed to think Walter was fit to carry his father's stethoscope. Landon had always found the younger Denbigh affable and kind. His practice seemed to require patience more than expertise, since most of his patients were lonely or worried more than they were sick. Not a bad gig, if you were that kind of doctor, but Landon wasn't and knew he never would be.

The door to the office swung open. "Landon—sorry to keep you waiting. Come on back."

He tossed the magazine onto the table and rose, stiff from the plane and car ride. "Walter," he said, extending his hand. "Thanks for seeing me."

Denbigh was six inches taller than Landon, rail-thin, with his father's angular face and sad, gray eyes. His arms and legs seemed too long for his body. *He had aged well,* Landon thought, though his wardrobe had never evolved: Top-Siders, khaki pants, a patterned shirt that looked like it shouldn't be worn with a tie, along with a knit tie that looked like it shouldn't be worn with anything. Landon had never seen him in a lab coat.

"It's my pleasure." He gestured vaguely toward the hall. In his office, they sat facing one another across an expansive wooden desk. A large window brightened the room but offered little more than an elevated view of the parking lot that serviced the hospital and the medical office building.

Before Landon could speak, Walter inquired about his health, expressing shock and regret upon hearing the news of the crash. As Landon would have guessed, it seemed his mother had not mentioned the tumor. She was superstitious and wouldn't tempt fate by revealing that her boy had "the cancer." His reassurances that he was doing fine drew a smile from Denbigh followed by a comment about how one's life can change in an instant. As if Landon didn't know.

"How's your mom holding up?" Denbigh asked. "She's had more than her share lately. Your grandmother's been sick, your crash, and now your father."

"Unfortunately, I think she's used to it. She's had more than her share for the last forty-five years."

"Have they been married that long? Your father's, what, sixty-four?"

"Yep. They've been together since they were kids basically."

Denbigh shook his head.

Landon couldn't let it go. "I know—spending your whole life with Eddie Ratliff."

"No, I didn't mean that," Denbigh said, flapping a bony hand in Landon's direction. "I just thought about forty-five years of marriage. I'll be seventy-five when I hit that milestone. You're not married, are you? Your mom would've mentioned that."

"No."

"And you're how old?"

"Just turned forty."

"Can you imagine forty-five years of marriage?"

Now Landon turned away, trying, hoping to imagine forty-five more years of life.

Denbigh cleared his throat. "Well, anyway, your dad seemed better this morning, but I couldn't get over to see him at lunchtime. Everyone's trying to work in an appointment before they leave on vacation, I guess. How'd he look to you?"

"Not too bad. He got up today and was giving the nurses a fit, so I think he's on the mend."

"Good. We'll let him try some liquids this evening, advance his diet in the morning, and let him go tomorrow if he tolerates breakfast and his pain isn't too bad."

"Yeah, I figured if I came out here, he'd get better right away. Guess I should've waited one more day." Denbigh looked a little confused. "I'm leaving on vacation Monday," Landon explained. "I've got stuff to do."

Denbigh propped his elbows on the desk and rested his chin on his interlaced fingers. "I'm sure you're busy, Landon, but don't underestimate how much your mother needs you. Your brother can't be around all the time, and your presence is a great comfort to her. Your father's glad to see you, too, although he might not show it."

"Pretty sure of that."

"He talks about you all the time. He's proud of you."

"I'll take your word for it." Landon shifted in his chair. "Listen, Walter, the reason I wanted to meet with you is, do you think there's any reason to suspect another diagnosis?"

"No, I don't think so. Pretty typical chronic pancreatitis, don't you think? You have something else in mind?"

"No, not really. Just thought we ought to think through the possibilities. Things get overlooked sometimes."

"No question about that. I haven't done much workup for a while. His last CT scan didn't show much. This is consistent with his typical pattern, although the flare-ups are coming more frequently." Denbigh dropped his hands, then crossed his forearms on the desk. "Let me ask you something. Is your dad still drinking?"

Landon squinted, trying to display disbelief. "Yeah. Why? Did he deny it?"

"Yes, and your mother did too. Does she know?"

"She told me, and then I saw it for myself when I was here in May."

Denbigh stared at the papers littering his desk, his jaw muscles pulsing. "Hmm. No offense, Landon, but I'm a little disappointed with your mother." He took no offense, actually found Denbigh's response generous—being misled by a patient or family member made a doctor's job much harder. He hadn't expected his mother to lie.

"When are you heading back to Charleston?"

"Friday, unless something happens. Why?"

"We've got to confront your father about the drinking, or this is going to kill him. I've talked to him. I wonder if you might do better."

Landon smiled. "You've got to be kidding. He's never listened to any of us about this."

"But he's been pretty sick, Landon. When's the last time you talked to him about his drinking?"

"Probably college. It never does any good."

"You're a doctor now. He's scared. Believe me, it just might work." Denbigh rose from his chair. "Your mother's covering for him. That won't help. You know where this is headed. Like it or not, I think it's up to you. A man-to-man conversation might make a big difference. I've seen it."

"I'll think about it," Landon said, hoping to convey more sincerity than he felt.

CHAPTER TWENTY-FOUR

As it turned out, Landon kept his word to Denbigh; he did think about it, far more than he had hoped to, for the next two days.

His father was discharged on Wednesday, and the ordeal of transferring him from bed to wheelchair to car to house wiped him out. He had lost more weight; his bony arms felt as brittle as twigs, and his shirt hung on his wasted frame as if he were a hastily dressed scarecrow. Landon felt him tense when he pried him from the car, using both arms hooked under his father's armpits to lever him up and out. His ribs seemed to have no meat on them. His mother offered little help, seemingly afraid of breaking off a limb if she held her husband too tightly. But they navigated the porch and guided him first to the bathroom and then into bed, where he eagerly accepted a pain pill and curled up for a nap.

His mother collapsed onto the sofa and accepted his offer to serve her tea without protest, an acquiescence to exhaustion that he had never before witnessed. With little coaxing, he got her to agree to lie down in his room. She was asleep in no time. He called Dale to let him know they were home and safe and that he could wait until tomorrow to come over, if he wanted. It was a long haul from Dale's house, so Landon knew that one less trip probably suited his brother just fine. Since he was working when Landon called, the odds of having a lengthy conversation were reduced from highly unlikely to negligible. They would do better tomorrow—maybe.

The refrigerator was understandably empty, and when he spotted his mother's grocery list on the counter, he decided to surprise her and do the shopping. He left a note and bypassed the local grocery in favor of the larger store in Deltaville, which was in range of a cell tower. Luna answered on the first ring.

"Hi, sweetie. I was hoping you'd call." Her voice was like soft music at the end of a hard day.

"Every chance I get," he said. "How was book club?"

"It was fine. I hadn't finished the book, so I was one of the people I usually complain about." Her laugh made him smile. "It went too late, though. How's your father? Did you talk to him yet?"

He took a deep breath. Luna had enthusiastically endorsed Denbigh's plan when they'd talked yesterday. "Not yet. We brought him home today. He and Mom are wiped out. They're napping, so I decided to pick up the groceries."

"Good for you, Landon. That's sweet; your mom will appreciate the help."

"Yep. I had an ulterior motive, though. I wanted to hear your voice."

He heard a soft moan, just a second or two, then, "I miss you too. So much. I'm counting the minutes until Friday. I'm thinking you'll need some personal attention." She delivered the last two words in a sultry whisper that had him squirming.

"I love how you think. In fact, I love everything about you." The ease with which he said that still made him shake his head.

"I love you too, Landon," she said. "Hurry home. But hey, don't you need to get shopping?"

"Yeah. Mom probably won't sleep too long. I'm not sure about Dad, though."

"When are you planning to talk to him?"

He felt himself tense. Then, he realized her tone was more curious than challenging. "Tonight. Dale's coming to dinner tomorrow."

"Wouldn't he be supportive?"

"Not sure. Dale's Dale. He's always just gone along. He might not want to deal with it. I'm sure Dad's drinking bothered him when we were kids, but you could never tell."

"Did you ever ask him?"

"Yes, I have, several times, I swear. If you think *I* don't talk much—"

"I believe you, Landon." Her voice was level and calm. "I know I was tough on you about Enrique, but believe me, I can imagine how hard this is, with your father. I want you to know that I think you're very brave to do this. I love you, and I'm proud of you."

He couldn't remember a thing either of them said after that.

His mother did not awaken until he was nearly finished putting away the groceries. He had found almost everything on the list. She smiled and helped with the last few items, planted a loving kiss on his cheek, then shooed him out of the way so she could begin preparing dinner.

His father was still snoring loudly. Landon had hoped to catch him before dinner in case eating caused some pain, which would make any serious conversation difficult. He finally convinced himself that waiting until tomorrow might be smarter anyway, since it was reasonable to expect improvement with time and there seemed to be no chance that he would sneak a drink tonight; even Eddie Ratliff wouldn't risk that.

Landon awoke before dawn the next morning, unsure whether his headache was the cause or result of poor sleep. Before New Orleans, he'd thought maybe the headaches had at last vanished, but now they were back—mild, to be sure, nothing like the gripping pressure he'd endured for weeks after the crash. Still, he had hoped that at least his brain had healed. His thumb felt better, and he hadn't thought about the rawness in his throat for some time, so maybe the headache was just a headache. Even the tumor was gone—for now anyway.

Besides, he had reason enough for a headache this morning. He wondered if his father would be up early. Morning had always been his best time, even though most of them must have been marred by hangovers. He remembered lying awake in his bedroom, listening to his parents talking over breakfast. He couldn't make out the words, but loved the rhythm of what seemed to be peaceful conversations. Sundays were the best. It was his father's only day off each week; he never slept in but spent the morning in his chair, drinking coffee and reading the paper while his mother scurried about, timing the morning meal to coincide with her children's preference for sleeping in, keeping her husband's coffee cup filled, and somehow finding time to work the crossword puzzle and thumb through the Sunday magazine. Landon was always the first child out of bed. He would sprawl on the rug at his father's feet, sifting through the pile of already-read sections in search of the comics and the sports page. Then he'd lie on his back, reading and occasionally glancing up at his father's relaxed face and trembling hands.

Every day could be Sunday for them now, although he had witnessed the changes time and illness had wrought. Having adjusted to retirement, his mother and father slept later, and the ritual of reading the paper seemed to have lost its novelty and urgency. They had all day now, every day. Still, his father was at his best in the morning, in the hour or two before his illness overcame the refreshment of rest and reestablished its primacy in the effort it took him to perform the most basic tasks of living, before his angry, scalded pancreas rebelled against the need to help digest whatever food he had managed to eat.

He might be up extra early today, after picking at dinner last night in the brief interlude between awakening from his nap and retiring to bed. He was clearly exhausted, giving Landon license to avoid any attempt at broaching the subject of his drinking. His mother's decision to go to bed early relieved him of any obligation to discuss the plan with her either, and that had suited him just fine. He doubted that she would support the idea of confronting her husband.

Landon had seen her let him have it many times, usually after he'd said or done something to one of the kids. He'd watched her banish him to the army cot in the shed, kept ready for just such an occasion. He guessed that his parents must have discussed the drinking when his father was sober, but never in front of the children. Molly had tried to bring it up, but his mother would never allow it, would never allow her children to disrespect their father, no matter how much he may have earned their scorn. Dale had never said anything to anyone about it, so far as Landon could tell.

His mother had given him more private time than she had Molly or Dale, and Landon had never wanted to waste precious moments talking about something he didn't understand and she didn't want to discuss. But as he got older, he struggled to justify her reticence, her acquiescence to the hellish nightmare of life with his father. How could she just accept his drunken violence, and how could she subject her children to it? Answers had never come; he had never asked her. And now she was lying to his doctor about his drinking, even after Al-Anon?

He lay there while daylight crept into the room, thinking about all the words he'd never uttered—to his mother or his father—hoping to find among them the words that might make a difference today.

CHAPTER TWENTY-FIVE

The aroma of fresh coffee enticed him to throw off the covers and head for the kitchen. His parents hadn't been up very long; dawn had yielded to morning before the squeak of their bedroom door and muffled conversation had signaled the start of their day.

"Thought you were going to sleep all day," his father greeted him, smiling. His voice was strong, and his eyes were clear and alert. As always, he was already dressed in khakis and a work shirt. Landon had noted on his previous visit that his father's work boots seemed to have been permanently replaced with rubber-soled slip-ons. "Look who finally crawled out," his father called to his mother, who was smiling and pouring Landon a cup of coffee.

"Good morning, baby," she said. "Pay no attention to Rip Van Winkle, there. I thought I was going to have to serve him lunch in bed today. He was snoring like a buzz saw until after sunup."

"Ah, hell, you didn't get up until I did." His father hadn't looked up from the newspaper, but Landon saw the grin he was half concealing.

"I was awake, Eddie. I didn't want to disturb you."

His father gave Landon an exaggerated wink. "Well, I think you've picked a pretty good day to be here, Son. Mrs. Van Winkle is well refreshed and ready to make you a breakfast that would keep a lumberjack going all day."

He accepted the cup from his mother and leaned into her hug. She smelled of castile soap. Like his father, she rarely emerged from her bedroom without being dressed for the day, but occasionally she relaxed and allowed herself the luxury of gardening clothes and a light sweater for a housecoat. Today was one of those days.

"What can I fix you, baby?" Her smile seemed brighter than the sunshine throwing rectangles across the kitchen wall.

"What's Dad having?"

His father looked up and shifted the paper away from his place setting. "I'm still on oatmeal. Prison food." He smiled. "The warden threw in some fruit and sugar today, though. Not too bad."

"Play your cards right, and you'll get some real food tonight, Eddie. I might let you stay up late with your boys too. How about some eggs and bacon, Landon?"

He settled in at the table and watched his mother spinning like a dancer from refrigerator to cabinet to stove, her arms curving gracefully through the air as if she were conducting a symphony.

"Iris," his father intoned from behind the paper. "Arthur Denko is dead."

Landon smiled. His father was reading the obituaries, one of his parents' rare playful rituals that dated back to his childhood. Landon had once asked him why he always read the obituaries; his father had smiled and replied, "I need to make sure I'm not in there." So now, Landon was pretty certain his father had never heard of Mr. Denko. He knew what was coming next. His father's mischievous glance confirmed his hunch.

"Who's Arthur Denko?" His mother asked without looking.

"Old man Denko's boy."

She turned then. Her sour expression couldn't conceal the joy in her eyes, mirrored in his father's naughty grin. For a moment, Landon thought he saw two teenagers who fell in love—or thought they did—a long time ago.

By midmorning, Landon realized he'd lost another opportunity to talk with his father about his drinking. In hindsight, perhaps he should have seized upon the remarkable goodwill that surrounded the breakfast table, but it had proven too easy to justify silence and revel in something resembling normal family life, if only for a little while. Now, his father's stomach was beginning to bother him, and it seemed cruel to confront him when he was suffering. So he readily accepted his mother's request to run some errands and drove into Deltaville feeling both relieved and ashamed but mostly just feeling like a coward.

He called Luna, even though he dreaded admitting his failure, but his fear of a scolding proved unfounded. Landon's first attempt went directly to voicemail; Luna had been on the phone with Sutter and seemed distracted when he finally reached her. But after briefly describing how she had talked her sister out of derailing the sibling getaway, she seemed to settle into a generous and forgiving mood and offered him encouragement and good wishes for success at dinner. She commented that Dale's presence might actually prove helpful.

He did not want to hang up but was due back home and lost service as soon as his car left the Deltaville corporate limits.

Left alone with his thoughts, he pondered a strategy for broaching the subject of his father's drinking. He might deny everything, and then how would Landon prove it? He thought of searching for a bottle, but that seemed sneaky, and he had no right to violate his parents' privacy—it wasn't his house anymore. Besides, a confrontation would surely upset his mother and spoil the dinner that meant so much to her.

Dinner was going to be late, which could be trouble in itself, since Landon's father had always preferred to eat early. When he was working, he arrived home hungry and usually drunk and had never been willing to subordinate his preferences to his children's schedules. The family dinner, never a bonding experience, became a rarity once Dale and Landon starting playing sports and vanished altogether when Molly entered high school. Now that his father was retired, there were no barriers to what seemed to Landon to be a late afternoon dinnertime.

But Dale was coming tonight, and everyone knew he would never consider leaving work early (everyone, including his wife, had been grateful that his daughter had been born on a Sunday so Dale could witness the birth). It seemed that his father had always given Dale a little more slack, and his elder son's dedication to work seemed to resonate with him, so Landon guessed his father wouldn't complain. His mother, tickled to have all her men under one roof for a meal, would be in her element, caring and preparing. He had just about convinced himself that they might have a supportive, constructive conversation, then concluded that this seemed about as likely as his father announcing he had joined Alcoholics Anonymous.

His father's familiar silhouette was visible on the porch when Landon pulled into the drive. The thrum of a ballgame crowd reached his ears when he exited the car. He paused, just for a moment, when his father's arm shot high into the air. He'd seen that greeting too many times.

"Hey, Son!" His voice was too loud, too enthusiastic, too cheerful. "Come on in. Sit down and listen to the ballgame with me. You want a beer?"

Landon scanned the tables; no sign of a can or bottle. His mother wouldn't have allowed that, he was fairly certain. He waved off the offer. "I'm fine, Dad. Who's winning?"

"Braves, two nothing, bottom of the second."

The sweet medicinal smell of bourbon breath wafted over him after his father's pronouncement. Landon's stomach was knotted and sour. He lowered himself into the recliner.

"Did you call that gal?" His father's gaze was wandering about as fast as Landon's mind, and he wore a grin that suggested nothing good. Landon felt as if he'd just passed the last Turn Back sign; he was picking up speed and could barely make out the roar of the waterfall.

He rose, groping for the chair arm and avoiding eye contact. "I couldn't reach her. Sorry, Dad, I think I'd better lie down for a bit. Something at lunch didn't agree with me, I guess." He headed for the door. "I'll be okay by the time Dale gets here."

He felt the squeezing weight of disappointment descending upon him as it had so often in the past. Back then, the optimism of youth had outweighed the lessons of memory, allowing him to hope and pray his father wouldn't be drinking, imagining what a normal, fun evening would be like. Landon could not recall ever being pleasantly surprised. He'd never gotten used to the disappointment— he'd just finally stopped hoping. Now his sense of betrayal buttressed his fading resolve; no matter what, he would speak up tonight.

Dale arrived right on time. Landon and his mother greeted him in the yard, just as he exited from the 1964 Chevy Stepside pickup he'd bought while Landon was in college. Over the years, Dale had replaced or rebuilt everything, added air-conditioning and decent seatbelts, and painted it Middlesex High School Charger blue.

Landon hadn't seen his brother since Christmas, but he noticed no changes. Dale had not inherited the angular, feral Ratliff features and physique. His mother always said Dale was "a Leonard," her mother's people, who were taller and stockier. Dale's body was thick and powerful looking, not sculpted by weight training but rather forged by hard, physical labor. His athletic grace had always surprised those seeing him on the field for the first time. Both boys had their father's thick, wiry hair, but Dale kept his cut shorter. To Landon, Dale had always been a dead ringer for John Riggins, the hero of the greatest Super Bowl win for the greatest Redskins team ever. And although his brother might have been pleased to hear that, it had always struck Landon as too weird to mention.

"Hey, Brother," Dale said now, releasing his mother from a hug that had come with a kiss on the cheek. He extended a callused hand that still carried the floral scent of the hand cleaner every mechanic used. "How you feelin'?"

"I'm good, Dale," Landon said. "How's Sally?"

"Fabulous. You wouldn't recognize her. Growing like a weed." He turned to his mother. "How's Dad?"

"He had a pretty good day," she said. "Looking forward to having his men home for dinner."

Landon caught Dale's glance and stifled a smile. He guessed that Dale's skeptical expression mirrored his own, but no sense spoiling his mother's obvious excitement with a cynical comment. Dale draped an arm around his mother's shoulders as they headed inside.

His father was waiting for them in the living room, stooped and pallid, clutching the back of the sofa for support, apparently determined to greet them from a standing position. He looked as pale and brittle as a potato chip as Dale shook his hand and patted him gently on the shoulder. His father did not object when Dale held on while he eased himself back onto the sofa.

"How was the traffic?" his father asked.

Dale checked his watch. "Not too bad, once I got out of Norfolk. Seems like it's always a mess in the afternoon."

"I wouldn't give you a nickel for that place," his father said. "You ought to move back up here."

Dale smiled in Landon's direction. "I gotta work, Dad. Sally's already taking all my money."

"They need good mechanics in Deltaville and Gloucester."

"Yeah, but they don't pay anything. We're dug in down in Norfolk now."

"How's Carla?" his mother asked. "I was hoping she'd come and bring that sweet baby."

"She's great, Mom," Dale said. "She would've come, wanted Landon to see Sally, but we'd get home too late for Sally's bedtime. Carla won't budge on that." He turned to his father. "Besides, by the time I picked them up and then got up here, the old man would be chewing on the furniture."

"I heard that," his father said. "My stomach thinks my throat's been cut now. Can we eat?"

Landon's mother catapulted from her seat. "Everything's hot and ready. Y'all come on."

She had prepared pork chops, Dale's favorite, with Landon's beloved mashed potatoes and enough side dishes to cover the table and the counter that divided the kitchen from the dining area. Two thoughts immediately entered Landon's mind: this was not a dream meal for someone with pancreatitis, and it was too bad Molly wasn't here. Neither thought would deter him from plowing into a meal that reminded him of home, or at least of what he had come to believe had been home, even if he couldn't pinpoint a specific memory. Steam from the hot food curled into the yellow light, forming a cocoon around his mother's table. This was her passion, her alchemy of love, her canvas, and Landon took it all in as if he were seeing a familiar exhibit at his favorite museum. His father and brother bent over their plates, his mother nibbling and smiling and flitting from chair to counter to stove to refrigerator, fetching one more thing she was certain someone might want, ensuring no glass dipped below half-full. She was in her glory, surrounded by her men.

"Come on, Mom, sit down and eat," Dale said finally, shaking his head and smiling at Landon.

"Don't worry about me," she said as she dropped into her chair for the fourth time. "I don't get to cook like this anymore."

"You guys still come up on Sundays?" Landon asked Dale.

"Some. We go to Carla's sister's place over in Dam Neck pretty often. She has the whole family over there most Sundays." He gave Landon a nod. "When you heading back, Brother?"

"I fly out tomorrow at noon. I'm heading down to Key West on Monday, for the holiday. You remember my roommate, Enrique? He has a place down there."

Dale smiled. "Tough break. You taking that new girl?" His eyes lit up. "Mom told me about her. Anything serious?"

His mother was blushing but couldn't hide her smile.

"We haven't met her yet," his father said. "I was starting to wonder if you'd ever settle down."

Now Landon smiled. "Hold on. Nobody said anything about settling down." He shook his head at Dale. "She's not going to Key West. She has a family get-together in California."

"Well, bring her out whenever you want," Dale said. "You can stay with us. Carla can't wait to meet her. We can go to the beach. I'd guess a California girl would go for that."

"Yeah, she likes the beach," Landon said. "We'll see how it goes." Word had spread fast; he guessed his mother and Carla talked pretty often. They got along well, and Carla was remarkably patient with his father. Now that there was a baby, Landon wondered if that would change. Maybe it already had. Landon and Carla had hit it off from the beginning. She'd love Luna. Landon wished she were here now, for a lot of reasons.

As dinner wound down, his father got quiet and began picking at his food. He had taken larger portions than usual and eaten about half. Finally, he excused himself to go to the bathroom, and when he returned, his eyes seemed a little shinier. Landon wasn't certain, but he didn't need to be. It was now or never.

"Dad," he said, swallowing hard. He was already backpedaling in his mind. "Dr. Denbigh asked me to talk to you." He hadn't wanted to invoke Denbigh, but his heart was racing. Courage had eluded him. Dale and his mother were looking at him. He tried to fix his gaze on his father, whose expression was like that of someone who is watching a show that isn't holding his interest. "He thinks, or at least thought you weren't drinking anymore, but now—"

"I'm not drinking."

His mother was staring into her lap. Dale's gaze had shifted to his father; his jaw was set and the hand holding a forkful of potatoes hovered above his plate.

"I'm not picking on you, Dad, and neither is Denbigh. We're doctors, and I'm your son. We want you to get well."

"Ask your mother. She'll tell you."

He did not want to make eye contact with his mom. He was fighting his cracking voice as it was. "I have, Dad. We've both smelled it on you."

His father's brow descended over increasingly vacant and unfocused eyes. Landon was certain he was drinking now but felt nothing except pity and fear. Mostly fear.

"I'm not attacking or accusing you. I just want you to know how bad it is for you. Your pancreas is really bad, and alcohol is poison for it."

"I'm not drinking, and you can tell Denbigh to kiss my ass," his father said. "You, too, Dr. Hotshot." Landon saw his father's hands trembling. "Okay, I take a sip now and then—so what? It helps the pain, and besides, I been drinking all my life. Your mom knew that when I married her." He turned to her. "I think I've done pretty good. Did your counseling friends put you up to this?"

"Mom had nothing to do with this," Landon said. His head was starting to hurt. "Denbigh asked me if I thought you were drinking, and I told him what I thought."

"So what do you think?" his father snarled. He had shrunk into his chair, a nasty sneer creasing his face. His shoulders were hunched, and his hands curled into pathetic little fists that threatened no one.

"He said he had talked with you, and he thought maybe you'd listen to me."

"I'm listening. What do you think?"

Landon felt his eyes filling up. His hands felt shaky, and as he tried to clear his throat, a thin moan escaped. "I think you're sick, Dad, and I know you've always liked to drink. I know it's hard to stop, and maybe you don't want to, but I wish you would." He looked around the table. "I think we all do."

"Let them speak for themselves," his father said. "I'm talking to you. They aren't on my ass about this—you are. I don't need any lectures, especially from my own son. I know I'm sick, and I know how to take care of myself. You're goddamn right I like to drink, and I don't drink nearly as much as I want to because I'm sick. I don't smoke much either because I'm sick." He got to his feet, holding the table with both hands. "I can't do shit anymore because I'm sick." His father stood there, weaving slightly, his watery, muddy gaze wandering. Finally, he settled on Landon again. "Now you're sick." He tried to smile, but it didn't take, and his mouth fell. "I hope it goes better for you." His voice was trembly, but his eyes flared with anger and he turned away, brushing off his wife's offer of help and disappearing down the hall toward his bedroom.

His mother sank into her chair. She wasn't crying. Dale was staring at something in the middle of the table, where it seemed to Landon the food had aged too quickly. The gravy had formed a feeble crust, like late-November ice on the pond, and the corn had congealed into an unappealing mass. Landon sensed neither solace nor support, but neither did he sense heartbreak or anger.

"I'm sorry," he said. "I didn't mean to ruin the dinner."

"You didn't ruin anything," Dale said. His strong voice drew Landon's eyes to his. "It was a great dinner, Mom." His eyes never left Landon's. "Brother, you did what the doctor asked you to. It couldn't have been easy. I guess I wouldn't expect anything different from Dad. He's sick, and things are slipping away from him."

His mother's hand found his. He feared crying and didn't respond to the caress. "You tried, Landon," she said. "That's all you can do. Your father will be okay. He just doesn't like being challenged, especially in front of or by his boys. I'm proud of you."

This wasn't as bad as he'd feared or as good as he'd hoped. It felt as if something had changed. He was glad for Al-Anon; without it, his mother would have folded, tried to gloss over the problem, anything to keep the peace. He felt as if Dale was looking at him differently. Landon had expected anger or frustration, maybe a scolding about his bad timing, but it hadn't come. Still, he felt hollow, as if challenging his father had cost him a piece of himself.

CHAPTER TWENTY-SIX

The next day delivered a sad ride to the airport after a quiet, grim morning. His father stayed in bed until just before it was time for Landon to leave, and had his mother not disappeared into the bedroom a short while earlier, he guessed there might have been no departing farewell. His father looked shriveled and hard, his eyes downcast as he offered a reluctant handshake and mechanical hug. "Let us hear from you," he murmured, then turned away. The door was closing as Landon wished him better health.

His mother's hug was a little shaky, but her eyes were clear, and she planted a firm kiss on his forehead. She had packed him a sandwich for the flight. He promised to bring Luna next time. He felt isolated on the plane—not the solitude he usually craved but rather a lonely, leprous isolation, as if he were unclean, shunned by those keeping a safe, wary distance.

He called Luna as soon as the wheels touched down in Charleston; apparently something in his voice betrayed him. She didn't press, just told him to hurry home—to her apartment, where she and Hazel needed a man's touch.

Hazel had to wait her turn. Luna answered the bell wearing an ankle-length, cotton shirtdress that clung to her wondrous form, showing nothing but revealing everything. She smelled like flowers and felt warm and curvy and eager and responsive. Her finger on his lips stifled speech while her other hand busied itself with the buttons on his shirt. She replaced the finger with her lips, then led him to the bedroom.

They made love slowly and tenderly while the afternoon sun threw rectangles across the bed. Luna nuzzled, murmuring and whispering, and he felt the knots in his back and neck unwind. His headache, along with all thoughts of home, vanished. Nothing mattered except the miracle that writhed and slithered under and over him, drowning him in pleasure, wrapping him in a cocoon of relaxation.

Luna got up afterward and released Hazel from wherever she had been imprisoned. He heard her shushing the cat's vexed whining, then she was back, her naked body sliding next to his under the sheet. He pulled her to him, and her head found his chest, where she planted a wet kiss and then cuddled in, her cheek rubbing against his chest hair. He kissed her scalp, aiming for one of many sharp angles in her part. Her head came up slowly, as if she were emerging from under water, strands of fiery-red hair spilling aside to reveal her huge eyes followed by her luscious, smiling mouth.

"That was pretty amazing, mister. Better than I anticipated."

"Oh, doubting my ability, huh?" He ran his fingers through her hair, clearing a spot on her forehead for a kiss.

"No, mine. I missed you so much. Afraid I might be too anxious."

"You didn't show it. You seemed about as anxious as a swan when I got here."

She smiled. "It was all an act. I wanted to jump your bones, but I thought you might appreciate some calmness."

"How did you know?" He shifted on the pillow so he could see her face better.

"You sounded tense on the phone. I figured things might not have gone well last night." Her fingers were dancing in his chest hair now. "So how was it?"

"Weird. I didn't handle it all that well. I was too wishy-washy, I think, but Dad didn't like it."

"Did he blow up?"

"Not really. He got angry and went to bed but nothing violent or anything. He was still pretty quiet this morning."

"What about your mom and brother?"

"Didn't say much, but they were okay afterward."

"Sounds like you gave them all something to think about." Hazel leapt onto the bed, sniffing and purring while she searched for a suitable place to plop down.

He hooked Hazel's ears with his thumb. She dropped like a stone against his unoccupied left side. "I guess. I don't know."

"I'm proud of you, Landon. How do you feel about it?"

He stared at the ceiling; a spider was working its way down the web it had constructed between two arms of the chandelier, toward a fly that had blundered in and stopped struggling. "Mostly like I've lost something, like I've done something wrong. I feel like I betrayed my dad. I know it sounds silly, but I don't feel right challenging him, even though I know I'm doing what's best for him."

"Do you think he'll stop drinking?"

"Not until it hurts too much."

Luna sat up, cross-legged, draping the sheet around her shoulders like a robe. "Well, maybe you made it hurt a little more."

"Yeah, and that's what bothers me," he said. "Doctors are supposed to relieve pain. Seems like maybe sons are too."

He hung around through a late-afternoon meal of chicken salad on pumpernickel. Then Luna had some last-minute errands to run, even though she had another full day before departing for her sisters reunion, and Landon needed to unpack, do laundry, and begin putting together his wardrobe for the tropical getaway. It would be his first visit to Key West; he was picturing Jimmy Buffet, and he'd never seen Jimmy in anything except shorts, a beach shirt, and flip-flops. Besides, it was a guys' trip; he didn't need to sweat over outfits.

He'd gotten his bags unpacked and the laundry going when he noticed the voicemail light. It was Amy: "Landon, if you get this message before Saturday morning, call me at home. Otherwise, I'll try to reach you Saturday."

Why hadn't she tried the cell? There were no missed calls. Her phone was busy twice, but he reached her on the third try. For the first time ever, Landon heard not a hint of joy or playfulness in her voice. "I'm sorry to tell you this, Landon, but Enrique entered rehab yesterday. I'm afraid the Key West trip is off."

"God, Amy, I'm sorry. What happened?"

"Nothing sudden. You saw him in Charleston. It's been going on for a while."

"Yeah, it seemed pretty bad, but … how'd you get him to go?"

"It wasn't me. I tried, over and over. He finally got caught by one of the nurses at the hospital. He was on call, and she smelled it on him. He could lose his license unless he completes rehab."

Landon couldn't believe it. "He's drinking while he's *working*?"

There was silence, then he heard Amy exhale. "You sound like Enrique's father, Landon. Why is it so shocking that he's drinking at work but not that he's drinking in front of his kids? I get the whole physician thing and think it's terrible, too, but frankly, I couldn't give a shit about that when I watch my kids cry themselves to sleep and see Hector hiding out in his room every night. I can't tell you how bad it's been."

"You don't need to, Amy. I've been there."

He was distracted for the remainder of the call and later wished he'd spent more time asking Amy how she was doing, although she seemed exhausted and tired of talking about it. She and the kids had already planned to visit her parents for the holiday, so they were packed and ready to depart in the morning. Since Enrique would not be allowed any visitors for an indefinite time, Amy was uncertain when they would return. Landon felt sure she would keep him posted and knew Luna would be on him to check in with Amy regularly.

He sat by the phone for a long time, the silence broken only by the soft ticking of the clock and the hum of the refrigerator. Time and life could be tough, even cruel. Now Enrique was sick—a drunk, of all things, and drinking on duty. He knew Amy was right about the kids, but still, a physician had taken a solemn oath. Enrique knew that; his father had drilled it into him since forever.

Amy *was* right, though; Landon remembered. Never knowing what to expect, feeling tense all the time, wondering why other kids got a normal dad. Watching his mother suffer and wondering why she put up with it, how she could let her kids go through it. How could a father, a husband, do that? Landon had learned about addiction as a medical student, had read the pamphlets from Al-Anon, and yet, he struggled to call alcoholism a disease. Why didn't the patients want to be cured? How many times had his father refused to consider treatment, the last time less than twenty-four hours ago? He was glad Enrique got caught. At least that would force him to get sober. Otherwise, he'd lose everything.

His head began to ache a little, and that reminded him that Dr. Schneider had been after him to get in for a follow-up appointment. Now Landon had an unexpected opening in his schedule. It was too late to call the office, but maybe he could reach Schneider on his cell phone. He'd work him in on Monday or Tuesday. His schedule was probably light anyway. A lot of people would be away for the holidays. But not Landon.

CHAPTER TWENTY-SEVEN

The news about Enrique would come as no surprise to Luna. She'd seen him during the visit, had confirmed her suspicions with Amy, and yet Landon felt funny about telling her that Enrique's drinking had finally caught up with him. Despite running late for their planned rendezvous, he dawdled on the walk to The Vendue, rehearsing what he would say, how he would break the news.

It seemed ironic—they were meeting for drinks. Alcohol, always a lurking, malevolent presence in his life, was once again an overt threat to someone he cared about. And it had played a role in ruining his nap, which had been tormented by a dream, a distortion of a memory that had haunted him for years. He was back on the football field, age nine or ten, waiting in the cruel November night for his father to come and get him after practice. Everyone else had been picked up; he'd sent the coaches away with phony reassurances, and now he was left alone, listening to the soft, grinding murmur of the timer that would soon extinguish the stadium lights and plunge him into blackness. Later, he'd learn that his father had passed out and forgotten him, but now he faced a long, terrifying trudge home through a half mile of woods, clutching and ominous in the night, the nearly bare limbs rattling in the wind like desiccated bones. His hands and eyes burned with the cold. He had never felt so utterly abandoned, but in the dream, the stadium lights bore down on him while he grieved that his father had missed the great tackle he'd made just before practice ended.

He had awakened troubled, not certain why. He remembered, way back then, wishing his father had been watching when he made the tackle. But that had been a fleeting wish, outweighed by relief that for once, practice had not been punctuated by his father's cursing that drew looks of disgust from other parents and fearful silence from his teammates. What Landon remembered most was embarrassment and isolation, tinged with confused anger. Why didn't he have parents who drove up in a clean, decent car with welcoming smiles and a kind word for the coach? Parents who cheered for their kids and for the others? Why didn't he get that? There were no answers then or now. He had learned self-reliance that night, a terrible lesson for a kid so young, but one that had served him, for good or ill, ever since.

He spotted Luna when he exited the elevator. She had chosen a table on the lower level, near the elevator but out of the sun that still had some fight left in it. In the moment before she turned and saw him, he had time to reflect on how lucky she made him feel.

"Yummy," she said in response to the unselfconscious kiss he greeted her with. "You should take a nap more often."

"That had nothing to do with the nap. It wasn't that good—the nap, I mean. The kiss was great."

The waitress had been watching for his arrival. Luna wanted something really cold, so they settled on a bottle of

Pinot Grigio that they knew would come nestled in a bucket of ice.

"So you didn't sleep much?" she asked, once they were alone again.

"No, I had a message from Amy when I got home, so I called her back. Enrique had to enter an alcohol rehab program."

Luna's brow furrowed. "What do you mean *had to*?"

"He got caught at work by a nurse. His license is at stake."

"Oh, wow. How are Amy and the kids?"

"She sounds tired. They're all headed to DC for a while."

She did not reply. A corner of her lip slipped into her mouth, and her gaze wandered out over the jumbled rooflines of the city. Landon sipped his water, waiting until she turned back to him. "You okay?" he asked.

She nodded. "Yeah, just sad for Amy and the kids. It's too bad it took getting caught at work. Sounds like there were plenty of clues at home. Did he go voluntarily?"

"I guess so. Why?"

"Well, it sounds like the license thing was a big driver. I get that, but it doesn't seem like a great predictor of successful sobriety."

"I don't know. It would be for me."

"You say that because you aren't addicted, Landon." She prodded his leg with her bare foot, which had abandoned its flip-flop. "And because you're addicted to work."

"Well, speaking of addiction to work, I called Schneider, and he can see me Monday. I could be back to work later next week."

"That's right—Key West is out."

He nodded, then watched Luna's eyes widen.

"Hey, I have an idea," she said.

"Come with you to California?" He pasted on a fake grin.

Her face fell into a slit-eyed mask. "Sorry, but I can absolutely verify that you are not one of the girls. Chicks only, my love." She paused while the wine arrived. They touched glasses and sipped, then she leaned in. "Maybe you should go back home."

He shook his head. "No chance. I was just there."

"You left a little unfinished business, it sounds like."

"It needs to be left alone for a while." The wine was fruity and cold. "I'll be fine here."

Luna stuck out her lip. "Sounds lonely."

He grabbed her hand. "I'd have been lonely in Key West." He was starting to miss her already.

By midnight on Saturday, he was starting to question his sanity. He lay awake in the stillness of Luna's bed, staring at the ceiling. He felt empty, shaky, and scared and knew there was no sense in it. Luna was beside him, enjoying the contented after-sex sleep they would ordinarily be sharing. In a few hours, it would be time to send her off on the trip she had been anticipating for weeks, and the thought of watching her go sucked the breath out of him.

Being alone scared him. After years of reveling in solitude, he had to admit that the prospect of days spent living in his wounded mind was unsettling. There was progress, no doubt. His symptoms were mostly gone, and those that remained were manageable. But so much else was gone too. Would he ever be able to concentrate, to think clearly about complicated problems? He still couldn't even remember his birthday, not that there was much to remember. Up until now, he'd been pretty good at staying busy, avoiding rumination about how much he'd lost. It had been an arduous journey, and now, his Sherpa was leaving him on his own.

He had closed the door on the idea of returning to Virginia when he called home midafternoon and his father refused to speak with him. His mother offered an unconvincing excuse, and Landon pretended to buy it, but it was clear that neither had fooled the other. His parents had no holiday plans. He invoked his doctor's appointment and the need to watch Hazel to buttress his argument against another trip home.

He had also tried without success to call Mike Fanning—he was probably still making his way back from Europe. It had been more than two months since Landon had worked. His colleagues probably wondered if he was ever coming back, and he didn't blame them. He was starting to feel like maybe he wasn't a doctor anymore. Maybe that's how Enrique was feeling.

He shifted slightly to try and relieve the ache in his thumb. Luna stirred just then. He heard the soft whistling sound of a sudden inhalation, then her head moved. He smiled. Her face rose up, ready for kissing. Her lips were soft and supple, even after an hour or more of sleep.

"Hope I didn't wake you up," he whispered.

She shook her head. "I'm glad I'm up. Were you awake?" She raised herself up on her elbow and touched a finger to his lips.

"Yeah, I was watching you sleep. I won't get to for a while, you know."

She ran her hand over his forehead, then locked her fingers into his tangled curls. "How's your head?"

"It's okay. Little headache but nothing bad."

"Maybe you should rest while I'm gone."

"Don't worry. There's nothing much else to do unless Schneider surprises me."

"You don't think he'll let you go back to work?"

He shrugged. His shoulder bumped pleasantly against the swell of Luna's breast. "Oh, I think he will, but probably not this week. There's nothing much going on. He's pretty conservative."

"You *are* still having headaches."

"I know, and I still can't remember everything. Maybe I should tell him I remember now."

"I hope you're joking, Landon."

"I am. Don't worry, I won't lie. I'm guessing some of the memories won't ever come back. I've seen that in some patients."

Luna untangled herself and slid out of bed. Hazel rose and stretched like an old woman, then padded off toward the kitchen. Landon thought Luna was heading for the bathroom, but instead she lit a candle she kept on the nightstand, bathing her naked body in a soft yellow glow that erased any thoughts of sleep from his mind. She smiled and crawled back under the covers, molding herself to his body once again. He rolled toward her, encircling her with his arm. The kiss she offered was quick; she was likely chatty rather than in the mood. She fluffed the pillow, then propped herself up, almost nose-to-nose. He couldn't suppress a smile, eager for whatever came next.

"Tell me what you remember from the day of the wreck," Luna whispered.

"I don't think it works that way," he said, smiling. "Talking about it doesn't bring the memories back."

"We'll see. Just tell me what you remember."

He rolled onto his back. "I don't really remember anything until I woke up in the hospital and you were there."

"What about before the crash? Can you remember getting in the car?"

"No."

"How about the night before?"

He shook his head. "No. I remember brunch the day before, but after that I can't remember. Maybe a couple things, but nothing—"

"Like what?" Her head had come up. He flinched at the sudden movement.

"Whoa. I don't know, Luna. Just vague thoughts. Nothing specific. Why?"

She smiled again, leaned in, and drew another kiss from him. "I want to tell you something. I've been waiting to see if you'd remember, but it doesn't seem like it's going to come back, so I want to tell you before I leave tomorrow."

Her smile made him feel a little better, but his chest was beginning to feel tight.

"It's nothing bad, sweetie." Her fingers on his cheek were gentle and reassuring. "I wanted to surprise you that night, for your birthday, so I came over to your place in the middle of the night. I woke you up."

"You did?"

"Yep. I had on a T-shirt and panties, and I had a bottle of wine and a balloon bouquet with me."

He smiled. "What? Are you kidding me?"

"I'm not. It was the first time we slept together."

His smile faded, and he saw his own disappointment reflected in Luna's wounded eyes. He pulled her to him, offered a quick kiss, and then held her, expecting tears that did not come. He pulled away; her eyes were dry and shining in the soft candlelight.

"I'm sorry, Luna. If I could make the memory come back, you know I would. But I wouldn't trade May thirteenth for anything. That's my memory of our first time, and I'll always cherish it." He traced her gentle smile with his fingertip. "I feel awful about my birthday, though—you've been living with this for so long. I wish you'd told me sooner."

"I didn't want to confuse you or make you feel bad. I even threw the bouquet out the day you were coming home. I didn't want to upset you."

"Such a sweet thing. I can't believe I can't remember it."

"I wish you could," she said, snuggling against his chest. "It's been hard. I kept hoping, but it's gone, I guess."

"Well, you could fill me in. Must have been pretty good— for both of us."

"You weren't complaining." She rose up on an elbow again. "It was the first time, so it was special."

He stroked her face again and let his thumb trace the outline of her lips, then the deepening smile crease at the corner of her mouth. "May thirteenth was special too. I'll never forget that."

She turned and blew out the candle, then crawled on top of him. He felt their bodies sink deeper into the mattress. He tilted his head to receive her kiss, returning her soft moan that vibrated into his mouth. His mind was struggling with what he'd lost, with what had been stolen from him, and with what he had now, right here. Luna's tongue found his ear. "How about a memory for while I'm gone?" she whispered, banishing all other thoughts, at least for now.

CHAPTER TWENTY-EIGHT

The sense of loss, of being cheated, began to dog Landon the next morning, though he kept it to himself while he and Luna had a farewell breakfast at Hominy Grill. Luna awoke craving a Charleston Nasty Biscuit, and since this was their favorite breakfast spot anyway, it was an easy choice. They beat the after-church crowd and sat inside. The bright sun provided them with an unnecessary excuse to sit side by side, backs to the window. He liked the feel of her shoulder against his while they shared the newspaper. He was missing her already, trying not to show it, and dreading the drive to the airport.

Luna cried when they said goodbye; her tears touched their parting with a sweetness that mingled with the sadness he felt on the drive home. As he had when he'd last left his parents' home, Landon felt empty, lost, abandoned, sick, and old, and couldn't say exactly why. She would be gone for only a week, and this trip meant so much to her. The Key West trip wasn't that big a deal; at least now Enrique was getting professional help, far better than any advice Landon might have offered. Charleston, Fourth of July—he ought to be able to entertain himself for seven days.

He didn't go back to Luna's right away; he would have to face her ghosts enough over the next week, and besides, Hazel was fed and would sleep away most of the day. He briefly considered napping as well, then piddled around his house instead. Dust that predated the New Orleans trip was everywhere, so he dusted and vacuumed, stripped the bed, and washed the sheets and what little laundry he had. He considered cleaning the refrigerator before realizing he was not quite that lonely.

Just before dinner, he walked to Luna's. Hazel was characteristically indifferent to his arrival, staring past him before stretching and sashaying off in the direction of the bedroom. Landon didn't want to spend time in there, so he filled her food and water bowls and sifted the litter pan. Everything was as they had left it that morning, and Luna had insisted on cleaning everything before her trip, so there really was nothing to do. He glanced into the bedroom, where Hazel mocked him by languishing on Luna's side of the bed. The room smelled of her perfume, and he wasted little time there before wishing Hazel a good night and locking up on the way out.

There was no message on the home phone, and he had already checked his cell twice, so he sat down to eat the pastrami sandwich he'd picked up on the way back. He glanced through the paper he and Luna had shared over breakfast. Seemed like long ago now. The sandwich was greasy, but the fries were crispy. Fortunately, he had bought some beer for Enrique and Amy's visit, and equally fortunately, they had drunk only wine. So now, he had a very cold six-pack all to himself.

The food was mostly eaten, and he was on his fourth beer when his cell phone rang. "Luna Quinn" was displayed across the screen.

"Hey, baby," he answered, wondering if the beer lent a little too much Elvis to his greeting.

"Wrong baby, Doctor, but I like the way it sounds." It was another female voice, sultry, with a throaty laugh.

He smiled. "You must be Fox."

"Wow. First I'm baby, and now I'm a fox. If I didn't know better, I'd think my little sister found herself a player." She waited a beat, then added, "This is me." She seemed to have lowered her voice. "Luna's in the bathroom. I've been wanting to call you, and she wouldn't let me, so in about a minute, you're going to hear screaming." Her self-congratulatory laugh confirmed her disinhibited state.

"So, how are you, Fox? It's nice to meet you, sort of."

"To be perfectly honest, Landon, I'm drunk, and so is my baby sister."

He heard Luna's muffled voice. It grew louder quickly. "What are you doing? Is that Landon?"

There was laughter, a yell, more laughter, and then finally, Luna's voice. "Hey, sweetie, sorry about my crazy sister."

"You're Lunatic, not me." It was Fox, her voice punctuated with more laughter.

"No problem," he said. "Not like you're interrupting anything. I was just sitting here, missing you."

"Ah, that's so sweet," Luna said. "I miss you too."

He heard an exaggerated *aw* in the background.

"We've had a little too much wine." Luna's words were noticeably slurred.

"No kidding," he said. "Good for you. I'm working on some beer here and feeling pretty good myself."

There were sounds of another struggle, screams and laughter, and then Fox was back on the line. "Listen, mister—I mean, Doctor, I mean, Landon. Now that we're on a first-name basis, I want to know what your intentions are toward my sister."

He ignored the now-familiar sounds of struggle. "Well, Mother Quinn, a player like me couldn't have anything other than bad intentions. I'm thinking of kidnapping her when she gets back and ravishing her by candlelight for a few days. After that, we'll see."

"Mmmm—I approve." Her voice became more distant. "Good choice, Lunatic. I like this guy."

"What did you tell her?" Luna asked, her voice now filling the phone.

"It's a secret," he said. "She'll tell you later. I just told her the truth."

"What's the truth?"

Her absence stabbed him all of a sudden. "I love you, Luna, and I miss you like crazy." He hoped he disguised the crack in his voice.

"I love you too, sweetie." There was another pause, then Luna giggled. "Listen, I'd better go before my sister hurts herself. I'll call you tomorrow night. What time is your appointment?"

"Two o'clock."

"That's eleven here. Okay, I'll call in the evening probably. We're leaving Tuesday morning, and I don't know if we'll have good reception after that."

"I'll try too," he said. "They must have cell towers in wine country for the millionaires."

It was freezing in Schneider's office. Landon perched on the examining table, wearing only his underwear and a flimsy gown. He stared at his skinny legs and blue feet—discolored, he knew, from the pressure of the table on the veins of his legs as well as the chill in the room. It pleased him to realize he was still thinking like a doctor, although he was waiting—and freezing—like the patient he was.

Ten long minutes later, Schneider burst through the door, his dingy white coat flapping around his bulk. "Ratliff, good to see you." His voice was too loud for the small room, but Landon had anticipated and prepared for it. He knew any sign of sound sensitivity would make Schneider suspicious, so he smiled and greeted the neurosurgeon with far more enthusiasm than he felt.

Schneider hovered beside the examining table, making Landon feel especially scrawny. "You look pretty good, Ratliff," he said, turning to retrieve the chart from the desk. He thumbed through his notes, making declarations as he went: "Let's see. It's been nine weeks since the crash. Your last tests showed improvement." He set the chart down and fixed Landon with a searching gaze. "I talked with Fanning. You tried office work, but it didn't work out, right?"

"Yeah. I wasn't able to concentrate."

"Is that improving?"

"I think so. I can read."

"How's your comprehension?"

"Good, I think. No one quizzes me, though."

Schneider smiled. "We'll do that today. You feeling pretty good?"

"Yeah. Most of the time."

"What do you do all day?"

He shrugged. "Depends. I've been traveling a lot the past few weeks."

"Where'd you go?" The conversation seemed to be tiring Schneider. He glanced behind him, then used his arm like a divining rod to locate the desk chair. He pulled it close beside the examining table and sat.

"Well, I went to New Orleans for my ablation, then to Virginia to visit my parents."

Schneider was nodding now. "That's right—the tumor. That was a surprise, huh? I guess it's good that we found it. The procedure went okay?"

"Yeah, I think so. Prognosis is good, although it's cancer, so who knows?"

Schneider froze, no longer making eye contact, staring instead at the wall. "That's true, Ratliff." His eyes moved upward and fixed on Landon's. "That's true." He tossed the chart on the desk and rose abruptly, fishing in his coat pocket before pulling out a reflex hammer. "How's your memory? Anything coming back?"

Landon stared across the room, waiting for the bright light to hit his pupils. "Not really. I can remember things up until the evening before the crash and then after I woke up in the hospital. Nothing in between."

"Does this light bother you?" Schneider was swinging the light back and forth. Landon shook his head. "So you haven't really recovered any memory?"

"No. My girlfriend has told me some things. She was with me the night before, but I can't remember it."

"Are you sensitive to noise?"

"Not anymore. That's gotten a lot better, just like the light sensitivity."

"Good. How's your balance?"

"Fine, I think. Haven't noticed anything."

"Headaches?" Schneider was tapping the hammer against Landon's knees now, making his legs jump each time. Landon could tell his reflexes were fine.

"Yeah, still having them, although they're getting milder. Annoying, mostly."

Schneider paused, his hammer poised like a tomahawk above Landon's left arm. "Do you have them every day?"

"Pretty much. Not all day, though."

"What do you do for them?"

"Depends. I'll lie down if I don't have anything to do. Most of the time, I just live with it until it goes away."

"Hmm." Schneider's brow was almost always knitted, but now it looked a little tighter. He tested Landon's strength and his ability to feel pinpricks and feathery touches. He had him lie down and close his eyes then tested his ability to tell if his toe was being moved up or down. He tested coordination and balance. "Your exam is normal, Ratliff," Schneider said afterward. "Those headaches concern me, though. Should be gone by now. Let's do some more tests today. See how your thinking is doing."

Ninety minutes later, Schneider led him into his office, where what used to be a desktop now held a dumpster load of papers and charts and unopened mail. He sagged into his throne-like desk chair and held up Landon's test results.

"Good news, Ratliff," he said. "Your tests look fine. I think your noodle is about as good as ever, which may not be saying much." He smiled, and Landon felt compelled to return the sentiment. It was a lame joke, but perhaps all a neurosurgeon had in him. "The headaches and the memory loss are a little concerning, though. Here's what I recommend: you can go back to work part-time beginning next week—but no clinical work yet."

"Come on, Al. I feel fine. A little amnesia isn't so bad, is it?"

"Not so good either." He interlaced his sausage-sized fingers and rested his hands on a stack of papers. "Look, Ratliff, I think you're okay, but let's go slow. We don't want to find out you're not quite well at a patient's expense, do we? I want to see you in two weeks and see how things are going. I'll confirm with Fanning, so don't try to shit me. If everything goes well, you can start back on rotation in August."

"But the schedule will be made. I won't be able to do anything except fill in."

"Perfect. You can ease back into it." Schneider rose and led him to the door. "Enjoy your holiday, Ratliff. Don't get too impatient. You had a very serious head injury, and it looks like you're going to recover fully." He held the door and gave Landon a clap on the shoulder. "Three months might seem like an eternity, but consider the alternative. The nursing homes are full of people who weren't as lucky as you."

By the time he left Fanning's office, Landon would have put "lucky" at the bottom of a long list of adjectives describing how he was feeling at that moment. First, on the walk over to the divisional offices, he discovered that he had missed a call from Luna while he was taking the interminable neuropsychiatric tests. Then there was Fanning, fresh from his European vacation. He was thrilled with Landon's progress report and looked forward to welcoming him back the following Monday. The clinical schedule was covered through September, so no worries. That wasn't what Landon had wanted to hear. Neither had he wanted to relive the New Orleans experience. He omitted any mention of his trip home, not wanting to dive into that emotional swamp. The conversation eventually landed on Luna, which made him miss her even more. Fanning invited him over to his house on the Fourth, but Landon begged off, inventing a story about plans to drive down the coast and give his convertible a proper workout.

Dinner seemed like a chore. The thought of eating alone in a restaurant was unbearable. He thought Hazel might like some company, but she quickly disabused him of that idea. So he prowled around Luna's kitchen, hoping something might spark his appetite, and found a bottle of Prosecco in the refrigerator. He took the first glass out on the piazza and briefly considered trying to roust Luna's weird neighbor, John. That thought, which Landon took as evidence of his desperation, and the swampy evening air drove him back inside, where he sat in the living room, surrounded by evidence of Luna's absence, and stared at the evening news.

Cat food hitting the bowl flushed Hazel from her lair. She ate indolently while Landon prepared his own dinner: two pieces of butter-moistened, perfectly browned rye toast. Two attempts to call Luna failed while the Proseco disappeared. Darkness descended along with his mood, until finally, he joined Hazel on Luna's bed, falling into a drunken sleep atop the comforter.

He awoke with a sparkling wine headache, a perfect accompaniment to the unwashed feeling of having slept in his clothes, including shoes and socks. He imagined himself homeless as he struggled to lift his expanded, painful head from the pillow. His cell phone was on the floor, the ringer silenced, with two voicemails from Luna. Her oldest sister had had car trouble on the way to meet them. Luna had tried to call his house—twice. She hoped his doctor's appointment had gone well. She had left an itinerary with phone numbers on her bulletin board. She saved the best for last: "I love you."

She sounded tired, not drunk. There was no giggling, no catcalls in the background. The first message had come in at 1:00 a.m., which was 10 a.m. in California. The second at 9:00 a.m.

Why hadn't she thought to call here? He checked her home phone. There were no messages, and the list of missed calls on the screen began three weeks ago. The ringer was set to its lowest volume, as usual, because Hazel didn't like it.

It was almost ten. Landon remembered they'd left early to beat the traffic out of San Francisco after they picked up Sutter. He couldn't reach Luna on her cell phone. He checked the itinerary tacked on the corkboard in the kitchen. The hotel was in Sonoma. Luna's atlas was in the kitchen drawer, and he found the place on the map. They probably wouldn't be there until evening, what with the stops along the way.

Landon's stomach was sour, his head hurt, and he smelled like dirty laundry. His head felt like one of the surgical gloves he used to blow up and give to kids on the pediatric ward when he was in medical school. Did his father feel this way most mornings? Why would *anyone* drink like this regularly, if it made you feel so bad? Then a more troubling thought occurred to him: *Why would an alcoholic's son ever do this?* No, he wasn't going there right now. His immediate needs included breakfast, aspirin, a gallon of water, a shower, and a nap. He dropped into a chair and stared at his phone. He had plenty of time.

Chapter Twenty-Nine

Landon's wake-up call, literally and figuratively, came from his mother a few hours later. Their conversation, which suggested that his father was still nursing a grudge, solidified his decision to stay in Charleston over the holiday. His own unexpected resiliency provided further encouragement about his ability to function independently; the hangover had vanished. One final, failed attempt to reach Luna sealed it. He was on his own and tired of wallowing in loneliness. The emancipation plan came to him immediately: he needed a trip to Salty Mike's.

Two-dollar drafts and decent bar food provided a siren song for overworked, underpaid residents. Medical students, single nurses, and college kids rounded out the typical clientele, along with sailors and tourists and a few local degenerates. Throw in live music and sunsets over the Ashley River marina, and it all added up to one of Landon's favored hangouts, at least before the crash. Mike's opened at three, which was perfect for the day-shift nurses and everyone getting an early start before a rare weekend off.

Not wanting to appear desperate for fun, Landon took his time getting ready; no sense being the first one in the door.

Besides, things never got going until four or after. Walking would kill more time and eliminate the risk of driving after drinking. He took a long, roundabout route across the peninsula, stopping first at Luna's to attend to Hazel. Despite the midsummer heat and humidity, he arrived at Mike's feeling invigorated. Schneider had recommended more exercise, said it helped with brain injuries. Maybe he wasn't up to running yet, but there was no reason not to take some long walks. On the way over, Landon had resolved to get moving. It wasn't as if he didn't have the time.

He had time for other things too. The procedure had been a success, so was he really a cancer patient now? A survivor, but how many people even knew? Except for a small scar, he didn't look any different. Today, he was Landon Ratliff, finally recovered from a bad car crash, heading back to work Monday. It was the Fourth of July holiday, and he was in Charleston—things could be a lot worse.

He circled the building, a two-story, nondescript structure tucked into the marina complex and separated from the river by a wide swath of fontina grass. The back deck was sparsely populated. The live music didn't start until six. It was still early. He turned north, thinking he'd wander up to the ballpark or maybe to the Citadel campus. It had been a while since he'd been there. He could get some more walking in, and the tidiness and order of the campus was comforting sometimes.

He hadn't gone two blocks before his mind starting drifting back to cancer and brain injury. Solitude suddenly seemed a bigger risk than a small bar crowd, so he reversed course again, determined to take a few steps in the direction of the guy he used to be.

The glare from the river-facing windows illuminated the back of the room, but the bar and tables remained enveloped in gloomy tavern light. There was a rank smell of stale beer and burned oil; rock music wafted through the room at pre-crowd volume while four guys were setting up to play on the stage in the corner. He recognized a girl at the bar, a social worker from the hospital, but he couldn't remember her name. She might know his, so he slid onto a barstool one removed from hers and ordered a beer.

"Dr. Ratliff," she said. The gamble had paid off. "How've you been? We've missed you."

"I'm fine." He smiled. "I'm sorry, but you're new, aren't you? I don't remember your name."

"Oh, that's okay. I started in March, and I just fill in in the ICU. I'm Shannon. We didn't work together much before the accident. Everyone misses you, though. When are you coming back?"

"Well, I'm starting back in the office Monday. Back on service next month."

"That's great." She introduced her boyfriend and his two friends, all students from the College of Charleston, hanging around for the holiday without definite plans or worry about making any. Landon remembered being that way long ago. The conversation honed in on the car crash pretty quickly, and since he was talking to college kids, he neither expected nor received any difficult questions about the impact on his life. He was right where he wanted to be, among those for whom bad or serious news was an intrusion, and his offer to buy the next round not only changed the subject but also elevated his status from victim to benefactor.

By 4:30 p.m., the crowd was swelling noticeably. Apparently anticipating the arrival of more colleagues, Shannon suggested a move to the deck before all the tables were claimed. She chose one of the largest, next to the rail. Landon waylaid the waitress and started a tab, waving off the protests from his adopted tribe. Things continued to look up when two physical therapists arrived, followed by several nurses who knew him well. The beer wasn't going down that well after a couple nights of heavy drinking, but he drank enough to at least begin feeling clever and witty. By the third round, though, he was nursing his beer. His stomach reminded him that he needed to eat. Everyone was ordering, so he got the fish and chips, and when he finished that off, he needed to pee. He was shaking his hands, cursing whoever was supposed to keep the towel dispenser filled, when a low, throaty chuckle from the ladies' room line stopped him in his tracks.

"Hope that's water you're shaking off." Terri Blair had snaked a hand between the buttons on his shirt, trapping herself in the fabric and forcing Landon to turn or else risk tearing his clothing. "Who you here with?" Her hand was either asking a question or delivering an invitation or both.

"Bunch of folks from the hospital are out on the deck," he replied. "I got a chair for you." She seemed to have grown several inches since their last meeting. His eyes roamed past her midnight-blue gauzy top and skimpy white shorts. She was wearing red sandals that strapped around her ankle and had a heel not made for walking. Her long legs were fiercely tanned. Everything about her screamed danger, but that had always been true, had always been what attracted him to Terri.

"Perfect. I came with Jenn and Emily—from the ICU."

He smiled. "Bring 'em over." He left her waiting and wandered back through the crowd.

He was grateful for Shannon's foresight. They had a plum table with a perfect view of the silvery river, framed by the fontina grass and a palm tree or two. The sinking sun was just beginning to tinge the sky. The James Island Bridge might have marred the scene, but Landon had grown used to seeing it, and it reminded him how fortunate he was to live in a busy city with such beautiful vistas.

By now, the table was nothing more than a landing place for cups and cans and baskets of fried food. A social version of musical chairs refreshed and replenished the occupants, and Landon took advantage of an exodus to the dance floor to claim four chairs along the rail. Jenn and Emily, familiar coworkers, arrived clutching colorful frozen drinks in tall island glasses. They greeted him with welcome enthusiasm.

"Where's Terri?" Landon asked, once they had settled into their seats.

Jenn fanned herself with a menu. "Not sure. She said she'd be right out."

"How've you been, Dr. Ratliff?" Emily asked.

"Fine. Feeling better every day. I'm coming back to work, in the office Monday. And what's with the *doctor* crap?"

Emily blushed. She was tall and thin, with auburn hair and caramel eyes. "Sorry. Landon."

"That's better. I didn't know you guys still hung out with Terri."

"We meet her here pretty regularly, now that she's back in Charleston," Jenn said. She was shorter, with an easy smile and more outgoing personality. Both she and Emily were top-notch nurses.

Terri arrived, right on cue, carrying a tray of Jell-O shots. "Let's get this sunset celebration started," she announced. It was an eager holiday crowd; no one demurred. Against his better judgment, Landon allowed Terri to feed him a shot, which tasted horrible, a gelatinous mixture of licorice, cough syrup, and burnt rubber.

He chased it with a long shot of beer, which was only marginally more palatable. "I thought you liked me," he sputtered.

Terri's grin spread like an oil slick on a calm bay. "Jägermeister. You'll get used to it, Doctor. It's good for you."

He was pretty sure he didn't want to get used to it. The toxic drink burned all the way to his stomach, then spread upward to his brain like a mushroom cloud. Just before his mind vaulted over the edge into space with no turning back, he had one last flash of insight.

"Here, Terri," he said, getting to his feet. "I'll get the next round. You sit here."

She accepted with a sidelong glance and a smile. He weaved through the crowd, grabbed a water at the bar, and headed out the front door, trading the saloon cacophony for the ponderous calm of the riverside twilight. The sky was a riot of pink, supported by the golden glow of the dying sun. The Ashley River was shimmering silver, framed by the boats and masts and palms.

It was still late afternoon in California, but he might get lucky. Luna's phone didn't even ring, so he tried the hotel. The Quinn party had not yet arrived. He declined the offer to leave a message. Luna was having a good time, and it was a holiday, after all. She could try him later or not. If he was gone much longer, Terri would come looking, and he didn't want to be found here. Besides, he owed his crew some shots, and he owed himself some fun.

Terri jumped up and took the tray from him when he returned. "Let me serve those for you, Doctor. Sit right down." She waved off his protest, then leaned in and whispered, "I thought you'd run off on me." A low, soft half laugh, half moan accompanied the glance that she left him to ponder while she distributed the shots.

"Take my seat, Terri," Landon offered when it was his turn. She frowned as he dodged her attempt to nudge him back into the chair. It seemed unwise to let her sit in his lap in front of all these people. Both her hands were occupied with shots.

"Here, let me feed you one." He relieved her of one of the shots as she dropped into the vacant chair. She clutched at his shirt but gave up and obediently tipped her head to accept her dose of trouble.

"Yum. Your turn, Doctor."

He shook his head and hoisted his beer can. "No thanks. That stuff tastes like gasoline. I'll stick with this."

Her chin dove into her shoulder, and she glanced sidelong at him. "Okay, lightweight. One of us has to drive, I guess."

He smiled. "And one of us has to drink." He tipped the second shot into her eager mouth. The feel of her lips and wandering tongue grazing his fingers reminded him that the guy he used to be never went to bars for the alcohol, anyway.

It was too dark to see much of anything. He was glad he'd paced himself drinking; he'd learned long ago that maintaining a tipsy state not only made him feel giddy and clever, but also enhanced tactile sensations. Terri's skin felt warm and enticingly damp. Her swaying hips caused her legs to brush against his, never disengaging for more than a second or two. With every breath, her breasts rose against his chest.

Earlier, he had allowed Jenn and then Emily to coax him onto the dance floor, where they had drilled him relentlessly in the fundamentals of shag dancing. All the while, Terri sat smiling and drinking until the band began a long, slow number, which seemed to be her cue to rise and lead him wordlessly to the dance floor for what had turned into a full-body sexy slow dance.

Her shoes, not fit for dancing unless a pole was involved, elevated Terri to the perfect height. His hands rested in the uncovered small of her back while her fingers roamed, alternately finding his ear or the hairs at the base of his neck. When her cheek grazed his, he tensed briefly, then felt her lips brushing his. She pressed closer, and a soft moan escaped from her lips.

Her mouth smelled and tasted like a stale ashtray.

He turned his head and pressed hers into his shoulder. The song would end soon; if he could just buy some time. Terri slithered against him, and her hand tucked into the back of his pants at his belt line. He held her tight, praying she wouldn't go for his zipper. At last, the lights came up, and he broke free, looped an arm around her waist, and guided her back to the safety of the table.

In the time it took Landon to swish the nasty taste of cigarette out of his mouth, he'd formulated a plan. Terri cooperated by bouncing out of her seat and announcing to the table that she had to use the restroom. A glance confirmed his hope—the line looked to be three or four women long. That would give him time.

The Irish goodbye would get him away quickly and leave no accomplices subject to Terri's legendary interrogation skills. No one would know anything. They'd probably assume he'd had too much to drink. He couldn't skip out on the bill, though, so after excusing himself to no one in particular, he located the waitress, detoured briefly to the bar and paid the tab to that point, then hustled out the door without looking back.

The night air was thick and still. Afraid to pause, he crossed the lot, still smacking his lips, trying to work up some saliva to dilute the musty taste of cigarette breath. He'd forgotten how much he disliked that taste and forgotten how the lure of uncommitted sex had allowed him to overlook it in the past. For a moment, he considered continuing north into the medical center complex, where cabs were sometimes waiting for a late fare, then thought better of it and headed east on Calhoun, never hazarding a glance backward until he was almost to the college.

What had he been thinking? Or more to the point, why hadn't he been thinking? He never wanted this. A little fun, sure, but had he really thought a night flirting and even grinding with a woman like Terri was okay? He couldn't blame the drinking, although he was beginning to think he needed to cool it. He hadn't had that much tonight. So what was he trying to prove? That he was still Landon Ratliff, free and easy Landon, out for a good time? That a car wreck, a head injury, a tumor, and most important, a fun, funny, smart, and beautiful redhead hadn't changed everything? No, he should have known what he knew for sure now: he wasn't that guy anymore, and thanks to the redhead, he was glad.

His phone buzzed. It was her.

"Hey, sweetie," Luna said. Her voice sounded far brighter and cheerier than he felt. He checked his watch—it was about 9:30 p.m. in California. "I'm so glad I caught you. We just got here. Whatcha doin'?"

"Nothing much. How's the trip?"

"Ahh. Okay, I guess. Sutter is being a pain in the ass, but nothing new there. Tule's car broke down coming through the mountains. That was a cluster, but we figured it out."

"That's good." He turned south on King, heading toward home. "I miss you. Hazel misses you too. She's fine, by the way."

"I miss you too. To be honest, I'm about ready to come home."

"I could pick you up," Landon said.

"Did I wake you up?" Luna asked. "I tried your home phone, but you didn't answer."

"No, I'm not home yet. I went out tonight, to Salty Mike's. You know, over by the marina. Just now heading home." One semihonest answer made him feel better, but not much. No cabs in sight. "What did you say?"

"I said I'm glad you went out. Was it fun?"

"It was okay."

"Are you drunk? You sound funny."

He took another peek. "No. Well, I had a little beer. Some people from the hospital were there, and they bought shots. I had one, but it was awful."

"Tell me what the doctor said. The suspense is killing me."

"Good news. Back to work part-time Monday, and then—"

Luna's screech made him jerk the phone away from his ear. "That's fantastic! Hooray, I've been hoping for this! Wait till I tell my sisters. They are probably so sick of hearing me talk about you, but I don't care." She paused for a breath, seemed to gather herself. "I'm so happy for you, Landon. I love you."

"Thanks, I love you too."

"Listen, I better get going. You get home safely and get to bed. Any plans for tomorrow?"

"Not really. I might go to the beach."

"No looking at girls in skimpy bikinis." She was laughing.

"Okay. You stay away from those surfer guys."

"That's *southern* California. I'm going to have to bring you out here."

He stepped aside to let a young couple pass. "Okay, Luna. Have fun, and call me when you can. I love you." He stared at the phone, his alcohol level seeming to plummet by the second. How could he have been so stupid?

He had felt free tonight, free of the worries and concerns that had dogged him for the past few months. But then he'd gone too far with a woman whose alcohol-fueled motivation was a night of pleasure, no strings attached. The same formula he'd followed for most of his adult life. Except now he wasn't obligation-free and didn't want to be. Another casualty of time, but one Landon thought he had happily accepted. How could he have done this? Why would he?

His mind was not capable of deep reflection, but he suddenly felt very tired. So he stood on the sidewalk, looking north, hoping to spot a cab looking for a fare. Maybe he'd get lucky. If not, a two-mile walk served him right.

CHAPTER THIRTY

Luna came home on Sunday. She had declined Landon's offer to pay the difference for an earlier flight. He was disappointed but recognized that his offer was only partially motivated by a genuine desire to see her. Guilt was an important contributor as well, but by Sunday he had wrestled with his conscience enough to arrive at a somewhat peaceful resolution. Most important, he had resolved not to confess.

In Landon's mind, he had made a mistake but had not gone too far and therefore was not required to make a full disclosure or confession that would only invite suspicion and damage the relationship unnecessarily. It had been an accidental meeting, and his judgment was impaired by loneliness and alcohol. He hoped he had learned his lesson about both. One thing was clear—the near-miss had resolved any lingering doubt about his self-identity. Gone was the emotionally distant womanizer seeking shallow, temporary gratification. That guy didn't exist anymore, and Landon was certain his transformation owed more to Luna than it did to his injuries and cancer.

The drinking was harder to rationalize. He'd been drunk or drinking every night since Luna left, another binge close on the heels of the sloshed weekend with Amy and Enrique and the trip to New Orleans. Since he had always been a careful drinker with occasional exceptions and now had a still-damaged brain and a friend entering rehab, not to mention an alcoholic father who'd turned their family life into a hellish nightmare, it seemed that he ought to know better.

By Saturday, he had recovered sufficiently to turn his attention to preparing for Luna's return. There wasn't much to do at her apartment, but he washed the few dishes he'd dirtied and remade the bed so it would be fresh and welcoming for her. While he was tidying up the piazza, the idea of fresh flowers came to him, so he ran to the florist and got a colorful arrangement in a white seashell bowl for Luna's kitchen.

On Sunday, he sifted and cleaned Hazel's litter pan—a job he would not miss—for the last time and supplied her with food and water. A trip to the grocery yielded the ingredients for one of Luna's favorite meals: cold pasta with shrimp and mandarin oranges. He was capable of making a salad to go with the pasta, and a quart of peach ice cream took care of dessert. He made a pitcher of fresh iced tea and added mint from Luna's container garden.

His breath caught in his throat when she appeared at the airport wearing his favorite pale-blue dress. Her smiling, freckly, crinkly-nose face beckoned to him, actually gave him goose bumps, and his legs were pulling him toward her as if she'd been gone for months or years. He reveled in the smell of her perfume, the milky feel of her skin, and then finally, the taste of her baby-soft lips.

"I missed you," she said. Her eyes sagged; they had lost a little of their usual sparkle.

"You look beautiful," he said. "Welcome home." He took her hand. "Things haven't felt right without you. Feels like home again."

She leaned her head against his. "It does. I wondered before this trip, but not anymore." She lifted his hand to her lips. "This is where I belong."

"Not California?"

She shook her head. A faint, confident smile lit her face. "No. Not anymore. I still love it, but it's not for me." She squeezed his hand. "I'll take Charleston."

He pulled her close. "Charleston is very glad to hear that."

The ride home was uneventful. Hazel was a cat's version of overjoyed to see Luna; she stared and stayed in the room while Luna teared up over the bouquet and the dinner plan. After another long kiss that suggested more than hello, Landon poured tea while Luna bundled Hazel into her lap for some cuddling on the sofa.

"I think Hazel is glad to see you," he said, handing Luna a glass topped with a fresh lemon slice.

"Such a sweet kitty. I missed her almost as much as I missed you."

He settled in next to Luna and focused on her neck; she leaned into his hand and closed her eyes while he massaged. Hazel took the hint finally and sashayed off like a prudish grandma when Luna's arm encircled Landon's neck. Her kiss was more tender than urgent but was just what he needed.

"How about a nap?" he whispered. Her smile seemed ambivalent but in no way threatening. "A real nap, I mean. I know you're tired. I'll leave you alone, I promise."

She leaned away. The corners of her mouth tilted downward. "That's no fun."

Landon stood and pulled her to her feet. "Don't worry. Once you've rested up, I plan to feed you and then get busy making you feel much better."

"It's a deal, Doc. I look forward to a long, slow recovery."

He led her to the bedroom. "Yes. It may take all night, but I'll give you my full attention."

They stretched out on the bed under a thin blanket, removing only their shoes. Luna's eyelids seemed heavy, and Landon watched as her breathing settled into a drowsy rhythm. Her placid face exuded serenity, echoing his own sense of total fulfillment.

He lay quietly, watching her, hoping she was dreaming of him, of them. The evening faded into twilight while they rested, until finally he eased himself out of bed to go and prepare dinner. He would let Luna sleep. Might make for a more energetic night, which sounded good to him, back to work tomorrow or not.

He woke her just before he put the pasta on to boil. She smiled and blushed when she saw the table settings, the bouquet, and a salad with sliced cucumbers and tomatoes arranged carefully on top. They sat and sipped tea while the pasta cooled in the refrigerator.

"Tell me about your trip," Landon said. "You haven't said much."

She shrugged. "It was okay. Not as good as I'd hoped, though. We're all so different. I'm not sure why I ever thought I could pull this off."

"You did pull it off."

"Well, I got everyone together, but it wasn't exactly a warm, fuzzy reunion."

"I think that might be asking too much." He rose and retrieved the pasta. "You broke the ice, so maybe next year will be better. Besides, it sounded like you and Fox were having a good time."

Luna smiled. "We did. I love her. She is so fun, even if she *is* obsessed with money and things. But I'm not sure there'll be a next year for this."

"Really? That bad?"

"Not awful, but it's a lot of work, and a lot of time and emotional energy. And Sutter and Tule, they just don't care. It's pretty obvious. Tule's all right—she's just the oldest, always was pretty independent, but we almost seem like strangers to her. Sutter's just a bitch. I'm sorry, but there's no other way to put it. She's mad at the world, and anything connected to her past is the enemy." She took a long swallow of tea. "Mom and Dad are at the top of her list, and we're right below them."

He tonged salad onto the plates, alongside the pasta. "What's bugging her?"

Luna pursed her lips, then shrugged. "Who really knows? It isn't just her sexuality. None of us care about that anyway. It's her whole life, the way she sees everything." She smiled broadly. "Fox told her she looks at life through shit-colored glasses."

Landon laughed and raised his glass. "Well, I say good effort. You got it done, and if it doesn't happen again, at least you tried. I can't imagine ever getting my brother and sister together."

For a few moments, they ate in silence broken only by Luna's moans of approval, accompanied by a tilt of her head and her soft hand stroking Landon's forearm. She was obviously famished, so he left her to the food. It was good to share a meal with her again.

"How's your father?" she asked. "Did you ever speak with him?"

He shook his head. "No. I talked to Dale on Wednesday morning. My parents went to his place for the Fourth. Dale said Dad's fine. My name comes up in conversation. He's still a little pissed about the drinking comments but getting better."

"You didn't talk with him on the Fourth? How about your mom?"

"Yeah, I talked with her, but my dad was resting, and she didn't want to disturb him. She said he wasn't eating well and seemed tired. Dale said he was all right, though."

"I bet your mom knows better."

"No doubt."

"You haven't talked to them since?"

"No. I was busy getting ready for you to come home." He hoped she'd let his lame excuse pass, but he knew better.

"You afraid to call him?"

"I don't know. Maybe. Not sure."

"How about tonight?"

"Tonight's for us." He refilled their glasses. "How was Sonoma?"

Luna paused. He figured her silence indicated that he was off the hook but only for the time being. Finally, she smiled. "It was beautiful. The weather was perfect, and the Merlot was fabulous. That was one thing we all agreed about. I'm shipping some back." She raised her hands above her plate. "This is so good, Landon. It was so sweet of you."

"My pleasure. Did your parents make it to the dinner?"

"Yes. We had a great vegetarian meal at one of the wineries. It was outside, at a long table under a pergola in the vineyard. Beautiful, and the food and wine were incredible."

"Sounds nice."

"It was. But of course, my parents found a way to make it weird. They talked incessantly about one of my old boyfriends. I guess they'd run into him recently."

"Old boyfriend?" He hoped he wasn't blushing. "Have you mentioned him?"

"I doubt it. I met him in college. We dated for a couple years."

"A couple years? That sounds serious."

Luna shrugged. "Off and on. Nothing seemed serious back then."

"Why'd you break up?"

"I met another guy and realized I didn't want to be tied down. Just didn't work out. You know."

"So is he still pining away for you?"

That comment earned him a flat-eyed look from Luna. "Are you serious? You sound like my parents. He's married."

"Happily?"

"Stop, Landon, please. I had to put up with my sisters kidding me about this for two days. I just thought it was weird, that's all."

"They just ran into him," he said, struggling to leave it alone. "Why is that weird?" Something didn't feel right to him. Was he jealous?

Luna was staring at him, her eyes full of—what? Not anger or pain. Not betrayal either, or was it? He waited, his throat dry, the memory of Salty Mike's arising unbidden in his mind.

"I thought it was weird," she said. "My mom always loved Dylan—that's his name, Dylan Graham—but it's been years, and she knows I'm involved with you."

He thought he was stone-faced, but Luna dispelled that notion when her eyes went wide. She reached over to stroke his face. Her hand felt soft and cool; he caught her thumb gently between his lips. "Are you okay, sweetie? Nothing happened."

He tried to sound casual. "That's your business. I didn't mean to pry."

"You weren't prying. Nothing happened. It *is* your business, and I want you to know."

"Did you guys talk about me?" He wanted to steer this conversation in another direction—fast.

"We did. Fox is a big fan. You really wowed her on the phone. Sutter was negative, as usual. Kept kidding me about trying to snag a doctor. Tule didn't say too much and neither did my father. Mom kept blabbing about Dylan."

"Why was she so crazy about him?"

Luna shrugged. "Probably because he was earthy, like her. She came to visit once when we were dating, and they hit it off, talking about baking their own bread or something. That stuff drove me crazy." She rose from the table and began collecting the plates. "I'm doing the dishes," she said. Her kiss carried a hint of onion and garlic. "You sit." Then she set the plates down and dropped into his lap, circling his neck with both arms. "I missed you so much, Landon," she whispered, planting soft kisses on his ear and cheek. She leaned back and stared into his eyes. Her freckled nose and smiling lips erased all doubts. The sharp stab of jealousy, a fair price to pay to assuage the guilt that had not completely vanished, was fading. He could deal with the guilt. There was no point in introducing doubt, because if he'd ever had any, he sure didn't now.

CHAPTER THIRTY-ONE

Work went fine on Monday; the office welcomed him back with a lunchtime celebration attended by most of the pulmonary division's physicians, including the new fellows and residents. The attending physicians were just back from holiday, so some of them hadn't yet welcomed the new trainees. This diverted some attention from Landon's return, which suited him and made the day fly by more quickly. Fanning had conspired with Schneider to establish a strict schedule for the first two weeks, so Landon had barely dented his email by the time Fanning shooed him home.

On Tuesday, he received a call from radiology. Dr. Lake's office had arranged a follow-up MRI to be done at MUSC on July 18. The scheduler, for whom this task was but one of many that day, collected the demographic information in a businesslike and compassion-free way, which again suited Landon. He was eager to shed the role of patient and return to his accustomed and more comfortable life, at least as much as his disease and its required monitoring would allow.

Later that afternoon he received a second call that would derail his return to normalcy.

"Your daddy is back in the hospital," his mother told him. She sounded more fatigued than fearful. "He woke up with yellow jaundice this morning. His stomach is hurting awful bad."

"Want me to come home?"

"No, baby. You just got back to work. I'll let you know what the tests show."

He was relieved and felt a little guilty for being so. Jaundice was worrisome, though. Might be from drinking, but his mother claimed he hadn't been drinking that much. The other possibilities were not good at all. "Okay, Mom," he said. "You doing all right?"

"I'm fine—worried and tired, nothing I'm not used to." There was a brief pause then, "Landon, listen. Carla's here. She and Sally are taking me out for dinner. Just us three girls. I'll call you tomorrow. You take care of yourself and hug Luna for me."

How had it never occurred to him? Worried and tired pretty much described his life for the past few months, and yet he hadn't connected those emotions to his mother, whose concerns, unlike his own, seemed directed almost exclusively to others—to her husband, her parents, and to him. No doubt to Molly, her lost daughter, whose absence from her life had to be a wound that refused to heal.

It had been so easy for Landon to justify his actions. After all, he called her every few days. He was a busy doctor, and besides, he'd bought her a car and sent money regularly. He lived far away. It wasn't as if he could just run up to Virginia whenever he liked. Dale was there; he was the one who always knew what to do. And now after the crash, well, a head injury and cancer ...

None of it sounded convincing. Excuses never did, whether they came from a resident who hadn't been diligent enough or from a self-absorbed son who didn't want to face up to his past. He owed his mother, and himself, more than this.

He awoke the next morning resolved to be the son both his father and mother needed. A son more like Dale, steady and dependable. He began by searching for his brittle, faded address book, rarely needed but not yet completely obsolete. The book had been a valuable reference for mailing Christmas cards during the brief period when he had felt obligated to send them. Just the place he might have written down Molly's phone number, if he'd ever had it.

He found the book, but it was no help, at least not for Molly's contact information. It contained the address and phone number for Dale's first apartment and for Mike Fanning's place in New Orleans. Just below that was Enrique's first house in Florida. That discovery reminded him he needed to check in with Amy, and after promising himself to do it later, he went ahead and called, a low-risk test of his nascent transformation. He got voicemail and left a message. Afterward, he refused to flog himself for the relief he felt at not having to actually speak with her; he was in new territory, and at least he had made contact. Amy would appreciate it, he hoped, and would surely return his call.

Dale might have Molly's number, but with their father once again in the hospital, such a request might cause more family chaos, and Landon most definitely did not want that. He had not spoken with Dale about Molly for years. It would not surprise him if he discovered that Dale had somehow kept in touch with her, although she never seemed to have any special relationship with Dale. Now, though, Landon wondered if he would have noticed such a relationship and had to conclude that he probably wouldn't have done so. Was it possible that his mother kept up with Molly too? He didn't think so, though he hadn't taken the time to talk with her about it. He had thought it too painful, too raw a subject, but for whom?

The answers to those questions would have to wait. On his third day in the office, Landon was making real progress on his email backlog. And then, late morning, the phone rang.

"Landon. Walter Denbigh." His tone drove any hope out of Landon's mind. "I need to talk with you about your dad."

A hole was opening up in Landon's chest. He reminded himself to breathe. "What did the tests show?"

"Well, the enzymes showed an obstructive pattern, so we did some imaging."

Landon knew Denbigh was spoon-feeding the news, allowing each sip to sink in before adding another dose. Obstruction meant something was blocking the liver, making its chemicals back up into the blood, causing jaundice. Might be gallstones, but Denbigh would have said that right away. "I'm listening, Walter. Go ahead."

Landon heard an exhale. "There's a mass, Landon. The CT isn't definitive, but it doesn't look good."

"Liver cancer?"

"Maybe. MRI is being done now, but I think he'll need a biopsy. I'd like to transfer him."

"To the VA?"

"No, probably to the Medical College of Virginia. The VA's been full and backed up most of this month. I think he'd be better off at MCV. The VA will approve it, I'm sure."

"Have you told my mom?"

"Not yet. I'm waiting on the MRI. I'll tell her this afternoon, on rounds."

"Is my brother with her?"

"No, I haven't seen him. He may have visited last night."

"Look, Walter." His voice was as shaky as his hands now. He tried to breathe through the anxiety, but the air didn't seem to want to go in or out. "I can be on the road in an hour or so. Can you wait until tomorrow to tell my mother? I'd like to be with her."

"I don't know, Landon. I talked with her this morning. She's expecting to hear something this afternoon. I don't want to stall or lie to her."

Landon knew he was right. "Well, maybe I can stop on the way and call so I can be on the phone when you tell her."

"Don't stress yourself. I don't want you driving any more distracted than you already will be. You'll be here, what, around seven?"

"Easily by then. I'm leaving as soon as I talk to my boss."

"Okay, let's plan to meet in my office at seven thirty."

"That's nice of you, Walter. Sorry to keep you late."

"It's no problem. I wish the news were better. I'll let your mother know when we're meeting."

He sat silently in his office after closing the door, searching without success for the imperturbability that he had cultivated during his training and throughout his career. He had things to do—speak with Mike, pack, break the news to Luna—but he couldn't, not right away. He sat trembling, his heart racing, tears filling his eyes. Nausea flared, but the feeling passed. An unsteadiness gripped him, as if he were on rough seas. His life, and everything in it, had come unmoored with one phone call, with three words: "There's a mass."

He'd heard them before, about a mass in his own kidney, and thought nothing could be worse than that. But that had been different. Scary, but buffered by astonishment. Harder to grasp and therefore easier to shrug off somehow. Denial was plausible, even in the face of evidence to the contrary. The news about his father was more like a feared visitor, finally come to call. A known threat, suppressed by its absence, but lurking nevertheless. His father had not heeded the warnings, had taunted the visitor. Even Landon had let his guard down, until at last, now here was the knock on the door. The visitor, come to collect. Landon knew what a mass in the liver meant. Barring a miracle, his father would die, and quickly.

He began typing "primary liver carcinoma" into the search bar on his computer screen and then stopped. He stared at the cursor—flashing, waiting, appearing, and reappearing—then closed the window and turned away. He didn't want to research the prognosis, didn't want to read about the treatment, didn't want to be the doctor. Not now. For now, for as long as he had left, Landon wanted to be his father's son.

Denbigh's face was sagging behind the kind smile he offered when Landon arrived at his office. His mother had walked over from the hospital and greeted him with a broken, needy hug lasting long enough to indicate that she suspected the worst. His decision to drive up had confirmed her fears. He had not formulated a plan to break the news to her; he would leave that to his father's doctor.

Despite his obvious fatigue, Denbigh's voice was even and reassuring, filled with the equanimity both he and Landon had been trained to maintain and for which Landon had developed a newfound appreciation these last few months. His mother's voice was halting and fragile. She shouldn't have been left alone all day, but Landon could not fault Dale, who probably didn't know the latest news. Carla was busy with Sally. Molly surely didn't know, but Landon couldn't think about her right now.

He listened to Denbigh setting the stage by telling the story of his father's illness, recounting familiar details, allowing his mother to begin to anticipate the answers she did not really want to acknowledge.

"The CT scan showed some kind of growth in the liver, which is probably what caused his jaundice," Denbigh said as he approached the climax of the story. "We did an MRI to try and see what was going on in more detail. The MRI shows a fairly large tumor in the center of his liver, in the area where the gallbladder and the veins of the liver come together."

The silence of his pause was suffocating. "I wish I had better news," Denbigh said, "but it looks like cancer." Another brief pause. "We'll need to do more tests to be certain, but the radiologist thinks it looks like cholangiocarcinoma, which means cancer of the bile duct."

Landon's chest seemed to cave in, as if he'd been kicked. He remembered caring for a patient with cholangiocarcinoma in medical school. Out of earshot of the patient, the attending physician had pronounced the disease "uniformly lethal."

Landon had learned later that the chances of survival were less than five in one hundred and that survivors were usually young, diagnosed early and by chance—a clinical story very much like his own. Not at all like his father's.

He watched Denbigh offering tissues, heard his mother's soft sobbing, but could not find the strength to be fully present. His mind was reeling, careening from medical school to the bedside of all the suffering patients he'd cared for, to their shattered families desperate for miracles, for comfort, for something. He heard his mother's questions, directed to both Denbigh and to him. He allowed Denbigh to answer; that was his job, though Landon knew he wouldn't be able to just play the role of the son.

"I think we need to transfer Mr. Ratliff to MCV," Denbigh said. "They've got more experience with this type of disease. They'll be able to decide which specific treatment is best for him."

"I agree with Dr. Denbigh, Mom," Landon said. Then, anticipating her next question, he asked Denbigh, "When do you think he should go?"

"I'll call tonight. He should be able to go first thing in the morning. He's strong enough to make the trip and the sooner the better. He'll need a biopsy to confirm the diagnosis before they can start on the treatment plan."

Landon expected more questions, but none came, and he couldn't think of any that would be helpful. Denbigh's chair squeaked softly as he stood. He circled the desk and laid a hand on Landon's mother's shoulder. "I'm going to step out for a few moments and let you folks talk in private. Take your time. I know this is difficult."

It got very quiet then. "Mom?" Landon asked, finally risking a glance at her.

"I'm here, baby." Her voice was stronger now, buttressed, he knew, by the need to be a mother. She reached for his hand. "I need a favor."

"Sure—anything, Mom. What is it?"

"It's Dale. He knows this is bad. Can you talk to him? I can't explain all this."

"Of course. I'll call him tonight."

He was surprised to see a hint of a smile cross her face. "You don't need to, baby. He'll be here in the morning."

"He's taking off work?"

"You did, Landon. When Dale heard you were coming, he made up his mind." She looked almost happy. "I thought you two might want to go fishing."

Landon nodded. The few deep conversations they'd had over the years had taken place in a boat. "Maybe so, Mom. I'll ask him."

"I already did. He thought it was a great idea."

CHAPTER THIRTY-TWO

The York River was smaller than he'd remembered. Sitting in the bow seat, facing backward toward Dale, who handled the outboard like a fine instrument, Landon took in the changes along the riverbank with more regret than he would have expected. Houses, yards, and docks had devoured the woods and fields where he and Dale had played as boys. Cigarette boats and sleek sailing vessels were tied up next to strings of garish-colored floats that laid claim to vast swaths of the river as private swimming areas.

The sky, like everything else in Landon's world, it seemed, had looked threatening all morning. He hoped it wouldn't rain because that would force him and Dale together, and history had taught him that Dale would shut down in that circumstance. Space and physical activity were prerequisites for serious conversation.

"Adams Creek?" Landon shouted above the roar of the outboard.

Dale nodded, then added, "Just south of there, in the marshes. I took some nice croaker a few weeks ago. Hope it's not crawling with boats."

He knew what Dale meant—the word got out whenever the fishing was good—but he also knew his brother wasn't one to talk about what he caught. He recalled Dale's standard reply to any queries about the quality of the fishing. He'd pause, raise his chin just a little, and say, "Oh, we caught a few." Landon had wanted to pull the stringer up and show off what they'd caught or complain about the lack of action, but Dale had stopped him the first time and never had to tell him again. That's the way it was with Dale. He needed to tell you only once.

The water was the color of weak coffee but clear. That was good for fishing. They had a foam cooler full of squid and a larger cooler full of sandwiches and drinks. Landon's old rod and Zebco 33 reel looked like an antique next to Dale's latest purchases. His brother could catch fish with a hand line, but fishing was his passion, and Carla indulged his infrequent requests for new equipment without complaint.

The marshes around Adams Creek were busy but only with wildlife. A great blue heron lifted off as they approached. Dale maneuvered the boat into position and signaled to drop the anchor. Dale always insisted on rigging up the rods before departing, so they only had to add squid to the hook, and their lines were in the water right away. It felt good to be out with his brother; they hadn't fished together for two or three years. Each time out reminded him that fishing and baseball had endured as the lights that illuminated whatever brotherly affection had survived through the years.

They fished in silence for a few minutes. Landon missed a light strike then wondered if it had been a snag instead. He was eager, as always, to impress his brother. Dale finally landed a croaker too small for eating. He unhooked it and tossed it back.

"Not going to keep it for bait?" Landon asked.

Dale shook his head. "Haven't seen any drum caught up here for a couple years. Too many boats now."

Leaden purplish clouds seemed to be descending to treetop level. Poor fishing and threatening weather might scuttle the trip, so Landon figured now was the time to continue the conversation he'd begun on the ride to the river.

"Dad's pretty sick, you know," he said, without facing Dale.

"Yeah, sounds like."

"Gonna be bad, I think."

"Cancer's like that, isn't it?"

Landon turned. Dale was squinting off toward shore. "What about you?" Dale asked. "How are you doing with yours?" He rotated his head so his gaze rested on Landon. The squint remained. "You aren't going to leave me, are you, Brother?"

Landon swallowed. He knew he'd just heard the closest thing to *I love you* that his brother was likely to utter. "No, man. You're stuck with me for a while. They took my tumor out. All of it. They can't do that with Dad's."

"You think he'll make it?"

"I don't know."

"Shit, I know you don't know, Landon. What do you think? You're a doctor."

Landon swallowed and stared into the water. "Most likely, he won't make it. This is a bad cancer, and his is pretty advanced."

Dale nodded, his mouth set in a thin line. "I sort of figured that. Does Mom know?"

"I think she does, but I haven't asked, and I haven't volunteered anything."

Dale reeled his line in and executed a perfect, looping cast that landed just short of the marshy grass, right where the fish would be. "Brother, you're in a tough spot. We all are, but you especially, being a doctor and all. We're looking to you for help, some guidance. Mom, particularly. I know it's difficult, but you're going to need to do it."

"Yeah, I guess so. It's hard to know sometimes, what to say and what not to."

"Isn't that what you do, though?"

"I'm not the doctor here, Dale. I'm a son, like you."

Dale looked at him and smiled. He shook his head. "Not exactly, Brother. It's never been quite like that."

Landon felt a stab of fear or something like it. "What do you mean?"

Dale was working his bait, raising his rod tip, then dropping it and reeling up the slack, letting the bait rise and fall from the river bottom. "You were always different, Landon. Smarter than the rest of us. We all saw it."

"We? You mean you?"

"I mean all of us. Mom, Dad, Molly. It wasn't just school either. You thought about stuff more, seemed to worry or brood or something. You still do. Always thinking too much, if you ask me." He reeled his line in and laid the rod against the gunwale. "Toss me a Coke, will you?"

Landon rummaged in the cooler, grabbed two cans, and handed him one. "I gotta tell you something, Dale."

Dale had a mouthful of Coke, so he tipped his head back quickly, eyebrows up.

"We never talk much, not like this, and I think we need to," Landon said. "At least I do." He didn't expect a response. "I've always admired the way you handle yourself, the way you can do things, fix things. I'm no good at that stuff. Everybody talks about how smart I am, but there's lots of ways to be smart. I was good at reading and going to school." Dale nodded and dipped his head, his gaze wandering away but working back to Landon, who took that as a sign of attentiveness. "I feel like I've kind of let Mom and Dad down and you too." He paused before continuing, "I haven't been around as much as I should have. You've been here, helping out, doing everything."

Dale shrugged. "I live here. You don't." He looked away. "You bought Mom that car, and that means a lot to her. I know you send money. I can't do that." He finished his drink and tossed the can into the bottom of the boat. "I don't know what to tell you, Landon. I don't understand the battles you fight inside your head, but I wish you could get past them. They aren't doing you any good. Mom appreciates the things you do, and so do I. Don't know about Dad, but none of us do. I hear him talk about you once in a while. He's proud of you, but he's proud, period, and that pride gets in the way a lot—so does the drinking." He looked around; Landon figured he was searching for something he wouldn't find in the boat. "It wouldn't hurt for you to come around more, maybe bring that new girl with you." He gave Landon a sidewise glance and a smile. "How's that going anyway?"

Landon made no effort to hide his smile. "Really good. I thought about inviting her this time, but I wasn't sure she could get away."

"Thinking again, huh? That's a surprise." Dale was smiling.

"I guess." He shrugged. "Anyway, she called last night. Her boss said they can cover for her whenever she needs to come." He shook his head. "I guess she wants to be here."

"She wants to be here for you, genius." Dale laughed. "How'd you ever get through medical school? She loves you, sounds like. You guys in love?"

"I think I am, Dale. I think she feels the same, but I'm not sure. How do you know? How'd you know with Carla?"

Dale peered into his face; his expression made Landon smile. Dale smiled back. "You can't calculate it. Stop thinking about it. You feel it. Don't you feel it? By the way you talk about her, it seems like you do. Sounds like she does too. Have you even told her you love her?"

"Of course. Lots of times."

"Well, that's a start. What does she say?"

"She says she loves me too."

Dale nodded, pushed his lips out, and gazed up at the sky, clearly having fun at Landon's expense. "Okay, let me take the Landon Ratliff approach and analyze this to death. You both say you love each other. Hmm."

"Okay, okay, you've made your point. Right again, Big Brother."

Dale picked up his rod. "Just stop thinking it to death. You're a good guy. A good woman would make a big difference in your life."

Landon cast toward the shore. "She already has."

"Bring her around. Mom and Carla want to meet her."

"Kind of a tough time to be meeting the family."

"It is, but if you want her to meet Dad, you probably ought to get her here."

He swallowed the lump that rose in his throat. "Yeah, you're right. We talked about that. Her class is over in a couple weeks. I think she can finish up."

They fished on without success, but Landon didn't care. His mind was on Luna and on his brother, and despite the circumstances with his father, he felt happy, almost elated about the conversation they'd had. Dale was fishing, once again giving nothing away, but there wouldn't be a better time, he knew, so he waited until they pulled in closer to shore and dropped anchor for lunch. He passed out sandwiches wrapped in waxed paper, then tossed a bag of chips a little too high and hard. Dale speared it before it went overboard.

"Still got those second baseman's hands, huh?" Landon teased.

"Yeah, and you still got that doctor's arm." Dale was laughing.

Landon took a bite of the sandwich: thick-cut bologna, lettuce, tomato, slice of onion, American cheese, and mayonnaise. Simple sandwich, but no one made it like his mother did. "Hey," he said while he chewed, "you ever hear from Molly?"

Dale shook his head and stared into the bottom of the boat. He had spread a napkin across his tackle box and now straddled his makeshift lunch table, where the sandwich and chips shared space with a second Coke. "No. I tried for a while. Carla still sends her a picture now and then and a

Christmas card. We don't get anything back. Her husband used to answer, but I guess Molly put a stop to that."

"You mean *Ian*?" Landon emphasized the name with a roll of his eyes.

"Yeah. He's okay, I think. About as okay as someone living in a commune can be."

"He never even came to meet Mom and Dad."

Dale chewed, letting his laugh exit through his nose. "You think Molly would have let him? No chance."

"What's Dad say about him?"

"If you leave out the cuss words, he doesn't say anything. He doesn't say anything about her either, at least to me. I guess he and Mom talk about it. I don't really know."

"Does she even talk to Mom? You'd think she'd get over it by now. Especially now. Does she know about Dad?"

Dale chewed another bite. His gaze was fixed on Landon, who wondered what was coming next.

"She speaks your language, too, you know," Dale said. "Have *you* tried to contact her?"

"No. I should have, I guess. I figured she didn't want to talk to me."

"You're probably right. I've never heard Mom say anything about hearing from her, and I think she'd let us know if she did. For myself, I feel better that I tried. Mom sent her a letter about Dad. I don't know if she read it. Hell, I don't know if she still lives at the same address."

"I should have tried."

"Still can. I don't think she's dead, but who knows? Ian would have told us that."

"I guess if she doesn't answer, I haven't lost anything."

Dale nodded. "I don't think you ever lose by trying to do the right thing."

Landon cleared his throat with a big swallow of Coke. He let the burn fade, then leaned closer to his brother. "I want to tell you something," he said. Dale's eyes came up, squinting again. "I admire you, Dale. Always have and still do. The way you've lived your life, everything you've taught me. I hope I get a little better at showing how grateful I am. I love you, man."

Dale smiled a crooked, closed-mouth smile, then stuck his work-hardened hand into the bag of chips. "Hell, I've created a monster. I just wanted you to stop thinking so much." He paused, clutching a handful of chips. "You're a good guy, Landon. I'm proud of you too. It's been hard trying to act like a family in this family, but that's not your fault or anybody's fault. Not even Dad's fault, I don't think. But even if it is, we don't have to keep doing what we've done. Let's just do better, all of us. That's all we can do."

A rumble of thunder put an exclamation point on Dale's speech, which had been long for him. The clouds had darkened and were scudding across the sky. Dale turned to the motor. "The fishing wasn't any good anyway," he said. "Sure not worth risking lightning."

"Yeah, let's head in," Landon said. "Think I'll pick up a card for Molly."

The motor roared to life with one pull. Dale gave Landon a thumbs-up.

CHAPTER THIRTY-THREE

Landon and his mother were up early the next morning. She made coffee, and they wandered among her flowerbeds, which had perked up after a night of rain. Her gardens contained no exotic specimens and would never appear on anyone's garden week tour but nevertheless reflected the love and care of a dedicated gardener. Watching his mother's face, knowing the concerns that plagued her, he concluded that the flowers gave as much as they got.

Afterward, she prepared breakfast while he sorted through the week's accumulated mail. His mother had asked him to open anything addressed to his father, who had not felt up to looking at mail for some time. One envelope caught his eye. It was addressed to Private Edward Ratliff, and "Save the Date—August 18" was printed in red block letters below the return address. It was from a post office box in Richmond.

He held up the envelope. "Mom, what's this?"

She turned from the stove where she was frying eggs. "You can open it, baby." She squinted as he carried it toward her. "Oh, I'll bet that's another invitation. Your daddy gets one every year. His army unit gets together in Richmond."

The envelope contained a thick stock invitation to dinner and a reception for members of the First Infantry, Fourth Brigade at the Jefferson Hotel in Richmond. Imprinted on the invitation was a green shield with a red "1" and underneath, the slogan "The Big Red One." The reply card had checkboxes for designating your battalion; one of the choices was the 75th.

Landon had not thought much about "seventy-five, dead or alive, for all time, sir," since his father had become ill. He thought again of New Orleans, of Amede Doucet, the homeless man who had taken the secret to his grave. It seemed likely his father would do the same.

"Did Dad ever go to this?" he asked.

His mother set a plate of bacon and eggs in front of him. "No, he never would go. I even offered to go with him, but he said no."

August 18 was more than a month away. His father wouldn't be well enough to go. He might not even be alive. Landon dug into his breakfast, swallowing the lump in his throat with toast dipped in egg yolk. His mother nibbled on toast slathered with strawberry preserves. She smiled at him; he knew it pleased her to feed her boys. He also knew there wouldn't be a better time to talk about Molly. After today, when they had to meet with the doctors at MCV, there might not be a good time for a while.

"You think Dad would mind if I went to the reunion?"

His mother shrugged. "I don't know. It's not for you, though."

"I know, but it might be nice to meet some of Dad's buddies, let them know about him."

"He wouldn't want them to see him like this, Landon."

"I wouldn't expect them to come see him, Mom. I'll bet they'd like to know about him, though. It's been forty years."

She sipped her coffee. "You might be right. Maybe you should go. I'd ask your daddy, though. He wouldn't want to be surprised."

"Maybe you should come with me."

The color seemed to drain from his mother's face; her expression hardened in a frightening way he had never seen. "No. I don't want to go there or anywhere that takes me back to that time. That war ruined your daddy. It hurt him in his mind worse than it did his body. He never got over it." She caught herself, as if she'd just awakened from a brief nap, and began stirring her coffee. "I only asked him about going once. I could see it in his face, how much it tortured him even to think about it." She looked up and smiled. "You go ahead. I know you want to know some things about your daddy, and I'm glad. He'll need me here anyway."

He hoped she was right, although by then his father might need lots of difficult care or none at all. Regardless, he'd lost his opportunity to bring up Molly. The war had intervened, and his mother needed a break, maybe the last break she'd have before her life, and all their lives, changed forever.

"This breakfast is great, Mom," he said, returning the smile he knew his words would coax from her.

The oncologist was as good as anyone could be, under the circumstances. He showed up on time, knocked before entering, and was respectful to everyone, especially to Landon's father. A short, slight man with thick glasses and even thicker hair plastered to his head like the hair on Molly's Ken dolls long ago, he introduced himself as Ravi Nubyam, not "Dr. Nubyam." Landon liked that. He also called himself The Cancer Doctor, avoiding medical jargon that might confuse his patient. His smile was tight-lipped and reserved, but his eyes conveyed kindness and concern.

Landon's father was tired and seemed sicker. Initially, Landon wondered if Dr. Nubyam's nationality (he guessed Indian) would be an issue, but his father either had no animosity toward his new physician or was too ill to show it. Dr. Nubyam's handshake was more a squeeze, but he maintained eye contact throughout and bowed somewhat deferentially to Landon as he greeted him. Landon's mother smiled and thanked him for coming; Dr. Nubyam held her hand, patting it with his other hand as he expressed his pleasure at meeting her. Then he pulled a chair to the bedside and sat very close to Landon's father, leaning in and asking about his comfort, focusing his attention for just a few moments on nothing else. When the conversation was finished, he touched Landon's father's shoulder gently and turned the chair to face outward, into the room, toward the other chair, where he motioned for Landon's mother to sit. Landon half leaned, half sat in the windowsill across the room.

"How did you two meet?" he asked, smiling as he glanced from Landon's mother to his father. His father managed a smile, while his mother seemed to take the cue and began the tale of their high school romance. This first question surprised Landon a little, but as the conversation unfolded, he recognized that Nubyam was doing what Fanning had taught him during his training: focus on the person rather than the disease if you want to provide the best possible care.

Nubyam shared his personal history as well. The son and grandson of physicians, he had grown up in Chicago never considering any other career, had gone to college and medical school at Michigan, and then had done his residency and fellowship at Vanderbilt. Landon mentioned the school's location in Nashville and his father's love of country music. That spurred a few minutes of animated conversation about the Ryman Auditorium and Hank Williams before Nubyam surprised Landon with his detailed discussion of Hank's exhibit at the Country Music Hall of Fame and Museum.

His mother's face relaxed noticeably, which pleased Landon, even though he knew it wouldn't last. Finally, Nubyam took a deep breath, leaned forward in his chair, and steepled his hands at his chin, elbows resting on his knees. "Now I need to share the results of the tests with you and discuss how to proceed with your treatment." He glanced from person to person, then settled his gaze upon Landon's father. "My plan is to tell you every detail, whether it is good news or bad, unless you say otherwise, because you need information in order to make good decisions, and because I respect you too much to withhold the truth."

Landon's father was nodding; his mouth was set in a thin line, and Landon thought his eyes betrayed a bit of fear or reluctance to hear what was coming. His mother was wringing her hands, but nodding as well.

"I'm afraid the news is not as good as I would have hoped," Nubyam said, pausing for a moment to let the pronouncement sink in. "The tumor has spread outside of the gall bladder ducts, into the surrounding tissues and veins that drain the liver. So it cannot be treated surgically with an operation."

"There's lymph node involvement?" Landon asked, unable to avoid the physician's role entirely.

Nubyam nodded. "Yes." He turned to Landon's father. "That means the tumor has spread to the lymph glands, which indicates more advanced disease."

Landon tried to appear impassive for his parents' sake, while Nubyam proceeded, as delicately and expertly as had ever been done, to deliver a death sentence to his father. And to his mother, who seemed to grasp the enormity of the news more quickly than did his father, who kept asking questions long after she had fallen silent. Nubyam offered chemotherapy, as Landon knew he would, and to his surprise, Landon found himself grasping for therapy that he knew would almost certainly fail, for anything that offered a glimmer of hope. When Nubyam began discussing experimental protocols, everyone perked up, and he saw his mother's eyes begging, pleading for a miracle. His father was more restrained, yet determined, unwilling to accept any finality whatsoever. Landon didn't blame him; in fact, he couldn't accept the stark probabilities either, at least not emotionally. His father would suffer terribly either way, so why not take the long shot?

It was only after Nubyam departed that Landon's rational mind reasserted itself, but by then it was too late. His mother and father were ready to take on the monster, certain that Dr. Nubyam would never let them down. He couldn't take his parents' hope away. He'd leave that to the monster.

His father was exhausted by dinnertime, and although Landon could not persuade his mother to skip evening visiting hours, he did convince her to bypass the cafeteria fare in favor of a restaurant in the vicinity of the MCV campus. Chinese food, which his mother loved and his father refused to eat, seemed like a good choice. In typical fashion, after claiming to have no appetite, she perked up while reviewing the menu and ordered a meal that would have adequately fortified one of Genghis Khan's warriors. Landon waited until the steamed dumplings arrived.

"Mom, don't you think we should let Molly know about Dad?"

His mother halted with a dumpling halfway to her mouth. She placed the fork carefully on her plate. "That's the first time you've mentioned Molly in years, Landon."

He nodded. "I know. I've been thinking about her. Dale and I talked about her yesterday."

A light seemed to come on in her eyes. "Have you tried to reach her?"

"No. I looked for her number at home but couldn't find it. I don't know if I ever had it. I bought a card yesterday."

"I don't think she has the same number she had," his mother said. "I can't remember when I spoke with her." She shrugged. "I don't know if she gets the letters I send. She quit writing back a good while ago."

"Seems like she ought to know about Dad. I can't believe she wouldn't care."

His mother swallowed, then dabbed her mouth. "It's a complicated thing. Your father hurt her really badly, and she blamed me for not being tough enough, I guess."

"What did she want you to do?"

"Leave him, I think. I wasn't going to do that. I wasn't raised that way." She took another dumpling. "Maybe I should have … I don't know. I did the best I could. I didn't think I'd have to choose and lose one of my babies." She bowed her head.

"Mom, I'm sorry. I don't mean to hurt you with this."

She waved him off. Her eyes were a little misty, but her voice was clear. "It's okay. I'm glad to hear you talk about her. She's your sister."

He set his fork down and reached for his mother's hand. "I've got to ask you, Mom—what did Dad do to her?"

She shook her head. "Nothing like that, Landon. I asked her once, before she left home. He never touched her, but she couldn't take the yelling and the way he embarrassed her in front of her friends. You remember, the same things he did to you and Dale."

"I remember when he hit Dale."

"Yeah." She got very quiet for a moment. "I told your father if he ever hit any of you again, I'd put him out for good." She patted his hand and withdrew her own. "That was a long time ago. Your daddy needs us now more than ever. And I think Molly should know. I sent her a letter last week. If you want to try to reach her, I wish you would."

"You think Dad wants her to know?"

"I would bet he does. It's hard to say. I know I would."

Her face was starting to sag; the strain of trying to decipher his father's mind was difficult for anyone to hide it seemed. He sipped tea while his mother picked at her dumpling. The restaurant was filling up with smiling, chatty people whose lives seemed so much less complicated than his own. It had been a long time since he'd felt carefree. He began to wonder if he ever had.

"I got a call today from the hospital in Charleston," he said just as the entrées arrived. "I was supposed to have my follow-up MRI on Wednesday. I forgot."

"Oh no. What are you going to do?"

"It's okay. It was just a routine test. I don't have to get it this week. I'll call Dr. Lake and explain what's going on. I can get it here. They'll send the images to him."

"Well, you'd better call him. Please take care of yourself, Landon. Please." Her hand found his again.

"I will, Mom. I promise. We're going to need each other."

"Have you talked with Luna?"

"Not today. I'll call her later tonight."

She smiled. "Your daddy talks about her. He wants to meet her. So do I."

He returned the smile. "You will. She's teaching a class that ends in a couple weeks. She asked about coming, but we're trying to figure out the best time."

"The sooner the better, I would think. Your daddy's pretty sick and liable to get sicker."

He nodded. "Yeah. Maybe she should come next weekend."

She picked up her fork. "You know best, Landon."

He stared across the room, wishing she was right.

CHAPTER THIRTY-FOUR

Luna wanted to come the following Friday, but Landon talked her out of it. The initial chemotherapy had ravaged his father, causing vomiting and general misery beyond what Landon had expected from past experiences with his own patients. Now his father's mouth was so full of sores he could barely tolerate water, much less eat, and he was too weak to get out of bed. What little energy he had seemed to be channeled into grouchiness and resentment of visitors, including his own wife. Landon's mother was exhausted and overwhelmed. All in all, it seemed a poor time to introduce them to his girlfriend. To his relief, Luna seemed to understand. Although it wasn't entirely clear that waiting another week would help, the doctors thought his father would have adjusted to the therapy better, so the plan was made for her to come then.

He did not share the other reason he was glad for the delay. He had scheduled the MRI for Thursday afternoon and did not want to risk processing devastating news while he was navigating the minefield of bringing a new woman to meet his family. Except for Darlene, his college sweetheart, Luna would be the only love interest he'd brought home.

Although he'd now been dating Luna almost as long as he'd dated Darlene, this relationship felt very different, and he didn't want distractions, at least none that he could control.

His worries were relieved when Lake called on Saturday with the news that the MRI was clean, no sign of tumor. He and Luna celebrated by phone, then he and his mother met Dale and Carla for a celebratory dinner. Carla demonstrated her compassion and insight by steering the conversation away from the grim realities at hand, honing in on Luna instead. Despite his initial discomfort, Landon soon relaxed and offered a series of descriptions and stories that clearly delighted his mother and made his brother smile more than he could recall in recent memory. Afterward, Landon reflected on the intuition that came so easily to Carla (and most other women, it seemed) and thanked her privately for giving everyone a break from their grief.

"I didn't do anything," Carla said. He noticed for the first time that her eyes were the same color as Luna's. "You did most of the talking."

He felt himself turning red. "Yeah, but I wouldn't have, if you hadn't asked."

"Oh, I bet you would've. You wanted to, seemed like." She crossed her arms. "You're in love, Landon—everyone can see that."

He smiled and shrugged, feeling as dopey as the first time he asked Darlene out on a date. He wasn't sure what everyone was seeing, but he didn't mind; he wasn't trying to hide it.

"You know what?" Carla asked. "I think she's a very lucky girl. I can't wait to meet her."

The second round of chemotherapy went somewhat better. The vomiting and diarrhea passed more quickly, and

Landon's father weathered it like the experienced cancer patient he had now become. His hair was falling out in clumps, and he seemed to be losing weight by the hour. The fatty tissues in his face were gone, leaving the skin stretched over the bones like a drumhead. As his father's head turned into little more than a covered skull, Landon noted that he began to more closely resemble the young man whose photo hung in the hallway at home, the young man who could not have guessed it would all come down to this.

And yet, his father was better, much better this week. He sat in a chair—only briefly because the effort exhausted him—and he ate some. There was something in his eyes. They seemed clearer, maybe because he hadn't had any whiskey in ten days.

Finally, on Thursday, after rebuffing Carla's offer to have Luna and Landon stay in Norfolk with them, his mother left the hospital and went home to make it ready for Landon's new love. Dale was working, of course, and Carla was home with the baby, so Landon was left alone with his father for the first time since he'd been in the hospital. He got his mother safely away, then dawdled his way back toward the oncology unit. Before he reached the room, he spotted Nubyam at the nurses' station and detoured, grateful for a plausible reason to delay going in.

"How does he seem to you?" Nubyam asked after steering him to a sitting area away from the staff. Landon guessed he had a ton of work yet to complete, but as usual, Nubyam gave his full attention to him.

"A little better, I think," Landon said. "He's getting used to the therapy. He seems more attentive."

Nubyam nodded. "Have you spoken with him?"

"I was just going in when I spotted you. My mom finally went home."

"Good. She seems exhausted." Nubyam interlaced his fingers and leaned closer. His eyes seemed to be searching for something. "I had a long talk with your father this morning. Your mother had gone for coffee, so it was just the two of us. I think what you're seeing is acceptance, Landon."

"What do you mean?" He knew very well what Nubyam meant, but the question allowed him to try and breathe through the vise that had tightened around his chest.

"He's getting weaker. The chemotherapy is proving to be very toxic for him. Oh, he's tolerating it better this week, but nevertheless, his functional performance is declining rapidly. I don't think—"

"But he was up in the chair today."

Nubyam let Landon's words hang in the air between them. Landon knew, and was certain Nubyam knew, they were the desperate, futile cry for a miracle that neither believed would come. Nubyam's eyes were softer now, kind and caring, full of the shared grief Landon had offered to other families in similar circumstances many times. It sure felt different from this angle.

"Your father knows he's dying, Landon. He's pondering whether to stop the chemotherapy."

"Does my mother know?" She hadn't revealed anything to him. Surely this would have come up?

"I don't know. I haven't spoken with her yet." He laid a hand on Landon's knee. "I know this is difficult. Remember, you're not his doctor. You're his son. Your family will look to you for guidance. Please feel free to refer them to me."

Landon stared at the floor. His eyes felt full. "What happens now?"

"For now, until your father decides otherwise, we'll continue the therapy. I told him if he becomes bedridden, though, it makes no sense to continue."

"What if he stops?"

"We've discussed that. He understands hospice care and would want to go home."

Landon felt unmoored, unsteady. He was restless, wanted to stand and pace but feared losing his balance, so he gripped the chair, wishing it had arms to lean on. "What do you think he should do?" he asked, stifling the urge to plead with Dr. Nubyam for comfort.

"It's his decision, but the treatment seems to be harming him, and at best, it would only provide him with an additional two to three months."

"But there's a chance it would be longer, right?" He pressed himself against the chair back, determined not to crowd Dr. Nubyam.

"There's always hope, Landon. I've seen miracles, but I can't cause them. Occasionally, there's an unexplainable remission, even a cure, but in my experience, those occur most often in younger, healthier patients." Nubyam leaned even closer, his dark eyes seeming to search inside of Landon. "I'll do whatever your father wishes. I'll answer his questions honestly, and if he asks my opinion, I'll tell him I think it's very likely his time is short, and he ought to make his remaining days as fulfilling as he can. It's up to him to determine what that means for him." He patted Landon's leg and rose from the chair. "You're welcome to come with me while I visit with your father, but perhaps you need a little time to collect yourself?"

Landon nodded. He wanted to stand, shake Nubyam's hand, thank him for all he was doing, but all he could manage was a glance and another nod. He felt Nubyam's hand on his shoulder. A squeeze, a pat or two, and then he felt the tears, blurring the image of the small man in a white coat walking away to go attend to his dying father.

The room was still and smelled of hand sanitizer. His father lay on his side, facing away from the door toward the windows that glowed with the light of a waning sunset. He turned when Landon approached the bed, grimacing with the effort of settling himself onto his back. His mouth was set in a line that tried to form something resembling a smile. "Hey, Son," he murmured. His voice was feeble.

"Hey, Dad." He pulled a chair up to the bedside. "How you feeling?"

His father gave a barely perceptible shrug. "About the same. Not throwing up, at least."

"How's the pain?"

"Not too bad."

There was no tray in the room. "Did you eat anything?"

"A little. The food's not very good."

"Want me to go get you something?" Landon felt fidgety; he didn't want to smooth the bedclothes or tuck them in around his father as he'd seen his mother do. He clasped his hands together and forced himself to focus on his father, who seemed to be looking past Landon with still, dry eyes that weren't really fixing on anything. "Dr. Nubyam said you could have anything you want."

His father closed his eyes. Landon thought he might drift off to sleep, but then an unmistakable smile creased his drawn face, and his eyes brightened. "You know what I'd really like?" he asked.

The first thing that flashed through Landon's mind was a shot of bourbon, but he pushed that aside. He leaned closer, drawn by his father's mischievous look, a look that used to presage a pretty good, usually dirty joke. "What do you want, Dad?"

"A strawberry shake from The Dairy Bar."

He should have guessed. He remembered the trips to The Diamond to see the Braves play, and how they'd always, always have to stop at The Dairy Bar on the way. Their strawberry shake seemed to be the only drink that rivaled whiskey for his father. Landon's memories of the place were mixed, tempered by childhood fears of his father's behavior and whether they would get home safely after his father had followed up the milkshake with several beers at the ballpark.

"I can run up there and get you one," he said. "A peanut butter and banana shake would taste pretty good."

His father waved that off. "Don't go to all that trouble. It's too far."

"It's nothing, Dad. I can be back in thirty minutes." He rose from the chair. "Want a ham sandwich?"

"Better not push it. Sounds awful good, though."

"How about I bring one anyway? You might want a bedtime snack." His father's silence seemed like agreement. He was neither smiling nor frowning, but his eyes seemed to be searching for something he'd lost.

He hurried from the hospital, happy to have something to do, even as he recognized that he was escaping, avoiding a conversation he didn't want to face. His father was excited; he still had some fight left in him. Maybe if he got better food. Not that country ham and ice cream represented high quality nutrition, but at this point, calories mattered more. He wondered if Nubyam had brought up hospice again. It seemed too early for that. Landon knew all about hospice, had recommended it many times, but now wasn't the time. Nubyam had told them this chemotherapy regimen held a lot of promise, that patients were living longer. Maybe only a few months, but still … maybe his father could get well enough to go fishing with him and Dale, maybe take in a Braves game. There was still time to make a few good memories. There had to be.

In the meantime, there were milkshakes. The calories wouldn't make a big difference, but if he got some pleasure from it and it didn't hurt him, what was the problem? Didn't he deserve something besides pain and doctors and nurses and chemotherapy? Didn't he deserve to smile, to enjoy himself? For a fleeting moment, it occurred to Landon that he was about to provide hospice care, but he put that thought out of his mind as quickly as he could.

CHAPTER THIRTY-FIVE

His mother insisted on accompanying Landon to the airport on Friday, explaining she did not want to meet "Landon's lady" in a hospital room, and wouldn't force her to make the long drive out to their home and then back to Richmond after traveling all day. He agreed readily, happy to see anticipation on his mother's face, knowing that his own precious time alone with Luna would come later.

She exited the jetway wearing a simple, yellow summer dress he hadn't seen before. Her hair was pulled up. The ever-present wayward tendrils of hair tickled his face in their post-kiss hug. He closed his eyes for a second and inhaled the sweet scent of Luna.

Her eyes were shining when he broke the hug and stepped aside. Luna's shoulders bunched in what he now recognized as her bashful shrug. Her head tilted, her arms came up, and she stepped toward his mother, whose eyes had become misty. The smile on her face left no doubt about her state of mind, though. There would be no handshake, although that would have been customary for both of them. They attached to one another like magnets, as if they'd been apart far too long. Then they separated, sort of, but held on, regarding one another through tears and smiles and murmurs that left him happily excluded.

Finally, they fully separated, and Landon's mother reached for him. She still held tightly to Luna's hand, but swept him up with her free arm and pulled him close. He reveled in the joyful hug, thinking back to his medical school graduation when he found her in the crowd after receiving his diploma.

For a second, he worried about the walk to baggage claim. Would his mother want to hold his hand? Would Luna think it weird? Then Luna's hand slid into his, and his mother took her place beside Luna, smiling and chattering like a squirrel.

After retrieving Luna's bag, they took a circuitous route to the hospital, driving first out to the University of Richmond. Luna loved campuses, and Landon thought this one the prettiest in town. He drove back down Monument Avenue, not certain what Luna would think of the statues of Confederate war heroes. She seemed to ignore them and was too busy chatting with his mother to notice the mansions in The Fan or anything in Shockoe Slip. He curtailed the tour and headed for the hospital.

As they approached the room, Landon's grip tightened on Luna's hand.

"Let me go in first and make sure he's ready," his mother said. "He's been looking forward to this all week."

Luna's lips felt cool and soft on his cheek. "It's okay, sweetie," she whispered. "Are you nervous?"

He nodded, then smiled. "Yeah."

"I'm glad." She shrugged. "Makes me feel important."

The door opened. "He's ready," his mother said, one arm extended as if she were welcoming visiting dignitaries to her home. The room was awash in sunlight. His father was propped up in bed by the elevated mattress and two spongy pillows that cradled his head. His hair was freshly combed. Both his arms lay flat atop bedclothes that had been folded crisply and tucked in around him. Landon recognized his mother's handiwork. His father's sallow, wasted face seemed transfigured by his eager eyes and genuine smile.

"Dad, this is Luna," he said, but she was already reaching for his hand, lowering herself into the chair that had been made ready for her.

"Hi, Doll Baby," his father said in a surprisingly strong voice.

Luna held onto his hand as she sat. "I'm glad to finally meet you. Landon has told me so much about you."

"Well, don't believe everything you hear." His father cut his eyes toward Landon and gave him a wink. "I hope you'll make up your own mind."

"I always do," she said. "I think we'll get along fine, Mr. Ratliff. Like father, like son, right?"

His father grew wide-eyed at that remark. "Careful. I don't want to come between you and my son." His attempt at a fake grimace made him cough. "You can call me Eddie."

"Well, Eddie, don't worry about coming between me and Landon. You remind me of him already, and that's totally a compliment." Luna's eyes were shining. Landon felt his face turning red. His father was looking at him in a way he'd seen somewhere but couldn't place. It made him smile, and he didn't mind feeling a little embarrassed. He felt his mother's hand on his back.

His father held Luna's hand, but his gaze wandered before settling on Landon's mother. "Us Ratliff men have been very lucky when it comes to picking women," he said. He turned back to Luna, who was smiling and nodding. "Have you met Carla yet?"

"Not yet." She hooked a wayward strand of hair behind her ear with her free hand.

"Dale did good." His father smiled. "Looks like Landon did too."

Landon began to wonder if Luna was feeling uncomfortable. The conversation seemed awfully familiar, but she never flinched. "Thank you, Eddie," she said. "You know what? I think you and Iris did better than good."

"That was her doing more than mine," he said, gesturing toward Landon's mother. His hand dropped heavily after a few seconds. His eyes closed briefly, but when they opened, he was smiling again. "It's nice of you to say so, though." He lifted his head from the pillow and turned toward Landon before settling back with a soft groan. Landon saw the look again and remembered. It was the look he'd seen on Enrique's father's face long ago, when he'd introduced Enrique to the crowd at a medical conference. Whether it was pride or love or both, it felt good and almost worth the wait.

Everyone seemed sorry to see Sunday afternoon arrive, his father most of all. Luna's presence had prompted him to perhaps overdo it on Saturday by sitting up in the chair for a couple hours, so he was unable to leave the bed to say goodbye, but he was alert and smiling when she kissed his cheek and told him she would see him soon.

"When?"

Landon smiled. He had expected the question, the same one asked by Dale, Carla, and his mother at one time or another today—in private, out of earshot of Luna. Landon's answer had been honest—he didn't know, and they hadn't discussed it, but the question had been on his mind since Saturday morning. He'd kept it to himself, fearing he might be pressing too much, not wanting to spoil the magic of the weekend. Her impending departure made him jittery and sad.

"We'll see," Luna said now. She held his father's hand a moment longer. "You take care of yourself and do what the nurses tell you."

"I will. Call me soon, okay?" His father's voice sounded hopeful, almost eager, like a child saying goodbye to his grandmother.

The rest of the goodbyes were full of smiles and happy tears. It all felt good, like a real family, Landon thought, although he caught himself feeling a bit scared by the unfamiliarity of that feeling.

The drive to the airport was short; he was glad they weren't in a hurry.

"*Well*," he said with extra emphasis, once they had left the parking garage and joined the light Sunday evening traffic. He wanted to appear calm, not too needy, not too eager, yet not too casual. He felt as if he were in quicksand. "I hope you know I didn't set you up."

"What do you mean?" Luna had been teasing the hairs at the base of his neck. Her hand froze as her eyes narrowed.

"Well, it seemed like they had us married off. That must have been uncomfortable for you."

Luna's eyes softened again. He saw just a hint of a smile.

"I enjoyed meeting your family, Landon. They made me feel welcome. I was a little scared at first."

"You were? I couldn't tell. You never said anything about that."

For a second, she was silent. He felt her hand start moving again. He risked a glance. Her head was tilted against his shoulder. "You never asked."

He mashed his lips together. "You're right, I didn't. I'm sorry."

"Don't be. You've got plenty on your mind. Besides, everyone was so nice. Even—maybe especially—your father."

"No kidding. I've never seen him like that. If I didn't know better, I'd swear he was hitting on you." He gave her a wide-eyed smile, just to let her know he was joking. "By the way, how'd it go with him this morning, one-on-one?"

"It was fine. How'd the family breakfast go?"

"I asked you first. Besides, I thought you would have interrogated me way before now. You losing your touch?" He turned and gave her a quick kiss on the arm.

"Careful, buster," she said. "I'll get my turn. It's not like we've had any time alone today."

"Yeah, I know. Sally would've thrown a fit if I tried to take you away, though."

Luna smiled. "What a cutie. Jeez, kids are a lot of work, though. I don't see how Carla does it."

"Momma Dale does his share too."

"He does. It's good to see. You wouldn't think that about him. He doesn't look the type."

Landon nodded. "I know. There's a lot more to him than meets the eye."

"He thinks a lot of you too."

That felt good, but he didn't need details. The fishing trip with Dale would stay with him a long time, and now Dale was clearly relying upon him to translate and navigate the family through what seemed certain to be his father's final weeks or months. Landon had all the affirmation he needed from his brother right now.

"Landon?" Luna's face had softened. If he had not been driving, he would have kissed her right then. "I didn't ask you about your father on purpose. I can only imagine how difficult this must be for you, and I think—I hope …" She squeezed his neck. He turned and flashed a smile that she returned. "I hope you know you can talk to me when you're ready. I'm always here to listen."

"I know," he said, and he did. He really did know, somewhere deep inside, and it felt warm and comforting and right. It felt safe. He knew he wanted to make Luna feel the same way, and to do that he needed to ask more questions, to speak more freely, and to listen. None of that came easily to him, but he no longer doubted that the payoff was worth the effort.

CHAPTER THIRTY-SIX

His father was alone, dozing, when Landon returned from the airport. He awoke when the hallway noise invaded the room; his arousal stifled Landon's plan to withdraw and go looking for the rest of the family.

"Hey, Dad, sorry I woke you," he said.

"No, I was waiting for you." His father fumbled with the bed control, which raised him into a sitting position. "Dale took your mom on home. She was pretty tired."

Landon paused beside the chair. "You want me to take off so you can sleep?"

"No."

"If you're tired, I understand."

"Sit, Landon, it's fine." His father offered a thin-lipped smile. "I was hoping we'd get a little time together. You've been pretty busy this weekend."

He wished he had some water. "Yeah, I was. I think Luna had a good time. Everybody seemed to like her."

"Who wouldn't?" His father's eyes were bright, as when he'd said goodbye earlier.

"I think she's sweet on you, Dad. I'm a little jealous about those phone calls."

His father smiled and then turned and stared out the window. In the silence, Landon felt his own heart hammering in his chest. His father's smile held firm when he turned back to him. "There might have been a time when I could have given her a run for her money, Son, but I don't think you have to worry about that anymore. Besides, that woman loves you, and if you're as smart as I think you are, you love her too."

He exhaled, relieving the pressure in his chest, hoping he wouldn't tear up. "I do, Dad. I'm glad you like her." He grabbed a tissue; his cracking voice had warned him he'd need some help. "Sorry." He dabbed his eyes.

"Don't be. I've cried a river full myself this week." He shifted in the bed, grimacing momentarily before settling his gaze on Landon once again. "Landon, I want to talk with you about my treatment."

Landon's mouth trembled. He mashed his lips together, told himself he was a doctor, but it was no good. Nubyam was right. He was not Mr. Ratliff's doctor, he was Eddie Ratliff's son, and no amount of training or experience would alter that.

"I talked with Dr. Nubyam this weekend," his father said. "He doesn't think the chemotherapy is doing much except making me sick."

Landon nodded. "Did he think something else might—"

His father raised his hand, just a little, then shook his head. The effort made him close his eyes. "No, Son, he didn't." A tear spilled onto his cheek when he opened his eyes. "I'm dying, Landon." His voice sounded fragile and thin. "We both know it. I don't have much time."

"You never know for sure, Dad."

His father smiled through his tears. "Doctors might not, but when it's you, you know." His eyes narrowed. "Your mom told me your tests turned out good. You're doing all right?"

"I think so. Everything looks fine. No sign of the tumor. I'll get checked again in a year or so, whenever the doctors tell me."

His father shook his head. "Doctors. Hard to get a straight story out of them." He was smiling again. "You listen to them and take care of yourself."

He scooted his chair closer and reached for his father's hand. It was skin stretched over bones. All the muscle that had gripped hammers and saws and rifles and bottles was gone.

"I want you to know how proud I am of you, how proud I've always been," his father said. "I wish I had told you, had shown you, a long time ago."

Landon gave in and let the tears flow, bowing his head, squeezing his eyes tightly. He felt his father's faltering grip, his thumb trying to provide comfort.

At last, he raised his head. His father was looking at him, his expression tired but tender.

"I love you, Dad."

"I love you too, Landon."

He rested his head on his father's bony chest and felt the skeletal arms encircle him. His father's heart was drumming away, keeping time with his own. How long had he waited, yearned for this moment with his father? Why had he, Landon, waited so long? He knew why, but now he no longer had to fear his father's response. Maybe it couldn't have happened earlier, but at least it had happened. At least it had happened.

"I got something else to tell you, Son."

He untangled himself and returned to the chair. His father's smiling face looked more tender than he'd ever seen it. "We heard from Molly."

"What? When?" He fumbled for words, wondering briefly if his father was kidding, but of course he wasn't.

"Nubyam told me this morning—she called his office on Friday."

"I don't get it. How did she know to call him?"

"Let me back up," his father said. He shifted in the bed and waved off Landon's offer of help. "Your mother's been writing her, every couple days, it seems like, but she never answers. Hasn't for a long time. Finally, Nubyam asked me if he could write and tell her about my cancer. He said he didn't expect an answer, he just wanted her to know."

"Did she call you?"

"No, I think that would be a stretch. Nubyam thinks she might, though."

"He's a good guy and a good doctor," Landon said.

His father nodded. "He is, and if he can get Molly to call, I'll get that miracle he keeps talking about."

CHAPTER THIRTY-SEVEN

Everything and everyone was prepared by Thursday, August 2, when Landon's father left the hospital. Landon and his mother had cried a little when they stayed up most of one night at home talking about how life would soon be very different. His mother no longer asked about other treatment options. She had spent many hours talking with Landon's father and with Dr. Nubyam. She knew almost as much about the disease as Landon did and a whole lot more about what course of treatment was consistent with his father's wishes. Dale was stoic about it, at least in front of Landon and his mother. Carla told him Dale was doing fine but had expressed profound sorrow that his father would not get to see Sally grow up.

And then there was hospice care, the unspeakable threat that had become their friend, little by little, as they witnessed suffering and struggle giving way to acceptance. Dr. Nubyam had guided them, first with a comment or two, then later with longer conversations with Landon's father and mother, and last with Landon, Dale, and Carla. But it was Eddie himself who ultimately convinced them by making the decision and making peace with it. Even then, Landon had been forced to confront his fears and biases and to admit to himself that acceptance was not the same as giving up. He was embarrassed but not surprised that Dale had figured that out first.

No one was surprised to learn that Molly had proven to be the most resistant to the idea of hospice care. Apparently, she had broken years of silence to express her dissatisfaction to both parents in a series of separate, private phone conversations that had begun with angry invective about Dr. Nubyam and the medical profession. His parents assumed that her anger reflected fear and some form of love, however. So overjoyed to reconnect with their lost child, they refused to judge, allowing her to verbalize her emotional and psychological struggle until the effort changed her—at least enough to give in. Acceptance seemed to come reluctantly and with a chip on its shoulder. It still wasn't clear whether she would come and see her father before he died.

Molly had not spoken with Landon or Dale and left no number where she could be reached. Landon learned from his mother that Molly had received the card he'd sent as well as letters from the rest of the family over the years. There was no further explanation. Nevertheless, the reconnection seemed to contribute substantially to the peacefulness that surrounded his father's transfer home into hospice care.

Once his father was settled into the hospital bed installed in the extra bedroom and after a reassuring visit from the hospice nurse, it became clear that his mother was up to the task of caring for her husband during his final weeks (Nubyam had predicted two to four). Dr. Denbigh made a house call on Friday evening and made himself available by phone at any time. So Landon made plans for a quick trip to Charleston.

He needed to talk with Mike Fanning, who had offered sympathy and encouragement during his prolonged absence. He figured that he'd used up his paid time off long ago and guessed that Fanning would be understanding. If not, he was prepared to take unpaid leave or resign to ensure that he would be home as long as necessary.

He left Sunday morning, figuring traffic would be lighter then. The drive offered private time that he'd expected to fill with reflections on his father's impending death, but his mind refused to cooperate. Instead, his own quiescent illness, lost in the soul-searing emotions of the past couple weeks, resurfaced like an enemy submarine that had been patrolling silently and was now emerging from the depths to declare its presence rather than its arrival.

He, too, was a cancer patient. While it wasn't always top of mind, never did he feel completely free, completely well. Every twinge in his back or the slightest discoloration of his urine was an unwelcome tap on his shoulder. The threat of recurrence hovered. The tumor was gone—or was it? It was undetectable, but that wasn't the same thing. He knew most cancers had nothing to do with exposure to a toxin. You didn't catch cancer—you developed it. Sometimes, repeated exposure to an irritant, like alcohol, could trigger it. But not always. Sometimes, something in your DNA simply went wrong—a random mutation, pure chance—and cells went crazy. Now he found himself wondering and worrying. Science, knowledge, and experience were of no use to him. He felt adrift. He might be cured, with no chance of ever getting kidney cancer again, but he would never know until something else got him, and by then it would be too late.

Luna shooed all thoughts of cancer out of his consciousness, consigning them to a locked closet deep inside his brain. She had wine and candles and Tony Bennett waiting, along with a dinner that could wait while they made love and languished in bed, catching up on what they had each missed during the past week's absence from one another.

He knew she had called his father midweek, so there really wasn't that much to catch up on, except the feel and smell and taste of her skin. That was plenty for him, and Luna wasn't complaining either. A break from thinking about and discussing his father's decline unto death was a relief. He also knew she'd been writing a lot, taking advantage of the two-week interlude between summer session and the start of fall semester. He'd learned early on how important this novel was to her and read *Sweet Thursday* out of curiosity and interest—in her more than in the story. But he'd subsequently learned that she didn't like to discuss her work, at least in the draft phase. She felt it was bad luck. One of her professors from graduate school was her reader and editor and critic and the only person who saw and discussed the drafts in any serious way. That left only affectionate and flirty banter for now, which seemed to be just what the doctor needed.

The evening passed too quickly, but the best sleep he'd had in at least a week reenergized him for the following day. Fanning had rearranged his schedule so they could linger over a long lunch and catch up. News of Landon's father was first, summarized in the car while Fanning drove to a café he and Sheila had discovered north of Cannon, near King Street.

"They make incredible soups and a great quiche," Fanning told him. "Sheila's after me about my weight again."

He thought the idea of soup in a dripping Charleston August was harebrained until he tried the peach gazpacho, a cold, vinegary blend of peaches and tomatoes that was perfect with a watermelon and beet salad and a warm baguette baked fresh on the premises.

"Wow, I'll have to bring Luna here," he said after the third moan-accompanied mouthful.

Fanning was grinning like a pelican with a bill full of fish. "It is extraordinary—and healthy." He interlaced his fingers and balanced his prominent chin on them, leaning in and looming over Landon as if he were the next course. "It sounds like things are going well with Ms. Quinn."

He nodded as he felt the blood rush to his face. "Really well. She's been a big help."

Fanning's eyes shone with what Landon now recognized as affection.

"So have you, Mike," he continued. "I can't tell you how grateful I am. This has been a long, difficult ordeal."

Fanning's grin faded. "It has, and you've borne it well. I assume you've had your follow-up study?" He waved his hands. "I don't want to intrude, of course."

"Not at all. I did have it. No sign of tumor. I'm cleared for another six months, and if that's okay, I'm clear for a year."

"Wonderful!" Fanning hoisted his glass of sweet tea and drank deeply. He clung to the glass after setting it down. His smile faded as he stared into the drink. "I'm so happy that crisis, at least, is behind you. I'm sure you know that the likelihood of recurrence is minimal now, although minimal isn't much comfort."

Landon shrugged. "It is, actually. I've read enough now to feel pretty hopeful about it. Not that I don't think about it, but with my dad, I've got plenty on my mind."

"Indeed." Fanning pushed his glasses up. His gaze became more probing than kind. "I need to discuss something with you, Landon—two things actually, and I'm afraid neither may be very welcome."

Landon had become accustomed to feeling unsettled, but he was caught off guard. He slid his trembling hands into his lap.

"I'll get right to the point. Your job is safe, and the dean has agreed to extend your leave for another month. He was happy to do it."

"Thank you, Mike. This is a big relief."

Fanning waved him off. "It's the right thing to do. Everyone agrees and wishes you the best." He laughed. "I'd be lying if I said there was no grumbling in the division, but you know how that is."

"Sure." Landon was waiting; he hadn't heard either of the two promised unwelcome things.

Fanning exhaled loudly. His shoulders sagged. "But I do have to let you know I've decided to reassign your administrative responsibilities."

"What?" He tried to remain impassive, to allow his brain to process before he tried to interpret. "What do you mean?"

"We're two months into the academic year, Landon. The fellowship—it needs attention, and you can't provide it right now." Fanning's hand was tapping the table, ticking off his justifications. Landon found it easier to look at than his friend's face. "Same thing with the vice chief. The business of the division won't wait. It's temporary, I assure you. Everyone knows these are interim moves."

That felt better, but not good. He felt as if he'd been shoved aside, even though he knew Mike Fanning would never betray him. He forced a thin-lipped smile and nodded. "Makes sense, Mike. I don't blame you, and it wouldn't matter if I did."

"Of course it would matter, Landon. How can you say that?"

"I'm sorry. I didn't mean it that way." He fumbled for his napkin and swiped at his mouth, wishing he could tuck that last statement back in. "I meant just what you said—the work needs to be done, and I'm not here. I can't expect everything and everyone to wait on me."

"I'm sorry too," Fanning said. "I didn't mean to snap at you. I've been dreading this, and I let my anxiety take over. I know how much your work means to you." He tossed his napkin onto the table. "If it was a little later, I'd suggest a cocktail. I have to tell you something else."

Landon felt like a fighter who can no longer defend himself. He didn't know whether to laugh or cry, but he did neither. He just waited.

"The dean wants to see you. This afternoon, if you can manage it."

His heart was racing ahead of his brain, which seemed as deconditioned as his body right now.

"I shouldn't tell you, but it seems cruel to prolong it now. He's going to relieve you as admissions committee chair."

"Can he do that?" He felt anger rising like a storm surge. "I'm on medical leave."

"Committee assignments aren't protected, Landon. Applications will begin arriving any day. Your return date is uncertain."

"Couldn't he wait and see?"

Fanning shook his head. "He doesn't want to take the chance. It isn't personal and certainly not a reflection of disappointment. He thinks highly of you."

The air rushed out of him, leaving him too spent to savor or even respond to Mike's last comment. He *was* adrift now, cut loose from everything that had anchored and defined him. Not only could he not take care of patients, now he couldn't even do the paperwork.

"He asked me to see if four o'clock would work for you. He can see you later if that's more convenient."

"Well, I know now. What's the point?"

"He didn't ask me to tell you. I think he'd be upset if he knew I did. I thought this would allow you to absorb the news and respond without anger."

He smiled. "If you didn't know me so well, I might be offended, Mike."

Fanning gave him a squeeze just above the wrist. His hand seemed the size of a baseball glove. "You are my wingman, Landon. Nothing has changed. I want you to be able to focus on what's most important right now. Your job will be waiting for you when you're ready, and I have no doubt the dean feels the same way."

The sting lasted long enough for Luna to hear him out. Her presence, murmurs of affirmation, and eyes filled with love were more than enough to prepare him for the meeting with the dean. Landon thought he played his own part admirably. He concurred with the decision, prioritizing the important work of the committee over his situation, and offered his personal recommendations for the dean's consideration. The dean thanked him for understanding and waved off his apology for failing to move the work forward; his best wishes seemed sincere although Landon would have appreciated more reassurance about his future role in the medical school. This chairmanship had been a plum assignment that might have led to an assistant dean position. Failure was failure, even if it wasn't his fault.

He kept that last thought to himself. This wasn't the time for self-pity. He had other things to do and not much time to do them, and he wasn't about to waste any time he had with Luna or with his father. He went home and sifted through the mail and newspapers she had dutifully deposited on his kitchen counter. The entire place was spotless, with fresh flowers sitting in a small, crystal vase on the coffee table.

He paid the bills, discarded the junk, and kept the newspapers to catch up on what he'd missed during his absence. Charleston was still his home, even if he had become an expatriate these past few weeks, but he really didn't know what was going on in the city or in the hospital, the medical school, all the places that had mattered so much to him before—before the crash, before his cancer, before his father's final illness. With another long drive approaching in two days, he knew he would have time to ruminate on all of this, but suddenly, he wasn't sure he wanted to. He wanted to see Luna, not waste any precious time with her, and then he wanted to be with his father and with his family. That was enough.

CHAPTER THIRTY-EIGHT

few days in Charleston flew by, and even though he
missed Luna before his car left the peninsula, Landon
felt ready to go. He was needed at home. The drive
once again gave him time to think, but this time his mind
stayed focused outward, on his family and eventually on the
reunion. It was now less than two weeks away, and he hadn't
yet mentioned it to his father. He still wanted to go, still
wanted to know what "seventy-five, dead or alive, for all
time, sir" meant. Time was running out on his ability to
get the answer from his father, who had always refused to
discuss it, and his mother wouldn't want him to bother his
father with something that haunted him. Besides, Landon
was pretty certain his father wouldn't give up that secret;
Vietnam was imprisoned behind a locked door in his mind,
and the key had been lost long ago. It seemed cruel to press
him about it. Maybe someone at the reunion would be able
to tell him.

His father's decline was obvious but not dramatic, at
first. He now needed help getting up to the bathroom, but
the trips were more infrequent as his appetite faltered. He
had stopped complaining about being helpless, and when

the bedside commode was brought in, he accepted that without complaint. When he wasn't sleeping, he spent long hours sitting with Landon's mother, the door usually closed. Landon refused to eavesdrop but heard the murmuring, and afterward, he saw how his mother looked more contented than he ever would have thought possible. She did not share, and he never asked her to do so.

He busied himself when he was alone with his father. The morning shave and sponge bath became something both men seemed to look forward to. He always made sure that either George Jones or Johnny Cash was on the CD player, and his father whispered along with the music while Landon freshened him up.

There wasn't much serious conversation. For Landon, being useful seemed an adequate expression of love, and he guessed that his father just didn't have it in him to pour out his heart, even on his deathbed. After all, he had told Landon he loved him and that he was proud of him. He had expressed regret for the wasted years, in his own way. What else was there to say? Landon didn't know either, but he saw the unspoken love in his father's eyes and hoped his father saw the same in his. Each evening, before he withdrew to allow his mother and father to share the end of another of their final few days together, he would squeeze his father's wasted hand and whisper, "I love you, Dad," and wait for the whispered reply he knew he'd remember for the rest of his life.

His mother mentioned the reunion on the following Tuesday, and Landon acknowledged the need to ask permission. She didn't bring it up again. Landon procrastinated out of fear of upsetting whatever peace his father was finding. On Friday morning, though, he knew he could wait no longer.

"Dad, your army reunion is tomorrow night." His father's eyes flickered, but otherwise, there was no response. "I was thinking about going. Luna wants to go too. She's coming tomorrow, remember?"

His father nodded, careful to wait until Landon was rinsing the razor. "What do you want to go there for?" he asked.

"I just thought it would be nice to let your buddies know how you're doing, maybe hear some stories about the war."

He felt what was left of his father's jaw muscles working beneath the razor. "If they tell 'em right, you won't want to hear 'em. They ain't no stories worth telling."

"That's okay, Dad. I'll bet they'd like to hear about you."

"What? That I'm dying of cancer?"

"Well, yeah. They might want to visit or something. Is there anybody you'd want to see? Someone I should look for?"

His father's gaze wandered off. Landon watched him going back in time for a half minute or so and wondered what he was seeing or remembering.

"No, I don't think so, Son. I don't even know who's still alive."

He awoke Saturday morning feeling lucky and nervous. Lucky, because he'd been able to take advantage of a late cancellation to secure a Sunday brunch reservation to go with the room reservation he'd made a month ago. The brunch would enhance their brief romantic getaway at a hotel that he guessed would become one of Luna's favorites.

He was nervous because his original plan had been quashed by Luna, who rejected the idea of proceeding directly to the hotel from the airport. Although her Sunday evening return flight allowed some time for visiting, she had promised his father she would see him Saturday, and besides, she had researched the hotel; check-in was at four o'clock. That meant two trips to Richmond and a cramped schedule prior to the reunion. He wished she had come Friday night, but a mandatory faculty meeting had compressed their weekend plans.

The ride back to Richmond late that afternoon began quietly. Landon was tired and preoccupied with thoughts of the reunion. Luna had been shaken by Eddie's decline but recovered quickly when her presence obviously buoyed his spirits. Once they'd left the house, however, she dropped her defenses and sobbed briefly, clutching Landon's hand. By now he had grown accustomed to grief and knew that it needed its time, that it was not something to be avoided or fixed but rather something to accept silently with love and patience and tissues—which he now kept in a box on his front seat at all times. He offered an occasional glance, a squeeze, and a broken smile that had become a familiar companion. Luna's free hand stroked his arm, and after ten miles or so, she wiped her eyes and kissed him lightly on the cheek.

"Better?" he asked without taking his eyes from the road.

"Yes. Thanks. I wasn't ready for that. He looks so weak."

He nodded. "He is. Gets a little worse each day, it seems like." He paused, giving his failing voice a chance to recover. "Nubyam said it would be like this."

"I guess I didn't think it would be this quick."

"You guys were blabbing away in there," he said, giving her leg a pat. He was eager to change the mood. "I thought I was going to have to bust in and break up the party."

She smiled. "He is so cute. What a flirt—I see where you get it."

"Now, now." He wagged his finger at her. "Don't be complaining. He just knows a hottie when he sees one." He stroked her hair, then let his hand drift over her cheek. He felt her lips brush his fingers. "As does his son."

"And like his son, he's putty in my hands."

That comment made him risk a glance. Luna was wearing the naughty, close-lipped, *I've got a secret* smile. Her eyes seemed bright as headlights.

"Whatever you do, don't ever play poker," he said. "What did you get out of him this time?"

"Just the name of his best friend in his army unit." A curvy stretch of road prevented any prolonged eye contact, but he swiveled his gaze from the road to Luna, who wore a satisfied, impish grin.

He shook his head. "I'll have to compile a list of questions for you. There are other things I'd like to know. How'd you get him to tell you?"

"I didn't. He just told me. I mentioned how excited I was to see the Jefferson Hotel, to stay there, and as I was leaving, he told me to look for Calvin Anderson."

"Did he describe him? What else did he tell you?"

"No, I didn't press him about it. I just told him we'd find him. I asked if there was anything he wanted us to tell him, but he didn't answer. I think he was already asleep."

Frustration or jealousy or something like that flashed through his mind; he could feel it on his face and didn't want

Luna to see it. He felt like a sulking child, upset because he'd been beaten to the punch. The news was welcome, but he wished his father had told him. Now he was about to face a room full of strangers, trying to find someone who might have the answers he wanted. He drove on, pondering which was worse: the possibility that Anderson wouldn't show or that they wouldn't find him in the crowd. Another glance at Luna erased the second possibility. Anderson might not attend, but if he did, Luna would find him.

CHAPTER THIRTY-NINE

L andon scanned name badges while he waited his turn
at the bar. Even in low light, it wasn't difficult work;
in deference to the advancing age of the veterans, the
last names on the badges were large enough to be read at a
distance. He spotted Luna chatting with a woman at a table,
a temporary pause in her quest for Calvin Anderson.

He and Luna were far younger than most of the guests,
but there were other descendants here and there, identified
by badges, that listed the name and rank of the veteran along
with his or her date of death. Since Landon had not followed
the instructions on the invitation, neither he nor Luna had
printed name badges and so his father's information was not
available on the hand-lettered badges that branded them as
last-minute attendees. These were trivial obstacles to Luna,
who had already breezed through half the room, introducing
herself and Landon to anyone who caught her eye.

She cut a striking figure in a black dress that adhered
to the "cocktail attire" instructions he had gotten from the
hotel after misplacing the invitation. He had heard Luna
retelling the story to Carla this afternoon, how she'd had
to threaten him with sleeping on the floor if he didn't find

out what they were supposed to wear, along with the saga of the boutique-by-boutique reconnaissance that Luna and her friend Diana had undertaken last week. She paired the story with a big smile and enough affectionate caresses to reassure him, and along the way he learned that she was wearing a banded sheath dress, though the details about her shoes had never taken hold in his mind.

None of that mattered now. He loved the way the dress tastefully highlighted Luna's figure, the way the neckline plunged, just a little, accentuating the curve of her neck and shoulder, and how the shoes showed off her fresh, perfect pedicure punctuated with Chanel Red Dragon polish—he remembered that. To him, the dress and shoes were pretty; Luna was beautiful.

"You're Eddie's boy, aren't you?"

The deep baritone came from a slim figure only an inch or so taller than Landon. He looked younger and healthier than most of the attendees and wore a jacket and tie along with a warm, welcoming smile. He was black, an unexpected feature that drove Landon to quickly confirm the name Anderson on the name tag pinned to the man's lapel.

"I am," Landon said, offering as firm a handshake as he could muster. "I'm Landon Ratliff."

"Calvin Anderson. I can't tell you what a pleasure it is to meet you." He covered the handshake with his other hand. His smile vanished. "I hope your father hasn't passed?"

Landon cleared his throat. "No, but he's very sick. Terminally ill, in fact."

"I'm so sorry to hear that. Cancer?"

"Yes. He's at home in hospice care. He asked me to look you up, tell you hello."

That drew another smile. "Good old Rat. I knew he'd never show up here. But you did, and I'm glad." He gestured toward the bar. "This calls for a drink."

Landon took a step back and dipped his head. "After you, Mr. Anderson. This is your evening."

"Calvin, please," he said, stepping up. "Martini. Up, with a twist," he told the bartender. "What'll you have, Landon? Is Landon okay?"

"Perfect. I'll have the same. I'm not driving anywhere tonight."

"Me neither. You married, Landon?"

He shook his head, noted Calvin's wedding ring. "No, but my girlfriend's here." He gestured toward the far side of the room and asked the bartender for a glass of white wine. "She's working the crowd, looking for you." He smiled. "But you found me instead. How'd you know it was me?"

Calvin smiled, his head scrunching down into his collar. "The name badge caught my eye, but then I knew. You stand just like Eddie always did. Built like him, too, and you've got his eyes."

"Is your wife here?" Landon asked. He accepted the drinks, and he and Calvin stepped aside. Luna was smiling and chatting with another couple near the dance floor.

"No, Elizabeth has a sister here in Richmond. She uses this trip to catch up with her. She says this is my thing. She's picking me up later."

"Are you sitting with friends? Why don't you sit with us? I don't know anyone." He began to move tentatively toward Luna, hoping he wasn't pressing too much.

Calvin smiled. "I'd be happy to join you. Thank you."

He led Calvin to Luna, pleased that he got to make the introduction. Luna was thrilled, too, and seemed unsurprised to hear that Calvin had spotted Landon. They chose an unoccupied table, but before they could sit, two other veterans greeted Calvin. He introduced both Landon and Luna, but it quickly became clear that neither of the newcomers had known Landon's father. Landon was grateful when they moved on after a short conversation.

"Have you seen anyone else from your unit?" he asked Calvin when they were alone again.

"Not yet. Didn't see many last year. Seems like the numbers get smaller every year."

"Do you come every year?" Luna asked.

"No—I try to, but my granddaughter was leaving for college two years ago, and I missed another time because I was sick."

"My dad's never come to this," Landon said. "Have you seen him since the war?"

Calvin shook his head. "No. Haven't had any contact with him. We didn't know each other that long, and all of it was under a lot of stress. I live in Abingdon, teach at Emory and Henry, and that's a pretty long haul. Your dad lives in Gloucester or near there, right?"

"Near Deltaville," Landon said.

"Right. We're not really beach folks, and when we did go, we always went to the Outer Banks, so I never really had much occasion to visit that area. No people there."

"I'm a teacher too," Luna said. She went on to explain her position and background. Calvin was attentive, asking questions, but Landon gradually drifted away from the conversation, wondering why two war buddies would never have taken the time to visit one another over a forty-year period. He knew the answer for his father, drowning in alcohol and his own demons. But Calvin? A college professor? It didn't make sense.

"How about you, Landon. What do you do?"

"I'm a doctor. Associate professor at the Medical University of South Carolina, in critical care medicine."

Calvin was smiling broadly now, his eyes shining. "That's wonderful. I bet old Eddie is proud of you."

"He really is," Luna said, before Landon could comment.

Waiters began arriving with dinner, and two more couples joined them at their table. Landon recounted his educational history, beginning with Old Dominion University, through medical school at MCV, and then his residency in Florida and New Orleans.

"I've got a cousin in New Orleans," Calvin said. "I haven't been back since Katrina."

"It's changed some since then," Landon said. "Luna and I were there in June."

"My first visit," she said. "I thought it was lovely."

"We enjoy it," Calvin said, "in small doses." His smile lit up the room again.

The chitchat continued through most of dinner, and Landon marveled at how different Calvin's life had unfolded compared with his father's. Calvin had gone to college on the GI Bill, earned his master's degree, and then went to work, first at a community college in Roanoke and then at Emory and Henry, where he'd been for more than twenty years. Born in Grundy to a coal-mining family, he, like Landon's father, had not strayed far from where he was born, except when his country drafted him and sent him halfway around the world to hell. The history came in sips; Calvin seemed more interested in talking about Landon and Luna and to the others at the table. The war talk was confined to the unit and dates of service, and then it was on to children, grandchildren, and other things.

When dessert was served, Landon began to worry. Calvin might disappear shortly after dinner. He'd had only one drink, no wine with dinner, and didn't seem like the type to hang around when the dancing started.

"Mr. Anderson?" he asked, just before everyone dug into the Key lime pie.

"Calvin. Or should I call you Doctor?"

Landon laughed. "No, don't do that. Sounds too much like work. Okay, Calvin, do you mind telling me about my father, about the war? I don't want to bring up bad memories, but he's never talked about it at all."

Calvin's smile faded. His face grew stony—not unfriendly or menacing but rather distant and searching. After a minute, he forced a close-lipped, nervous smile. "I'm not surprised to hear that, Landon. The war was hard on all of us, especially your father."

"Why do you say that?" Luna asked.

"Eddie was different—jumpy and angry. He didn't want to be there. None of us did really, but most of us thought we were doing the right thing. It was 1966, you know, most of the anti-war stuff hadn't really started, and most of us just accepted it. Not Eddie. He saw through it, thought we were wasting our time and getting killed for nothing. Especially after Mick got killed."

"Mick? Dad never mentioned him."

Calvin laid his napkin beside his plate. "They're going to start playing music shortly, and we won't be able to hear a thing. How about we adjourn to the lobby bar?" He moved behind Luna's chair. "After you," he said with a sweep of his hand. "I'm buying."

As they crossed the lobby, Landon felt Luna's hand on his shoulder, then encircling his back. He slowed and leaned in, felt her lips brush his cheek. "I hope we're not pushing him too hard," she whispered.

"Yeah, I know, but it's now or never." He turned to face Luna. "He'll stop if it gets too painful. I hope it doesn't, though."

They found an empty table. Calvin ordered brandy. Landon asked for the same. Luna went along, giving him a wide-eyed smile and a shrug when he glanced at her.

"To Eddie Ratliff and Robert Oaks," Calvin said. Landon and Luna touched their glasses to his. "Two finer men I have never known."

The brandy burned—in a good way. Landon wondered how Luna was faring, but she never flinched. "Was Oaks Mick?" he asked.

"Yes. Your dad was Hank. I'll bet he never told you that, did he?"

Landon shook his head.

Calvin smiled again, a vague, broken grin. His eyes seemed to be searching for something he didn't want to find. "I was Ray—Ray Charles. Your dad was Hank Williams, and Rob was Mick Jagger. Rob was only eighteen, just a kid. We all were, I guess, but at least Eddie and I were married, had kids. Mick never got the chance.

"We all went in country at the same time, and at first there wasn't much to do. So we cut up to pass the time, listened to our music, and argued about whose music was best. Just joking, you know, and pretty soon we were Ray and Hank and Mick." He shook his head. "Hard to imagine, but we had some good times—for a little while."

"What happened to Mick?" Landon asked. "If you don't mind telling us."

Calvin said nothing, just looked at Landon with vacant eyes, and then the light came on again. "I don't mind. It's been a long while since I talked about Mick or any of this. It took a lot of therapy. When I was done, I didn't want any more of it, but now I think you need to know, and I think I want to tell it. I think I *can* tell it, and that feels good."

Calvin's eyes shifted from Landon to Luna and back again. "It was Operation Birmingham." After another sip, he pursed his lips and smiled. "That's awful good. Anyway, we were in Tây Ninh Province near the Cambodian border. Flew us in, told us the Viet Cong were training there, that we were going to engage a large force, destroy them. Never happened. We fought the jungle mostly and burned bags of rice. Found supplies but not many men. Just about every day, snipers would pick off one or two of us. We'd light up the jungle for a few minutes, and then it'd be over. We might find a couple of dead VC, or find none, and one or two of our men would be shot up or dead."

"Is that what happened to Mick?" Luna asked.

"Yeah. We'd only been there about a week. We were on patrol, crossing a clearing that wasn't more than a hundred yards across. Mick was between me and Eddie. Took a round in the neck. We killed the sniper in five minutes, but Mick was dead before the medic could get to him. We watched him die, Eddie and me.

"It was one guy. No army, no supplies, no nothing. He had to know he was going to get killed, but he took one American with him. Something went out of Eddie that day, and it wasn't long until he got it too."

"Another sniper?" Landon was glad to feel Luna's hand in his.

"No. Your dad got it in a real firefight. That was a battle. Went on for hours. I thought we were all going to die. First real battle for all of us, I think. Wasn't my last one, but it was Eddie's.

"We were patrolling along the Cái River when all hell broke loose. It was early in the morning, already hot, four or five days after Mick got killed. The VC opened up with artillery, machine guns, mortars, everything. It was coming from everywhere. I thought we were surrounded at first. Guys were shooting in every direction. Then our platoon leader got us straightened out, but you couldn't see anybody to shoot at.

"Finally, airstrikes wiped out most of their artillery, and we moved on the machine guns. It was mid-afternoon before we finished them off. We found fifty or sixty dead VC. They might have carried off a bunch more when they left."

"How did my father get wounded?" Landon asked.

Calvin smiled. "I don't know for sure. It wasn't like the movies, where everyone's gathered together. It was every man for himself when the shooting started. Bullets and smoke and fire were everywhere. The noise was deafening, but you could hear men get hit. I didn't see Eddie, but I heard him go down, hollering and cussing. I saw a medic going for him, and then I kept moving, kept my head down. If you raised up, the machine guns would get you. I took a round in the pack that day.

"Eddie's leg was pretty tore up. I saw him before they airlifted him out. He had machine gun wounds and some shrapnel. I knew he wasn't coming back."

"Did you talk to him?" Landon wasn't sure why he asked that, but he wanted to learn all he could.

"No. They'd given him morphine, and he wasn't really coherent, you know." Calvin finished off his brandy. "We lost four guys that day and had twelve wounded."

"This was 1966, you said?" Luna asked.

Calvin nodded. "Thirtieth April. Never forget that day."

"That's my birthday," Landon said.

"Exactly one year later," Luna added.

"You're kidding," Calvin said, then smiled. "That's one way to turn an unhappy anniversary into something positive. It's funny—April thirtieth is also the date we pulled out of Vietnam for good." He raised his empty glass. "Your birthday's been a big day, Landon."

Luna was staring into the remains of her dessert. Landon guessed she was thinking what he was thinking: the corner of Broad and Meeting Streets. He nodded and touched his glass to Calvin's. "It definitely has."

"What was Eddie like back then, before he got wounded?" Luna asked, her voice full of music that wanted a different mood.

"Oh, Eddie was angry but funny too. He didn't want to be there, but when you got him talking about his wife and kids, showing off the photos we all carried, his eyes would light up, and you'd see the guy inside, hidden by the angry man.

He was mad at the world, seemed like. Still, we had some good times, talking about what we'd do when we got back. If we got back." Calvin's eyes seemed to cloud over again. "How'd Eddie do, Landon? After he got home?"

"Not so well. He drank way too much. My mom says the war ruined him."

"I worried about that. Could tell he was a drinker. That's ruined a lot of men."

"Can I ask you something else?" Landon didn't wait for a reply. "What does seventy-five, dead or alive, for all time, sir' mean?"

"Did you hear your dad say that?" Calvin's broad smile caught Landon off guard.

He nodded. "Yeah, and another guy too. Did you know Amede Doucet?"

"Doucet? Yeah, I knew him. Not well. Big Cajun—came in country just before I mustered out. Seemed like a good guy."

"Well, he ended up homeless on the streets of New Orleans," Landon said. "Drank himself to death. I met him on my first trip there. He said that seventy-five thing but wouldn't tell me what it meant."

"Neither would your dad, right?"

"Right. And neither will you, right?"

Calvin kept smiling. "No, I'll tell you. I'm over all that shit." He turned to Luna. "Excuse my language—all that stuff. That was our company commander's idea. He was gung ho, right out of West Point, and wanted to build morale or camaraderie or something. He always told us if we got hurt or captured, that was all we'd say, that it would carry us through, but we should never reveal its meaning to anyone else. Eddie always made fun of it. Said it was a pile of you-know-what." He shook his head. "Doucet, too, huh? I guess you never know what sticks with people."

"Yep," Landon said. "Told me it was a secret."

Calvin seemed to be elsewhere, staring across the room, but he wasn't gone long. His gaze was piercing when he turned to Landon. "Secrets can eat you up, Landon. Too many good men are holding secrets from back then. The military does that all the time. I guess they have to, to get men to do things no sane person would do. But those secrets isolate you, keep you bottled up, and that's no good. I made up my mind a long time ago. I was done with keeping secrets."

It got quiet then. The muffled music from the ballroom drifted across the lobby. Landon wanted a drink, and Luna's brandy was barely touched, so he excused himself to go fetch another round. Calvin declined and scooted closer to Luna so they could chat in Landon's absence.

When he returned, Calvin rose from his chair. "It's time for me to get on." He offered his hand to Luna. "It's been a pleasure meeting you, Luna." He shook Landon's hand vigorously, then offered a quick man hug. "Landon, I can't tell you how good it is to see you—Eddie's boy." He shook his head. "Never thought I'd be talking to Eddie's boy."

"Come and visit him," Landon said. "He'd enjoy seeing you."

Calvin grimaced, a close-lipped maneuver that seemed designed to capture and reshape words before they escaped. "I don't know. I don't think Eddie would want me to see him like he is now."

"He won't be around much longer, I'm afraid," Landon said.

Calvin's smile was his brightest yet. "Oh yeah, he'll be around." He patted his chest. "Old Hank's right here, right next to Mick. Give him my best."

"Thanks for talking with us," Landon said. "Hope we didn't stir up too many bad memories."

Calvin shook his head. "Not at all. It's part of my history, like it or not. I wouldn't wish it on anyone, but it helped make me who I am today. I'm one of the lucky ones." He nodded, waved, and turned toward the exit.

Landon slid his arm around Luna's waist and watched Calvin disappear into the lobby crowd. "My dad wasn't," he said.

Luna excused herself to go find the restroom. He welcomed the time to collect his thoughts. He felt as if he'd found his father's diary, only to discover that most of the pages were blank. Still, he'd learned a little. He had no trouble picturing his father angry, but it sounded as if he'd recognized the futility of the war sooner than most, and that surprised Landon. As did the story of his father's parental pride, though he'd heard that before, from others. And he knew very well that when Calvin heard him bragging, Landon was not yet one of those children.

He glanced up and spotted Luna wandering through the lobby, admiring the marble columns and the grand staircase. He watched her dawdle, knowing she was giving him some private time, and when he finally caught her eye, he motioned her over.

"I was getting lonely," he said unconvincingly, then added, "thanks."

Luna leaned in and kissed him. He tasted fresh lipstick. "You're welcome. I thought you might like a few minutes." She smiled a crooked smile. "That's all you're getting, though."

"Calvin's a great guy," he said, then shook his head. "A Black guy. I never would have guessed."

"Why? Does that matter?"

"Not to me. I guess not to my dad either."

"Is Eddie a racist?"

He wasn't sure how to answer that. Luna's face betrayed no horror or disgust, so he knew he was on firm ground with her, but still, the answer seemed complicated. "I guess he is, at least the way most people I grew up with were. I mean, he used the N-word all the time when I was a kid. Everybody did. I mean, I never saw him mistreat anyone except us, and he was nice to the black people we ran into, but we never socialized with them, and I couldn't imagine him having black friends." He paused for a sip. "Honestly, the only friends he ever had that I saw were drinking buddies. Sounds like Calvin might've been the best friend he ever had. A black guy."

"You think he was ashamed? That's why he never told you?"

"I doubt it. Calvin said it took a lot of counseling for him to be able to face what he'd been through. Too bad my dad didn't have the self-awareness to get some help."

"Hmm." Luna was smiling around the rim of her glass.

"What?"

"I don't know—seems like the Ratliff men have some difficulty recognizing the value of psychotherapy. I guess I didn't know it was genetic."

"Checkmate," Landon said, happy to have been bested again.

CHAPTER FORTY

Halfway to the restaurant, Luna began to regret her decision to forego the taxi. It was a short walk, but the sweltering evening threatened the breezy, carefree look she had labored to achieve for her first meeting with Diana since the fall term began two weeks earlier.

Time had flown by, between trips to Virginia and the start of the school year. When Diana called her on Monday, it only then occurred to her that she hadn't even thought of Diana for some time. Amidst a flurry of apologies on both sides, they agreed to a dinner meeting for Thursday. Diana surprised Luna by choosing the Peninsula Grill, a place she and Landon had considered for one of their first dates, back when they had the time and freedom to ponder restaurant choices. Was that really only seven months ago?

Diana was waiting in the Champagne Bar. Her incandescent smile, highlighted by the muted bar lighting, and her warm, genuine hug allayed Luna's worries immediately. It had been too long, but nothing was lost. She felt the burdens of the past weeks float away, at least for a little while.

"It's so good to see you," Diana said, motioning for Luna to sit. "I ordered some Pinot Grigio for us. I hope you don't mind—it's so hot."

"This looks perfect."

A silver bucket of ice held a corked bottle. The waiter materialized before they could unfold their napkins. "Will you be dining in the bar, ladies?" The pale-yellow liquid swirled into the glass and caught the light from one of the wall sconces. She felt her neck and shoulders relax.

"No, we have a reservation at seven in the dining room," Diana told him. She waited until he had excused himself with a nod and a smile. She raised her glass. "To the end of August. Good riddance, I say. Let's hope we have an early fall."

The wine was cold and tasted like pears. The first sip seemed to go straight to her brain, making her wish she'd eaten more lunch. "Wow. This is delicious, Diana."

That drew a closed-mouth smile, followed by a head tilt. "Glad you like it. You look beautiful. You must be exhausted. How are you?"

"I'm fine. Tired for sure. The last month has been crazy." She sat up straighter and raised her glass. "Enough of that. It's wonderful to see you—I've missed you. How are you?"

Diana touched her glass to hers. "I'm good. Very good, now that you're here." After a sip, she leaned closer, her eyes searching.

"What?" Luna asked, unable to contain a smile.

"You look like a woman in love, Luna."

Luna gave her a head tilt, brow wrinkled, still smiling, though.

Diana sat back and tossed her free hand in the air, as if she were shooing a fly. "I don't know. Call me crazy, but I remember having lunch at your place in the spring. Things were tough then, too, and you were confused and worried and unsure about your relationship. Now, things might be even tougher, but your eyes tell a different story. Maybe I'm wrong?" She plopped her elbow on the table and planted her chin in her hand. Her eyebrows arched as she chuckled under her breath, just loud enough for Luna to hear.

"No question. I'm totally in love, but I think we've been through this?"

"I know." Diana's brows arched high above her impish eyes, drawing a smile from Luna. "But I enjoy hearing you say it and seeing it on your face." Diana's smile drifted away. "How's Landon?"

"He's being very brave. It's so hard—I can't tell you. He's taking care of his father and his mother. His father has turned out to be a sweetheart—he's crazy about me, and he's funny. I guess sickness can take the meanness out of you."

"What's the prognosis?"

"Not good. He's going downhill fast. He can't get out of bed without help. He's really weak." She felt her throat tightening. She raised a finger and took a sip.

"Sorry," Diana said. "This must be so hard."

"Yeah, but I'm glad I can be there. I'm going back tomorrow for Labor Day weekend. It sounds like it won't be much longer."

"Why? How do you know?"

She shrugged. "You don't, really—not for certain. But on Tuesday, Landon said his father couldn't use the bedside commode anymore. He's only taking sips of water. The doctor said that's what happens near the end."

Diana's free hand was pressed to her throat. "It sounds horrible."

"It really isn't." Luna shook her head. "It's hard, but it's beautiful in a way. He's where he wants to be, and the whole family is with him, as much as possible. Landon's mom is such a trooper. I think this time has helped heal some wounds for all of them." She sat forward and took another sip. "Oh, I haven't told you this. Landon has a sister he hasn't seen or spoken to in years."

"You're kidding."

"I'm not, and now *she's* even talking with her parents. Not with Landon or Dale—that's his brother—but it's a start. I'm hoping she'll visit before Landon's father dies."

"Surely she will?" The fun had definitely disappeared from Diana's face. Luna wondered if she should change the subject.

"We'll see. It's her loss if she doesn't." She glanced around the room. "I love this place. It's dark and cool and perfect."

Diana nodded. The smile was back. "It is. One of our favorite places to eat in Charleston actually. Mark never says no to this place."

"How is Mark? *Where* is Mark? You could've brought him, you know."

"Shake yourself, Luna. I'm not going to spoil our first dinner together in, what, months? Anyway, it would be tough to bring him. He's in London, or I guess on his way to Frankfurt by now."

"I used to like the time apart," Luna said. "I thought it kept me sane." She swirled her wine, staring into the glass. "Now I just miss him."

"Well, give it some time. I used to miss Mark too. Now I like the time apart. I guess everything comes full circle, doesn't it?"

By the time she and Diana split a slice of coconut cake, Luna was tipsy, full, and nearly as satisfied as she'd been the morning after the reunion. Diana had extracted every shareable detail about that trip; it seemed the Jefferson Hotel (and Richmond) was one of the few places Diana had never visited. Luna felt sure she would check that one off her list in the near future.

Most of a second bottle of wine was gone when Diana reached across the table and laid her hand on Luna's wrist. "I need to tell you something."

She sat up straighter. Diana's change of expression had dampened her buzz considerably. "What is it? Are you okay?"

"Yes, yes. You've had your share of sickness in your life. I'm fine." Diana cleared her throat. "But I need to tell you … I guess there's no other way but to just tell you … I'm leaving Charleston."

"*You're* leaving?" Luna frowned. "Are you getting a divorce?"

Diana recoiled into her chair. "No! Why would you say that?"

She shrugged. "I don't know. Too much wine?"

Diana laughed then, a deep, quiet, shoulder-shaking laugh that drew a smile from Luna, who already felt as if she were losing her closest friend.

"You've got to visit—you and Landon. I'm going to miss you so much."

"Where the heck are you going, and why? What am I going to do?"

"Europe." Diana nodded slowly, her eyes wide with excitement, letting the news seep into Luna's brain for a moment. "Frankfurt actually. At least, that's where our apartment will be. Mark's heading up his firm's Frankfurt office."

"Germany?" She scrunched her nose.

"Frankfurt is a beautiful city," Diana said. She drained her glass. "Besides, Mark will be so busy, and traveling, so I plan to spend most of my time seeing the sights. I already have plans for Amsterdam and Brussels and a spring trip to Paris. We're spending Christmas in Vienna."

"Christmas? When are you moving?"

Diana's face fell. "We leave October tenth. I told the dean yesterday. My last day is September thirtieth."

"That's only a month." Luna stared into the remains of the cake. When she looked up, Diana was watching her, her head tilted slightly, a hint of a smile on her lips.

"I thought you'd be excited for me."

"I am, Diana. I'm sorry. I guess it's all about me, huh?" She raised her glass, then realized that Diana's wine was gone. "Congratulations. What a great opportunity." She felt her eyes filling up and tried to look away, but Diana's hand caught hers.

"Luna, look at me." Diana's eyes were watery. "You're going to be fine. I'm flattered that you think you need my help, but you don't—not anymore. Besides, they have phone service in Europe, you know, and whether you like it or not,

I plan to call you regularly just to keep up with the gossip around here.

"I spoke with the dean about you too. He agrees that you've proven yourself, but we both want you to have a resource. Why don't you think about that, and let me know? I'll be glad to ask whoever you choose."

She nodded. Her career, a promotion, all seemed trivial right now; she wasn't ready to think about any of that. Her best friend was leaving. "Do you already have an apartment?"

"Just something temporary, furnished. It'll be fine until I find something. We're storing our stuff." Diana leaned closer. "The invitation is genuine, Luna. You and Landon have to visit me. Promise?"

Diana insisted on paying, and Luna couldn't muster the energy to argue. They walked together to the market, where taxis were sometimes found, and Diana got lucky. Luna figured a walk would burn off some of the wine and get her ready for a snuggle with Hazel. She reminded herself to take some ibuprofen and drink lots of water before bed.

She hadn't gone far when her phone buzzed. *Probably Diana,* she thought while digging through her purse, but it was Landon.

"Sorry to bother you," he said. "How was dinner?"

"You're never bothering me, sweetie. It was fine. Diana is moving to Europe."

"Oh jeez, I'm sorry."

Something in his voice jolted her out of her self-absorption. "Landon, what's wrong?"

"It's Dad. He's slipping away, I think. "Walter came by tonight and—"

"Oh, I'm so sorry." The crack in his voice had brought tears to her eyes. "I wish I was there."

"Me too."

"I can try to get an earlier flight tomorrow." She hoped he wouldn't agree to that. She had no idea how she'd cover her class. She felt guilty all of a sudden.

"No, don't do that. Walter said he thought it would be a few days anyway."

"What happened?"

"Nothing dramatic. He just isn't awake anymore."

"Wasn't he all right this morning?" She tried to recall their conversation from earlier.

"Seemed to be. He's been declining all week, like I told you, but now, well, I guess he's …"

"I love you, Landon. I'll be there as soon as I can." In that instant, she knew where she belonged. It wasn't a place or a city, and it had nothing to do with her job. Diana would be fine, and so would she.

CHAPTER FORTY-ONE

Carla had invited Landon and Luna to spend Labor Day with her family, water-skiing and picnicking, but it didn't happen. Landon appreciated the kindness and hopefulness that came with the invitation, but as the weekend hours passed, his father remained unconscious. By Saturday afternoon, his breathing had become more irregular; he required intermittent doses of morphine to help him rest quietly. All desperate hopes for a miracle seemed to have vanished. His mother welcomed a parade of visitors, most of whom stood around awkwardly and offered their best ineffective words of comfort while his father's life ebbed away.

Landon had watched many people die. Some had gone quickly from heart attacks or blood clots, and others had lingered, gradually succumbing to infection or some other insult that overwhelmed their immune system. Some had died of cancer. None of these had been family members, and of course, none were his father.

On Sunday afternoon, he and Dale, exhausted from the previous night's vigil, had fallen asleep watching the Braves game. Luna woke him. Her tears jolted him into alertness. "I think you'd better come," she said.

They all crowded into the small bedroom where his father's breathing had become noisy and irregular. "The hospice nurse said it would get like this," his mother said. "She's on her way."

He and Dale flanked their mother, each encircling her with one arm. He and Luna held hands, her head resting against his shoulder. His father looked shrunken and small, his collapsed face appeared youthful despite the ravages of disease. His eyes were half-open, staring into space as if he were already gone. The room was still, the silence broken by a gasping breath every thirty seconds or so. Luna sniffled and dabbed at her eyes.

Finally, his mother broke free and kneeled beside his father, cradling his head and speaking softly. "It's okay, Eddie, we're fine. We're all fine, and you will be too. You can go now. Go be with God." She leaned forward and touched her lips to his forehead.

Landon felt himself coming apart. He couldn't look at Dale, didn't want him to see him like this. He pulled Luna closer. An occasional muffled sob wracked her trembling body.

Dale stepped forward and laid a hand on his father's chest. "It's okay, Dad. I love you." He wiped away a tear and pulled Carla close.

It was Landon's turn. He knew it, had known this moment would come, and yet was not at all prepared for it. The world—his world—was shifting and would never be the same. Luna stepped away, releasing him, and he reached for his father's hand. He dared not squeeze too hard. Tears blurred his vision, but now he didn't care. He laid his head on his father's chest, heard the heartbeat, strong and even, and knew that he was hearing the coda, that the symphony of his father's life was drawing to a close. He waited for another agonal gasp and then whispered, "I love you, Dad." The effort seemed to sap his strength. His mother and Luna helped him to his feet. His father took another breath, and then, after a long pause, another one.

No one moved for a minute or so. Then his mother stepped forward. "I think he's gone," she said and turned to Landon. He knew the family was looking to him for confirmation. He felt no pulse at the neck or the wrist. Once again, he laid his head on his father's chest. It was silent now. He nodded. Luna and Carla gathered his mother, who finally gave in to silent tears. Dale reached for him, and he dropped all pretense, sobbing into his brother's shoulder while a strong arm clutched him tightly around his back.

Then it was Luna who held him, stroking his hair and whispering between sobs. Finally, he saw his mother's face and gave in to his grief once again, wrapped in the hug that had shielded him from the man whose death had now turned him loose to fend for himself.

When the hugging was finished and the tears spent, everyone stood around waiting for someone, probably his mother, to do something. It seemed as if someone ought to say something, but Landon had never been much of a speaker, and the only prayer he could think of was grace. He smiled, keeping it to himself, as he thought of his father at the dinner table, kidding his mother by hastily mumbling, "Good bread, good meat, good God, let's eat," whenever he wanted to tease her about saying grace.

Dale nudged him and motioned toward the door with his head, pointing at their mother, who had lowered herself into the bedside chair. Landon nodded, and they gave her some private time.

Carla and Luna immediately busied themselves in the kitchen, trying to find storage space for all the food that had been deposited by well-meaning family and friends. Dale headed for the front door; Landon guessed he would find refuge in his truck, maybe take a drive, but he hadn't invited him along, and he didn't want to go—didn't want to be with anyone just now. He headed out the back door, hoping Luna wouldn't follow him, and she didn't.

The back porch wasn't large enough for sitting. It was nothing more than a square platform with wooden railings. He remembered sitting on those railings when he was a kid, eating an apple or a cookie on late summer evenings. He had felt like King Kong astride the Empire State Building back then. Now he saw that he wasn't more than seven or eight feet above the sloping backyard that fell off toward the marsh.

The sky was fading to twilight, and a soft, warm breeze had come up. Clouds—their undersides just tinted a fading pink—glided effortlessly across the sky, as if nothing had just happened. Couldn't they stop, just for a minute? Birds sang their evening song, squirrels chattered before bedding down, and across the way, an owl announced himself. The wind blew. Between the clouds, he saw a star or two begin to appear. The world was going on about its business.

CHAPTER FORTY-TWO

arilyn, the hospice nurse, arrived before Landon's mother emerged from the bedroom. She greeted everyone before joining her at the bedside. They were behind closed doors for a few minutes, and then Marilyn summoned everyone into the room. His father's eyes were closed now, his hair was combed, and his bedclothes had been smoothed and tucked in around him. He looked peaceful.

His mother welcomed them with a hug, then situated herself between Dale and Landon. Marilyn said a prayer and asked if anyone else had something to say. His mother spoke in a clear voice: "Eddie was my husband and the father of my children. He wasn't the easiest husband or father, but I loved him, and I want you all to know how much he loved you. He told me to be sure to tell you that. He knew he hadn't done right by you, but he tried his best. His best wasn't always that good."

He felt tears filling his eyes again as he smiled at his mother's understatement. It didn't matter now; he knew his father hadn't tried hard enough and knew a little more about why, but it didn't matter now. His father was gone, and Landon would give anything to have him back, just for a little while.

"He taught me a lot," Dale was saying. "I loved him, even though I didn't understand him or the things he did. He did what he could, I guess."

"Landon?" Marilyn asked. "Would you like to say something?"

He felt Luna's hand on his back. He nodded. His mother's broken smile was heartbreaking. "He was my dad. It wasn't easy, but I wasn't the easiest son either. I wish things had been better. I'm glad I got to know him better these last few weeks. I used to cringe when I acted like him, but now I know he's in me, and I'm glad."

Carla and Luna spoke about how kind he'd been to them. Molly was in Landon's mind. She hadn't come to see him before he died. He felt no anger, only sadness for what she would have to live with.

"Eddie asked that we sing 'Amazing Grace' here, in this room, before his body is removed," Marilyn said. "It was his favorite hymn." She passed out the lyrics. It was difficult to fathom. Landon had never heard his father sing a hymn; he had only entered a church when the occasion, or more precisely, Landon's mother had demanded it.

Carla and Marilyn carried the song. Dale and Landon had inherited the Ratliff/Leonard unfamiliarity with key, pitch, and timbre, and like their mother, murmured so softly that their lips hardly moved. Luna took a less timid approach, wandering somewhere in the vicinity of the right key.

"There's one more song Eddie requested," Marilyn said, after the last note of the hymn had faded. He stifled a groan. "No more singing," Marilyn said with a smile. "Eddie wanted us to listen to this one." She reached for his mother's hand. "This was Eddie and Iris' song."

Landon knew—it had to be Hank Williams. He had watched his parents dance to it a few times. He wondered if his mother would break down, but she didn't. She smiled and swayed while Hank sang "I'm So Lonesome I Could Cry." Her eyes were closed, and he guessed she was traveling back to high school, when they were young and naïve and crazy about each other, never dreaming of everything that life had waiting for them, everything that led to this.

There wasn't much to do after that. His mother phoned her parents and Reverend Koenig, her boss and pastor. Marilyn had already phoned the funeral home. Two men arrived, wrapped the body in a sheet, and wheeled it out the door to a waiting hearse. Landon stood in the front yard alone, watching until the taillights vanished behind the pines. Marilyn stayed to review the funeral plans. Everything was done; his father had long ago squelched any thought of burial in Arlington National Cemetery. He did not want the military headstone. The casket was a simple, pine box selected during a bedside conversation with Marilyn. The Leonard family plot, purchased by grandfather Leonard fifty years earlier, suited him fine; it was a pretty churchyard plot with tall hardwood trees and well-tended shrubs. A low headstone that would mark the graves of Eddie and Iris Ratliff was expected to be in place within a couple of weeks.

So Labor Day passed pretty quietly. Sally kept everyone busy and brought reluctant smiles to their faces. Landon felt as if he ought to be doing something, but he didn't know what. Luna was there with a touch or a smile. He knew she wouldn't try to make things better; she was there to listen, but he didn't have anything to say.

In the afternoon, he ventured out to the shed. Luna and Carla had taken Sally down to the water, and Dale had driven his mother to Deltaville. The shed had always been his father's private place, as well as his cell when he misbehaved. The cot was still there; he wondered when it had last been used. His father's hand tools hung on hooks above the workbench, which had accumulated a thick layer of dust. He grabbed the hammer that he bought as a present for his father's fiftieth birthday, a sixteen-ounce Estwing rip hammer with a leather handle. His father had wanted one for years or at least said he did. Landon recalled being surprised at how inexpensive it turned out to be when he finally got around to purchasing it. But his father had loved it, showed it off to his friends, and cared for it as if it were an expensive violin, cleaning the handle with saddle soap and conditioning the leather every week.

The hammer was hefty. He sniffed, searching for his father's scent, but the handle smelled like worn leather. Although the tools would rightfully go to Dale, who knew how to use them, Landon figured this one belonged to him. Suddenly, an image of turkey buzzards circling in the sky above the marsh came to him. He replaced the hammer on its hook. He and Dale could discuss this later.

After dinner, his mother gathered everyone around the kitchen table to discuss the funeral. "Your daddy didn't want a long funeral," she told Dale and Landon. "He wanted to skip the whole thing, but Marilyn explained that the funeral wasn't really for him, and that convinced him."

"Sounds like the dad I knew," Dale said. He was smiling, shaking his head.

"If either of you boys want to speak, you can. I'm not trying to pressure you, but Reverend Koenig needs to know so he can finalize the service."

Landon wasn't sure. He ought to speak, but what would he say? That for most of his life, his father was a source of fear and anger and sadness and pain? Or that for the past couple of months, his father had finally been nice to him? That the process of dying seemed to have been good for him? Nothing felt right and true.

"I'm not sure I do, Mom," Dale said. I've kind of said what I had to say, and I don't like talking in front of people."

"That's fine, honey." She patted his arm. "Landon?"

He remembered in that instant. "I'd like to read something, Mom. The Sullivan Ballou letter."

For a moment, he thought he'd hurt her. His mother's eyes filled with tears, and she bowed her head. When she looked up, though, she was smiling. "I'd forgotten about that. Thank you for remembering." She fished a handkerchief from her skirt pocket. "That would be really sweet."

"Good going, Brother," Dale said.

Luna looked puzzled. "Did you watch the Ken Burns series on the Civil War?" Landon asked. She nodded. "Remember at the very beginning, there's a letter from a Union soldier to his wife, just before the Battle of Bull Run? He talks about how he regrets not being able to see their sons grow up and how he will be with her, in the breeze, after he dies?"

Luna pressed her lips together. "I was a teenager. Sutter was into it."

"My dad always said it was the best thing he'd ever heard about bravery and about war and death."

She smiled. "Sounds perfect."

"We still have the CD, right, Mom?" he asked. "Or did Dad wear it out?"

"It's here, baby," she said. He didn't try to hide the tear that spilled onto his cheek.

His mother cleared her throat. "Now, I have something else to tell you. Molly is coming to the funeral."

He looked at Dale, who was looking at him.

"I called her late last night. She'd asked me to, and she wants to come. I didn't want you boys to be surprised when she shows up."

"When's she coming?" Dale asked.

"I think just for the service. I don't know for sure. I told her I'd call her tomorrow, when everything's finalized, but I wonder if I should call her tonight. She may want to speak."

"Are you kidding, Mom?" Landon asked. "After all these years, she wants to pop in and offer a tribute?" He felt Luna's hand on his forearm. His mother's eyes were narrowing. Dale was watching him. "I'm sorry, but I just don't think that's right. She didn't even come to say goodbye."

Things got very quiet. His mother looked as she always looked when Landon had gone too far. Usually, that look was followed by a quiet "Landon," but not this time. He worried that he'd hurt her, but she didn't look broken or even wounded. She seemed to be waiting.

Dale jumped to his feet. "Come on, Brother. Let's go for a ride."

Carla stared at the table. Luna forced a smile that looked painful. He rose and followed his brother out to his truck.

They hit the main road before Landon found his voice. "What do you think, Dale? Am I way off base here?"

"I don't know, Landon. It's a complicated thing, no doubt. I have mixed feelings about it. Let's get us a soda."

Dale rolled his window down. Landon followed his lead. There was the slightest hint of fall in the air, enough to cut through the humidity and make the traveling wind refreshing. Their speed would have enabled conversation, but Landon knew Dale's last statement was his way of putting things on pause while he thought things through. He needed more time, and so did Landon. Dale had probably known that.

They rode in silence for a mile or so. The tree frogs were audible even over the growl of the truck engine. Dale pulled into the dirt-and-gravel lot that fronted Henry's Store, their source of candy and snacks since they were kids.

"I got this," Dale said. "Dr. Pepper, right?" Landon paused with his door half-open, then nodded and pulled it shut without an argument.

It was almost dusk, and a whip-poor-will was tuning up. Other birds joined in. Then from beyond the pines, over toward the marshy creek, came a harsh, barking call. The birds seemed unconcerned.

Dale handed him a Dr. Pepper through the open window, along with a honey bun. He smiled, grateful that his brother had remembered his favorite snack from long ago. He guessed that Dale's tastes, like his own, had evolved over the years but hoped this was a nod to their shared past. When he saw Dale clutching a package of Twinkies along with a Coke, he confirmed his hunch.

Darkness was falling fast, aided by a stand of tall pines surrounding Henry's and a thick blanket of clouds that had moved in. Rain was forecast for tomorrow.

"Night heron," Dale said when the barking birdcall cut through the drone of tree frogs again. "He's stalking over in Wilton Creek, I expect."

The honey bun tasted more like sweet cardboard than he had remembered. The ice-cold Dr. Pepper was as good as ever, the perfect accompaniment to his nostalgic treat.

"You better now?" Dale asked, his mouth full of Twinkie.

He smiled and nodded. "I guess."

"Look, Brother, I'm no expert and probably the worst at giving advice, but here's how I see it. Dad's gone now, and life's never going to be the same. I already feel it, don't you?"

"Yeah, I do."

Dale popped the second Twinkie into his mouth and shifted in the seat so he was facing Landon. He crossed his leg under the steering wheel and laid his knee across the seat. "So how do you want it to play out?"

"What do you mean?" He wasn't quite sure where Dale was heading with this.

"Well, it seems like Mom and Dad had made some peace with Molly. Can't you?"

"It doesn't seem right, Dale. She didn't even come to see him."

Dale raised his free hand, letting it hang in the air between them. "She's got to live with that one, Brother. You don't."

"I don't have to like it, though. I don't have to pretend it's okay."

"You don't have to judge it at all. The way I see it, this is between Molly and Mom right now. She hasn't talked to me or to you, unless you haven't told me."

He shook his head. "Molly hasn't said anything to me."

Dale shrugged. "So it isn't our thing, until she makes it ours—or you do."

"So you're just going to ignore her?"

"No." There was something between pain and astonishment in Dale's voice. Something that made Landon look. His brother's brow was furrowed. He was looking at him the way he used to when Landon couldn't understand how an engine worked. "That would hurt Mom. I'm going to greet her like the prodigal daughter and then let her take the lead. See where it goes."

Landon clenched his jaw. This didn't seem right.

"Let it go, Brother," Dale said. "It's her battle. She created this mess, with a ton of help from Dad. Now she's trying— at least a little—to do what's right. She should be at his funeral—you know that. What she's done up to now is hers to own, not yours. She owes us all, but this one is for Mom, and Mom deserves it. Besides, what's the worst that happens? She leaves, and we never see her again? Is that going to ruin your life?

"It's going to be different, Brother, and not all the different will be bad. You'll be back in Charleston anyway. Molly might or might not visit you, but we will, and Mom will. If this makes Mom happier, isn't that reason enough? Stop overthinking it. Just let it happen."

He knew Dale was right. As usual.

"Don't let her ruin your time with Mom or with saying goodbye to Dad. This is our chance to try and make the rest of our lives different. I don't know about you, but I wouldn't mind having my sister back in my life." He shifted under the wheel and turned the ignition. When the roar of the engine settled into a loud drone, they headed for home.

Darkness had descended fully now; clouds of bugs swirled in the headlight beams. The air was noticeably cooler. Landon rolled up his window and stared into the unbroken night. The lightning bugs were long gone for this year.

"What do you think she'll say about Dad?" Landon asked without turning.

"You're the one who used to hang around with fortune-tellers, Brother. You tell me."

He smiled at his brother. "That was a long time ago, Dale."

Dale nodded, kept his eyes on the road. "Right now, seems like everything was."

CHAPTER FORTY-THREE

It rained off and on for the next two days. Molly did not come. Landon never asked his mother about her arrival, but Luna made sure he didn't keep his feelings about Molly to himself. By Tuesday night, he had put his anger away.

He and Luna drove to Gloucester for lunch on Wednesday. Landon needed to get out of the house. His mother's sister was arriving from Raleigh after lunch, and so his mother declined their invitation to join them. He was secretly glad; time alone with Luna had been scarce, and by bedtime each night he was too exhausted to take advantage of what little private time they had.

He stopped the car once they had rounded the first bend, out of sight of the house. Luna looked puzzled as he unhitched his seat belt, then smiled as he leaned in for a long, deep kiss.

"That's better," he said. Her finger traced a line down his nose; he caught it between his lips and gave it a loud smooch. He hoped his eyes looked like Luna's, which were telling him all he needed to know right now. "I love you, Luna," he whispered, just in case. "I'm so glad you're here."

Her murmured response was smothered by their hug. He held on, inhaling her scent, feeling as if his battery had just been recharged. When they finally unwrapped themselves, Luna looked refreshed too.

"When are you planning to go back to Charleston?" she asked after they accelerated onto Route 33.

It struck him then that he hadn't asked about Luna's plans. She had classes to teach. She should have left on Labor Day, but he had never thought to ask.

"I'm here until Sunday," she said, after waving off his apology. "I talked with the dean last Thursday after you called, and he thought it was best to go ahead and arrange coverage for me, just in case."

"I'm really sorry, Luna. I should have asked before."

Her hand slid from his elbow to his shoulder. "I think you've had other things on your mind. It's okay. What are your plans, though, if you've thought about those? I'm not pushing you."

"No, it's okay. I need to call Mike. I haven't even told him about Dad yet." He shook his head. "I feel like there's so much to do, but nothing makes any difference. Seems like nothing matters—except you."

Her hand caressed the back of his neck. "That's sweet. This must be very hard."

He rubbed her arm, and his hand found hers. "It's hard for you too," he said. A long, straight stretch gave him the opportunity to glance at her. "I can't tell you how grateful I am that you stayed this week."

She smiled—a sweet, slow, syrupy smile. "You just did."

"Sunday seems about right for me too," he said. "Mom's doing well, and Dale and Carla are here."

"Your mom is amazing."

"Yeah, I've been thinking. I wonder if all this is in some way a relief. I don't want to sound awful, but my dad was hard on her, and she's got Al-Anon now, and well, maybe this will be good in some ways. Does that sound terrible?"

"No, not at all. I think your mom will make the best of her new life. She'll be able to spend time with her granddaughter, and if things with Molly go well, maybe she'll have other grandkids to spoil too."

"She could visit us in Charleston." He hoped he hadn't stumbled on *us*.

"Yeah, I talked to her about that a little yesterday. I think she will, but she doesn't like traveling as much as she used to."

His mother had been to Charleston only once. Landon had always attributed that to his father, but his mother was nearly sixty-five now, and they hadn't been easy years.

"I wonder if she'll stay in the house," Luna said.

"Why would you say that?" His reply struck him as a little too sharp. "I'm sorry. Did she say something about moving? I didn't mean to snap at you."

She waved him off. "No problem. She hasn't mentioned it, but you just said this might all be a relief. Maybe she'll make some changes."

He pulled up to the light at Route 17. The pause allowed him to look at Luna, who had turned and was waiting for him. "She's pretty isolated there," she said, "and Dale and Carla are in Norfolk."

"Her parents live close by," he replied. "She does a lot for them."

She shrugged. "We'll see. It's her decision. I just wondered, is all."

The light changed, and he eased out onto the highway heading south into Gloucester. He hadn't considered the possibility of his mother moving. He couldn't imagine her in Norfolk, but why not? A smaller house—maybe even an apartment. She was getting older. What would it be like to stay with memories of her dead husband everywhere? There must be some good memories; there sure were a lot of bad ones.

"You okay, sweetie?" Luna's hand found his shoulder again.

"Yeah, just thinking. Mom moving seems weird."

"Does it bother you to think about that?"

He shrugged. "I don't know. Just another new world, I guess." He glanced at her. "Must be a lot worse for her."

Luna's mouth quivered; her eyes seemed watery. "It must be so hard for all of you. It makes me scared."

"Of what? I'm okay, Luna. We'll all be fine."

"I know, but it must be harder when your relationship hasn't been as good as you would have liked. That's the way it is with my parents too."

He nodded. "Yeah, I guess. It's probably hard when you've been really close too. I don't know. This is the only way I've ever known. I don't think you're ever ready for your parents to die, unless they die in their sleep—healthy, happy, and one hundred years old."

"Well, my parents seem happy," she said. She had fished a tissue from the box and was dabbing at her eyes. "Not sure about the healthy part. I guess we'll find out when they need us, if they ever do."

He wanted to say something comforting, but he knew Luna's parents were essentially Nomads. They weren't always easy to locate, and their calls to Luna seemed random and unpredictable. Something could happen without any of the girls knowing. He gave her leg a pat without taking his eyes off the road. "It's hard, sweetheart, no matter what."

They rode in silence for a while. A few raindrops speckled the windshield. They had an umbrella, but Landon was hoping for a waterside lunch. He wanted to eat outside. The clouds were moving pretty fast, and there was a patch of blue sky off to the west. They might get lucky.

Luna broke the silence when the speed limit changed, houses and businesses and traffic lights marking the approach to Gloucester. "So Sunday, huh? Would you like to avoid a trip to the airport?"

He smiled. "You bet. It'll cost you to use your ticket later, though."

She leaned in. He felt her lips on his cheek, her hand on his leg. "You'll owe me," she whispered. "I'll make you pay me back, somehow."

They stopped at a light. He let his head fall back against the headrest. A smile creased his face. He was still alive.

Everyone seemed edgy Thursday morning, the first fine, sunny, almost crisp morning of the year. Landon had awakened early and found his mother sitting alone with a cup of coffee. For the first time in his memory, she obeyed his silent command to stay seated while he poured himself a cup and then joined her at the table.

"Didn't you sleep?" he asked.

"I did. I've been waking up a little earlier since your daddy passed. I didn't feel like reading this morning."

"Reading anything good?"

"I've been rereading *Huckleberry Finn*. Feeling a little nostalgic, I guess."

He smiled. That book was their favorite, the one he and his mother would retreat into whenever things got really bad at home. When she read it to him, they would disappear down the mighty river on a raft, just the two of them.

"Did Molly like to read?"

"When she was small. More than Dale, but not like you."

Not like I used to, anyway, he thought.

"Is she coming today?" he asked.

"Yes. Reverend Koenig said she met with him yesterday, about the service."

He felt his mother's eyes on him. He stared into his cup briefly, then gave her his best fake neutral look, figuring she wouldn't buy it. "What do you think she'll say?"

"No idea, Landon. I imagine she's scared and embarrassed. She'll be facing a lot of family and friends, and she's turned her back on all of them."

"You think she'll make a scene?"

"Probably not. She sounds more grown-up on the phone, and besides, she's been making a scene for twenty-five years. She's probably tired." She laughed, covering her mouth with her hand, then gave in and really laughed, bowing her head and letting her shoulders bounce. He couldn't help joining in, and they leaned into one another, working to keep silent so as not to awaken Luna.

"You okay, Mom?" he asked when they were finally spent. She was wiping her eyes on a napkin.

"I'm fine. Poor thing—she's spent a lot of energy being mad."

"I didn't mean about Molly, Mom."

"Oh. I'm all right, baby. I miss your daddy something awful, but I've had time to prepare for this. I knew it was coming."

"What are you going to do? Luna asked me if you were going to stay here."

She smiled. "She's really something. I like her a bunch." She drained her cup and rose for a refill, then carried the pot over and topped off Landon's cup. "I'll never leave Virginia. My people are all here. My mom and dad need me too."

"How about Norfolk?"

"I've thought about that. Carla has asked me. I sure wouldn't mind watching Sally more often. She's a pistol."

"Would you like Norfolk, though? It's a big city."

"I'd like anywhere my kids are, Landon." She stared off through the windows, into the darkness. "I'm trying not to get ahead of myself, but I keep thinking maybe Molly will actually come around now, bring her kids. I hardly know my own grandchildren."

"We'll come visit you, Mom. As often as we can."

She reached for a napkin but couldn't hide her smile. "It's nice to hear you say *we*, Landon."

The phone rang while Luna was in the shower. It was Reverend Koenig, asking for Landon's mother, who was getting dressed and ready early, as usual. "Molly is at the church," she told him after she hung up. "She came early to see your daddy in private."

"So she's leaving?" he asked.

"No, of course not. She wants me to come and visit with her before everyone else gets there."

He threw his hands up. "Sure, why not? She hasn't seen you in ten years, hasn't seen any of us. Now she breezes in and—"

"Let it go, Landon." She tilted her head and smiled. "She's here. She wants to see me. Someday you'll have children, and then you'll understand."

He exhaled, then pasted on a smile. "Want me to drive you?"

"I've been driving by myself a long time. You all wait for Dale and them. Come on a little early, though. You might want to visit with Molly without a lot of other folks around."

For once, he remembered to keep silent. That didn't last long, though, once Luna joined him at the table. She wanted to know how he felt, and truthfully, he felt fine. The events of the day seemed surreal, almost as if he had a part in a play. He wasn't nervous. It felt good to sit at the table with Luna, just the two of them. He wasn't nervous about seeing Molly either. It would be strange, he guessed, but his mother was right; today would be much harder on Molly, and he didn't need to make it worse. Luna reminded him to pay attention, to try and remember the day for his father's sake and for himself.

He did pretty well for most of the morning, but when Dale showed up in a suit, he felt his throat and chest begin to tighten. His mouth got dry, and he felt fidgety. A hint of a headache—the first in a while—began to plague him.

They rode to the church in Carla's SUV, which accommodated Sally's car seat and two additional passengers without difficulty. Dale was driving, alone with his thoughts. Landon, who had declined Carla's offer of the front seat, held Luna's hand and tried to avoid eye contact as a clammy fog descended on his mind and body. He felt Luna's fingers stroking his and offered an occasional faux-brave smile that he knew would not fool her. She said nothing but stayed close. Carla's attention was divided between Sally and Luna, their chitchat providing a diversion that Landon appreciated.

He spotted Molly when he and Luna entered the sanctuary. She looked much older than he expected; rail-thin, her face and skin betraying the smoking habit she'd obviously never kicked. He felt his heart pounding and stuffed his shaking hands into his pockets while he watched Dale give her an awkward hug and a kiss on the cheek. He followed suit, clearing his throat before returning her mechanical "hey" and sharing a hug that felt something like the hugs he'd gotten from his grandmother's sisters when he graduated from college.

There followed some equally awkward and forced conversation among the three of them; he felt as if they were all sharing information that masked and avoided the questions and answers they really wanted. Molly tried to be gracious to Luna, but the effort was clearly too much for her. She wasn't rude, and Luna seemed to take no offense, but Molly's social skills, never her strong suit, had not been honed by years of living on a communal farm.

The transformation in his mother was obvious. Her brood was intact, even with her husband gone, and her face radiated hope that was in no way diminished by the clumsy reunion. Landon endured the awkwardness, but could not help wondering if crushing disappointment might not magnify his mother's grief once the funeral was over. For now, though, her hope, along with Luna's and Dale's counsel, helped contain any anger that might otherwise have surfaced.

Mourners began arriving before long. The novelty of his sister's reappearance was quickly replaced by a suffocating unease that brought Landon no satisfaction. His distress must have been obvious to Luna, who guided him to his seat with whispered reassurances that felt as welcome as an unexpected summer breeze.

He quickly found himself drifting away, retreating into the place that had allowed him, over the years, to bear witness to awful suffering, death, and grief without becoming overwhelmed by it all. There had been times when he'd wondered about the emotional cost of becoming a physician, but today was not one of those times. Today, he fell into that state of detachment as if it were his bed at the end of a long, exhausting journey.

There were words spoken about death, about God, about life, and about his father. They sang "Rock of Ages," his mother's favorite, and the pastor read Psalm 23 and spoke briefly about the triumph of eternal life over death. When Landon's turn came, he walked unsteadily to the pulpit and pulled his typed notes from his jacket. He introduced the letter and then read it in what he later remembered as a halting voice that he wished had conveyed more bravery. When he returned to his seat, Luna was weeping silently. She laid her head on his shoulder.

Molly was next. Landon would not remember everything she said, but he remembered the final lines: "I spent much of my life wondering why my father didn't do a better job, why I got cheated, never thinking that maybe he felt the same way about me. Now I realize we both were who we were. We both could have done better. We had a difficult relationship, but I'm glad we at least had time to tell each other that we wished things had been different, that we loved each other, and that we forgave each other. He taught me more than I ever gave him credit for."

She left right after the graveside service, promising everyone she would return for Thanksgiving and bring her family. Her daughter's birthday was tomorrow, and there was a party after school, and she had to drive four hundred miles. She was hoping to make it to Pennsylvania by tonight.

"You're coming home for Thanksgiving, right?" she asked Landon. They were circling each other around Molly's car. He knew another hug was coming, and Molly looked no more eager or prepared than he felt. "I hope you'll bring Luna." He flinched when she leaned in but could not miss the brightness in her eyes. "She's a keeper." He returned her smile and then wrapped his sister in the first real hug they'd shared since before he could remember.

CHAPTER FORTY-FOUR

October 31 began with the happiest birthday wake-up Luna had ever experienced. It was wonderful to wake up snuggled against Landon's chest, pressed into the crook of his arm that had come to fit her so comfortably. They made love as the darkness gave way to dawn. Then, while he showered, shaved, and dressed, she languished in bed, thinking back to Landon's birthday morning, when she'd crept out and ridden home on her bike, satisfied and full of anticipation. So much had happened since then. Before Landon left for work, there were playful hints about a surprise gift, but by then she had felt the need to get moving.

She had canceled class, a midweek gift to her students, who were beginning to delight her with the quality of their writing. This would be the first time she'd ever canceled class for her birthday, but she justified it easily. After all, how could she claim to need to work when Diana had flown in from Germany to help her celebrate?

Diana had called on Saturday morning; her home in Charleston was closing, and she scheduled it to ensure she would be there to help celebrate Luna's big day. She first suggested lunch, thinking Luna would be working, then delightedly agreed with Luna's last-minute plan to clear the day. Luna won the argument over where to eat brunch, negotiating a plan to eat at her place while allowing Diana to bring the food. Eating at home would provide privacy for the big news Luna had been dying to share with someone.

Landon had been busy interviewing residency candidates on Monday and Tuesday, so her place was clean, and Luna had everything ready when Diana rang the doorbell precisely at ten o'clock. She carried a small bottle of something, along with a small bouquet of asters, mums, and sedum in muted fall colors that compensated for the absence of falling leaves Luna bemoaned every autumn in Charleston. It was just cool enough to justify a fire, and Luna had lit scented candles to provide a fallish atmosphere. Diana's flowers were the perfect finishing touch.

She teared up when she saw her friend. It had only been a few weeks, but she missed her smile and her shining eyes terribly. She needed someone to talk to. Fox was too far away and too caught up in herself. Diana was different, able to step outside herself and really listen. Luna needed that.

They hugged for a long time, holding on and saying nothing. *Unusual for both of them,* she thought.

"Let's have a drink," Diana said. "I brought Prosecco, just a glass apiece, since it's your big day." She began working the wire cap off the cork. "I promise, no references to your age. Besides, it's just a number."

"I don't care," Luna said. "Thirty, thirty, thirty. I thought it would bother me—God knows I've worried about it enough, but now that it's here, it really doesn't."

"To my favorite teacher and wonderful friend," Diana said, raising her glass. "Happiest of birthdays and many, many more."

The bubbles tickled her nose. "Thank you, Diana. It's so wonderful to see you. Thanks for coming."

"I wouldn't have missed it. You're the only Halloween baby I know. You must have some great costumes—and stories. By the way, your present will be late. I had to order it."

Luna waved her off. "I'm not a big Halloween fan. My parents used it as an excuse to not throw me parties, and I sort of blamed Halloween for that. And I certainly don't need a present. You came all this way." She took a second sip, then raised an eyebrow. "I do need to eat, though. Weren't you in charge of the food?"

"I ordered from Toast, thank you very much." Diana curtsied, then took a long sip. "They deliver. Brunch will arrive at ten thirty. You're going to love it. Have you eaten there?"

"No. Sounds perfect." She motioned toward the fire, past the table she had prepared inside. "We could sit on the piazza, but I think it's a little chilly."

"I haven't been warm since I left Charleston," Diana said. She settled into the Morgan armchair next to the hearth. Luna took a seat on the sofa.

"So how is Frankfurt?"

"It's cold and dreary right now. Unusually so, I'm told by the natives. Just my luck." Diana shrugged. "But I don't want to talk about that. I need a break." She sat forward, almost knee-to-knee with Luna. "Tell me. How's Landon?"

"He's doing really well, I think."

"Back to work?"

"Yes. He actually did his first week on the clinical service—taking care of patients—last week. He was tired, but it went well."

"How's he doing about his father?"

"He's okay. He misses him, and once in a while, he'll get choked up, but I think that's pretty normal. His mother and brother are doing well. We've been back to visit once."

"How about his sister? *That* sounded weird."

She grimaced and scrunched her shoulders. "Yeah, not sure about that yet. Probably take some time to see how it turns out. But she's spoken with her mother several times, and she wrote Landon a letter. He wrote her back. Anyway, we're all supposed to be getting together at Thanksgiving, at his mother's house."

Diana's smile unfurled around the rim of her glass. Her playful eyes caught the reflection of the firelight. Luna heard the faintest "hmm" and knew what was coming. "Sure sounds like things are good."

Luna wasn't sure why she was blushing, but she didn't care. She just nodded and let her smile give it all away. "Things are fabulous, Diana. I can't believe it. I love his family. His mother is so nice and sweet. His brother's wife, too, and—what?"

Diana was laughing now, trying to avoid choking on her last sip. She coughed once, pressed her hand to her chest, and then recovered. "I was asking about you and Landon. I didn't realize you were part of his family now."

The doorbell rang just then. She raised a finger. "Hold that thought, Diana. I think the food is here."

The arrival of brunch diverted them for a bit. Diana unpacked the food, offering commentary on each selection—

French toast with peach syrup, and shrimp etouffee with grits and fried green tomatoes. They divided each dish, tasted and moaned, and finished the Prosecco.

"What are your plans for the rest of the day?" Diana asked.

"A mani-pedi this afternoon. Maybe a nap first." She raised her glass. "I'm not used to day drinking anymore."

Diana waved a hand. "Good for you. What are you two doing tonight?"

"Landon has it all planned out. Dinner at the Muse and then—"

"Ooh, that's the new place over by the college, isn't it?"

She nodded. "Yeah, just opened last month. Supposed to be great Italian, and it's small and romantic."

Diana's grin was unmistakably conspiratorial. "Perfect."

"And then we're going to the Pavilion Bar."

"The rooftop?"

"No. Too cold for that. We're going to the lobby bar, to snuggle on a sofa and listen to jazz. Maybe dance a little."

"New dress?"

"Already took care of that—last week, before you called." Luna gathered the remnants of the meal, shooing Diana back into her seat. "If I'd known you were coming, I'd have waited for you. I found the cutest dress at Finicky Filly."

"Love that place. I was there yesterday. How about this weekend? It's been too long since we ravaged the boutiques together."

Luna sank back into her chair. "That would be fun. Saturday might work."

"Hmm." The playful grin was back. "Waffling about shopping. You're sounding more and more like an old married lady, honey."

Luna wagged a finger in Diana's face. "None of that kind of talk now. You've been watching too many chick flicks. Things are way too unsettled for marriage talk. In fact, I have some news to tell you."

Diana's smile faltered but didn't collapse entirely. "What do you mean? Not more bad news, I hope?"

Luna shook her head. She was enjoying this. "No, not at all. Landon's fine. I'm fine."

"What is it? What's unsettled?"

"Well, Landon is thinking about moving to Virginia, to be closer to his family."

"When? What about you? Are you going?"

The wine had made Luna giggly. Now she gave in and leaned over her plate, laughing; it wasn't long until Diana joined in.

"None of this is settled yet," Luna said. He's planning to talk to the people at MCV in Richmond next month. He might look at Norfolk, too, although that wouldn't be as academic as he wants. If he moved, it would be next summer. He wants to finish out the academic year here."

"What about you?"

Luna shrugged. She was enjoying this a lot.

"You haven't discussed it? He hasn't asked you?"

"Okay, he has. He asked me if I would consider moving, and I said maybe."

Diana looked as if she wasn't buying this. "Maybe ... so which schools are you looking at?"

"Don't jump to conclusions, Diana. I'd miss Charleston. I love my job."

"Of course you do—more than anything or anybody." Diana's head was bobbing, her brows knitted in a mock serious, hilarious way. She beckoned toward Luna with one hand. "Come on, which schools?"

Luna suddenly wished there were more Prosecco. "University of Richmond looks the best so far."

Landon changed at home, moving quickly so as not to spoil the mood too much. Luna had seemed a little miffed when he left her at her place while he went to retrieve her present. While a little shift in her mood would enhance the surprise, he didn't want to risk losing the romance of an intimate candlelit dinner, though truthfully, if his present didn't restore a romantic mood, then he had badly misjudged their relationship.

At her suggestion, he'd left a change of clothes for tomorrow at her place. An extra supply of toiletries now resided there permanently, so he had only to grab the present and get back so the rest of the evening could unfold.

Halloween provided perfect cover. No one would look twice at a man in a T-shirt and "Happy Birthday" boxers tonight. Most of the trick-or-treaters were home by now, but he might well be heading to or from a private celebration with a back seat full of balloons and a bottle of champagne on the driver's seat. The portable spotlight might take some explaining, though.

Luck was with him; a car was pulling away from the curb less than two blocks from Luna's apartment. He made two trips, first setting up the spotlight in the small yard below Luna's piazza, then returning for the balloons and champagne.

When all was ready, he called Luna. Her breathless answer sounded more anxious than angry. "Hey, babe," he said, trying to sound breezy and unconcerned. "Come on out on the balcony." He watched for the muted slash of light from her candlelit apartment, then split the night with the glare of the spotlight, which caught her smiling face peering over the rail.

"Happy Birthday, baby. Thought I'd repay you for the memory I lost."

He dropped the champagne bottle so he had one hand free to gather her up at the bottom of the stairs. She bounded into his hug; her kiss was hungry and happy and perfect.

"Come on," he whispered, leading her to where the bottle lay on the grass.

"Landon?" she asked. "Don't you want to come inside? Someone might see you."

"Nope. Let 'em." He spread his arms and spun, feeling the weight of the balloons as they formed a centripetal circle above his head. "I'm going to release the bouquet—for you. The spotlight will let you follow them up into the night sky."

Luna's shoulders were bunched. Landon felt certain she was blushing. He pulled her closer into the glare from the spotlight. Her squinting, smiling face made him wish he'd thought to bring her some sunglasses.

"Happy Birthday, Luna Quinn," he announced. "Your love and boundless spirit have helped me through some tough times. I love you as big as the universe, as far as these balloons will fly."

He released the balloons. Luna's head tilted as she followed them into the light beam. He kept his eyes on her, knowing she was watching the bouquet disperse and scatter, each balloon exiting the beam of light, becoming a shadow and disappearing into the star-dappled night.

All except one.

The lone red balloon hovered, drawing her glance, which moved quickly to him, then back to the balloon. Her eyes traveled down the string, then gaped when she recognized the counterweight, twisting and turning in and out of the bright beam. It was a perfect keyhole sand dollar and next to it, a large diamond ring that caught and scattered light onto Luna's dress.

Her mouth fell open. Landon watched her rise up onto her toes as he dropped to one knee.